Christian and Pliable in the Slough of Despond

Pilgrim's Progress

The lions in the path

Pilgrim's Progress

John Bunyan

With More Than 100 Original Illustrations

Printed in the United States of America

www.anekopress.com

Aneko Press books are available at discounted prices for ministries and other outreach.
Find out more by contacting us at info@lspbooks.com

Aneko Press, Life Sentence Publishing, and its logos are trademarks of

Life Sentence Publishing, Inc.
P.O. Box 652
Abbotsford, WI 54405

FICTION / Christian / Classic & Allegory

Hardcover ISBN: 978-1-62245-331-3

Paperback ISBN: 978-1-62245-239-2

Ebook ISBN: 978-1-62245-240-8

Audiobook ISBN: 978-1-62245-293-4

10   9   8   7   6   5   4   3

Available where books are sold

Contents

Lord Hate-good

Part 1

Great Heart

The First Stage

As I walked through the wilderness of this world, I came upon a certain place with a den,[1] and lay down to sleep. I fell asleep and dreamed. In my dream, I saw a man clothed with rags standing in a certain place, with his face turned from his own house. In his hand he held a book, and he bore a great burden upon his back. (*For my iniquities are gone over my head; as a heavy burden they are too heavy for me.* – Psalm 38:4) He opened the book, and as he read, he wept and trembled. Unable to contain his emotions any longer, he broke out with a mournful cry. "What shall I do?" (*O LORD, how long shall I cry, and thou wilt not hear; and raise my voice unto thee because of the violence, and thou wilt not save? Why dost thou cause me to see iniquity and cause me to behold grievance and destruction and violence before me, in addition to those that raise up strife and contention?* – Hab. 1:2, 3)

Christian reading his book

In the midst of this dilemma, he returned home, but he restrained himself as he pondered his true feelings. At first, even his wife and children were unaware of his distress; but he grew more and more troubled. Finally, his wife asked, "What's the matter?"

He could no longer stay silent. He told his wife and children what he

---

1   Bedford jail, in which the author was imprisoned for conscience' sake.

had learned from the book and how it troubled his mind. "Dear," he said to his wife, "and you my children, I love you dearly." He looked from one to another. "A burden lies heavily upon me." He took a deep breath and let it out slowly. "You see, I've learned that our city will be burned with fire from heaven. I'm afraid we are all doomed … even you my sweet children, unless I can find some way of escape, but I haven't found any way."

His wife and children didn't believe a word of what he said to be true and looked at him as if he'd lost his mind. They hoped a good night's sleep would settle his frenzied thoughts. With this hope in mind, his family hurried him off to bed, but his mind remained just as troubled in the night as it was during the day. He tossed and turned with tears and sighs until the sky brightened with the dawn.

His family looked at him with concern. They could see he hadn't slept. "It's worse and worse." He started to talk to them again about what he learned in the book. At first they tried to console him, but as he went on, their faces hardened with anger. Finally, they had enough and answered him gruffly with harsh words. Sometimes they even ridiculed him, and other times they scolded him. Finally, they just ignored him.

Christian goes to his bedroom to pray

It saddened him to see them like this. In fact, he pitied them. He'd often go to his bedroom to pray for them as a way to soothe his misery, or he'd walk alone through fields while reading or praying.

One day he walked in the fields while reading his book and he became so distressed that he burst out crying. "What shall I do to be saved?" (*What must I do to be saved? And they said, Believe on the Lord Jesus Christ, and thou shalt be saved.* – Acts 16:30b, 31)

He looked this way and that as if he would run, but instead he stood still. He didn't know which way to go. As he stood there a man named Evangelist walked up to him and asked, "Why are you crying?"

He answered, "Sir, I've read in this book I'm holding that I am condemned to die and after that comes judgment (*And as it is appointed unto men to die once, and after this the judgment* – Heb. 9:27); and I find that I am not willing to do the first (*Before I go, to not return, to the land of darkness and of the shadow of death; land of darkness, as darkness itself, and of the shadow of death, without any order, and where the light is as darkness.* – Job 10:21, 22), nor able to do the second." (*Can thine heart endure, or can thine hands be strong in the days that I shall deal with thee? I the LORD have spoken it and will do it.* – Ezek. 22:14)

Then Evangelist said, "Why aren't you willing to die, since this life is riddled with so many evils?"

The man answered, "Because, I fear that this burden upon my back will sink me lower than the grave and I shall fall into Tophet [Gehenna]." (*For Tophet is ordained of yesterday for the king of Babylon, it is also prepared; he has deepened and enlarged the pile of her fire and much wood; the breath of the LORD like a stream of brimstone kindles it.* – Isa. 30:33) "And Sir," the man said. "If I'm not fit to go to prison, then I am not fit to go from judgment to execution." Distress wrinkled his brow. "The thoughts of these things make me cry."

Evangelist studied the man. "If this is your condition, why are you standing here still?"

The man shrugged. "Because I don't know where to go."

Evangelist handed him a parchment roll and on it were the words "Flee from the wrath to come." (*But when he saw many of the Pharisees and Sadducees come to his baptism, he said unto them, O generation of vipers, who taught you to flee from the wrath to come?* – Matt. 3:7)

The man read it and looked carefully at Evangelist. "Where must I flee to?"

Evangelist pointed his finger over a very wide field. "Do you see the wicket gate over there in the distance?" (*Enter ye in at the narrow gate, for the way that leads to destruction is wide and spacious, and those who follow it are many; because narrow is the gate, and confined is the way which leads unto life, and there are few that find it.* – Matt. 7:13, 14)

The man squinted. "No."

Evangelist points the way to the wicket gate

Evangelist asked, "Do you see the shining light in the distance?" (*We have also the most sure word of the prophets, unto which ye do well that ye take heed, as unto a light that shines in a dark place, until the day dawns and the morning star arises in your hearts. – 2 Peter 1:19*)

"I think I do."

Evangelist said, "Keep that light in your eye and go up directly to it. If you do, you will see the gate. Upon arrival at the gate, when you knock you will be told what you should do."

In my dream the man began to run. He hadn't run far from his own door when his wife and children noticed what he was doing and cried out to him. "Come back! Come home!"

The man put his fingers in his ears and ran on. "Life! Life! Eternal life!" (*If anyone comes to me and does not hate his father and mother and wife and children and brethren and sisters, and even his own life also, he cannot be my disciple. – Luke 14:26*) He didn't turn to look at his home or family behind him (*Escape; for thy soul, do not look behind thee, neither stop thou in all the plain; escape to the mountain, lest thou be consumed. – Gen. 19:17b*), but fled towards the middle of the plain.

His neighbors also came out to see him run. (*All my friends watched to see if I would stumble. Peradventure he will deceive himself, they said, and we shall prevail against him, and we shall take our revenge on him. – Jer. 20:10b*) The man continued to run even though some of his neighbors mocked him. Others threatened him, and some joined with his family and cried for him to return. Among those neighbors calling for him to come home, two decided to grab him and forcibly drag him back. The name of the one was Obstinate and the name of the other Pliable.

The man had run a good distance ahead of them, but they were determined to pursue him. They chased after him and a short time later they overtook him.

"Neighbors, why have you come after me?" the man asked as he caught his breath.

"We have come after you to persuade you to go back with us."

The man shook his head. "I can no longer live in the City of Destruction. I know I was born there and have lived my whole life there, but I've seen the truth of living and dying there. Sooner or later, you will sink lower than the grave, into a place that burns with fire and brimstone. Don't go back! Come with me," the man pleaded with his neighbors.

"What?" Obstinate looked at him eyes wide with surprise. "And leave our friends and our comforts behind?"

"Yes," Christian said (for that was the man's name). "All you leave behind isn't worthy to be compared with the tiniest portion of that which I am seeking to enjoy. (*We look not at the things which are seen, but at the things which are not seen, for the things which are seen are temporal, but the things which are not seen are eternal. – 2 Cor. 4:18*) If you come with me, you'll hold it yourself and fare as well as me, because where I go there is more than enough. (*And when he came to himself, he said, How many hired servants of my father's have abundance of bread, and I perish here with hunger! – Luke 15:17*) Come with me and you'll see I'm speaking the truth."

Obstinate's brows knit into furrows of confusion. "What are the things you seek, since you leave all the world to find them?"

"I seek an incorruptible inheritance," Christian answered. "It's pure and untarnished, and it never fades. (*Unto the incorruptible inheritance that cannot be defiled and that does not fade away, conserved in the heavens for you. – 1 Peter 1:4*) And it is laid up in heaven where it is safe (*But now they desire a better country, that is, a heavenly one; therefore, God is not ashamed to be called their God, for he has prepared for them a city. – Heb. 11:16*), to be given at the appointed time to those who diligently seek it." He extended the book toward Obstinate. "Read it if you will, in my book."

"Tush." Obstinate held up his hand and with a flick of his wrist said, "Away with your book. Will you go back with us or not?"

Christian shook his head. "No, I will not. I have laid my hand to the plough and will not look back." (*No one having put his hand to the plough and looking back is fit for the kingdom of God. – Luke 9:62*)

Obstinate motioned with a sweeping gesture toward his neighbor, Pliable, to join him. "Come, Pliable, let's turn around and go home without him." He shrugged. "There's a company of these crazy-headed, vain and conceited men, who think they are wiser in their own eyes than seven men."

Pliable didn't move. He said, "Don't berate him. If what the good Christian says is true, the things he seeks are far better than the things that hold our attention. I'm inclined to go with him."

Obstinate threw his arms in the air. "What? Another fool! Listen to me and go back. Who knows where such a brain-sick fellow will lead you? Go back, go back," he pleaded. "It's the wise thing to do."

"No," Christian said to Obstinate. "Come with your neighbor Pliable. The things I spoke of are real, plus there are many more glories too. If you don't believe me, read this book." He extended the book toward Pliable this time. "You'll find truth in what it says, and it's all confirmed by the blood of Him who made it." (*For a testament is confirmed by the death: otherwise it is not valid as long as the testator lives. From which came that not even the first one was dedicated without blood. For when Moses had read every commandment of the law to all the people, taking the blood of calves and of goats, with water, and scarlet wool, and hyssop, he sprinkled both the book and all the people, saying, This is the blood of the testament which God has*

Obstinate turns back

commanded unto you. Moreover he sprinkled with blood both the tabernacle and all the vessels of the ministry. – Heb. 9:17-21)

Pliable looked from Christian to Obstinate. "Well, Obstinate, I think I'll go along with this good man and cast my lot with him." He turned his attention to Christian. "My good companion, do you know the way to this desired place?"

"I've been directed by a man whose name is Evangelist, to hurry to a little gate, where we shall receive instructions about the way."

Pliable found that to be agreeable. "Come then, good neighbor. Let's be going."

The two of them headed off together while Obstinate stood in his place. "I am going back home," he called after them. "I will not be the companion of such misled, weird fellows."

In my dream, when Obstinate had gone back, Christian and Pliable walked along the plain of Ease and Christian talked with his traveling companion. "So how do you feel Pliable?" he asked. "I am so glad you were convinced to come along with me. If Obstinate had felt what I have felt of powers and terrors … of what is yet unseen, then I'm sure he would not have turned his back on us as he did."

Pliable hungered to know more. "Since it is just the two of us, Christian, tell me more. What are the things you spoke of, and how are they to be enjoyed? Where are we going?"

Christian struggled to put his thoughts into words. "It is easier to comprehend them with my mind, than to explain them verbally. But since you're asking I will read of them in my book."

Pliable pointed at the book. "So you think the words of your book are absolutely true?"

Christian nodded without any doubt. "Yes, of course. It was made by Him who cannot lie." (*For the hope of eternal life, which God, who cannot lie, promised before the times of the ages.* Titus 1:2)

"Very well. Try to tell me of these things. What are they?"

Christian motioned with his hand as he explained. "There is an endless kingdom to be inhabited and everlasting life to be given us, in order that we may live in that kingdom forever." (*For, behold, I create new heavens and a new earth; and the former shall not be remembered, nor come into mind.* – Isa. 65:17)

"Brilliant! And what else?"

"Well, there are crowns of glory to be given us and garments that will make us shine like the sun in the skies of heaven." (*Then shall the righteous shine forth as the sun in the kingdom of their Father.* – Matt. 13:43)

"That is very pleasant news. What else?"

"There shall be no more crying, nor sorrow; for He who owns the place will wipe all tears from our eyes." (*He will destroy death forever; and the Lord GOD shall wipe away every tear from off all faces; and the rebuke of his people he shall take away from off all the earth: for the LORD has determined it.* – Isa. 25:8)

"And who will be there with us?" Pliable wondered out loud.

"There will be seraphim and cherubim ... (*And I beheld, and I heard the voice of many angels round about the throne and of the animals and of the elders; and the number of them was ten thousand times ten thousand, and thousands of thousands.* – Rev. 5:11) ... creatures that will dazzle your eyes. You'll also meet with thousands and ten thousands who have gone before us to that place. Everyone there will be loving and holy; with everyone walking about in the sight of God and standing in his presence with everlasting acceptance. In a word, there we shall see the elders with their golden crowns (*And round about the throne were twenty-four thrones, and upon the thrones I saw twenty-four elders sitting, clothed in white raiment; and they had on their heads crowns of gold.* – Rev. 4:4), and the holy virgins with their golden harps. (*And I saw and, behold, the Lamb stood upon Mount Sion and with him a hundred and forty-four thousand, having the name of his Father written in their foreheads. And I heard a voice from heaven as the voice of many waters and as the voice of a great thunder; and I heard the voice of harpers harping with their harps; and they sang as it were a new song before the throne and before the four animals and the elders; and no one could learn that song but the hundred and forty-four thousand, who were redeemed from the earth. These are those who are not defiled with women, for they are virgins. These are those who follow the Lamb wherever he goes. These are redeemed from among men, being the first fruits unto God and to the Lamb. And in their mouth was found no guile, for they are without blemish before the throne of God.* – Rev. 14:1-5)

"And we'll see men, who were cut into pieces by the world, burnt in flames, eaten of beasts, drowned in the seas, all because of their love for the Lord of the place (*Blessed are those who suffer persecution for righteousness' sake, for theirs is the kingdom of the heavens.* – Matt. 5:10);[2] all will be well and clothed with immortality as with a garment." (*For in this we groan, earnestly desiring to be clothed upon with our house which is from heaven.* – 2 Cor. 5:2)

"Just hearing all this is enough to overwhelm me. But are these things to be enjoyed? And how is it we get to share in all this?"

"The Lord, the governor of the country, has recorded these things in this book." Christian patted the book for emphasis. (*And he said unto me, It is done. I AM the Alpha and the Omega, the beginning and the end. I will give unto him that is thirsty of the fountain of the water of life freely.* – Rev. 21:6) The fact is, if we are truly willing to have it, He will give to us freely."

Pliable's face brightened. "Well, my good companion, I'm glad to hear of all these things. Come on, let's pick up our pace."

Christian let out a long sigh. "I cannot go any faster, because of this burden on my back."

Now in my dream, as the two of them ended this talk, they drew near to a very muddy bog in the midst of the plain, but they didn't see it. In quick order, they both fell into the mire. The name of the marshy slough was Despond. Here, they wallowed for a time until they were totally covered with the slime and mud. Because of the burden on his back, Christian began to sink.

Pliable asked, "Ah, neighbor Christian, where are you now?"

"Truthfully, I don't know."

Pliable felt offended and his face grew red. "Is *this* the happiness you told me about? If we are stuck in the likes of this dirty goo right at the start, what can we expect between this …" He lifted his arms and let them slap the mud. "… and our journey's end? If I get out of this mess with my life, you'll be going on alone to possess the brave country, for I will return home."

With this he struggled desperately and finally climbed out of the mire on the side of the bog nearest to his house. Once out, he didn't even turn to help Christian. In fact, he didn't even say good-bye. Instead, he walked away covered in filth and headed straight toward his house. Christian never saw him again, so he was left to tumble in the Slough of Despond alone. But

---

2   Original: *He that loves his life shall lose it, and he that hates his life in this world shall keep it unto life eternal* – John 12:25.

Christian struggled through the muck little by little toward the side of the bog farthest from his house … the side next to the wicket gate. He finally reached that side, but he couldn't get out because of the burden he carried on his back. But in my dream, a man came to him whose name was Help.

"What are you doing here?" Help asked Christian.

"Sir, I was encouraged to go this way by a man called Evangelist." Christian pointed a muddy finger toward the wicket gate. "He directed me to that gate over there, so I might escape the wrath to come. And as I headed toward it, I fell in here." He flicked mud from his fingertips into the mire.

"But why didn't you look for the steps?" Help asked.

"We were talking[3] and I never thought to look for stairs."

Help reached out toward Christian. "Then, give me your hand."

Christian reached out and grabbed his hand and Help pulled him out of the mucky mire (*He brought me up also out of the pit of hopelessness, out of the miry clay and set my feet upon a rock and straightened my steps.* – Psalm 40:2), and set him upon solid ground.

"Now go on your way."

In my dream, I stepped toward the man who plucked Christian out of the slough and asked, "Sir, why isn't this hazard fixed so poor travelers can cross it safely, since it is on the way from the City of Destruction to the gate over there?"

"This miry slough is a place that can't be repaired. It is a low-lying place where the scum and filth that comes with the conviction of sin drains and collects as the traveling sinner becomes aware of his lost condition. It is the fears, doubts, and discouraging apprehensions about oneself that arise in his soul.

"The King is not happy that this place remains so bad. (*Comfort ye the tired hands and strengthen the knees that tremble. Say to those that are of a fearful heart, Be comforted, fear not; behold, your God comes with vengeance, with recompense; God himself will come and save you.* – Isa. 35:3, 4) Based on the direction offered by His Majesty's surveyors, His workers have also tended to this patch of ground for more than two thousand years, to see if it could possibly be fixed." Sadness filled Help's eyes. "To my knowledge, at least twenty thousand cartloads have been swallowed up by this mire. Cartloads of millions of wholesome instructions have been delivered at

---

3   Original: Fear chased me so hard I bolted this way and fell in.

all seasons from all around the King's dominions. It is said these instructions are made of the best materials in order to create good solid ground in this place, if it could be fixed. But this is the Slough of Despond, and it will remain so even after they have done all they can.

"By the direction of the Lawgiver, there are certain good and substantial steps placed through the very midst of this bog to offer a sure way, but

Help draws Christian out of the Slough of Despond

this place spews out so much filth and changes with the weather, so that these steps are hardly seen. And often when men find the steps, they grow dizzy from their own guilt and their feet miss the steps and they become covered and stained with mud. But the steps are there and the ground is good once they get in at the gate." (*In all thy ways acknowledge him, and he shall direct thy paths. –* Prov. 3:6)[4]

Now in my dream, by this time Pliable arrived home to his house and his neighbors came to visit him. Some of them called him a wise man for coming back, and some called him a fool for endangering his life by going with Christian in the first place. Others just made fun of him and mocked him for his cowardliness.

They said, "If I had started this adventure like you did, I wouldn't have been so timid as to quit after just a few difficulties." Pliable sat cringing among them at these words, but after a little time passed he gained some confidence. When his neighbors saw his regained confidence they turned against poor Christian instead and ridiculed him behind his back. However, even though they were no longer talking about him, their words against Christian concerned Pliable.

Now as Christian walked alone, he spotted a man in the distance crossing the field to meet him. Eventually their paths met and the gentleman introduced himself as Mr. Wordly Wiseman. He lived in the town of Carnal Policy, which was a large town close to Christian's hometown.

Worldly Wiseman acted as if he had foreknowledge of Christian's leaving the City of Destruction, as if the leaving of Destruction was a topic of much gossip, not only in the town where he lived but that the news seemed to have spread to other places too. Because Worldly Wiseman had an inkling of his coming, he had spotted Christian's arduous approach. When Worldly Wiseman observed Christian's sighs and groans and the like, he engaged him in sympathetic conversation.

"Greetings, good fellow. Where are you traveling burdened in this manner?"

"Burdened manner, indeed! I think it's as large a burden as any poor creature ever had to carry!" Christian said. "And where am I going you ask? Let me tell you, sir. I'm on my way to that distant wicket gate." Christian

---

4   Original: *Moreover as for me, in no wise should I sin against the LORD in ceasing to pray for you, but I will teach you the good and the right way –* 1 Sam. 12:23.

nodded in the direction of his goal. "For there, I've been told, I will gain entrance to the place that will rid me of my heavy burden."

"Do you have a wife and children?" Worldly Wiseman asked.

Christian nodded. "Yes, yes I do. But I am so weighed down by this cumbersome burden that I can no longer enjoy their company like I used to. In fact, it makes me feel more like I don't even have a family." (*But this I say, brothers, the time is short; for the rest, let those that have wives be as though they had none. – 1 Cor. 7:29*)

Mr. Worldly Wiseman

Worldly Wiseman studied Christian for a moment. "Will you listen to me if I give you advice?"

Christian considered his answer. "If it's good advice, I will, because truthfully I'm in need of some wise advice."

Worldly Wiseman said, "Then I would advise you to get rid of that burden as fast as you can, because as long as you have it you'll never have peace of mind or be able to enjoy the blessings God has bestowed on you."

"That's exactly what I want to do ... to be rid of this heavy burden. But I can't get rid of it on my own, and I don't know of any man in our country who can take it off my shoulders, so I'm headed this direction as I told you for that very purpose: to get rid of my burden."

"So who told you to go this way to get rid of your burden?" Worldly Wiseman asked.

"A man who to me appeared to be a very great and honorable person. As I remember it, his name is Evangelist."

Worldly Wiseman's face puckered in a sour expression. "I most certainly condemn this man for his advice. There isn't a more dangerous and trouble-some way in the world to travel than the way he has told you to go. You'll certainly learn this the hard way if you listen to his advice. In fact, by the looks of things, I'd say you've already experienced some of this difficulty. Isn't that the dirt and grime of the Slough of Despond I see on you? What you don't realize is that slough is just the beginning of the sorrows you'll experience if you listen to that man. Other pilgrims who have gone that way could very well tell you the truth of that experience.

"Listen to me. I am older and more experienced than you. If you continue in this direction you are likely to experience wearisomeness, pain-fulness, hunger, perils, nakedness, sword, lions, dragons, darkness, and, in a word, death, and who knows what else." Worldly Wiseman looked Christian directly in the eye and said, "These things are certainly true and have been confirmed by the testimonies of many pilgrims just like yourself. So why should a man so carelessly place himself in danger by listening to a stranger like this man Evangelist?"

"You don't understand, sir," Christian replied. "This burden on my back is more terrible to me than are all the things you have mentioned." He shook his head. "No, I've given this thought, and I don't care what perils I meet along the way, as long as eventually I can be delivered from my burden."

The older man asked, "How did you come by your burden in the first place?"

Christian raised the book in his hand. "By reading this book."

Worldly Wiseman's lips thinned with disgust. "I thought so. The same thing has happened to you as to other weak men, who meddled with things too high for them. They are suddenly distracted and confused just like you, and it's humiliating. I can see the same thing has happened to you. And the problem is they turn to desperate measures to obtain what they know very little about."

"Oh no," Christian replied. "I know what I would obtain. I'd receive relief from my heavy burden."

"But why do you seek relief this way, by putting yourself in the path of so many dangers to get it? If you had enough patience to listen to me, I could tell you how to find what you're looking for without all the risks you'll run into along the way you're choosing to go. You see, the remedy

I'm suggesting is nearby and, instead of dangers, it offers safety, friendship, and contentment."

Christian eagerly looked to Worldly Wiseman. "Please, sir, tell me this secret."

"Why, the answer lies just a short distance away in the village named Morality. There ask after a gentleman by the name of Legality. He's a very judicious man, and a man of a very good name. He has skill to help men off with such burdens as yours from their shoulders. In fact, according to what I know, he has helped many pilgrims a great deal in this way.

"Besides that, he has the skill to cure those who are somewhat over-wrought and irrational about their burdens. You can go to him and be helped right away. His house isn't quite a mile from here. And if he isn't home himself, he has a son who is friendly and easy to get along with, whose name is Civility. He can assist you in the same way as his father. You can be relieved of your burden there!"

A broad smile softened his features. "If you decide not to go back to your former home, which I would recommend, you can send for your wife and children to come here to this village. Here we have suitable houses just waiting for someone to move in to them, and they are reasonably priced. The living standards here are good, though a little expensive, but high quality. We have everything you need for a happy life, plus, along with an environment you can enjoy, you would be in the company of honest neighbors who are financially secure and live a good life."

Christian was torn as what to do, but decided if what Worldly Wisdom said was true then his advice was the wisest to take. "Sir," he said. "How do I find my way to this honest man's house?"

Mr. Worldly Wiseman pointed toward a steep nearby hill. "Do you see that high hill over there?"

Christian nodded. "Yes, clearly."

The older man said, "You must walk up that hill, and the first house you come to is his."

So Christian turned from his current path to go visit Mr. Legality's house for help. But as he approached the hill it seemed to be steeper than he first thought. It rose so high that the side of it hung above him. It raised fear in him to venture further, for he was afraid the hill could fall on his head. He stood there trying to figure out what to do and his burden seemed heavier than ever, much heavier than when he had set out from his home.

Flashes of fire erupted from the side of the hill. (*There were thunders and lightnings and a thick cloud upon the mount and the voice of the shofar exceeding loud, so that all the people that were in the camp trembled. And all Mount Sinai smoked because the LORD had descended upon it in fire,*

Christian at Mount Sinai

and its smoke ascended as the smoke of a furnace, and the whole mount quaked greatly. – Exod. 19:16, 18) The sight filled Christian with dread that he would be burnt. Sweat beaded across his brow as he trembled with fear. (*And so terrible was the sight that Moses said, I exceedingly fear and quake.* – Heb. 12:21) He began to be sorry that he had taken Worldly Wiseman's advice, and just then he spotted Evangelist coming to meet him. While he was relieved to see the man, at the same time the blush of embarrassment heated his face for he had ignored the man's advice.

As Evangelist drew near, Christian could see the man was annoyed and ready for a serious talk. "What are you doing here, Christian?" he asked.

Christian didn't know what to say, so he just stood there without a word.

Evangelist took in a deep breath and let it out slowly. "Aren't you the man I found crying outside the walls of the City of Destruction?"

Christian looked at his feet and nodded. "Yes, I am the man."

"Didn't I give you directions to the little wicket gate?"

"Yes, you did, dear sir."

"Then how is it you turned aside so quickly? You are going the wrong way."

Christian shuffled his feet. "Soon after I left the Slough of Despond, I met a gentleman. He seemed like he cared about me and persuaded me I could find a man in the village who could remove my burden."

"What did he look like?"

"He looked like a gentleman," Christian said with a shrug. "He dressed like one and talked like one. I didn't want to go to the village, but with all his fine words this gentlemen eventually talked me into following his advice. So I came here, but as I drew close to this hill, and saw how it hangs over the way, I stopped. I was afraid it could fall on my head."

"Exactly what did the gentleman say to you?"

"Well, he asked me where I was going and so I told him."

"What then?" Evangelist asked. "What did he say next?"

"He asked me if I had a family. I told him I did, but I explained how this burden on my back weighs me down so much that I can't take pleasure in them like I used to."

"And what did he say after that?"

"He told me to get rid of my burden quickly. I explained that was what I was trying to do … that I sought relief. I described how I was traveling to the gate ahead so I could learn how to get directions to reach the place of deliverance. He said he would show me a better way that was closer and not fraught with all the dangers and difficulties as the way you set me in. He told me how to get to another man's house … one who knows how to take off burdens like mine." Christian looked away. "So I believed him and turned from the way you had advised me to go, in hopes I might soon be relieved of my burden. But when I came to this place …" He pointed toward the looming hill. "… and saw things as they are, I stopped dead in my tracks with fear and didn't know what to do."

"Just stand still for a little while," Evangelist said, "so I can show you the words of God."

So Christian stood trembling as he listened to what Evangelist had to say.

"Make sure you don't refuse Him who speaks to you, Christian, for if Israel did not escape judgment when they didn't listen to Him, how much more will we not escape if we turn away from Him when He speaks to us from heaven? (*See that you do not refuse him that speaks. For if those who refused him that spoke on earth did not escape, much less shall we escape, if we turn away from him that speaks from the heavens. – Heb. 12:25*)

"And besides that, He tells us that the just shall live by faith; but if any man draws back, His soul shall have no pleasure in him." (*Now the just shall live by faith, but if any man draws back, my soul shall have no pleasure in him. – Heb. 10:38*) Then Evangelist pointed at Christian. "You are the man who is running into this misery. You have begun to reject the direction offered by the Most High and to draw back from the way of peace. In fact, you are teetering at the point of being in danger of eternal punishment and damnation."

Christian fell down at his feet as dead and cried, "Woe is me, for I am ruined!"

Evangelist caught him by the right hand and said, "Men will be forgiven their sins and blasphemies. (*Therefore I say unto you, All manner of sin and blasphemy shall be forgiven unto men, but the blasphemy against the Spirit shall not be forgiven unto men. – Matt. 12:31*) Don't be faithless but believe." (*Then he said to Thomas, Reach here thy finger and behold my hands and reach here thy hand and thrust it into my side and be not unbelieving, but faithful. – John 20:27*)

Christian revived a little and stood up trembling again before Evangelist who said, "Pay careful attention to the things I am going to tell you. I'm going to show you who it was that deluded you, and who it was he sent you to. The man who met you is one Worldly Wiseman and rightly is he called by this name, partly because he has an appetite only for the doctrine of this world. (*They are of the world; therefore, they speak of the world, and the world hears them.* – 1 John 4:5) This is why he always goes to the town of Morality to church, because he loves the doctrine taught there because he thinks it saves him best from the cross. (*For many walk, of whom I have told you often and now tell you even weeping, that they are the enemies of the cross of Christ* – Phil. 3:18).[5] Because he is of this carnal temperament, he seeks to oppose my ways even though I am doing the work of an evangelist.

"Now there are three things in this man's counsel that you must utterly detest. First is his ability to turn you from the way you should go and get you sidetracked. The second is the way he works to portray the cross as odious to you, and lastly, that he points you in the direction which leads to death.

"You must despise his ability to turn you from the way, and yes, even the fact that you consented to his proposal. To do so is to reject the counsel of God in favor of the counsel of a Worldly Wiseman. The Lord says, 'Strive to enter in at the straight gate,' (*Strive to enter in at the narrow gate; for many, I say unto you, will seek to enter in and shall not be able.* – Luke 13:24) the gate to which I send you; 'for strait is the gate that leads to life, and few are those who find it.' (*Enter ye in at the narrow gate, for the way that leads to destruction is wide and spacious, and those who follow it are many; because narrow is the gate, and confined is the way which leads unto life, and there are few that find it.* – Matt. 7:13, 14) This wicked man has turned you away from this little wicket gate and from the way that leads to it. He has almost brought you to destruction! For this reason, you must hate his ability to turn you from the way, and in the same way you should loathe yourself because you listened to him.

"Secondly, you must detest his zeal to make the cross as offensive to you; for you are to prefer it more than the treasures of Egypt. (*Choosing rather to suffer affliction with the people of God than to enjoy the pleasures of sin for a season, esteeming the reproach of the Christ greater riches than the treasures in Egypt.* – Heb. 11:25, 26)

"Besides, the King of Glory has told you that the one who saves his

---

5   Original: *Brethren, if anyone is overtaken in a fault, ye who are spiritual restore such a one in the spirit of meekness, considering thyself lest thou also be tempted* – Gal. 6:1.

life shall lose it. And he who comes after Him, and doesn't hate his father, mother, wife, children, brothers, sisters, and even his own life cannot be his disciple. (*If anyone comes to me and does not hate his father and mother and wife and children and brethren and sisters, and even his own life also, he cannot be my disciple.* – Luke 14:26) Consider that Worldly Wiseman has worked diligently to persuade you to believe the King's advice will lead to your death, while the truth says you can't have eternal life without following the King's advice. As a result, you must abhor this doctrine circulated by Worldly Wiseman.

"Thirdly, you must hate the fact that he told you to follow the way that leads to death. In the same way you must consider the one he sent you to, and how he is unable to deliver you from your burden. You see, while it was promised that Legality could make the job of removing your burden easier, the fact is that he is the son of the Bondwoman who is in bondage along with her children. (*Tell me, ye that desire to be under the law, have ye not heard the law? For it is written that Abraham had two sons, the one by a bondmaid, the other by a freewoman. But he who was of the bondwoman was born according to the flesh, but he of the freewoman was born through the promise. Which things are an allegory; for these women are the two covenants: the one from the Mount Sinai, which begat unto slavery, which is Hagar. For this Hagar or Sinai is a mount in Arabia, which corresponds to the one that is now Jerusalem, which together with her children is in slavery. But the Jerusalem of above is free, which is the mother of us all. For it is written, Rejoice, thou barren that bearest not; break forth into praise and cry, thou that travailest not: for the desolate has many more children than she who has a husband.* – Gal. 4:21-27) You see, she represents Mount Sinai ...."* Evangelist gestured with an open hand toward the overhanging mountain. "The very thing you feared would fall on your head.

"Now if she and her children are in bondage, how can you expect to be made free by them? This Legality isn't able to set you free from your burden. No matter what Worldly Wiseman told you, the fact is that no one has ever been rid of his burden by him ... nor is he likely to be able to do so in the future."

Evangelist spoke from his heart with great passion. "You cannot be justified by the works of the law, because it isn't how one follows the law or the good things they do that rids one of their burden. This makes Worldly

Wiseman nothing more than an illegal guide and Mr. Legality a cheat. As for Legality's son Civility, he is full of hot air. With his smirking facade he is nothing but a hypocrite." Evangelist shook his head. "He can't help you. Believe me, there is nothing in what he says. You've heard of these intoxicated men, who dream up ways to deprive you of your salvation by turning you from the way in which I had set your path."

After this, Evangelist called aloud to the heavens for confirmation of what he had said. In reply I heard a voice and witnessed fire spewing from the mountain under which poor Christian stood. It made the hair of his flesh stand up. The voice cried out, "Those who trust in the works of the law are under the curse. For it is written, 'Cursed is every one who doesn't continue to do every aspect of the law which is written in the book of the law.'" (*For as many as are of the works of the law are under the curse; for it is written, Cursed is every one that continues not in all things which are written in the book of the law to do them.* – Gal. 3:10)

Christian thought he was going to die and began to cry out with an agonizing wail. He even cursed the time he met with Worldly Wiseman and called himself a fool a thousand times over for listening to that man's advice. Shame filled him. To think that this gentleman's arguments were nothing more than fleshly advice and yet caused him to forsake the right way. He scolded himself for being so foolish and came to his senses. He paid attention once again to what Evangelist said and had the sense to follow his guidance.

Christian looked to Evangelist and asked, "Sir, what do you think? Is there any hope? May I now go back to the way that leads to the wicket gate? Or will I be abandoned for what I've done and sent back to where I came from riddled with shame? I am sorry I ever listened to this man's counsel. May my sin be forgiven?"

Evangelist looked at him with a serious expression. "Your sin is very great, for you have committed two evils. You abandoned the way that is good, and you chose to walk in forbidden paths. Yet the man at the gate will receive you, for he has good will for men. But be careful not to turn aside again, because if you do, you may perish altogether when his wrath is ignited." (*Kiss the Son lest he be angry, and ye perish from the way when his wrath is kindled in a little while. Blessed are all those that put their trust in him.* – Psalm 2:12)

The Second Stage

hen Christian prepared to go back to the way. Evangelist kissed him and encouraged him with a smile. "God speed, Christian."

Christian hurried on his way and spoke to no one as he walked. Even if someone asked him a question, he was careful not to give them an answer. Instead, he went on like one walking on forbidden ground. He just didn't feel safe yet. In fact, he wouldn't think himself safe till he returned to the way which he had left to follow Worldly Wiseman's counsel. Finally, he reached the gate. Over it a sign read, "Knock, and it shall be opened unto you." (*Ask, and it shall be given you; seek, and ye shall find; knock, and it shall be opened unto you.* – Matt. 7:7)

He knocked with urgency more than once or twice. "May I now enter here?" he asked. "Will He within open to wretched me, even though I have been an undeserving rebel? If you let me in, I won't fail to sing His lasting praise!"

At last a serious-looking man named Goodwill came to the gate. "Who is there?" he asked. "And what do you want?"

Christian hung his head. "It is me – a poor burdened sinner. I come from the City of Destruction but am going to Mount Zion so I may be delivered from the wrath to come. I have been told, sir, that this gate leads to my destination. Are you willing to let me enter?"

"I am willing with all my heart," said he. With that he opened the gate.

Christian moved to step through the gate and to his surprise, Goodwill tugged him forward and hurried him inside. Christian stared at him in disbelief and straightened his jacket and asked, "What's the meaning of this?"

"A little distance from this gate there is erected a strong castle of which Beelzebub is the captain," Goodwill said. "From that castle both he and those with him shoot arrows at those who come up to this gate. It is their hope that those who arrive at this gate may die before they have the chance to enter in."

Christian pressed his lips into a thin line as he considered the man's words. He said, "I rejoice and tremble," for he was both relieved and thankful for the favor shown him.

Once he was inside the gate, Goodwill asked him, "Who directed you here?"

"Evangelist told me to come here to the gate and to knock, as I did. And he told me that you, sir," he nodded toward Goodwill, "would tell me what I must do."

Christian knocking at the gate

"An open door is set before you and no man can shut it."

Christian let out a sigh of relief. "Now I begin to reap the benefits of the risks I took and the dangers I faced in getting here."

Goodwill glanced to see if any others had come with Christian. "How is it that you came alone?"

Christian placed his hands on his hips, arms akimbo, and shrugged. "None of my neighbors saw their danger as I did."

"Did any of them know of your decision to leave Destruction to come this way?"

Christian nodded. "Yes, my wife and children knew what I was doing. When they wouldn't come with me I started out without them. They called after me to turn back. Along with them, some of my neighbors also stood crying and calling after me to return home, but I put my fingers in my ears and so came on my way without them."

Goodwill's brow furrowed. "Didn't any of them follow you and try to persuade you to go back?"

"Yes, a couple of neighbors did come along at the start. Both Obstinate and Pliable walked with me at the beginning, but when they saw that they couldn't get me to change my mind, Obstinate went back home complaining and denouncing me. Pliable came with me for a little ways."

"And why isn't he here?"

"Truthfully, we pressed on together until we came to the Slough of Despond, into which we both suddenly fell. My neighbor Pliable became so discouraged by that experience that he refused to go any farther. After struggling for a time in the miry bog, he finally reached the side nearest to his house and climbed out. He told me I should possess the brave country alone on his behalf, and he went in the direction of Obstinate while I proceeded to this gate."

Goodwill shook his head with regret. "How sad for poor Pliable. You mean to say he has such little appreciation for the celestial glory to come that he didn't consider it worth running the few risks and difficulties necessary to obtain it?"

Christian nodded. "It is true. What I have told you about Pliable is the sad truth." Christian hung his head again. "But to tell you the truth, I'm really no different from him myself. If the truth be told, he went back to his own house, but I also turned aside to go in the way of death when I believed the persuasive carnal arguments of one Worldly Wiseman."

"Oh, did that man prey upon you? Did he deceive you by offering an easy way to rid yourself of your burden by the hands of Mr. Legality? They are both cheats. Do you mean to say you followed his advice?"

Christian looked up at him sheepishly and nodded. "I went as far as I dared to locate Mr. Legality, until I came to the mountain that stands by his house. I feared it would fall upon my head, so when I saw that, I was forced to stop."

"It is just as well you escaped it, or it may have dashed you to pieces," Goodwill said. "That mountain has been the death of many and will be the death of many more."

"To tell you the truth, I don't know what would have become of me there at the mountain if it hadn't been for Evangelist's arrival just about the time I was feeling sorry for myself and rather depressed. It was by God's mercy that he came to me again, because if he hadn't I would never have come here to this place." He made a wide sweeping gesture with his arm taking in the area on that side of the gate. "But I have come now, unworthy as I am, and more deserving of death by that mountain than I am of being here talking with my Lord. Oh, what an undeserved favor it is for me to gain entrance here!"

"We don't object to any entering here, no matter what they have done in the past before they come here. In no way are they cast out. (*All that the Father gives me shall come to me, and he that comes to me I will in no wise cast out. - John 6:37*) Therefore my good Christian, come and walk with me a little distance, and I will teach you about the way you must go. Look ahead of us. Do you see this narrow way? That is the way you must go. It was established by the patriarchs, prophets, Christ, and his apostles. The way is straight. Follow it, for this is the way you must go."

"Straight?" Christian asked. "You mean to tell me there are no turns or bends – no detours in the way, by which a stranger may lose his way?"

"Oh yes, there are many side paths that connect to this narrow way, but they are crooked and wide. You must distinguish the right way from the wrong, by paying attention to which is straight and narrow." (*Because narrow is the gate, and confined is the way which leads unto life, and there are few that find it. - Matt. 7:14*)

Then, in my dream, I saw Christian ask Goodwill, "Can you help me off with this burden on my back?" For it was impossible for him to get rid of his burden without help.

Goodwill told him, "As for your burden, be content to bear this load until you come to the place of Deliverance, for there it will fall from your back of its own accord."

Goodwill shows Christian the way

Such news encouraged Christian, and he began to prepare himself and seriously consider the journey before him. Goodwill told him, "When you've traveled some distance from the gate, you will come to the house of the Interpreter. Knock on his door and he will show you excellent things."

Christian didn't waste any time. He said good-bye to his new friend. Goodwill wished him traveling mercies and sent him on his way.

Christian followed Goodwill's directions until he came to the house of the Interpreter. He didn't hesitate to approach the door and knock. To his dismay, no one came to the door, so he knocked again and again. Finally he heard footsteps from the other side of the door and a man opened the door a crack. "Who's there?"

Christian shuffled his weight from one foot to the other. "Sir, I'm a traveler, who was advised by an acquaintance to call on the good man who lives here in this house for my benefit. So, I'd like to speak with the master of the house, please."

The man turned and called to the master of the house, who came to the door and asked Christian, "What is the reason for your visit?"

"Sir," Christian began. "I am a man who has traveled from the City of Destruction, and I am on my way to Mount Zion. I was told by the man who stands at the gate at the head of this way, that if I called on you here at your home that you would show me excellent things – things helpful to me on my journey."

The Interpreter opened the door wide. "By all means come in." He ushered the pilgrim in with an inviting gesture. "I will show you things which will benefit you in your travels."

He commanded his servant to light the candle. With the glow of the flame casting a yellow puddle of light around them, the Interpreter led the way and told Christian to follow him. The three of them stepped into a private room. "Open the door," the Interpreter said to his helper. The man did as he was told. When the door opened Christian saw upon the wall the picture of an important man wearing a very serious expression. His eyes were lifted up to heaven. The best of books – the Bible – was clenched in his hand. The law of truth was written upon his lips, and the world was behind him. A crown of gold hung above his head, and he stood like one pleading with men.

Christian looked from the picture to the man of the house. "What does this mean?"

The man answered while still looking at the picture. "The man pictured here is one of a thousand who can produce children (*For though ye may have ten thousand instructors in Christ, yet ye shall not have many fathers, for in Christ Jesus I have begotten you through the gospel.* – 1 Cor. 4:15), labor in birth with children (*My little children, of whom I travail in birth again until Christ is formed in you.* – Gal. 4:19), and nurse them himself when they are born. Just as you see him with his eyes lifted toward heaven and holding the best of books in his hand, with the law of truth written on his lips, this is to show you that his work is to know and unfold dark things to sinners.

"In the same way, notice how he stands pleading with men and how the world is cast behind him. And see the crown which hangs over his head? These things are to show you that by despising the things in this present world and considering them less important, all for the love and devotion he has for his Master's service, he is sure to have glory for his reward in the next world."

The Interpreter looked at Christian. "I have showed you this picture first, because the man shown here is the only man whom the Lord of the place where you are going has authorized to be your guide. When you come across difficult situations in your journey, consider these things I have shown you. Think and ponder them so that if someone should meet you along the way and pretend to lead you along the right path, that you will recognize that in reality their way would lead to death."

Then he took him by the hand, and led him into a very large parlor full of dust, as if it had never been swept. The Interpreter called to a man and told him to sweep. The man grabbed a broom and swept and in so doing stirred a thick cloud of dust into the air. The dust grew so dense it almost choked Christian. The Interpreter then spoke to a woman who stood nearby. "Bring some water here and sprinkle the room." The woman did as she was told and the entire room was easily swept and cleaned.

Christian asked, "What does this mean?"

The Interpreter answered, "This parlor is the heart of a man who was never sanctified by the sweet grace of the gospel. The dust is his sin and inward corruption which has defiled the whole man. The one who began

Interpreter shows Christian the room full of dust

to sweep at first is the law, but she who brought water and sprinkled it is the gospel.

"Now while you saw the room fill with the great cloud of dust when first swept, the dust flew about in such a way that the room could not be cleansed and its dust almost choked you. This is to show you that the law, instead of cleansing the heart from sin, does in fact arouse it. (*So that without the law I lived for some time; but when the commandment came, sin revived, and I died.* – Rom. 7:9) It also gives it greater strength (*The sting of death is sin, and the power of sin is the law.* – 1 Cor. 15:56), and causes sin to flourish in the soul (*Moreover the law entered that the offence might abound. But where sin abounded, grace did much more abound.* – Rom. 5:20), for even as the law uncovers sin and forbids it, it does not provide the power to subdue it.

"In the same way, the woman you saw sprinkle the room with water which made it easy to clean – this is to show you that when the gospel comes with its sweet and precious influences and indwells the heart, just like the dust settled by sprinkling the floor with water, sin is also vanquished and subdued and the soul made clean, through faith. Consequently, the soul becomes a suitable place for the King of Glory to inhabit." (*Now to him that is able to confirm you according to my gospel and the preaching of Jesus Christ, according to the revelation of the mystery which was concealed from times eternal but now is made manifest, and by the writings of the prophets, by the commandment of God eternal, declared unto all the Gentiles, that they might hear and obey by faith.* – Rom. 16:25, 26)

Besides this, I saw in my dream the Interpreter take Christian by the hand, and lead him into a little room. Here two little children sat, each in their own chair. The name of the eldest was Passion and the name of the other Patience. Passion seemed to be very discontented but Patience remained quiet and calm.

Christian asked, "What is the reason for Passion's unrest?"

The Interpreter answered. "The governor of these children would have him wait for his best things until the beginning of the next year, but he wants his inheritance now. Patience, however, is willing to wait."

Then I saw a person come to Passion and bring him a bag of treasure. He poured it out at his feet. The eldest child scooped it up and rejoiced and at

Passion and Patience

the same time laughed with scorn at Patience. However, a short time later, he had wasted all his wealth and had nothing left but rags.

Christian turned to the Interpreter again and asked him to explain the meaning of these things more carefully.

The Interpreter said, "These two lads portray the passion of the men of this world and what is to come. Here you see Passion must have all of his inheritance, this year, which represents this present world, for so are the men of this world. They must have all their good things now. They can't wait till next year, that is, until the next world for their portion of good. That proverb, 'A bird in the hand is worth two in the bush,' holds more authority with them than all the divine testimonies of the good of the world to come. But as you saw for yourself, he quickly wasted it all and was left with nothing but rags. So will it be with all such men at the end of this world."

Christian nodded. "Now I see that Patience has superior wisdom in many ways. First of all, because he waits for the best things. Second, because he will also have the glory of his inheritance, when the other has nothing but rags."

"Yes," the Interpreter agreed, "but you may add another reason as well. It is the glory of the next world that will never wear out, while the good things of this world will vanish. Therefore Passion had no reason to laugh at Patience, for he had his good things first; however, Patience will have the last laugh at Passion for Patience eventually will receive his best things which last forever. For he who is first must yield to the one who is last because his good things vanish, while the one who is last will have his time to come but gives place to nothing, for there is nothing to follow.

"He who has his inheritance first, uses it and spends it; but he who has his portion last, has it forever. Therefore it is said of the rich man, 'In your lifetime you receive your good things, and likewise Lazarus evil things; but now he is comforted, and you are tormented'" (Luke 16:25).

"Then that means it is not good to crave things of this present world but to wait for things to come," Christian said.

"That is true. The things that are seen in this world are temporary, while things not seen are eternal. (*We look not at the things which are seen, but at the things which are not seen, for the things which are seen are temporal, but the things which are not seen are eternal.* – 2 Cor. 4:18) However, even though this is true, since things of the here and now and our fleshly desires are so closely related to one another, and because things to come and our carnal desires are opposed to one another, it is the present things and fleshly desires with which we so quickly establish a relationship, while distance is maintained between our desires and the things to come."

Then I saw in my dream that the Interpreter took Christian by the hand, and led him into a place where a fire burned in a fireplace in the wall. A man stood by it, continually throwing buckets of water on the flames trying to quench it. However, the fire only burned higher and hotter.

Again, Christian asked, "What does this mean?"

The Interpreter answered, "This fire is the work of grace that has been kindled in the heart. The man throwing water on it to extinguish and put out the flame is the Devil. Even though he continues to pour water on the fire, you can see the fire burns higher and hotter. Let me show you the reason for this."

The Interpreter led Christian behind the wall to the other side of the fire, where he saw a man with a container of oil in his hand. The man continually poured oil from the container secretly into the fire.

"What does this mean?" Christian asked.

The Interpreter answered, "This is Christ, who continually maintains the work already begun with the oil of his grace in the heart. By this grace, in spite of what the Devil can do, the souls of his people still prove to be gracious. (*My grace is sufficient for thee; for my strength is made perfect in weakness. Most gladly, therefore, I will rather glory in my weaknesses that the power of Christ may dwell in me. – 2 Cor. 12:9*) The man you saw who stood behind the wall to maintain the fire – this was shown to teach you that it is hard for those who are tempted to understand how this work of grace is maintained in the soul."

In my dream I watched as the Interpreter took Christian by the hand again and led him into a pleasant place where a beautiful stately palace stood. Now Christian was greatly delighted when he saw the striking building, but he was even more impressed at the sight of people walking around the top of the palace dressed in gold.

Christian looked wide-eyed at the Interpreter and asked, "May we go inside?"

Without a word, the Interpreter led him closer to the door of the palace. A big group of men stood in a knot in front of the entrance. They all wanted to enter but they seemed to lack the courage to do so.

A little distance from the door a man sat at a side table equipped with a book, his ink bottle, and quill. His role was to take the names of those who were determined to enter the palace. Christian's attention drifted to men posted at the doorway dressed in armor. They stood blocking the way and their clear intent was to prevent those who wanted to enter from getting in, even if it required violence. Christian pondered the meaning of all this.

Finally, when all the men cowered back away from the door for fear of the armed men, Christian spotted one man who appeared very resolute. He strode up to the man who sat at the table and said, "Sir, write down my name."

As soon as the name was recorded in the book, the man drew his sword, put a helmet on his head, and rushed toward the palace door where the armed men opposed him with deadly force. But the valiant man was not discouraged at all and fought fiercely, cutting and hacking his opponents. He both received and administered many wounds to those who attempted to keep him out (*Confirming the souls of the disciples and exhorting them to*

The man of stout countenance fights his way into the palace

remain in the faith, and that we must through much tribulation enter into the kingdom of God. – Acts 14:22); nevertheless, he cut his way through them all and pressed forward into the palace. Those inside cried out with a joyous voice, even those who walked upon the top of the palace.

They said, "Come in, come in; eternal glory you shall win."

So he went in and was clothed with garments similar to those worn by the citizens of the palace. Christian smiled and said, "I think I certainly know the meaning of this. Now, let me go forward."

The Interpreter shook his head. "No, you must stay until I have shown you a little more. After that you be on your way." The Interpreter reached and took Christian by the hand again and led him into a very dark room where a man sat in an iron cage.

The man appeared very sad. His eyes stared downcast at the ground, his hands folded with his fingers intertwined. He sighed as if his heart would break.

Christian looked from the sad man to the Interpreter. "What does this mean?"

"Talk to him." The Interpreter pointed to the man in the cage.

Christian looked to the man and asked, "What are you doing here?"

The man answered, "I am what I was not once."

"What were you once?"

The man said, "I was once an attractive and thriving professing Christian (*Those on the rock are those that when they hear, receive the word with joy, but these have no root, who for a while believe and in time of temptation fall away. – Luke 8:13*), both in my own eyes and in the eyes of others. I at one time was totally convinced I was on my way to the Celestial City. I even had joyous thoughts about my arrival there."

"Well, what are you now?" Christian asked.

The man let out another sigh. "I am now a man of despair and am held captive by it, just as this iron cage portrays. I cannot get out! Oh, how depressed I am now, because I cannot get out!"

"But what happened? How did you end up in this condition?"

"I neglected to watch and be sober. I loosened the restraints that kept my lusts in check. I sinned against the light of the Word and the goodness of God." With each statement his voice grew more troubled. "I have grieved the Spirit and He is gone. I flirted with temptation and the Devil came to me. I have provoked God to anger and He has left me. I have so hardened my heart that I cannot repent."

Christian tore his eyes from the man in the cage and looked to the Interpreter. "Is there no hope for such a man as this?"

"Ask him." The Interpreter nodded toward the caged man.

The man in the cage

Christian did as the Interpreter suggested and asked the man, "Do you have any hope that you will not be kept in the iron cage of despair?"

The man's eyes stared at the floor again. "No, none at all."

"But why? Don't you know that the Son of the Blessed is very merciful and compassionate?"

"I have crucified Him again by my life. (*Crucifying again for themselves the Son of God and putting him to an open shame. –* Heb. 6:6) I have despised His person. (*But his citizens hated him and sent an embassy after him, saying, We will not have this man to reign over us. –* Luke 19:14) I have despised His righteousness and regarded His blood as an unholy thing. I have acted spitefully to the spirit of grace (*Of how much greater punishment, suppose ye, shall he be thought worthy, who has trodden underfoot the Son of God and has counted the blood of the covenant, with which he was sanctified, an unholy thing and has done despite unto the Spirit of grace? –* Heb. 10:29); therefore, I have shut myself out of all the promises of God. Now there remains for me nothing but threats, dreadful threats, truthful threats of certain judgment and fiery indignation, which shall devour me as an enemy."

"Why? For what reasons did you bring yourself to this sorry condition?"

The man's eyes looked up for a moment. "For the lusts, pleasures, and profits of this world. It was the lure of the enjoyment of these things that I promised myself increasing pleasure." His eyes dropped to stare at the floor again. "But now every one of those things bites and snaps at me. They gnaw at my soul like a burning worm."

"But can't you repent and turn from this despicable condition?"

The man shook his head slowly. "No, for God has denied me repentance. (*For it is impossible that those who once received the light and tasted of that heavenly gift and were made partakers of the Holy Spirit and likewise have tasted the good word of God and the virtue of the age to come, and have backslidden, be renewed again by repentance. – Heb. 6:4-6*) His Word gives me no encouragement to repent. Yes, he is the one who has shut me up in this iron cage. Even if all the men in the world tried to let me out, they would not be able.

"Remember this man's misery," the Interpreter warned Christian. "And let his sorry state be an everlasting warning to you."

Christian moistened his dry lips. "Well, this is a most fearful situation! May God help me to watch and to be sober, and to pray that I may shun the cause of this man's misery. Sir, is it not time for me to go on my way now?" For Christian was quite ready to put this experience behind him.

"Wait just a little longer. I want to show you one more thing, and then

The man dreams

you can go on your way." The Interpreter took Christian by the hand again and led him into a bedchamber where he saw a man getting out of bed. The man got dressed, but as he put on his clothes he shook and trembled.

Christian asked, "Why does this man tremble like this?"

The Interpreter turned and asked the trembling man to explain the reason for his shaking.

The shaking man said, "This evening I was fast asleep. While I slept, I dreamed. In the dream I saw the heavens grow extremely black. Lightning streaked across the sky followed by a most-fearful thunderclap. It was terribly frightening and distressing. So I looked up in my dream, and the clouds rolled across the sky at an unusually fast rate. Among the noise of the storm, I heard the great blast of a trumpet and saw a man sitting upon a cloud served by thousands of heavenly beings in the midst of a flaming fire. Even the heavens were ablaze.

"A voice called out saying, 'Arise, you who are dead and come to judgment.' And with that the rocks shattered, the graves opened, and the dead who were in them came forth. Some of them were ecstatic and looked upward with joy on their faces, but others cringed and tried to hide under the mountains.

"Then I saw the man who sat upon the cloud open the book. He invited all the world to draw near, but the fierce flame that surrounded him kept the people at a safe distance, much like the distance between a judge and prisoners at the bar in this world. (*Marvel not at this, for an hour shall come when all that are in the graves shall hear his voice, and those that have done good shall come forth unto the resurrection of life; but those that have done evil, unto the resurrection of judgment.* – John 5:28, 29)

"Those who attended the man sitting on the cloud were ordered to 'Gather together the tares, the chaff, and stubble, and cast them into the burning lake.' (*For, behold, the day comes that shall burn as an oven; and all the proud, and all that do wickedly shall be stubble; and the day that comes shall burn them up, said the LORD of the hosts, that it shall leave them neither root nor branch.* – Mal. 4:1)

"Just then the bottomless pit opened very near where I stood. Smoke billowed and spewed from the mouth of the pit along with coals of fire and hideous noises. The heavenly attendants were commanded to 'Gather my wheat into the storehouse.' (*Whose fan is in his hand, and he will thoroughly purge his threshing floor and will gather the wheat into his storehouse, but the chaff he will burn with fire unquenchable.* – Luke 3:17) And with that I saw many caught up and carried away into the clouds, but I was left behind. (*For the Lord himself shall descend from heaven with a shout, with the voice of the archangel, and with the trumpet of God; and the dead in Christ shall rise first; then we who are alive and remain shall be caught up together with them in the clouds, to meet the Lord in the air, and so shall we ever be with the Lord.* – 1 Thess. 4:16, 17)

"I wanted to hide myself, but I couldn't because the man who sat upon the cloud kept his eye on me. All my sins flooded into my mind and my conscience accused me on every side. (*For when the Gentiles, who do not have the law, do by nature that which is of the law, these, not having the law, are a law unto themselves; which show the work of the law written in their hearts, their conscience also bearing witness, accusing and also excusing their reasonings one with another.* – Rom. 2:14, 15) At this point I woke up."

The shaking man's answer raised another question in Christian's mind and he asked, "But what made you so afraid of what you saw?"

"Why, I thought that the Day of Judgment had come," the man said. "And I was not ready for it! But the thing that frightened me most about it was that the angels gathered up several people around me and left me behind. Plus the pit of hell opened its mouth just where I stood, and my conscience distressed me because the Judge always kept his eyes focused on me with the look of angry disapproval upon his face!"

Then the Interpreter said to Christian, "Have you considered all these things?"

"Yes, and they challenge me with both hope and fear."

"Well, keep all these things in mind, so they may prod you to move forward in the right direction," the Interpreter said.

Then Christian began to make serious preparation for moving forward on his journey.

Then the Interpreter said, "I pray the Comforter will always be with you, good Christian, to guide you in the way that leads to the Celestial City."

With that Christian went on his way, saying, "Here I have seen things rare and profitable, things pleasant and dreadful; things to make me not easily moved. Let me think on these things I have begun to accept and to understand the purpose for which they were shown me. And let me be thankful, to you good Interpreter."

Christian's burden falls off

The Third Stage

———∽———

ow in my dream, the highway on which Christian was to travel was fenced in on both sides with a wall called Salvation. (*In that day they shall sing this song in the land of Judah; We have a strong city; God has appointed saving health for walls and bulwarks. – Isa. 26:1*) The burdened Christian ran up this way, with great difficulty because of the load on his back.

He ran like this until he came to a place where the road climbed up a small hill. At the top of the hill stood a cross and a little below at the bottom was a stone tomb. In my dream, just as Christian came up to the cross his burden loosened from his shoulders and fell off his back. It tumbled and continued to do so down the hill until it came to the mouth of the tomb where it fell inside and was seen no more.

Christian was so glad and overjoyed and in his excitement he said, "He has given me rest by his sorrow and life by his death."

He stood still for a while and looked with astonishment at the cross. It surprised him that the sight of the cross released him of his burden. He looked and looked again as tears ran down his cheeks. (*And I will pour upon the house of David and upon the inhabitants of Jerusalem the Spirit of grace and of prayer, and they shall look upon me whom they have pierced, and they shall mourn over him as one mourns for his only son, afflicting themselves over him as one afflicts himself over his firstborn. – Zech. 12:10*) Now as he stood looking and weeping, behold, three Shining Ones approached him and greeted him with "Peace be to thee."

The first of the Shining Ones said to him, "Your sins are forgiven." (*He was wounded for our rebellions; he was bruised for our iniquities – Isa. 53:5*)[6]

The second stripped Christian of his rags and clothed him with a complete change of clothes. (*And the angel answered and spoke unto those that*

---

6   Original: *When Jesus saw their faith, he said unto the paralytic, Son, thy sins are forgiven thee – Mark 2:5.*

The three Shining Ones

stood before him, saying, Take away the filthy garments from him. And unto him he said, Behold, I have caused thine iniquity to pass from thee, and I have caused thee to be clothed with new raiment. – Zech. 3:4)

The third placed a mark on Christian's forehead (*In whom ye also trusted, hearing the word of truth, the gospel of your saving health; in whom also after ye believed, ye were sealed with that Holy Spirit of the promise. – Eph. 1:13*), and gave him a scroll with a seal upon it. The third Shining One said,

"Look on this as you run, and deliver it when you arrive at the gate of the Celestial City."

With that the Shining Ones went their way.

Christian jumped for joy, leaping into the air three times, and went on his way singing:

"Thus far did I come burdened with my sin,
  No one could ease the grief that I was in,
Until I came here. What a place this is!
  Is this place the beginning of my blessedness?

Is this the place the burden fell from my back?
  Is this the place where the strings that bound it to me broke?
Blessed cross! Blessed sepulchre! Blessed rather be
The Man who there was put to shame for me!"

I saw in my dream that Christian continued on his way until he came to the bottom of the hill. There he saw three men fast asleep next to the road with chains attached to their heels. The name of the first was Simple, the second was Sloth, and the third was called Presumption.

When Christian saw these three pilgrims sleeping on the ground he walked over to them, hoping he might be able to awaken them. He said, "You are like those who sleep on the top of a mast (*Yea, thou shalt be as he that lies down in the midst of the sea or as he that sleeps at the rudder.* – Prov. 23:34), for the Dead Sea is under you, a gulf that has no bottom. So wake up and get moving. If you are willing I will help you get your shackles off."

He also told them, "If he who goes about like a roaring lion (*Be temperate and vigilant because your adversary the devil, as a roaring lion, walks about, seeking whom he may devour.* – 1 Peter 5:8) comes by, you will certainly become a prey to his teeth." With that they glanced at him and replied like this:

Simple said, "I see no danger."

Sloth said, "Just let me sleep a little more."

And Presumption said, "Every tub must stand upon its own without the need of assistance." And so the three of them lay down again to sleep and Christian decided it best to continue on his way.

But it troubled Christian to think of the three men in such obvious danger. It also bothered him that they didn't appreciate the kindness he freely offered them. First of all he awoke them, plus he volunteered to help them off with their shackles.

As Christian reflected on this troubling encounter he spotted two men tumbling over the wall, on the left-hand side of the narrow way. They hurried to catch up to him. The name of the one was Formalist, and the name of the other Hypocrisy. Like I said, they caught up to Christian, and he started a conversation with them.

"Gentlemen," Christian said. "Where did you come from and where are you going?"

Formalist and Hypocrisy explained that they were born in the land of Vain-glory and were going to Mount Zion to receive praise.

Christian looked from one man to the other and asked, "Why didn't you enter at the gate which is located at the beginning of this way? Don't you know that it is written, that 'he who doesn't come in by the door, but climbs up some other way, that person is a thief and a robber'?" (*Verily, verily, I say unto you, He that enters not by the door into the sheepfold, but climbs up some other way, the same is a thief and a robber.* – John 10:1)

"That may be true," they said. "However, our countrymen have agreed

Formalist and Hypocrisy coming into the way over the wall

that this gate you mentioned is too far away. So we usually just make a shortcut of it and climb over the wall at this point just as we have done."

Christian looked at the wall and back at his new traveling companions. "Won't this custom of yours be looked at as a trespass against the Lord of the Celestial City to which we are headed and so be considered a violation against his revealed will?"

Formalist and Hypocrisy said, "You don't have to trouble yourself about that. Our manner of climbing over the wall is a well-established custom. In fact, many witnesses have testified that it is an accepted route which has been well established."

"The real question is: Will your established practice stand up to investigation in a court of law?" Christian asked.

"We believe so." The two men assured Christian. "Our tradition has been accepted for a long time – more than a thousand years. Without a doubt it will be admitted as a legal ordinance by any impartial judge. And from a practical standpoint, what difference does it make how we get on this way as long as we get onto it? If we are in, we are in. From what you've told us, you're in by way of the wicket gate and we by tumbling over the wall. So what makes your present condition any better than ours?"

"I walk by the rule of my Master," Christian explained. "You, however, walk by the uninformed working of your imagination. You are already considered thieves by the Lord of the way. Therefore, I have little doubt that you will not be found to be legitimate travelers at the end of the way. You entered by your own devices without His direction, and you will leave by yourselves without His mercy."

To this they made almost no answer other than to tell Christian to mind his own business. Then in my dream, I saw each of the men continue to walk with Christian without talking much with one another, except that they explained their laws and ordinances to Christian. "We are as conscientious in obeying them as you," they said. "Therefore, we don't see where you differ from us, except for the coat you are wearing. Most likely that was provided by your neighbors, to hide your shameful nakedness."

Their words troubled young Christian. He said, "You will not be saved by obedience to laws and ordinances, since you did not come in by the door. (*Knowing that a man is not justified by the works of the law, but by the faith of Jesus Christ, even we have believed in Jesus Christ, that we might be justified by the faith of Christ, and not by the works of the law; for by the works of the law shall no flesh be justified.* – Gal. 2:16) And as for this coat I wear, it was given to me by the Lord of the place where I go – the Celestial City.

"You are right that it was given to me to cover my nakedness. And let me say that I accepted it as a token of kindness to me for I had been dressed in nothing but rags. Besides, it brings me comfort as I travel. I think about how the Lord will recognize me when I come to the gate of the Celestial City, because I wear His coat, a coat He gave me freely in the day that He stripped me of my rags.

"And perhaps you didn't notice it, but I have a mark on my forehead. One of my Lord's most intimate associates placed it there the day my burden fell off my shoulders. I'll tell you this, too. They also gave me a sealed scroll to read for comfort as I go on the way. I was told to turn it in at the Celestial Gate, as a token of my authorization to enter. However, I doubt you want any of these things since you didn't enter in at the gate."

When he said this they didn't answer him but only looked at each other and burst out laughing. Then I watched as they all pressed on, but Christian walked on ahead of them. He decided to walk alone and not to talk with these strangers any longer. Instead, he talked to himself, sometimes with great sighs and sometimes voicing contentment. As he traveled he was often refreshed by reading the scroll that one of the Shining Ones had given him.

They all went on till they came to the foot of the hill. At the bottom of the hill stood a spring and an intersection with two other roads besides the one which came straight from the wicket gate. One road turned to the left and the other to the right at the bottom of the hill, but the narrow way continued straight up the hill called Difficulty.

Christian walked over to the spring (*They shall never hunger nor thirst; neither shall the heat nor sun smite them: for he that has mercy on them shall lead them, even by the springs of water he shall feed them.* – Isa. 49:10), and drank to refresh himself and then started running up the hill. He said, "Though the hill is high, I still desire to walk up it. I don't care how difficult it is, because I understand that it leads to the way of life. Cheer up heart and don't grow faint or fear, because even if it is difficult, it is better to go this way because it is the right way, for while the wrong way is easier, it ends in anguish."

Formalist and Hypocrisy also arrived at the foot of the hill. They paused to consider the hill and how steep and high it was, as well as the fact that there were two alternative ways to go. They assumed that these two easier ways would meet up with the narrow way on the other side of the hill and decided to each choose one of the alternative roads. The name of one of those roads was Danger and the name of the other Destruction. So one turned to take the way called Danger, which led him into a vast woods and the other took the way to Destruction, which led him into a wide field full of dark mountains where he stumbled and fell, never to rise again.

Christian climbing the hill Difficulty

I looked toward Christian to see how far he had made it up the hill, but the steepness of the hill had caused him to slow his pace from running to walking and from walking to clambering on his hands and his knees.

Now about halfway to the top of the hill Christian came to a pleasant shady resting place made by the Lord of the hill for the refreshment of weary travelers. So as Christian reached this resting place, he sat down to rest awhile. While he sat, he pulled his scroll from his chest pocket to read it for comfort and reassurance. He paused to take a fresh look at the new coat that had been given to him when he stood by the cross. After reading and being encouraged, he grew drowsy and fell fast sleep and was delayed there until it was almost sunset. While he slept his scroll fell out of his hand and someone came up to him and shook him to wake him. The person said, "Go to the ant you sluggish person; consider her ways, and be wise" (Prov. 6:6). At this, Christian arose with a jolt and started on his way, racing ahead until he came to the top of the hill.

Now when he reached the top of the hill two men came running toward him in full flight from the opposite direction. The name of the one was Timorous and the other Mistrust.

Christian greeted them with a question. "Sirs, what's the matter? You are running the wrong way!"

Timorous answered, "We were going to the city of Zion and made it up this Hill Difficulty, but the further we go, the more danger we encounter! So we decided to turn around and are returning home again."

Mistrust nodded his agreement. "Yes, this is true! Just ahead of you, lying directly in the way is a couple of lions! We weren't sure if they were awake or asleep, but we couldn't bear to think of what would happen if we came within their reach. They'd pull us in pieces!"

Christian looked wide-eyed at the two men. "You make me afraid," he admitted. "But on the other hand, where else would I flee for safety? If I go back to my home in the City of Destruction, it is destined for judgment and awaiting fire and brimstone. I would certainly perish there.

"However, if I can get to the Celestial City, I am sure to be safe there. I must press onward. To go back is nothing but death, but to go forward … though I may fear death, life everlasting is beyond it. I will still go forward."

Mistrust and Timorous just shook their heads and ran down the hill, while Christian continued forward on his way.

As he went Christian pondered what he had heard from these men, and he felt for the scroll in his pocket so he might read it to be assured and comforted. To his surprise his fingers searched his empty pocket. The scroll wasn't there! Panic filled him and he became very distressed. He didn't know what to do, for he turned to the scroll for relief from his fears, plus it was his authority for entering into the Celestial City. At this point he became so perplexed he didn't know what to do.

Then he remembered falling asleep at the shady resting place halfway

Christian meets Mistrust and Timorous

up the Hill Difficulty and figured out what had happened. He fell to his knees and asked God for forgiveness for his foolish neglect. Then, without delay, he went back down the hill to look for his scroll. His heart was full of sorrow every step of the way. Sometimes he sighed, sometimes he wept, and he often chided himself for being so foolish as to fall asleep in that place. After all, it had been established for the purpose of modest refreshment from his weariness.

He traveled back down the hill further and further, carefully looking on this side and on that. His eyes eagerly searched for any sight of the scroll which had given him comfort so many times in his journey. He continued his downhill journey until he reached the shady resting place where he sat and slept. At the sight of this place his sorrow multiplied with the fresh reminder of his evil of sleeping. (*Therefore let us not sleep, as do others; but let us watch and be sober. For those that sleep in the night, and those that are drunken are drunken in the night. But let us, who are of the day, be sober, putting on the breastplate of faith and charity, and for a helmet, the hope of saving health.* – 1 Thess. 5:6-8)

In this way, he went on regretting his sinful sleep, saying, "Oh, wretched man that I am, that I should sleep in the daytime! That I should sleep in the midst of difficulty!" A small sob escaped his lips with his breath. "That I should so indulge myself as to allow rest for the ease of my flesh … to sleep in the place which the Lord of the hill built only for the relief of the spirits of pilgrims!

"I have taken these needless steps even in the same manner as Israel was required to do. It was for their sin that they were sent back again to wander in the wilderness by way of the Red Sea. In the same way, I am forced to walk this way again with sorrow, a way which should have only been walked with delight had it not been for this sinful sleep. How much farther along I might have been on my way by this time! Instead, I am forced to walk these steps three times instead of once. And now the night is about to overtake me since the day is almost spent. Oh, if only I had not slept!"

By this time he finally arrived at the shady resting place again, where for a while he sat down and wept. But at last, Christian remained downcast until his eyes fell upon the scroll! His fingers trembled with excitement as he snatched it up and thrust it into his pocket next to his heart.

I can't begin to say how joyful Christian was when he recovered his scroll.

For this scroll was the assurance of his life and acceptance at the desired sanctuary of the Celestial City. So with the scroll safely tucked away in his pocket, he thanked God for directing his eye to the place where it lay and with joy and tears focused on moving forward in his journey.

Oh, how nimbly he climbed the rest of the hill! Yet before he reached the top, the sun had set upon Christian. It made him all the more aware of the foolishness of his sleeping and how it had delayed him. He again began to grieve. "How sinful you are, oh sleep! Because of you my journey which should have been in the light has been overtaken by the night! I must walk without the sun. Darkness covers the path of my feet, and now I must listen to noises of miserable creatures, all because of my sinful sleep!"

Now the story Mistrust and Timorous had told him came to mind along with how they were frightened by the sight of the lions. Then Christian said to himself, "These beasts prowl in the night for their prey. If they should meet up with me in the darkness, how can I possibly avoid them? How can I escape being torn in pieces by them?" He nervously went on his way growing more jittery as he went. While he complained about his unhappy circumstances, he lifted up his eyes and spotted a regal palace directly ahead of him. The name of it was the palace Beautiful, and it stood to one side of the highway.

In my dream, Christian hurried along the way toward the palace, in hopes that he might get lodging there. However, before he had gone far, he entered into a very narrow passage which was about two hundred and twenty yards long, off the Porter's lodge. He carefully proceeded through the restricted path keeping his eyes alert as he went, and there he spotted two lions standing in the way. He thought, *Now I see the dangers that caused Mistrust and Timorous to turn back and flee.* (The lions were chained, but he did not see the chains that constrained the ferocious beasts.) Fear filled him and he thought about going back, just as they did, because at that moment he thought there was nothing ahead of him but death.

But the porter at the palace lodge, whose name was Watchful, noticed Christian's hesitation and that he looked as if he might go back. The porter cried out to him. "Is your strength and courage so small? (*And he said unto them, Why are ye so fearful? How is it that ye have no faith? – Mark 4:40*) Don't be afraid of the lions, for they are chained. They are placed there to test your faith at this point in your journey. They also show clearly those

Christian passes the lions

who have no faith. So stay in the middle of the path and you will not be harmed."

Then I saw Christian go forward, though he still trembled with fear of the lions. He took care to follow the porter's directions and stayed to the middle of the path. The lions roared and snarled, but they did him no harm. He clapped his hands with joy and went on till he stood before the palace gate where the porter awaited him.

Then said Christian to Watchful, "Sir, what is the purpose of this house? And may I stay here for the night?"

The porter answered, "This house was built by the Lord of the hill, and he built it for the relief and security of pilgrims." The porter looked directly at Christian and asked, "Where are you from and where are you going?"

"I have come from the City of Destruction," Christian said, "and am going to Mount Zion. But now that the sun is set, I would like, if I may, to stay here tonight."

"What is your name?"

"Now my name is Christian, but originally my name was Graceless. I was born of the race of Japheth, whom God will persuade to dwell in the tents of Shem." (*God shall enlarge Japheth, and he shall dwell in the tents of Shem; and Canaan shall be his slave.* – Gen. 9:27)

The porter's eyes narrowed. "But how is it that you have arrived so late? The sun has already set."

Christian looked away for a moment, too ashamed to meet the porter's eyes. "I would have been here sooner, but worthless man that I am, I slept in the shady resting place that stands on the Hill Difficulty! Even in spite of that, I would have been here much sooner, except that while I slept I lost my scroll of certification. When I reached the top of the hill I felt for it in my pocket. When it wasn't there, my heart was filled with sorrow and I was forced to go back to the place where I had overslept. I finally found it there and pressed forward on my journey once again. Now at this hour, I have come this far."

The porter said, "Well, I will call out one of the virgins of this place. If she likes what you have to say she will invite you to join the rest of the family, according to the rules of the house." So Watchful, the porter, rang a bell. At the sound of the bell a serious but beautiful young woman named Discretion came out of the door of the house and asked, "Why have you called me?"

The porter answered, "This man is on a journey from the City of Destruction to Mount Zion; but he's weary and seeing that the sun has set he asked if he might stay here for tonight. So I told him I would call for you, and that after talking with him you would decide what seems best according to the rules of the house."

Then the young woman asked Christian, "Where are you from, and where are you going?" He told her, and she also asked him how he got into the way, and he told her. Then she asked him what he had seen and met with in the way, and he told her all that as well. Lastly, she asked his name.

He said, "My is Christian, and I have a greater desire to stay here tonight, now that I understand this place was built by the Lord of the hill for the relief and security of pilgrims."

So she smiled and tears brimmed in her eyes. After a slight pause she said, "I will call for two or three more of the family. So she ran to the door and called to Prudence, Piety, and Charity, who came out to meet him. Following a little more conversation with him, they invited him inside to meet the rest of the family. Many of them met him at the threshold of the house and warmly welcomed him inside saying, "Come in, you who are blessed of the Lord. This house was built by the Lord of the hill specifically for the purpose of entertaining pilgrims such as you."

Christian bowed his head in respect and followed them into the house. Once inside, he sat down and they gave him something to drink. They agreed that until supper was ready, to make the best use of time, some of them should have a conversation with Christian regarding specific matters. So Piety, Prudence, and Charity were chosen for this discussion and they began to talk with him.

Christian is asked about his journey

"Come, Christian," Piety said. "Since we have shown love to you and received you into our house tonight, let's talk about all things that have happened to you in your pilgrimage. Perhaps talking about these things will help us better ourselves."

"I'm thankful for your good will, and I am glad your attitude is so friendly."

Piety asked, "What made you decide to take to a pilgrim's life in the first place?"

"I was driven from my native country by a dreadful message that unavoidable destruction would consume me, if I continued to live in the City of Destruction."

"But how did it happen that you came from your country in this direction?" she asked.

Christian told her that it was what God wanted. "For when I was fearful of destruction hanging over me, I did not know which way to go. But by chance a man by the name of Evangelist came to me as I was trembling and weeping. He directed me to the wicket gate. If he hadn't, I would never have found it, and so he pointed out the way that has led me directly to this house."

Piety's brow furrowed in thought. "But didn't you come by the way of the house of the Interpreter?"

"Oh yes." Christian nodded, eager to share the experience. "The things I saw there are most memorable! They'll stick with me as long as I live. Three of the things I saw especially made an impact. The first is how Christ, in opposition to Satan, maintains His work of grace in the heart. The second is how the man in the iron cage had sinned himself quite out of hope of God's mercy, and the third is the dream of the man who thought in his sleep that the Day of Judgment had come."

"Did you hear him tell his dream?"

"Yes," Christian said. "I thought it a dreadful revelation. It made my heart ache as he told it, and yet I am glad I heard it."

"Was this all you saw at the house of the Interpreter?"

Christian shook his head. "No. He took me to a place where he showed me a stately palace, and how the people in the palace were dressed in gold. Then a courageous man cut his way through the armed men who stood at the door to keep him out, and once he did, he was commanded to come inside and win eternal glory. My heart and mind were totally overwhelmed at the sight of these things. I would have stayed at that good man's house for a year, except I knew I had farther to go."

"What else did you see along the way?"

"See? Well, I had only gone a little farther when I saw One, as if in my mind, hanging upon a tree bleeding. The very sight of him made my burden fall off my back. For I had groaned under a very heavy burden, but it dropped off my back just like that." He snapped his fingers. "I had never seen such a thing, and it surprised me. While I stood looking up, for I couldn't stop looking, three Shining Ones came to me. One of them declared that my sins were forgiven; another stripped off my rags and gave me this embroidered coat I'm wearing, and the third set the mark you see upon my forehead and gave me this sealed scroll." He pulled the scroll from his pocket and showed it to her.

"But you saw even more than this, didn't you?"

Christian thought about it for a second and said, "The things I have told you were the best, but I did see some other interesting things. For instance, I saw three men, Simple, Sloth, and Presumption, lying asleep beside the way by which I came. They wore shackles upon their heels. But do you think I could awaken them? It was almost impossible!

"I also saw Formalist and Hypocrisy come tumbling over the wall instead of entering by the wicket gate and they pretended to be headed to Zion. But they were quickly lost, and even though I warned them, they would not believe. However, the hardest thing for me was getting up this hill, and it was equally difficult to muster the faith to get by the mouths of the lions. I'm telling you, if it hadn't been for the good man, Watchful, the porter who stands at the gate, I'm not sure that I wouldn't have gone back down the hill. But I thank God I am here and thank you for receiving me."

Prudence jumped into the conversation and said, "I have a few questions I'd like you to answer. First, do you sometimes think of the country from which you came?"

"Yes." He let out a sigh. "But not with fondness. I think of where I came from with much shame and loathing. And the truth be told, if I had yearned for that country I might have taken opportunity to return there by now. Instead, my heart desires a better country, that is a heavenly one." (*And truly, if they had been mindful of that country from which they came out, they might have had time to have returned. But now they desire a better country, that is, a heavenly one; therefore, God is not ashamed to be called their God, for he has prepared for them a city. – Heb. 11:15, 16*)

Prudence took in a deep breath and let it out slowly. "Don't you carry some memories of the things you did there and the people you talked to?"

"Yes, I do, but greatly against my will, especially deep inside my carnal thoughts and reasoning. You see all my countrymen, as well as myself, delighted in debating about such things. But now all those things only grieve me. If I could control my thoughts, I would choose never to think of those carnal things ever again. But even if I was able to do that which is best, that which is worst would still live within me." (*For that which I do, I do not understand, and not even the good that I desire is what I do; but what I hate, that is what I do. So that, desiring to do good, I find this law: evil is natural unto me. – Rom. 7:15, 21*)

Prudence tilted her head slightly to the side. "Did you sometimes find that those things related to personal carnality were overcome, yet at other times were cause for great puzzlement and confusion?"

"Sure, but those times of victory over carnality happened infrequently. However, when they did happen, it was truly golden."

"When you experienced such precious times in overcoming carnal annoyances, can you remember how you obtained these victories?"

"Yes, there are several means. For instance, when I think and meditate on what I saw at the cross, that will do it. And when I look at my embroidered coat, that will do it. Plus, when I read and study the scroll I carry in my pocket next to my heart, that will do it. When my thoughts are warmly stimulated about where I am going, that will do it too."

Prudence pressed him further. "And what is it that makes you so desirous to go to Mount Zion?"

Christian's eyes grew wide and dreamy. "Why, I hope to see Him alive who hung dead on the cross. And … and there I hope to be rid of all those things that remain as an annoyance to me. There at the Celestial City, they say there is no death (*And God shall wipe away all tears from their eyes; and death shall be no more neither shall there be any more sorrow nor crying*

Christian is instructed at the palace Beautiful

nor pain; for the former things are passed away. – Rev. 21:4); and there I shall dwell with such companions as I like best. For, to tell you the truth, I love Him because he released me from my burden, and I am weary of my inward sickness. In view of this, I prefer to be where I shall die no more, and in the company of others who shall continually cry, 'Holy, holy, holy.'"

Charity glanced around and looked back at Christian. "Why didn't you bring them along with you?"

He hung his head and wept. "Oh, how willingly would I have brought them! I have a wife and children ... and neighbors, but all of them were utterly against my going on pilgrimage."

Charity pursed her lips. "But you should have talked to them and should have attempted to show them the danger of staying behind."

Christian gestured with his palms up as he shrugged. "I did!" He let his arms drop. "I also told them what God had shown to me about the destruction of our city, but they looked at me like one telling a joke and they didn't believe me." (*And Lot went out and spoke unto his sons-in-law, those who were to marry his daughters, and said, Up, get you out of this place; for the LORD will destroy this city. But he seemed as one that mocked unto his sons-in-law.* – Gen. 19:14)

"And did you pray to God that He would bless them with understanding of your warning to them?"

"Oh yes," he nodded fervently. "I prayed with much love. You must know that my wife and poor children were very dear to me."

"But did you tell them of your own sorrow and fear of destruction? I expect that the prospect of destruction was clear enough to you."

Christian ran his fingers through his hair. "I did! Again and again and again! They could also see my fears were very real by my expression, by my tears, and also in the way I trembled under the anxiety of the judgment that hung over our heads! But even all this wasn't enough to get them to come with me."

"But why on earth wouldn't they come? What did they have to say for themselves for why they would not come?"

Christian wiped his hand across his face and looked at the ground. "Well, for one thing, my wife was afraid of losing what she has in this world. And my children?" He looked up at Charity. "Well, they were absorbed with the foolish pleasures of youth. So because of these types of things and other distractions, they left me to wander in this distressed frame of mind alone."

The young woman's face grew more serious. "So with all your efforts to persuade your loved ones to depart from the City of Destruction and come with you, did your futile, empty manner of life discourage them from acting on your advice?"

Christian's lips drew into a grimace. "I admit I cannot commend my life. I am well aware of my many failings. I also know that a man, by the way he lives his life, can quickly invalidate whatever arguments or advice he presents to others for their own good. Yet this I can say, I was very careful to avoid behavior on my part that would be considered disgraceful. I hoped to avoid giving them any excuse that would turn them against the idea of going on this pilgrimage. In fact, for this very behavior, they criticized me, saying I was too strict and that I denied myself of things (for their sakes) in which they saw no evil. I can honestly say that if what they saw in me hindered them, it was my own great kindheartedness in being careful not to sin against God or of doing any wrong to my neighbor."

Charity's head bobbed slightly in understanding. "Even as you say, Cain hated his brother because his own works were evil and his brother's righteous (*Not as Cain, who was of the wicked one and killed his brother. And why did he kill him? Because his own works were evil, and his brother's righteous. – 1 John 3:12*); and if your wife and children have been offended at you for this reason, they show themselves to be unyielding toward what is good. You have delivered your soul from accountability for their blood." (*Yet if thou warn the wicked and he does not turn from his wickedness nor from his wicked way, he shall die for his iniquity; but thou hast delivered thy soul. – Ezek. 3:19*)

Now I saw in my dream, that they sat talking together like this until supper was ready. When it was time to eat, they sat down to a table filled with good substantial foods and robust wine. All their conversation around the table was about the Lord of the hill and included what He had done and the purpose behind it. For instance, they talked about why He had built that house. By what they said, I understood that He had been a great warrior and had fought with and slain him who had the power of death (*Forasmuch then as the children are partakers of flesh and blood, he also himself likewise took part of the same, that through death he might destroy him that had the empire of death, that is, the devil, and deliver those who through fear of death were all their lifetime subject to slavery.* – Heb. 2:14, 15), but not without great danger to Himself which made me love Him all the more.

Christian continued the conversation as he ate. "For, as they said, and as I believe, He lost a lot of blood doing this. But He did it all in the glory of grace and with a motive of pure love for His country."

Besides this, some of the others around the table said they had spoken with Him following His death on the cross. Plus they testified that they heard from His own lips that He is such a lover of poor pilgrims that no one else is like Him in the whole world.

To make their point they gave an example of how He had stripped Himself of His glory so He might do this for the poor. Those who had heard from Him confirmed that He would not live in the mountain of Zion alone. They also talked of how He had made many pilgrims into princes, even though by nature they were born beggars and their nature originated from the dunghill. (*He raises up the poor out of the dust and lifts up the beggar from the dunghill to set them among princes and to make them inherit the throne of glory. For the pillars of the earth are the LORD's, and he has set the world upon them.* – 1 Sam. 2:8)

In this way they spoke together till late at night and after they had committed themselves to their Lord for protection, they each went to bed. They put Christian up in a large upper bedchamber with a window that opened towards the sunrising. The name of the room was Peace, where he slept until dawn.

When he awoke that morning, he sang joyfully.

> *"Where am I now? Is this the love and care*
> *Of Jesus, for the men that pilgrims are,*
> *Thus to provide that I should be forgiven,*
> *And dwell already the next door to heaven!"*

So in the morning they all got up and after more conversation, they told Christian he should not leave until they had shown him the distinctive features of that place. First they brought him into the study, where they showed him records of the greatest antiquity. There, in my dream, they showed Christian the bloodline of the Lord of the hill. It showed that

He was the Son of the Ancient of Days and came from an eternal generation. These records also revealed more fully the deeds He had done and the names of many hundreds whom He had recruited into His service. They also showed how He had placed them in such dwelling that would never pass away by undergoing decay or the passing of time.

They read to Christian the worthy acts that some of His servants had done

Then they read to him some of the notable deeds performed by some of His servants, including how they had subdued kingdoms, brought about righteousness, obtained promises, stopped the mouths of lions, quenched the violence of fire, and escaped the edge of the sword. Yet out of weakness they were made strong and became valiant in the fight, and turned foreign armies to flight. (*Who by faith won kingdoms, wrought righteousness, obtained promises, stopped the mouths of lions, quenched the violence of fire, escaped the edge of the sword, recovered from infirmities, were made valiant in battle, turned to flight the armies of foreign enemies.* – Heb. 11:33, 34)

Then they read another part of the records of the house which revealed how willing their Lord was to receive any person – no matter what kind of person they were – into His favor. This even included people who had in the past offered excessive insults to His character and accomplishments.

Along with these, several other historical documents provided accounts of many other famous events which Christian also viewed. These records included things both ancient and modern, along with prophecies and predictions concerning specific matters that are certain to be fulfilled, both to the dread and amazement of enemies and the comfort and relief of pilgrims.

The next day they brought Christian into the armory, where they showed him a variety of military weapons which their Lord had provided for pilgrims. There was a sword, shield, helmet, breastplate, all-prayer, and shoes that would not wear out. The great supply was enough to outfit as many men for the service of their Lord as there are multitudes of stars in the heavens.

They also showed him some of the military equipment which some of His servants had used to accomplish wonderful things. They showed him Moses' rod, the hammer and nail with which Jael slew Sisera, the pitchers, trumpets, and lamps too, with which Gideon put the Midian armies to flight. Then they showed him the ox-goad which Shamgar used to slay six hundred men and the jawbone with which Samson did such mighty feats. They also brought out the sling and stone with which David slew Goliath of Gath, and the sword their Lord would eventually use to kill the man of sin on that day of final victory over the predator. Besides these items, they showed him many excellent things that delighted Christian very much. They finished and at the end of the day they went to bed again.

Then I saw in my dream, on the following day that Christian got up expecting to head out on his journey, but those in the palace invited him to stay for one more day. They said, "If the day is clear, we will show you the Delectable Mountains, for they will further add to your comfort, because they are so much nearer to the Celestial City than where you are now."

So he agreed to stay, and the next morning they brought him to the top of the house and said, "Look south." When he did, he saw a range of very pleasant mountains a great distance away. They were covered with beautified woods, vineyards, fruits of all sorts, as well as flowers. Springs and fountains flowed freely and the place was very appealing to look at. (*He shall dwell upon the high places: fortresses of rocks shall be his place of refuge: bread shall be given him; his waters shall be sure. Thine eyes shall see the king in his beauty: they shall behold the land that is very far off.* – Isa. 33:16, 17)

Christian asked, "What is the name of the country?"

"Immanuel's Land," they said. "For true pilgrims, it offers the same character as this hill on which the palace is located. When you go there, from that vantage point you may see the gate of the Celestial City, which the shepherds who live there will make appear."

Now he gave thought to leaving the next day and of making preparations, but his companions said, "First, let's us go back into the armory."

So they did, and when Christian walked into the room, they equipped him from head to foot with fully tested weapons, just in case he should be assaulted on the way. Once he was well outfitted, he walked out with his friends to the gate. There he asked the porter, "Have you seen any pilgrim pass by?"

The porter answered, "Yes I have."

"Tell me, do you know his name?" Christian asked.

"I did ask him his name and he told me it was Faithful."

"Oh, I know him!" Christian said. "He is my townsman, my near neighbor! He comes from the place where I was born – the City of Destruction. How far do you think he is ahead of me?"

The porter thought for a moment and said, "By this time he has probably passed beyond the foot of the hill."

"Well, good porter, the Lord be with you and increase your blessings for all the kindness you have shown me."

The Fourth Stage

hen Christian headed out, but Discretion, Piety, Charity, and Prudence decided they would go with him to the foot of the hill. So they walked on together while reiterating their former discussions on their way to the bottom of the hill.

Christian said, "While it was difficult coming up the hill, so far as I can see, it is even more dangerous going down."

"Yes," Prudence agreed. "So it is. For it is a hard matter for a man to go down into the Valley of Humiliation, as you are doing now without slipping along the way. It is for this reason that we decided to accompany you down the hill." So they continued together down the hill, and though Christian walked very carefully, he still slipped a time or two.

Then I saw in my dream, that when Christian and his good companions reached the bottom of the hill, his companions gave him a loaf of bread, a bottle of wine, and a cluster of raisins and said farewell to him and he went on his way.

While Christian was among his godly friends, their precious words offered plenty of amends for all his grief, and when they let him go he was clad with northern steel from top to toe. But it didn't take long for Christian to be hard pressed, in this Valley of Humiliation. He had only gone a little way before he spotted a foul fiend coming across the field to meet him. The fiend's name was Apollyon, which means destroyer.

Fear filled Christian. His mind raced trying to figure out what to do. Should he go back or stand his ground? As he considered his options he thought about retreating, but he had no armor for his back. If he ran away and turned his back to the fiend it might give his foe a greater advantage, making it easier to pierce him with his darts. So Christian determined to stand his ground and risk confrontation with the enemy. He was out of time, and it was the best thing to do.

So he continued on and Apollyon met him. The monster was hideous and clothed with scales like a fish. They were his pride. He also had wings like a dragon, feet like a bear, and out of his belly spewed fire and smoke, and his mouth was like the mouth of a lion. When he came up to Christian, he eyed him with disdain and began to question him.

The fiend asked, "Where did you come from, and where are you going?"

Christian swallowed his fear and said, "I have come from the City of Destruction, which is the place of all evil, and I am going to the city of Zion."

Christian goes down into the Valley of Humiliation

"From Destruction you say. Then that means you are one of my subjects, for all that country is mine. You see, I am its prince and god." Apollyon's eyes narrowed. "So how is it, then, that you have run away from your king? If it wasn't for my plans for you to serve me more, I would strike you to the ground with one smashing blow right now for such an act."

Christian stood his ground. "I was, indeed, born in your dominion, but your service was hard and your wages such as a man cannot live on, for the wages of sin is death. (*For the wages of sin is death, but the grace of God is eternal life in Christ Jesus our Lord.* – Rom. 6:23) So when I reached adulthood, I did what thoughtful people do; I looked for a way that I might perhaps improve myself."

Apollyon looked down on Christian with eyes hooded with pride. "No prince worthy of his title releases his subjects easily, and I am no different. I am not ready to lose you as yet; but since you have complained about your service and wages, let me encourage you to go back home. I personally promise that what our country can afford I will give you."

Christian shook his head. "I can't do that. You see, I have already yielded myself to another – even to the King of princes. How can I in all fairness go back with you?"

One side of Apollyon's thin upper lip curled. "You have done exactly as the proverb says, 'exchanged a bad for a worse.' However, it is quite common for those who have professed themselves to be His servants to give Him the slip after a while and return to me. Do this and I promise all will be well."

Christian stood his ground. "I have given Him my faith and sworn my allegiance to Him. How can I possibly go back on my word and not be hanged as a traitor?"

"Think about it. You did the same to me and yet I am willing to forget about it, if you will turn again and go back to Destruction," Apollyn responded.

Christian raised his palm toward the fiend. "No. What I promised to you happened when I was but an immature youth. Besides that, I regard the Prince, under whose banner I now stand, to be the One able to absolve me of your charges."

He let his hand drop and looked Apollyon directly in the eye. "And yes, He is also able to pardon the things I did in service to you. Besides that, oh destroying Apollyon, to tell you the truth, I like His service, His wages, His servants, His government, His company and country better than yours. So stop trying to change my mind. I am the Lord's servant, and I have made up my mind to follow Him."

A wisp of smoke curled from Apollyon's nostrils. "That's all well and good, but think of what it will be like when your spirits are low and you have so much to get done." He paused dramatically and raised the boney-looking ridge above his right eye. "You are aware that, for the most part, His servants come to a wretched end because they are transgressors against me and my ways.

"How many of them have been shamefully put to death? And you consider His service better than mine, even though He has never come from that heavenly place where He is, to rescue any of His servants out of their enemies' hands? On the other hand, the world knows I am nothing like that. Look at how many times I have delivered those who faithfully served me, either by my power or the use of fraudulent schemes, even when they were taken by Him and His followers! And so will I rescue you in the same way, Christian."

"You don't understand," Christian said. "His present restraint in delivering them is deliberate and with purpose. It is to test their love and prove whether they will be loyal to Him to the end. And as for the shameful end you say is their destiny, that isn't an end, for they are assured of receiving future glory. In fact, they don't expect deliverance now. Instead they are content to wait for their future glory, and they will have it when their Prince comes in His glory along with the angels."

Apollyon jabbed his pointed finger in Christian's direction. "You have already been unfaithful in your service to Him, so how is it that you think you are going to receive wages from Him?"

"Tell me, Apollyon, in what ways have I been unfaithful to Him?"

"Very soon after setting out from Destruction you were quickly discouraged, when you were almost choked in the Slough of Despond." He raised his boney finger to track just how unfaithful the pilgrim had been. "You also made several wrong attempts to be rid of your burden, when you should have waited until your Prince had taken it off." He ticked off his point on a second finger. "Plus, you sinfully overslept; you lost your precious possession; and you almost turned back at the sight of the lions." He ran out of fingers on which to count Christian's missteps and dramatically threw his hand in the air with a flare to make his point of just how unfaithful Christian had been. "And when you talk about your journey, and of what you have seen and heard, inwardly you desire personal praise for all you say and do."

Christian glanced at the ground. "All this is true; in fact there is much more that you left out." He looked back at Apollyon. "But the Prince whom I serve and honor is merciful and ready to forgive. But besides these wrongdoings which I committed in your country where I was brought up and educated in them, I have groaned under and repented of them. As a result, I have received a full pardon from my Prince regarding these crimes."

Apollyon broke into a furious rage, saying, "I am an enemy to this Prince! I hate His person, His laws, and His people." He spit the words as if they left a bad taste in his mouth. "I have come out here to purposely oppose you."

Christian did not back away. He said, "Apollyon, be careful of what you are doing, for I am on the King's highway, the way of holiness. So watch yourself."

Apollyon defiantly straddled the entire width of the way blocking Christian's way. "I am not afraid in this," the fiend hissed. "Prepare to die; for I swear by my infernal den that you will go no further, for here will I spill your soul." Without warning he hurled a flaming dart at Christian's breast, but Christian lifted the shield in his hand and deflected it and so avoided the danger.

Christian drew his sword, for he saw it was time to rouse himself to action. Apollyon quickly responded by throwing darts as thick as hail, and even with all the skill he could muster Christian could not deflect them all. Apollyon inflicted wounds to his head, hand, and foot. Christian retreated a little, and Apollyon pressed more forcefully. Yet Christian took courage and resisted as fearlessly as he could. This agonizing combat lasted for more than half a day, until Christian was almost exhausted. For you should know that because of Christian's wounds, he inevitably grew weaker and weaker.

Then Apollyon spotted his opportunity. He began to press closer to Christian, wrestled with him, and threw him hard to the ground. Christian's sword flew out of his hand. Apollyon's teeth showed in a sneer. "I am sure of you now." The fiend drew closer, intending to inflict a mortal wound.

Christian began to despair for his life. But, as God would have it, while Apollyon prepared to make his final blow to destroy this good man, Christian nimbly reached out his hand and gripped his sword. He cried out, "Don't rejoice against me, oh my enemy, for when I fall, I shall arise" (Micah 7:8).

With that Christian gave Apollyon a deadly thrust. The fiend drew back, like someone who had received a fatal wound. Christian recognized the opportunity and moved in on him again, saying, "Even so, in all these things we are more than conquerors, through Him who loved us" (Rom. 8:37).

Apollyon spread his dragon wings and quickly took to the air and flew away, until Christian no longer saw him. (*Submit yourselves, therefore, to God. Resist the devil, and he will flee from you.* – James 4:7)

Now, unless you had seen and heard the intensity of this combat, like I did, you can't imagine the yelling and hideous roaring Apollyon made throughout the fight. Along with that, he spoke like a dragon! And on the other side of the fight, sighs and groans burst from Christian's heart. I had never seen him give so much as one pleasant look throughout the hellish fight, until he knew he had wounded Apollyon with his two-edged sword. Then a smile brightened his face and he looked up! But it was the battle itself that was the most dreadful sight I ever saw.

So when the battle was over Christian declared, "I will give thanks right

Christian defeats Apollyon

here and now to Him who has delivered me out of the mouth of the lion, that is Apollyon." He followed this with words of gratitude saying, "Great Beelzebub, the captain of this fiend, made plans for my ruin, and with this in mind he sent out Apollyon fully equipped and in a rage. And the hellish fiend fiercely engaged me, but blessed Michael helped me and by the blow of my sword I quickly made him fly. Therefore to Him let me give lasting praise and thank and bless His holy name always."

Then a hand appeared to Christian offering some leaves from the tree of life. He accepted them and applied the leaves to the wounds he had received in the battle. His wounds healed immediately. Christian took time to sit down in that place to eat bread and drink from the bottle which had been given to him for refreshment. Once finished, he headed out to continue his journey with his sword drawn in his hand. He said, "Who knows if there might be some other enemy at hand." But the remainder of his journey through this valley remained quiet, and he experienced no more trouble from Apollyon.

Now at the end of this valley stretched another called the Valley of the Shadow of Death. It was necessary for Christian to go through it, because the way to the Celestial City lay in that direction. Now, this valley was a very solitary place. The prophet Jeremiah describes it like this: "A wilderness, a land of deserts and pits, a land of drought, and of the Shadow of Death, a land that no man [but a Christian] passes through, and where no man dwells" (Jer. 2:6).

Now here Christian was tested more severely than in his fight with Apollyon, as you shall see in the following account.

I saw then in my dream, that when Christian reached the borders of the Shadow of Death, he met two men. They were children of the spies who had delivered an evil report about the good land and who quickly determined to go back. (*And they brought up an evil report of the land which they had spied out unto the sons of Israel, saying, The land, through which we have gone through to spy it out, is a land that eats up its inhabitants; and all the people that we saw in it are men of a great stature.* – Num. 13:32)

Christian spoke to the two men asking, "Where are you going?"

The two said, "Back! We are definitely going back! And truthfully, we would have you do the same, if you value life or peace."

"Why?" Christian looked out at the valley. "What's the matter with the way ahead?"

"Matter!" the two said together. "We were going that way just as you are and went as far as we dared. In fact, if we had gone on a little further we wouldn't be here to bring you the news."

"But what did you encounter?" Christian wanted to know.

The men looked at each other and back at Christian. "Why—why we were almost in the Valley of the Shadow of Death, but by good fortune we looked ahead of us and saw the danger before we came to it."

Furrows of frustration gathered between Christian's brows. "What! What did you see?"

"See! Why, the valley itself." They leaned close and almost whispered.

The Valley of the Shadow of Death

"It's dark as pitch and we also saw hobgoblins, satyrs, and dragons of the pit." They stood a little straighter and looked over their shoulders. "We also heard things in that valley like a continual howling and yelling, sounds of a people in misery too great for words; people bound in affliction and irons. Besides all that, discouraging clouds of confusion hung over that valley while death spread his wings and hovered over it. In a word, it was a completely dreadful sight being surrounded with nothing but disorder." (*Land of darkness, as darkness itself, and of the shadow of death, without any order, and where the light is as darkness. –* Job 10:22)

Christian slowly exhaled. "While I haven't seen what you describe, it doesn't change the fact that this is my way to the desired haven." (*Our heart is not turned back, neither have our steps declined from thy way though thou hast sore broken us in the place of dragons and covered us with the shadow of death. –* Psalm 44:18, 19)

The two men shrugged. "If it is still your way, be that as it may, but we will not choose it for ours."

So they parted ways, and Christian went on his way, with his sword still drawn and ready in his hand, for fear he might be assaulted.

Then I saw in my dream an overview of the valley. As far as it reached on the right was a very deep ditch. It is this ditch into which the blind have led the blind throughout time and have both perished miserably. On the left there was a very dangerous bottomless quagmire. If a man should fall into it, even a good man, there is no bottom for his foot to stand on. King David once fell into that quagmire and would no doubt have been smothered if it wasn't for He who was able who plucked him out. (*Deliver me out of the mire, and let me not drown; let me be delivered from those that hate me and out of the deep waters. –* Psalm 69:14)

Walking in the dark, Christian was careful to avoid the ditch on the one hand, but the way was so narrow it put him at risk of tipping the other way into the mire on the left. In the same way, if he tried to avoid the mire, without great caution he found himself on the brink of falling into the ditch. In this way, he went on. The effort brought one sigh after another, for besides the dangers of the ditch and the quagmire, the pathway was so dark, that he often couldn't see where his next step would land.

Now in about the middle of this valley I observed the mouth of hell. It stood hard against the narrow way. When Christian saw it, he wondered what he should do because of the flames and smoke that poured from it, not to mention the sparks and hideous noises. These things had no respect for Christian's sword such as Apollyon had shown. He was forced to put up his sword and to take another weapon, called all-prayer. (*Praying always with all prayer and supplication in the Spirit and watching in this with all perseverance and supplication for all the saints.* – Eph. 6:18)

Christian cried out, in my hearing, saying, "Oh Lord, I beg you to deliver my soul!" (*Then I called upon the name of the LORD, saying, O LORD, I beseech thee, deliver my soul.* – Psalm 116:4)

So Christian went on like this a long time as he continued on the way, yet the flames still reached towards him while doleful voices continued their unsettling calls, and rushed back and forth to the point that he sometimes thought he would be torn in pieces or tramped upon like mire in the streets.

He made slow progress over several miles surrounded by these frightful sights and dreadful noises. He finally reached a place where he thought he heard a group of fiends approaching to meet him. He stopped. His thoughts raced as he tried to figure out the best thing to do. He played with the idea of turning back, but then again he thought he might be halfway through the valley by now. He remembered how he had already overcome many perils and that the dangers of going back might be much more than those going forward. So he made up his mind to go on. Yet the fiends seemed to draw nearer and nearer to his location. When it seemed they were almost on him he cried out with a most fervent voice, "I will walk in the strength of the Lord God!" With that, the fiends drew back and came no further.

One thing I shouldn't forget to mention is how poor Christian looked so confused. As I watched him, it was like he didn't even know his own voice. Just when he came to the mouth of the burning pit ,one of the wicked ones sneaked up behind him. It whispered softly into his ear with many suggestive and distressing blasphemies. Christian thought these blasphemies had originated in his own mind, and it troubled him deeply. As he continued on his journey, the thought that he could possibly blaspheme the One who loved him so much weighed heavily on him. In fact, it tested Christian more than anything he had met with before. If he could have helped it, he would not have done it, but he didn't have the foresight to either stop his ears or to understand the real source of these blasphemies.

When Christian had travelled in this depressed condition for a significant amount of time, he thought he heard the voice of a man on the way ahead of him, saying, "Though I walk through the Valley of the Shadow of Death, I will fear no evil, for you are with me." (*Yea, though I walk through the valley of the shadow of death, I will fear no evil: for thou art with me; thy rod and thy staff shall comfort me. – Psalm 23:4*)

As a result, gladness filled Christian's heart for these reasons:

First, because he gathered from what he heard, that others who feared God were in this valley along with himself.

Secondly, since he understood that God was with them, even in such a dark and dismal place, he reasoned that his invisible presence was with him, in spite of the hindrances of such a place. (*Behold, he shall pass before me, and I shall not see him; and he shall pass on, and I shall not understand him. – Job 9:11*)

Thirdly, he hoped to catch up and enjoy some fellowship with the man ahead and thought about calling to him, though he didn't know what to say, for he had also thought himself to be alone.

Finally, the light of morning dawned and Christian said, "He has turned the shadow of death into morning." (*Look unto him that makes the seven stars and Orion and turns the shadow of death into the morning and makes the day dark with night, that calls for the waters of the sea and pours them out upon the face of the earth: The LORD is his name. – Amos 5:8*)

Now in light of the new day, he looked back, not because he wanted to go back the way he had come, but to see more clearly what hazards he had navigated through in the dark. He could see the ditch perfectly on the one side and the quagmire on the other, along with just how narrow the way was which lay between them. He could also see the hobgoblins, satyrs, and dragons of the pit, but they kept their distance. Apparently, after the break of day, they were reluctant to come near. Yet he saw them in fulfillment of that which is written, "He reveals deep things out of darkness, and brings to light the shadow of death" (Job 12:22).

Christian was greatly encouraged that he had made it through all the dangers of his solitary journey so far. He could now see these dangers, though he feared them more than ever, because the light of day exposed them. So the rising sun offered even more mercy to Christian, because it is important to note, that though the first part of the Valley of the Shadow of Death was dangerous, this second part which stretched ahead of him was, if possible, far more dangerous.

From the place where he currently stood he could see that throughout the remainder of the valley the way was full of snares, traps, gins, and nets. Along with that, the depths were so full of pits, pitfalls, deep holes, and unsafe ledges that if it had been dark now, like it was when he came to the first part of the way, even if he had a thousand souls, they all would have been lost. But as I said, the sun was now rising. Then said he, "His candle shines on my head and by his light I go through darkness" (Job 29:3).

Christian made it to the end of the valley walking in the light. Now I saw in my dream, at the end of the valley lay blood, bones, ashes, and mangled bodies of men, even of pilgrims who had gone this way earlier.

Christian enters the second part of the Valley of the Shadow of Death

While I pondered the possible reason for such remains, I spotted a little cave ahead of me, where two giants, Pope and Pagan, lived in old times. It was by their power and tyranny that the men whose bones, blood, ashes, and other remains lay in this place were cruelly put to death.

But Christian passed by this place without much danger, and it somewhat surprised me. But I have learned that Pagan has been dead many a day. As for the other, though he is still alive, because of his old age and many shrewd conflicts from his younger days, he has grown so crazy and stiff in his joints that he can do little more than sit in his cave's mouth, grinning at pilgrims as they go by, and biting his nails in frustration because he can no longer intercept them.

So Christian went on his way, but he didn't know what to think of the old man sitting at the mouth of the cave, especially because Pope was unable to approach him though he spoke to him saying, "You will never mend, till more of you are burned." But Christian held his peace, and smiled as he went by and suffered no harm. Then he sang a song.

"Oh world of wonders (I can say no less),
That I should be preserved in that distress
I have met with here! O blessed be
The hand that from it has delivered me!
Dangers in darkness, devils, hell, and sin,
Did surround me, while I this vale was in.
Snares, pits, traps, and nets did lie
About my path, that worthless I
Might have been caught, entangled, and cast down;
But since I live, let Jesus wear the crown."

The Fifth Stage

———— ⌀ ————

ow as Christian went on his way, he came to a slight incline designed to allow pilgrims to see more easily ahead. From up there, Christian went along and looking up he saw Faithful in the distance, intent on his journey.

Christian cried out loudly to get his attention. "Here, here, look here! Wait, and let me catch up to you and I will be your companion."

At that Faithful looked behind him.

Christian cried out again, "Wait, wait until I catch up to you!"

But Faithful answered, "No, I travel with my life at stake and the avenger of blood is close behind me."

This reply somewhat moved Christian. He mustered all his strength and quickly caught up with Faithful. In fact, he accidentally ran past him so that the last became first. A smile brightened Christian's face with a sense of self-congratulation. He felt proud because he had gotten ahead of his brother, but he didn't pay attention to his feet. Suddenly he stumbled, fell to the ground, and he couldn't get up – that is, until Faithful came up to help him.

Then I saw in my dream, that the two of them went along together very lovingly toward one another, and enjoyed a delightful conversation about all the things that had happened to them in their pilgrimage.

Christian began in this way. "My honored and deeply loved brother, Faithful, I am glad I have caught up with you and that God has so strengthened our spirits that we can walk as companions in this so pleasant a path."

Faithful looked over at Christian as they walked. "Dear friend, I had thought of enjoying your company even from our town, but you did get quite a start ahead of me. Because of that I was forced to come this far on my own."

"How long did you stay in the City of Destruction, before you set out after me on your pilgrimage?"

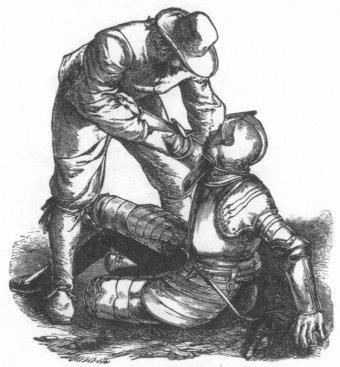

Faithful helps Christian

"Till I could stay no longer," Faithful admitted. "After you left, there was a lot of talk about how our city would be burned to the ground with fire from heaven, in a short time."

"Is that right? Did your neighbors really talk like this?"

Faithful nodded. "Yes, for a while it's what everybody talked about. At least for a while."

A slight frown creased Christian's brow. "Did no one else but you come away from Destruction to escape the danger?"

Faithful shrugged with his hand palm up and let it fall to his side in resignation. "Like I said, there was a lot of talk going on, but I don't think they really believed it. In the heat of the conversation, I heard some of them ridicule you. They even talked about your pilgrimage like they disapproved of it. In fact, they described it as a desperate journey. However, I believed, and still do, that the end of our city will be with fire and brimstone from above and as a result I decided to make my escape."

"Did you hear anyone talk about neighbor Pliable?"

"Yes, Christian. I heard that he followed you until he came to the Slough of Despond, where some said he fell in. He wouldn't say anything about it, but I'm sure he was thoroughly covered with the foul dirt of that place."

"And what did the neighbors say to him?"

"Since he returned, he has been the subject of considerable derision, from all sorts of people. Some mock and despise him, and hardly anyone will give him work. He is seven times worse off now than if he had never left the city in the first place."

The news troubled Christian. "But why were they so set against him, especially since they also despise the way he abandoned?"

Faithful's lips thinned to a straight line. "They say things like 'hang him,' 'he's a turncoat,' he wasn't true to his profession.' I think God has stirred them up to hiss and jeer at him, and make a proverb of him 'because he hath forsaken the way.'" (*And I will persecute them with the sword, with the famine, and with the pestilence, and will give them over as a reproach to all the kingdoms of the earth, as a curse, and as an astonishment, and a hissing, and an affront, unto all the Gentiles where I have driven them: because they did not hearken unto my words, said the LORD, which I sent unto them by my slaves the prophets, rising up early and sending them; but ye did not hear, said the LORD. – Jer. 29:18, 19*)

"Did you have a chance to talk with him before you left?"

"I saw him once in the streets," Faithful said, "but he stayed to the other side of the street, like he was ashamed of what he had done. So I didn't really speak to him."

Christian glanced down at the ground. "I have to say when I first set out I had hopes for him." He looked back at Faithful with sadness in his eyes. "But now I'm afraid he will perish in the overthrow of the city. For it has happened to him just as the proverb says, 'The dog returns to his vomit, and the sow that was washed to her wallowing in the mud'" (2 Peter 2:22).

Faithful nodded. "I agree. I have the same fears for him. But who can hinder that which will be?"

"Well, neighbor Faithful," Christian said. "Let's talk about something else. About things that concern us more immediately. Tell me now, what have you met with and experienced thus far along the way? Because I know you have undergone some things that would be worth recording."

Faithful didn't hesitate to answer. "I escaped the Slough of Despond which I understand you fell into, and I reached the gate without suffering that danger. However, I met with a woman whose name was Wanton, who intended to do me harm."

Christian said, "It's a good thing you escaped her snare. Joseph was tested by her in Egypt, and he escaped her as you did; otherwise it would have cost him his life. (*And it came to pass about this time, that Joseph went into the house to do his business, and none of those of the house were there within. And she caught him by his garment, saying, Lie with me; and he left his garment in her hand and fled and got outside. And it came to pass when she saw that he had left his garment in her hand and had fled forth.* – Gen. 39:11-13) But what did she do to you?"

Faithful and Wanton

"Unless you experience talking with her yourself, you can't begin to imagine how flattering her words were," Faithful said.

"So she didn't promise you the things of a moral excellence?"

Faithful shook his head. "No, not at all. She promised things of a carnal and fleshly nature, promising all sorts of sensual pleasure."

"Phew!" Christian let out a low whistle. "Thank God you escaped her, because those despised by the Lord shall fall into her pit." (*The mouth of strange women is a deep pit; he that is abhorred of the LORD shall fall therein.* – Prov. 22:14)

"True enough," Faithful agreed. "But to tell the truth, I'm not sure I entirely escaped her or not."

"Why do you say that?" Christian wanted to know. "I trust you did not consent to her solicitation … did you?"

"No, I did not defile myself with her. For I remembered an old writing that I had read, which said, 'Her steps descend down to Hell.' (*Her feet go down to death, her steps uphold Sheol.* – Prov. 5:5) So I shut my eyes to prevent myself from being bewitched by her seductive looks. (*I made a covenant with my eyes; why then should I look upon a maid?* – Job 31:1) Then she became angry and railed on me, and I quickly went on my way."

"Did you meet with any other assaults on your way?"

Faithful continued to give his account as the two of them walked. He said, "When I came to the foot of the hill called Difficulty, I met with a very aged man, who asked me who I was, and where I was going. I told him I was a pilgrim, going to the Celestial City.

"Then the old man said to me, 'You look like an honest fellow; would you be content to live with me if I pay you?'

"So I asked his name and about where he lived. He said his name was Adam the First and that he lived in the town of Deceit. (*That ye put off everything concerning the old way of life, that is, the old man who corrupts himself according to deceitful desire.* – Eph. 4:22) I asked him about what type of work, and exactly what wages he offered. He told me that his work offered many delights and that his wages would make me a full heir in his family.

"I asked him for further details about his household and what other servants he had. He explained how his house was maintained with all the luxuries of the world, and that his servants were his own children. I asked how many children he had, and he said that he had but three daughters, the Lust of the Flesh, the Lust of the Eyes, and the Pride of Life. (*For all that is in the world, the lust of the flesh and the lust of the eyes and the pride of life, is not of the Father, but is of the world.* – 1 John 2:16) He went on to say that I could marry them if I wished to do so. Then I asked how long he would expect me to live with him, and he said as long as he lived himself."

"So what did you decide?" Christian asked. "Did you finally end up making an agreement between the old man and yourself?"

"Well, at first I felt somewhat inclined to go with the man, because his offer seemed very fair and quite appealing. However, on looking at his forehead, as I talked with him, I saw these words written there: 'Put off the old man with his deeds.'"

"So how did you end up responding then?"

"A burning-hot thought came into my mind. It told me that whatever he said, and however he flattered, that once he lured me to his house he would sell me as a slave. So I insisted that he stop talking to me, for I had no intention to even go near the door of his house. Then he scorned and insulted me. He told me he would send a certain person after me who would make the way ahead bitter to my soul. So I turned to go away from him, but just as I turned to proceed on my journey, he took hold of my flesh and jerked me back with such force that I thought he had pulled a part of me to himself. At this I cried out in pain. 'Oh wretched man!' (*O wretched man that I am! who shall deliver me from the body of this death?* – Rom. 7:24) So I went on my way up the hill.

"Now, when I had walked halfway up the hill, I looked behind myself and saw someone coming after me, moving as swift as the wind. He overtook me just about the place where the shady resting place is located."

"That's the place where I sat down to rest," Christian said. "But being overcome with sleep, it was there that I lost this scroll out of my chest pocket as I slept."

"But, let me tell you the rest of the story, good brother," Faithful said. "Just as soon as the man overtook me, without a word, he knocked me down to the ground and left me lying there like one dead. But when I revived a little and came to my senses, I asked him why he had treated me this way. He said it was because of my secret fondness for Adam the First. With that, he struck me again with another deadly blow to my chest and beat me down to the ground. So once again I lay crumpled at his feet as if dead. When I came to myself the second time I cried to him for mercy, but he said, 'I don't know how to show mercy,' and with that he knocked me down to the ground again. It was clear he would have finished me off, if it hadn't been for a man who came by at that time and demanded that he stop his assault."

"Who was this man?"

Faithful said, "At first I didn't recognize him, but as he went by, I noticed the holes in his hands and in his side: Then I concluded that he was our Lord. So I continued up the hill."

"That man who overtook you was Moses," Christian explained. "He doesn't spare anyone; nor does he know how to show mercy to those who disobey the law."

Faithful nodded his agreement. "I know well that what you say is true, because this was not the first time we had met. He was the one who came to me when I lived securely at home in the City of Destruction. He told me he would burn my house down over my head if I stayed there."

Christian thought of his time in the palace at the top of the hill and asked, "Didn't you see the house that stood on the top of the hill, on the same side of the way where Moses met you?"

"Yes," Faithful said. "And lions, too, before I reached it. But, as for the lions, I think they were asleep, for it was about noon and they seemed to be asleep. Because I had so much of the day before me, I passed by the porter of that house and came down the other side of the hill."

"He told me that he saw you go by," Christian said. "But I wish you had stopped at the house and stayed a while. They would have showed you so many rare treasures that you would remember until the day you die. But tell me, did you meet anyone in the Valley of Humility?"

"Yes, I did." Faithful's brows knit together at the memory. "I met with a certain man by the name of Discontent. He was intent on persuading me to go back with him. For he reasoned that the valley was altogether without honor and to go ahead was the way to displease all my friends – Pride, Arrogancy, Self-Conceit, Worldly Glory, and others whom he knew. He said they would be very much offended if I made such a fool of myself as to wade through this valley."

"How did you answer him?" Christian asked.

"I told him that although all those he named might claim to be my friends, and rightly so since they were my relatives in the flesh, that since I became a pilgrim they have disowned me. And I have in the same way rejected them. Therefore they are no more to me than if they had never been of my lineage.

"And as for this valley I told him that he had quite misrepresented it, because humility comes before honor and a haughty spirit before a fall. Therefore, I said to him, I would rather go through this valley to obtain honor which the wisest highly value, than to choose what he esteemed to be worthy based on our affections."

"Did you meet with anyone else other than that in that valley?"

"Yes, I did. I met with a man by the name of Shame; but of all the men I met on my pilgrimage, he, I think, bears the wrong name. He would not agree, but after a little debate and other evidence I'd say this bold-faced Shame would better be called Shameless."

"Why, what did he say to you?" Christian asked.

"What did he say? Let's see. He objected to and railed against religion

Faithful is disowned by his relatives

itself. He said it was a pitiful, low, sneaking business for a man to value religion. And he said that a tender conscience was an unmanly thing." Faithful let out a heavy sigh. "He even when on to say that for a man to be mindful of his words and ways, actually curtails his intimidating freedom and the boastful spirits of the times which the heroes of these times freely display. Such actions, according to him, would make men the object of ridicule.

"He also objected because, according to him, only a few of the mighty, rich, or wise, ever held the same opinion as me. He also ridiculed the thought of being invited to become fools and to voluntarily hazard the loss of all for who knows what as being something accepted by very few. (*But those things which were gain to me, I counted loss for Christ. And doubtless I even count all things as loss for the excellency of the knowledge of Christ Jesus my Lord, for whom I have suffered the loss of all things and do count them but dung, that I may win Christ and be found in him, not having my own righteousness, which is of the law, but that which is through the faith of Christ, the righteousness which is of God by faith.* – Phil. 3:7-9)

"Plus he objected to the low standard of living and conditions the pilgrims submitted themselves to and even sneered at the way in which they lived and their ignorance and lack of understanding in all natural sciences. He also pressed me on a great deal more issues besides what I've told you. Things like how it was a shame to sit whining and mourning under a sermon, and that it was a shame to return home sighing and groaning under the conviction of that sermon. He even said it was a shame to ask from my neighbor forgiveness for petty faults or to make restitution when I have stolen from anyone.

"He said religion made a man appear to be strange to those who are great, because it's not normal to become concerned over a few vices, which he called by finer terms. He pointed out how such thinking gives pilgrims a perception that causes them to respect the lowest of society, solely because they belong to the same religious fraternity. He finished by asking me, 'Is this not a shame?'"

Christian asked the same question he'd asked earlier. "And what did you say to him?"

Faithful's brows arched in question. "Say? To tell you the truth, I didn't know what to say at first. He pressed me so hard my face burned with embarrassment. And of course Shame brought that up as if I had become ashamed and almost beaten in defeat. But finally I began to consider the fact that that which is highly esteemed among men is an abomination to God. (*And he said unto them, Ye are they who justify themselves before men, but God knows your hearts, for that which is highly esteemed among men is abomination in the sight of God.* – Luke 16:15) And as I thought more about it, I realized that this Shame was describing what men are, but he had nothing to offer me about what God or the Word of God reveals. I also thought about the Day of Judgment. We won't be doomed to death or life according to the boastful spirits of the world but according to the wisdom and law of the Highest.

"With this in mind, I focused on the fact that what God says is indeed best. It doesn't matter if all the men in the world are against it. So seeing that God prefers his religion; seeing God prefers a tender conscience; seeing that those who make themselves fools for the kingdom of heaven are wisest, and that the poor man who loves Christ is richer than the greatest man in the world who hates him, I turned to Shame and said, 'Depart, you who are an enemy to my salvation. Should I listen to your words which are contrary to my sovereign Lord? If I did that how would I be able to face him at his coming? (*Whosoever therefore shall be ashamed of me and of my words in this adulterous and sinful generation, of him also shall the Son of man be ashamed when he comes in the glory of his Father with the holy angels.* – Mark 8:38) Should I now be ashamed of his ways and servants? If I did that how could I expect his future blessing?'

"But this Shame proved to be a bold villain. He was clingy and I had a hard time shaking him from my company. He haunted me like a shadow and continually whispered in my ear countless other weakness he attributed to religion. I finally told him that it was useless to continue in this manner, because the very things he despised were those things that I see the most glory. So finally I got past this persistent one and when I had finally shaken him off I began to sing.

"*The trials that those men do meet with,*
*   Who are obedient to the heavenly call,*
Are many and various, and suited to the flesh,
*   And come, and come, and come again afresh;*

That now or some time else we by them may
Be taken, overcome, and cast away.
O let the pilgrims, let the pilgrims then,
Be vigilant and quit themselves like men."

Christian clapped Faithful on the back and said, "I am glad, my brother, that you so bravely withstood this villain. For I agree with you, that of all the people you met he has the wrong name. How bold he is to follow us in the streets and attempt to put us to shame before all the world in order to make us ashamed and embarrassed concerning that which is good. But if he was not so daring, he would never attempt to be this bold. But let us continue to resist him, for aside from all of his bold boasting he promotes himself as a fool and nothing else. Remember that Solomon said, 'The wise shall inherit glory, but shame shall be the promotion of fools.'" (Prov. 3:35)

Faithful agreed and said, "I think we must cry to Him for help against Shame so we might be valiant for truth upon the earth."

"I agree. What you say is true," Christian said. "Besides those you've already mentioned, did you happen to meet anybody else in that valley?"

Faithful shook his head. "No, I didn't. In fact, I enjoyed sunshine all the rest of the way through that first valley as well as through the Valley of the Shadow of Death."

"Then it was far better for you compared to what I experienced. For it was much worse for me. Almost immediately upon entering the Valley of Humiliation, I endured a dreadful battle with that foul fiend Apollyon."

Faithful looked at Christian with wide eyes.

Christian nodded. "Yes, I thought he would surely have killed me, especially when he struck me down and attempted to crush me under his weight. He seemed intent on crushing me to pieces. When he threw me down, my sword flew out of my hand and he said, 'Now I will surely destroy you.' But I cried out to God and he heard me and delivered me from all my troubles.

"Then I entered into the Valley of the Shadow of Death and from that point I had no light for almost half the way through that terrible place. Again and again, I thought I would be killed, but finally morning broke with the rising of the sun. With the light of day, I went through that place with far more ease and quiet."

I saw in my dream that as they went on Faithful happened to look to one side of the way and saw a man whose name was Talkative. He walked for a distance beside them, because in this place there was enough room for them all to walk side by side. He was a tall man and more handsome at a distance than when close at hand. To this man Faithful addressed himself in this manner as they drew near.

"Friend, which way are you going? Are you going to the heavenly country?"

Talkative said, "Yes I am headed to that very same place."

"That's good," Faithful said. "I do hope you will join us."

"By all means! I have every intention of being your traveling companion."

Faithful motioned for him to join them. "Come on with us then and let's spend our time talking about things that are profitable."

"Certainly, certainly." Talkative stepped in line with them. "To talk about things that are good is most enjoyable with you or anyone else. I am glad I have met someone inclined to such discussions. To tell you the truth, there are few who care to spend their traveling time in this way. Instead, they rather discuss things that are quite unprofitable. In fact, this is something that has often troubled me."

"Indeed!" Faithful agreed. "That is something to be disturbed about, for the things worthy of conversation are the things of the God of heaven."

"I certainly admire your attitude," Talkative said. "For you speak with conviction; and I might add, what else is so pleasant and so profitable as to talk about the things of God? For instance, if a man delights in such wonderful things as that, what could be more pleasurable to talk about than the history or mystery of such things? Or if a man loves to talk about miracles, wonders, or signs, where else will he find such things so delightfully recorded and so sweetly penned as in the Holy Scripture?"

"That is true," Faithful admitted, "but the real purpose of such discussion is that we should be benefited by such things in our talk. That should be our intended focus."

"That's exactly what I said," Talkative went on. "Because talking of such things is most profitable, since by so doing a man may gain knowledge about many things. For instance, generally speaking he may gain knowledge about the futility of earthly things and the benefit of things above. More specifically, he may learn the necessity of the new birth, the insufficiency of our works, the need of Christ's righteousness, etc.

"Besides, by such talk of religion a man may learn what it means to repent, to believe, to pray, to suffer, or the like. Plus by such profitable discussion, a man may learn about the great promises and consolations of the gospel and with such knowledge find personal comfort. Along with this, a man may learn to refute false opinions, to vindicate the truth and also to instruct the ignorant."

Faithful said, "This is true and I am glad to hear these things from you—"

"Unfortunately," Talkative broke in, "the lack of this perspective is the reason so few understand the need of faith and the necessity of a work of grace in their soul, in order to obtain eternal life. As a result they ignorantly live according to the works of the law, by which no man can enter the kingdom of heaven."

Faithful quickly jumped in as Talkative took a breath. "But, do allow me to say that heavenly knowledge of these truths is the gift of God. None can attain these things by human effort, let alone just talking about them."

"I know all this very well," Talkative said with a dismissive wave of his hand. "For a man can receive nothing unless it has been given to him from heaven; all is of grace, not of works. I could quote a hundred Scriptures that confirm this."

"Well, then." Faithful looked Talkative in the eye. "What one good topic shall we discuss at this time?"

"Whatever you like! I'm willing to talk about heavenly things or earthly things, moral things or evangelical things, sacred things or secular things, past things or future things, foreign things or domestic things, essential things or incidental things, provided that the discussion is for our profit."

Faithful was becoming impressed with his new traveling companion and stepped closer to Christian, who had been walking by himself all this time. Faithful leaned closer to Christian and said, "What a brave companion we have here! Surely this man will make a very excellent pilgrim."

A slight smile played across Christian's lips. "This man, with whom you are so taken, will captivate a multitude with his words provided they are not familiar with him."

"You mean to say you know him, then?"

"Know him?" Christian asked. "Yes and better than he knows himself."

"Seriously? Then tell me who he is."

"His name is Talkative. He lives in the town we come from. I know Destruction is large, but I'm surprised you don't know who he is."

Faithful scratched his head. "Whose son is he? And exactly where does he live?"

"He is the son of one Say-well," Christian said. "He lived in Prating-Row, and all who know him call him by the name of Talkative of Prating-Row. In spite of his eloquent manner of speaking, he remains a wretched fellow."

"Well, he seems to be a rather attractive man."

"Yes," Christian agreed. "That's how he appears to people who are not well acquainted with him. He looks best from a distance, but close up is really quite ugly. You're saying that he is an attractive man brings to my mind what I have observed in the work of a painter, whose pictures look best at a distance; but up close they are not so good looking."

Prating Row

"Are you joking?" Faithful asked. "Since you smiled I'm thinking maybe you're just joking."

"Sorry you mistook my smile, because God forbid if I should make this a laughing matter or that I should accuse this man falsely. I'm going to tell you more about him so that you understand why I say what I say.

"This man will accept any company as long as he is allowed to talk. Though he will now talk with you, in the same way he will enjoy a conversation in a tavern. And the more he drinks the more things he has to talk about. Religion has no place in his heart, or house, or conversation. All that he stands for depends on his mouth. His religion is to make a noise with it."

"I can't believe it. That means I have been greatly deceived by this man."

"Deceived! Hah! You may be sure of it. Remember the proverb, 'They say to do but do not do.' (*Therefore, whatever they bid you to observe, observe it and do it, but do not act according to their works, for they say and do not do it.* – Matt. 23:3) But the kingdom of God is not in word, but in power. (*For the kingdom of God is not in words, but in virtue.* – 1 Cor. 4:20)

"He talks about prayer, of repentance, of faith, and of the new birth; but he only knows how to talk about them. I have visited his family and have observed him both at home and abroad, and I know what I say is the truth. His house is as empty of religion as the white of an egg is devoid of flavor. There is no prayer offered in his house, nor any sign of repentance for sin. Yes, even an animal serves God far better than Talkative.

"To all who know him, he is the very stain, reproach, and shame of religion. (*Do not catch me away with the wicked, and with the workers of iniquity, who speak peace to their neighbours, but evil is in their hearts.* – Psalm 28:3)[7] Because of his reputation, the neighborhood in which he lives hardly has a good word to say about him. The common people who really know him say, 'A saint abroad and a devil at home.'

"His poor family would agree with me. He is an impolite and mean-spirited person, and such a bitter complainer and unreasonable man with his servants. They are at a loss as to how speak to him or fulfill their duties. Men who have any dealings with him say, 'It is better to deal with a barbarian trader than with him,' for fairer dealings they shall have at their hands. This Talkative, if possible, will go behind their backs to defraud, entice, and outsmart them.

"Besides, he brings up his sons to follow in his steps. If he finds what he calls a foolish timidity in any of them (this is what he calls the first signs of a tender conscience), he calls them fools and stupid blockheads. For this reason, he will rarely employ them or even recommend them to others. In my opinion, his wicked lifestyle causes many to stumble and fall and will be the ruin of many more, unless God intervenes."

"Well, my brother," Faithful answered. "From what you say I am

---

7   Original: *For the name of God is blasphemed among the Gentiles through you, as it is written. For circumcision verily profits if thou keep the law, but if thou art a rebel to the law, thy circumcision is made into a foreskin* – Rom. 2:24, 25.

compelled to believe you. Not only because you have personally known him, but because you offered your report with a Christian attitude. I can't imagine that you've told me these things out of ill-will, but rather see your motive is your love for the truth."

"If I didn't know him any more than you, I might have thought of him the same way you did at first. If I had received such information from the hands of those who are enemies to religion, I would have thought it to be slanderous. Unfortunately, the names and reputations of good men often suffer and are defamed by such messages as his. This isn't just my opinion. I can prove him guilty of all these things and many more that are just as bad. Besides, good men are ashamed of him. They can neither call him brother nor friend and for those who know him, the mere mention of his name makes them blush."

"Well," Faithful said, "I see that saying and doing are two things. From now on, I shall more carefully observe this difference."

"They certainly are two separate things and as different as the soul and the body. Think of it like this. The body without the soul is nothing but a

Talkative at home

dead carcass, so just *saying* these things without doing them is, in the same way, dead. The soul of true religion is the practical part. 'Pure and undefiled religion before God the Father is this, to visit the fatherless and widows in their affliction and to keep oneself unspotted from the world' (James 1:27). Talkative isn't aware of this. He thinks that hearing and saying alone makes a person a good Christian. As a result he deceives his own soul.

"Hearing is like the sowing of the seed. Talking alone isn't sufficient to prove that fruit is actually in the heart and life. And let's be perfectly clear. On Judgment Day men shall be judged according to their fruit. (*But he that was planted in good ground is he that hears the word and understands it and who also bears the fruit and brings forth: one a hundredfold and another sixty and another thirty.* – Matt. 13:23) At that time the question won't be, 'Did you believe?' but instead will be, 'Were you doers or talkers only?' It is by this that they will be judged.

"The end of the world is compared to our harvest (*Let both grow together until the harvest, and in the time of harvest I will say to the reapers, Gather ye together first the tares and bind them in bundles to burn them, but gather the wheat into my barn.* – Matt. 13:30), and you know how it is at harvest. Men notice nothing but fruit and anything that is not of faith cannot be accepted. I'm saying this to help you see how insignificant the profession of Talkative will be at that day."

Faithful pondered Christian's words and said, "This brings to my mind what Moses described about the beast that is clean. (*Nevertheless these ye shall not eat of those that chew the cud or of those that divide the cloven hoof: the camel and the hare and the coney, for they chew the cud, but do not divide the hoof; therefore they are unclean unto you; and the swine, because it divides the hoof, yet does not chew the cud, it is unclean unto you. Ye shall not eat of their flesh nor touch their dead carcase. These ye shall eat of all that are in the waters: all that have fins and scales shall ye eat, but whatever does not have fins and scales ye may not eat; it is unclean unto you. Of all clean birds ye shall eat.* – Deut. 14:7-10) Talkative is such a one who chews the cud – he seeks knowledge. He chews upon the Word, but he divides not the hoof. He does not separate himself from a sinful lifestyle, but like the hare he retains the foot of the dog or bear and therefore remains unclean."

"For all I know," Christian said, "you have spoken the true sense of the gospel from these texts. And I will add another thing which Paul says. He calls some men sounding brass and a tinkling cymbal and this includes those who are great talkers. (*Though I speak with the tongues of men and of angels and have not charity, I am become as sounding brass or a tinkling cymbal. – 1 Cor. 13:1*) He explains this further in another place where he describes them as 'things without life-giving sound.' (*And even things without life giving sound, whether flute or harp, except they give a distinction in the sounds, how shall it be known what is played or harped? – 1 Cor. 14:7*) He's talking about things without life; that is, without the true faith and grace of the gospel. Consequently, pilgrims who base what they say on such things shall never be placed in the kingdom of heaven among those who are the children of life. For the children of life remain true in what they say as if it were the tongue or voice of an angel."

Faithful scratched the crown of his head. "Well, now I am sick of his company. What shall we do to be rid of him?"

"Just take my advice," Christian said. "Do as I tell you, and you shall find he will quickly become sick of your company, too. That is unless God touches his heart and converts it."

"What would you have me to do?"

Christian gestured in Talkative's direction just a little ways before them. "Go to him and enter into some serious discussion about the power of true religion. Once he is agreeable to this topic, ask him directly whether this thing is set up in his heart, house, or daily behavior."

Then Faithful stepped forward again, and fell in line with Talkative. "Hello, how are you?"

Talkative smiled. "Thank you for asking. I'm well. Though I did think we should have been able to talk a great deal by this time."

"Well," Faithful said. "If you're willing, we can have some profitable discussion now. And since you left it up to me to come up with the topic, let it be this. How does the saving grace of God display itself when it lives in the heart of man?"

Talkative said, "I notice that our talk must be about the power of things. Well, this is a very good question, and I shall be more than willing to answer you. So accept my brief answer as follows. First, when the grace of God dwells in the heart, it causes a great outcry against sin. Secondly–"

"No, hold on." Faithful stopped him. "Let's consider each item one at a time. To make it clear I think you should have said that it shows itself by persuading the soul to abhor its sin."

A slight frown wrinkled Talkative's brow. "Why, what difference is there between crying out against and abhorring sin?"

"Oh, a great deal!" Faithful said. "A man may cry out against sin in principle; but he cannot abhor it except by virtue of a godly aversion against it. I have heard many cry out against sin in the pulpit, but who still live with it without any problem in their heart, house, and everyday life.

"Joseph's mistress cried out with a loud voice, as if she had been godly and virtuous, but in reality she would have willingly committed adultery with him. (*And it came to pass, when he heard that I lifted up my voice and cried, that he left his garment with me and fled and left.* – Gen. 39:15) Some cry out against sin, even as the mother cries out against her child when she scolds it as rude and naughty but then quickly changes to hugging and kissing the same child."

"Hmmm," Talkative's eyes narrowed. "I see you're trying to be clever and catch me."

"Not at all," Faithful said. "I am only trying to set things right. So what is the second thing you were going to mention as proof of a work of grace in the heart?"

"Great knowledge of gospel mysteries."

Faithful said, "This evidence should have been first, but first or last, it is also false. For knowledge, great knowledge, may be obtained in the mysteries of the gospel, without any work of grace in the soul. You see, even if a man has all knowledge, he may still be nothing, and so, consequently, not be a child of God. (*And though I have the gift of prophecy and understand all mysteries and all knowledge, and though I have all faith, so that I could remove mountains, and have not charity, I am nothing.* – 1 Cor. 13:2)

"When Christ said, 'Do you know all these things?' and the disciples answered, 'Yes,' he added, 'Blessed are you if you *do* them.' He doesn't lay the blessing in the *knowing* of them, but in the *doing* of them. You see there is a knowledge that is not accompanied with doing. Such a person is 'he who knows his Master's will and doesn't do it.'

"A man may have knowledge like an angel and yet not be Christian. So your sign of knowledge as evidence is not valid. Indeed, to *know* is a thing that pleases talkers and boasters, but to *do* is what pleases God. Not that the heart can be good without knowledge. However, there are two sorts of knowledge, knowledge based on the bare speculation of things, and knowledge which is accompanied with the grace of faith and love, which compels a man to do the will of God from the heart. The first serves the talker; but without the other, the true Christian is not content. 'Give me understanding, and I shall keep Your law. Yes, I will observe it with my whole heart'" (Psalm 119:34).

"You are trying to trip me up again. This discussion is not for edification."

"Well then," Faithful said. "Offer another example of clear evidence of this work of grace in the heart."

Talkative shook his head. "No; not this time. I will not give you another example because I can see we won't agree."

Faithful asked, "Well, if you won't, are you willing for me to do it?"

"Fine, feel free."

Faithful nodded his thanks and said, "A true work of grace at work in the heart is evident to the person himself as well as it is to the people around him. To the one who has it, it brings conviction of sin, especially the defilement of his new nature and the sin of unbelief for which he would be damned, if it weren't for the mercy at God's hand by faith in Jesus Christ.

"This perspective and sense of these things work in him a sorrow and shame for sin. (*Therefore I will declare my iniquity; I will be sorry for my sin.* – Psalm 38:18) Plus he finds the Savior of the world revealed in him, along with the absolute necessity of living for and with Him to the end of life. Through this he discovers a hunger and thirst for Him who has made the promise.

"Now, according to the strength or weakness of his faith in his Savior, so is the joy and peace he experiences. And so is his love of holiness, his desire to know Him more, and also to serve Him in this world. But though it reveals itself in this way, yet because of a person's own corruption and abused reason, they misjudge this matter for they are unable to understand this work of grace. For this reason, the one who has this work going on in their heart is required to use very sound judgment, before he can firmly conclude that this is a work of grace. (*We who are Jews by nature, and not sinners of the Gentiles, knowing that a man is not justified by the works of the law, but by the faith of Jesus Christ, even we have believed in Jesus Christ, that we might be justified by the faith of Christ, and not by the works of the law; for by the works of the law shall no flesh be justified.* – Gal. 2:15, 16) For others, this work of grace is externally evidenced by a confession of faith in Christ which comes from a genuine experience. And secondly it is evidenced by a life that is in agreement with such a confession.

"Now if you have any objections to this brief description of the work of grace and its evidence in true religion, then let me hear them right now. But if you don't, then let me propose another question."

Talkative said, "Now is not the time for me to object, but instead it is the time for me to hear what you have to say, so go ahead and pose your second question."

"All right, this is it," Faithful said. "Have you experienced this and does your life and conversation match up with what you say? Or do you place your faith in words or the things you talk about but not in the truth and without a care for how you act? If you are so inclined, please answer me on this, but only say what you know the God above will say is true along with what your conscience can justify. For it isn't the one who commends himself that is approved, but the one whom the Lord commends. Besides, to say you are one thing, when by your conversation and lifestyle all your neighbors tell you that you lie – this is a great wickedness."

Talkative blushed, but he recovered and said, "You now focus on experience, conscience, and God. I didn't really expect this kind of discussion, and I am not inclined to give an answer to such questions because I am not accountable to you, unless you've taken it upon yourself to be my examiner. However, even if you decided to do that, I would refuse to make you my judge. I do wonder why you decided to ask me such questions."

"Well," Faithful said, "because I noticed your eagerness to talk and talk but then understood you had no basis for your words. It was nothing but speculation on your part. Besides, to tell you all the truth, I have heard that you have a reputation as a man whose religion is based solely on talk, and that the way you live makes what you profess nothing but a lie.

"They say you are a spot or stain among Christians and that religion suffers because of your ungodly conversation and lifestyle. Some have already stumbled because of your wicked ways, and more are in danger of having their faith shipwrecked because of the way you practice your religion. For your religion involves meeting at a tavern and promotes qualities such as covetousness, uncleanness, swearing, lying, making friends with worldly people, and more. The proverb that describes a harlot is also true about you. 'That she is a shame to all women.' In the same way, you are a shame to all genuine Christians."

Talkative's lips turned down at the corners into a slight frown. "Since you seem quick to listen to what others have to say about me and to judge so rashly, I can't do anything but come to the conclusion that you are an irritable or depressed person who is not fit to carry on such a conversation. So with that I say farewell."

Christian came up to Faithful and said, "I told you how this would end. Your words and his lusts could not agree. He preferred to walk away from your company than to reform his life. But he is gone, so let him go. The loss is his. And he has saved us the trouble of breaking away from him, for if he had continued to walk with us, he would have been nothing but a blot on our reputation. Besides, the apostle says, 'Separate yourself from such people.'" (*Therefore come out from among them, and be ye separate, saith the Lord, and do not touch the unclean thing; and I will receive you* – 2 Cor. 6:17)

Faithful nodded his understanding. "I'm still glad we had this opportunity to have this short discussion with him. Perhaps he will think about it again. But even if he doesn't, I have spoken clearly with him about these matters, so if he perishes without the truth, I am innocent of his blood."

Christian agreed. "You did well to speak so frankly with him. Very little of this faithful dealing with men happens these days. When it does, it often makes true religion a stench to many who are nothing more than talkative fools. That's because their religion is only in word, and their conversation is morally corrupt and proud. And with so many of this type being admitted into the fellowship of the godly, they confuse the world, blemish Christianity, and grieve the sincere. I wish all men would deal with such imposters as directly as you have done. Then perhaps they would be made more agreeable to the truth. Either that or the fellowship of true Christians would prove to be too hot for them."

Faithful said, "How Talkative showed off all he knew at first! How bravely he spoke! How he presumed to drive down all before him! But as soon as I talked about the work of grace within the heart, like the moon that's waning, so he too diminished and faded. And it will be the same for everyone unless they know the work of grace in their heart."

Thus the two of them walked along talking about what they had seen along the way. It made the way easy, which would have otherwise proven to be tedious to them, for they were now making their way through a wilderness.

The Sixth Stage

ow when they almost passed through this wilderness, Faithful happened to look behind at the way they had come and spotted someone coming after them. He recognized the man but asked Christian to be sure his eyes weren't playing tricks. "Who is that coming after us?"

Christian looked and said, "It is my good friend Evangelist."

"Yes, and my good friend too," said Faithful. "For it was he who directed me to the way that leads to the gate."

With that Evangelist walked up and joined them. He said, "Peace be with you, dearly beloved, and may there be peace to those who have helped you."

Christian clapped his friend on the back. "Welcome, welcome, my good Evangelist. Just seeing you again reminds me of all your earlier kindnesses and tireless efforts for my eternal good."

"Yes! A thousand times welcome," Faithful said. "Oh, sweet Evangelist, how desirable is your fellowship to us poor pilgrims!"

Evangelist offered them a broad smile. "How have you fared, my friends, since the last time I saw you? What have you encountered, and how have you behaved yourselves?"

Christian and Faithful told him about all the things that had happened to them along the way, including the many difficulties they had endured up to this point in their travels.

"How glad am I to hear it!" Evangelist said. "Not glad that you have met with trials but that you have proven yourselves to be victors over them. And for this reason, despite your many weaknesses, you have been enabled to continue in the way to this very day.

"I can't tell you enough about how well pleased I am about this, for my own sake and yours. I have sown and you have reaped. The day is coming, when both he who sows and they who reap, shall rejoice together (*And he that reaps receives wages and gathers fruit unto eternal life, that both he that sows and he that reaps may rejoice together. –* John 4:36), that is, if you hold out to the end.

"'For in due time you shall reap, if you do not grow weary.' (*And let us not be weary in well doing, for in due season we shall reap if we faint not. –* Gal. 6:9) The crown of reward is before you and it is an incorruptible one, so run in a way that you may obtain it. (*Know ye not that those who run in a race indeed all run, but one receives the prize? So run, that ye may obtain it. And every man that strives for the mastery is temperate in all things. Now they do it to obtain a corruptible crown, but we, an incorruptible one. I therefore so run, not as unto an uncertain thing; so I fight, not as one that beats the air; but I keep my body under, and bring it into subjection, lest preaching to others, I myself should become reprobate. –* 1 Cor. 9:24-27)

"Some people have set out for this crown, but after they have gone a great distance another comes in and takes it from them. 'Therefore, hold fast to what you have and don't let another take your crown.' (*Behold, I come quickly; hold fast that which thou hast, that no one take thy crown. –* Rev. 3:11) You are not yet out of the gunshot range of the Devil, for 'you have not yet resisted to the point of blood as you strive against sin.' Let the kingdom always be before you, and without wavering believe regarding the things that are invisible. Let nothing in this world come between you and the crown.

"Above all, pay attention to your own hearts with their lusts, for they are 'deceitful above all things and desperately wicked.' Set your faces with flint-like resolve since you have all power in heaven and earth on your side."

Christian thanked him for his counsel and encouragement, but added that he and Faithful desired him to speak to them more, for they hoped for something helpful to take them the rest of the way. For they knew very well that he was a prophet and that he could tell them about things that might happen to them as well as how they might resist and overcome them.

So Evangelist agreed and said, "My sons, you have heard in the Word of the truth of the gospel that you must go 'through many tribulations to enter into the kingdom of heaven.' And again, that 'in every city, bonds and afflictions await you.' For this reason, you can't expect to travel far on your pilgrimage without encountering them in one way or another. You have already experienced a measure of this truth and more will immediately follow.

"For now, as you see, you are almost out of this wilderness. You will soon arrive at a town that you will see directly in front of you. In that town you will be severely assaulted by enemies, who will make every attempt to kill you. You may be sure that one or both of you will seal the testimony you hold with blood. In spite of this, 'be faithful unto death and the King will give you a crown of life.'

"Whoever dies there, although his death will be unnatural and his pain great, yet he will have an advantage over his companion. First of all, he will arrive at the Celestial City sooner, but secondly, he will also escape many miseries that the other will meet with during the rest of his journey. But when you arrive at this town and all that I have related to you comes to pass, then remember your friend, and behave like men, and 'commit the keeping of your souls to God with good conduct as to a faithful Creator'" (1 Peter 4:19).

Then I saw in my dream, that when Christian and Faithful got out of the wilderness, they immediately saw a town before them, and the name of that town was Vanity. In that town is promoted a fair called Vanity Fair. It is held all year long and is called Vanity Fair because of the name of the town. For the town is brighter than vanity (*Surely the sons of Adam are vanity, and the sons of nobles are a lie; to be laid in the balance, they are altogether lighter than vanity. – Psalm 62:9*), and also because all that is sold there, and all who come there, are worthless. As the saying of the wise says, 'All this world promotes is vanity.' (*But if a man lives many years and rejoices in them all; yet if afterwards he remembers the days of darkness, for they shall be many, he shall say that everything that shall have happened to him is vanity. – Eccles. 11:8*)

This fair is not a newly erected business but is actually an ancient enterprise. Let me tell you about its origins.

Almost five thousand years ago, there were pilgrims walking to the Celestial City, just like Faithful and Christian are doing. So Beelzebub, Apollyon, and Legion, with their associates, perceived by seeing the path made by the pilgrims on their way to the city, that the course lay through this town of Vanity. They planned to set up a fair here; a fair at which all sorts of vanity could be sold amid festivities open and ongoing the whole year. Therefore, at this fair they sell such merchandise as houses, land, trades, places, honors, promotions, titles, countries, kingdoms, lusts, and pleasures of all sorts, including things such as harlots, wives, husbands, children, masters, servants, lives, blood, bodies, souls, silver, gold, pearls, precious stones, and much more.

And along with all this, at this fair there is constant, round-the-clock entertainment like juggling, cheats, games, plays, clowns, mimics, tricksters, and rogues, and other amusements of every kind.

Here visitors can also find free offers that include thefts, murders,

Vanity Fair

adulteries, perjuries, and all of them are available in various shades of a blood-red color.

As in other fairs of less importance, there are several lanes and streets with representative names, where certain categories of merchandise are marketed. In the same way, at this fair you have the proper places, lanes, and streets, which bear names of countries and kingdoms. It is in these places that the goods of this fair are easily found. There is the Britain Row, the French Row, the Italian Row, the Spanish Row, the German Row, all of which offer a variety of vanities for sale. But, just like other fairs, where one commodity dominates the market, here too the most sought-after of all the fair is the merchandise of Rome, for it is greatly promoted. Some like our English nation and others have taken a dislike for this huckstering.

Now, as I said, the way to the Celestial City lies through this town, with its lusty fair which is held year-round. Those who think they are going to avoid this city will still have to go out of the world. The Prince of princes Himself, when He was here, passed through this town on His way to His own country during a time when the fair was in full operation. I believe it was Beelzebub, the chief lord of this fair, who invited Him to buy some of his vanities. Yes, he would have made Him Lord of this fair, if only He would have shown him reverence and bowed to him as He went through the town. (*Beloved, think it not strange when you are tried by fire (which is done to prove you) as though some strange thing happened unto you* – 1 Peter 4:12)[8]

Plus, because he was such a person of honor, Beelzebub escorted him from street to street, and showed him all the kingdoms of the world in a brief amount of time, so that he might, if possible, lure that blessed One to lower Himself and buy some of his vanities. But he paid no attention to the merchandise, and therefore left the town, without spending so much as one cent upon these vanities. (*Again, the devil took him up into an exceeding high mountain and showed him all the kingdoms of the world and the glory of them and said unto him, All these things I will give thee if thou wilt fall down and worship me.* – Matt. 4:8, 9) So this fair is of ancient origins and is a longstanding and very large fair.

When the Pilgrims arrived they were clothed with garments different

---

8   Original: *We are fools for Christ's sake, but ye are prudent in Christ; we are weak, but ye are strong; ye are honorable, but we are despised* – 1 Cor. 4:10.

from any available at that fair. When the people saw them, they stared at them and talked about what manner of people they might be. Some said they were fools (*For we are made a spectacle unto the world and to angels and to men. We are fools for Christ's sake, but ye are prudent in Christ; we are weak, but ye are strong; ye are honorable, but we are despised. – 1 Cor. 4:9, 10*); others said they were lunatics; and some, that they were strange and unusual.

Secondly, the great crowd wondered at their clothing and in the same way they were curious about their speech, for few could understand what they said. They naturally spoke the language of those who have sworn allegiance to the Lord Almighty, but those who ran the fair were men of this world. So from one end of the fair to the other, the people seemed barbarians to each other. (*But we speak the wisdom of God in a mystery, even the hidden wisdom, which God predestined before the ages unto our glory, which none of the princes of this age knew (for had they known it, they would never have crucified the Lord of glory). – 1 Cor. 2:7, 8*)

Thirdly, and this astonished the merchants, was how these pilgrims placed such little value on all the wares being sold. They didn't even care to browse, and if venders called out to them to buy their wares, they put their fingers in their ears, and cried, "Turn away my eyes from beholding worthless vanity," (*Turn away my eyes from beholding vanity, and cause me to live in thy way. – Psalm 119:37*) and they looked upward, signifying that their trade and commerce was in heaven. (*For our citizenship is in heaven, from where we also look for the Saviour, the Lord Jesus Christ: Who shall transform our vile body, that it may be fashioned like unto the body of his glory, according to the working by which he is also able to subdue all things unto himself. – Phil. 3:20, 21*)

One mocking merchant observed the strange behavior of Faithful and Christian and said to them, "What will you buy?"

The pilgrims looked at him with serious expressions and said, "We buy the truth." (*Buy the truth and sell it not, also wisdom and instruction and understanding. – Prov. 23:23*) With this answer, the merchant and others took the opportunity to deride the men even more; some mocked, some taunted, some spoke with reproach, and some called for others to strike them. It turned into a noticeable commotion and grew into a great disturbance, to the point that everywhere you looked the fair was in disorder.

As a result, word quickly reached the governor of the fair. He came down right away and appointed deputies from some of his most trusted friends. He put these in charge of investigating what happened and to examine the pilgrims about why they had nearly overturned the fair.

So Faithful and Christian were taken for further investigation. Those who presided over the proceedings asked them where they came from and where they were going, and why they were wearing such unusual clothing.

Faithful and Christian told them they were pilgrims and strangers in the world, and that they were going to their own country, which was called the heavenly Jerusalem (*For those that say such things declare plainly that they seek their native country. But now they desire a better country, that is, a heavenly one; therefore, God is not ashamed to be called their God, for he has prepared for them a city.* – Heb. 11:14, 16), and that they had done nothing to cause the men of the town or the merchants to mistreat them or to delay their journey.

The only exception they could think of was when the merchant had asked them what they would buy, and they had responded that they would buy the truth. But those who were appointed to investigate the uproar did not believe them. They thought the two pilgrims were nothing more than madmen and lunatics who came for the purpose of throwing the fair into confusion. Therefore, they took them and beat them, smeared them with dirt, and then put them into a cage as a spectacle in front of all the men of the fair. There the two pilgrims lay caged for some time as objects of sport, malice, or revenge from the men of that place. All the while the governor of the fair laughed at all that happened to them.

But the pilgrims remained patient, and did not return abuse for abuse. Instead, they offered a blessing while speaking good words for bad and showed kindness in the face of brutal treatment.

Some men in the fair noticed their example. These men were more observant and less prejudiced than the rest. They began to restrain and accuse the disreputable men for their continual mistreatment of the captives.

This made the disreputable sorts all the more angry, and they flew into a rage at those trying to hold them back. They counted them as bad as the caged pilgrims, and accused them as accomplices worthy of the same mistreatment.

In response the others replied that as far as they could see, the caged men were quiet, sober, and harmless. They went on to say that many others who attended their fair were more worthy of being put into the cage and ridiculed, than the men whom they had mistreated in this way. A variety of opinions were exchanged from both sides, while Christian and Faithful behaved themselves, acting very wisely and soberly the whole time. But the words exchanged turned to blows between the opposing groups, and they did harm to one another.

Faithful and Christian were once again dragged before their examiners and charged as guilty for causing the disturbance in the fair. As their punishment they were beaten unmercifully, hung in irons, and led in chains up and down the lanes of the fair as an example and warning to others who might think to speak on behalf of the pilgrims or to associate with them.

Even in all this Christian and Faithful behaved with increasing wisdom and with much meekness and patience amid the humiliation and shame heaped upon them. With such behavior they won several of the men in the fair to their side (though the number was few in comparison to the rest).

Christian and Faithful are brought to trial

This generated even more rage in the aggressive opponents, to the point that they sought the death of the two captives.

With this they announced, "This cage and the irons are not a sufficient penalty for what these men have done. They should die for the damage they have caused and for deceiving the men of the fair."

Then Christian and Faithful were imprisoned in the cage again, until the process of the law decided what should be done with them. So they locked their feet fast in the stocks inside the cage.

With their feet locked in the stocks, they recalled what their faithful friend Evangelist had told them. It helped them accept their current circumstances and to be assured that the sufferings and trials they were experiencing were exactly what he told them would happen to them. With this in mind, they now comforted each other in that whoever would suffer death, he would have the advantage. In his heart, each man secretly wished that he might be the one, but they committed themselves to the all-wise and sovereign purposes of the Almighty, and with much contentment they rested in the condition in which they found themselves, while waiting to see how they would be disposed of.

When a convenient time was determined, the prisoners were brought forth for their trial, in order that they could be found guilty and condemned. They were brought before their enemies and were formally accused. The judge's name was Lord Hate-good. Their indictment was essentially the same accusation, but it had been changed slightly in content. It read: "That they (Christian and Faithful) were enemies to, and disturbers of, the trading of the fair and that they had caused commotions and divisions in the town, and had, in the process, gained supporters for their most-dangerous opinions, in contempt of the law of their prince."

Then Faithful answered that he had only spoken against that which had asserted itself against Him who is higher than the highest. He went on to say, "As for causing a disturbance, I made no such thing, for I am a man of peace. As for the supporters who were won to us, they were persuaded when they recognized our innocence and that we spoke the truth. As a result they turned from what was worse to what is better. And as to the prince you talk about, since he is Beelzebub, the enemy of our Lord, I defy him and all his angels."

Then it was proclaimed that anyone who had anything to say in support for their lord the king against the prisoner at the bar, they should immediately appear to testify and bring forth their evidence. So three witnesses came forward: Envy, Superstition, and Pickthank.

These three were then asked if they knew the prisoner at the bar and what they had to say in support of their lord the king and what had been done against him.

Envy stepped forward first to give his testimony. He said, "My lord, I have known this prisoner a long time and verify upon my oath before this honorable bench, that he is–"

Lord Hate-good

"Hold on a moment," the judge said. "First administer the oath to him."

So they swore him in to tell the truth, and he continued his testimony. "My lord, this man, in spite of his credible name, is one of the vilest men in our country. He shows no regard for the prince, nor his people, laws, or customs. Instead, he does all he can to persuade all men with his disloyal notions, which he tends to call principles of faith and holiness. And in particular, I heard him say once myself that Christianity and the customs of our town of Vanity were diametrically opposed to each other and could not be reconciled. By this statement, my lord, he not only condemns all our praiseworthy deeds, but also us for doing them."

Then the judge asked. "Do you have any more to say?"

"My lord," Envy answered. "I could say much more, but I don't want to weary the court with every detail. However, if necessary, when the other gentlemen have given their evidence, to avoid any lack of evidence that would allow the prisoner to go free, I will expound on my testimony against him at that time."

So Envy was told to stand by in case further testimony was needed.

Then they called Superstition to the stand and told him to look at the prisoner. They also asked, "What can you say for your lord the king against the prisoner?" Then they swore him in and he began to give his testimony.

"My lord, I am not friends with this man, nor do I have any desire to know him better. However, I do know that he is a very lethal person from a discussion I had with him the other day in town. During our conversation, he distinctly said our religion was worthless and that it in no way could be a means to please God. My lord, you know very well what follows from such sayings, namely, that we are presently worshiping in vain and as a result our sins remain, and finally in the end we shall be damned. So that's what I have to say."

Then Pickthank was sworn in and he began to tell what he knew on behalf of their lord the king, against the prisoner at the bar. "My lord, and all of you gentlemen, I have known this fellow a long time and have heard him say things that should not be spoken. For he has denounced our noble prince Beelzebub and has spoken shamefully of his honorable friends, whose names are, the Lord Old Man, the Lord Carnal Delight, the Lord Luxurious, the Lord Desire of Vain Glory, my old Lord Lechery, Sir Having Greedy, along with all the rest of our nobility. And the prisoner has also said that if all men thought as he did, that not one of these noblemen would reside in this town any longer. And besides this, he hasn't been afraid to revile even you, my lord, who are now appointed to be his judge. He has called you an ungodly villain, and along with this he has used many other similar and slanderous names to smear the good names of most of the nobility of our town."

When Pickthank had finished giving his account of the evidence against Faithful, the judge turned his attention to the prisoner at the bar and talked to him directly. "You deserter of the truth! You heretic and traitor! Have you heard what these honest gentlemen have testified against you?"

Faithful asked, "May I speak a few words in my own defense?"

"You contemptible, good-for-nothing vagrant! You don't deserve to live a moment longer! Instead you should be put to death immediately, right here, right now. Yet, so that all men may see our gentleness toward you, let us hear what you have to say."

Faithful tipped his head and said, "First let me address what Mr. Envy has said. I want to clarify that I never said anything except that what rules, laws, customs, or people are against the Word of God, these are diametrically opposed to Christianity. If I have said anything in this regard that is incorrect, please point out my error and convince me otherwise. For I stand before you ready to recant my foolishness if you can do so.

Faithful speaks in his own defense

"As second, I'd like to address the charge that Mr. Superstition has made against me. I can only say this, that for true worship of God there is a divine faith required, but there can be no divine faith without a divine revelation of the will of God. Therefore, anything added into the worship of God that is not in agreement with divine revelation, is nothing but human faith; a faith that will not result in eternal life.

"And concerning what Mr. Pickthank has said, while avoiding those abusive terms I have been accused of using, I must still say that the prince of this town, with all the riotous crowd of low people and his attendants which were named by Mr. Pickthank, are more fit for being in hell than in this town and country. And so the Lord have mercy upon me."

Then the judge addressed the jury, who had been nearby and listening and observing all that was said and done. "Gentlemen of the jury," the judge said. "You see before us this man who has been at the center of a great uproar in this town. You have also heard what these worthy gentlemen have testified against him. In the same way, you have also heard his reply and confession. Now it rests in your heartfelt decision whether he should live or die. Before you decide, I think it is right that I should instruct you in our law.

"In the days of Pharaoh the Great, a servant to our prince, there was an act instituted that addressed the danger posed by false religion and those who would cause it to multiply and grow throughout the country. It decreed that their males should be thrown into the river. (*Then Pharaoh charged all his people, saying, Every son that is born ye shall cast into the river, and every daughter ye shall give them their lives. –* Exod. 1:22)

"A second decree enacted during the days of Nebuchadnezzar the Great, another of our prince's servants, declared that whoever would not fall down and worship his golden image should be thrown into a fiery furnace. (*And whoever does not fall down and worship shall the same hour be cast into the midst of a burning fiery furnace. –* Dan. 3:6)

"And yet another decree in the days of Darius, established a period of time during which any who called upon any god but him should be cast into the lion's den." (*All the presidents of the kingdom, magistrates, governors, great ones, and captains have agreed in common accord to promote a royal decree and to confirm it that whoever shall ask a petition of any God or man for thirty days, except of thee, O king, he shall be cast into the den of lions. –* Dan. 6:7)

The judge waggled his finger in Faithful's direction and said, "Now, this rebel has broken the substance of these laws, not only in thought, which is not an indictable offense, but also in word and deed which must not be tolerated.

"Concerning the law of Pharaoh, it was made known by public decree to prevent trouble before it actually happened. But in this case," he nodded toward Faithful, "a crime is apparent. With regard to the second and third precedents, you will notice how the prisoner argues against our religion in much the same way. For this treason, which he has already confessed, he deserves to die as a criminal."

Then the jury, whose names were Mr. Blindman, Mr. No-good, Mr. Malice, Mr. Love-lust, Mr. Live-loose, Mr. Heady, Mr. High-mind, Mr. Enmity, Mr. Liar, Mr. Cruelty, Mr. Hate-light, and Mr. Implacable went out to deliberate and consider a verdict. Each individual offered their private verdict against the prisoner and they unanimously concluded that he was guilty. First, the foreman of the jury, Mr. Blindman, said, "I see clearly that this man is a heretic."

Then Mr. No-good added, "Away with such a fellow from the face of the earth."

"Yes!" Mr. Malice agreed. "For I hate the very looks of him."

Mr. Love-lust jutted his chin forward and declared, "I could never tolerate him."

"Nor I," said Mr. Live-loose. "For he would always be condemning my lifestyle."

"Hang him, hang him!" Mr. Heady shouted out.

"A sorry hooligan," said Mr. High-mind.

Mr. Enmity nodded his agreement. "My heart boils with anger against him."

"He is a rogue," said Mr. Liar.

"Hanging is too good for him," Mr. Cruelty added.

"Let's dispose of him immediately," Mr. Hate-light suggested.

Then Mr. Implacable said, "If I were to be given the whole world, still I could not be reconciled to him. Therefore I say we deliver our verdict and find him guilty and deserving of death."

And so they did. Faithful was condemned to be returned to his prison cell and there to be put to death by the cruelest method they could think of. So they led him away, to do with him according to their law. First they scourged him, then they beat him, then they lanced his flesh with knives. After that, they stoned him with stones, then pricked him with their swords, and last of all they burned him to ashes at the stake. And so Faithful came to his earthly end.

Now I noticed a chariot and a couple of horses waiting for Faithful beyond the crowd. As soon as his adversaries executed him he was taken up into the chariot, and carried directly up through the clouds with the sound of a trumpet, taking the most direct route to the Celestial Gate. But as for Christian, he found relief during this agonizing situation when he was sent back to prison. He remained for a time, but He who overrules all things, having the power of their rage in His own hand, worked things out in such a way that Christian, after that time, was set free and allowed to continue on his way.

As he went he said, "Well, Faithful, you have faithfully professed unto your Lord, with whom you will be blessed. When faithless ones, with all their worthless delights are crying out under their hellish plights, sing, Faithful, sing, and let your name survive. For though they have killed you, yet you are alive."

Faithful is burned at Vanity Fair

Christian and Hopeful enter into a brotherly covenant

The Seventh Stage

———ॐ———

ow in my dream I watched Christian press forward on his journey but not alone. For now he was joined by another pilgrim by the name of Hopeful. (He was so named after watching Christian and Faithful and how they behaved and what they said.) Hopeful joined Christian, and the two of them entered into brotherly covenant and agreed to be companions because of the testimony to the truth Hopeful had witnessed, especially during the suffering Christian and Faithful had endured at the fair. For Faithful had died to make a testimony to the truth and another, by the name of Hopeful, arose from his ashes to be a companion with Christian in his pilgrimage. This Hopeful also told Christian, that there were many more of the men in the fair who would follow him after some time.

Shortly after they departed from the fair, they caught up to a man walking ahead of them, whose name was By-ends. They asked him, "Sir, what country are you from? And how far are you traveling in this direction?"

"I'm from the town of Fair-speech," the man said. "I am going to the Celestial City." But he didn't mention his name.

"From Fair-speech?" Christian said. "Is there any good that lives there?" (*When he speaks fair, do not believe him, for there are seven abominations in his heart. – Prov. 26:25*)

"Yes," By-ends said. "I certainly hope so."

"Then, sir, what name may I call you?"

By-ends said, "I am a stranger to you, and you to me. If you are going my way, I shall be glad to have your company, and if not, I must be content."

"I've heard of this town of Fair-speech, and from what I remember, they say it's a wealthy place."

"Yes, I can assure you that it is; and I have very many rich relatives and friends there."

"May I be so bold as to ask who they are?"

"To be honest, almost the whole town." By-ends shrugged. "In particular, my Lord Turn-about, my Lord Time-server, my Lord Fair-speech (from whose ancestors the town first took its name). Also there is Mr. Smooth-man, Mr. Facing-both-ways, Mr. Any-thing. The parson of our parish, Mr. Two-tongues, was my mother's own brother. And to tell you the truth, I have become a gentleman of good quality, though my father's grandfather was nothing but an oarsman for hire. He would look one way and row another. I gained most of my estate by the same occupation."

"Are you a married man?"

By-ends nodded. "Yes; and my wife is a very virtuous woman, the daughter of a virtuous woman. She was my Lady Feigning's daughter; therefore she came of a very honorable family. As a result she has a high level of breeding and she carries herself impeccably, to both prince and peasants. It is true, our religion somewhat differs from those of the stricter sort, but only in two small points.

Lady Feigning's daughter

"First, we never strive against the wind and tide. Second, we are always very fervent in following Religion who parades silver slippers. We love to walk with him in the street when the sun shines and the people applaud him."

Then Christian stepped a little to one side to speak with Hopeful. "It comes to mind that this fellow is in fact By-ends, of Fair-speech; and if it is true, we have quite a scoundrel in our company, the likes of which is often found in all these parts."

Hopeful said, "Ask him to be sure. I would think he shouldn't be ashamed of his name."

So Christian sidled up to By-ends once again and said, "Sir, you talk as one who knows more than all the world, and, if my guess is right, I surmise your name to be Mr. By-ends of Fair-speech. Is it not so?"

"This is not my true name," the man said. "But it is a nickname given to me by some who could not put up with me." He let out a sigh. "I must be content to tolerate it as a reproach, just as other good men have done before me."

Christian didn't let the subject rest. "But were you responsible for situations that caused men to call you by this name?"

"Never, never! The worst I ever did that might have caused them to give me this name was when luck was on my side. I made profitable judgments at the right time. But if I'm to be criticized for these times that are by chance, then I choose to count them as blessings rather than to let the hatred of such men force me to bear a malicious load of hatred."

Christian's eyes narrowed. "I was sure you were the man I had heard about, and to be honest, I fear this name more appropriately belongs to you than you might want us to think."

By-ends dismissed the comment with a wave of his hand. "Well, you can think whatever you like. I can't help what you think. However, you'll find me a fair-minded companion, if you will still allow me to travel with you."

"If you want to go with us, it will require you to go against wind and tide, which I understand goes against your convictions. You must also embrace Religion in his rags as well as when he wears his silver slippers. You must stand by him, too, even when he is bound in shackles, as well as when he walks the streets with applause."

By-ends' expression soured. "You must not impose this on me or coerce my faith. Respect my freedom and allow me to go with you."

"No," Christian said. "We'll not travel another step together, unless you agree with what I propose."

"Never," By-ends said. "I shall never abandon my long-held principles, since they are harmless and profitable. If I'm not allowed to go with you, then I must do as I did before you caught up with me. I'll just travel by myself, until someone else overtakes me who will be glad to have my company."

Now I saw in my dream that Christian and Hopeful moved ahead of Mr. By-ends, and they made sure to keep their distance. However, one of them looked back and saw three men following Mr. By-ends. These three caught up with him, he made them a very low bow, and they also gave him a friendly compliment. The men's names were Mr. Hold-the-World, Mr. Money-love, and Mr. Save-all.

Mr. By-ends had formerly been acquainted with all three of them, for in their younger years they were friends in school and had been taught by one Mr. Gripeman, a schoolmaster in Lovegain, which is a market-town in the county of Coveting, in the North. This schoolmaster taught them the art of getting, either by violence, cheating, flattering, lying, or by putting on a guise of religion. These four gentlemen had attained much of the art from their master and had each become a master who could have run such a school themselves.

Well, when they had greeted each other, Mr. Money-love said to Mr. By-ends, "Who are they up there on the road ahead of us?" For Christian and Hopeful were still within view.

By-ends said, "They are a couple of men from a distant country, who to their way of thinking are going on pilgrimage."

Mr. Money-love looked slightly confused. "That's unfortunate! Why didn't they stay, so we might enjoy their good company? For I should hope we are all going on pilgrimage."

"I agree," By-ends said. "But the men walking ahead of us are so rigid and they are in love with their own ideas. As a result, they don't really value the opinions of others. Even if a man is godly, if he doesn't jump in with them in all things, they quickly thrust him out of their company."

Mr. Save-all said, "That is bad, but we read of some who are excessively righteous, and such men's rigidness obliges them to judge and condemn everyone except themselves. But tell me, what and how many were the things in which you differed?"

"Why, they in their headstrong manner believed it is their duty to rush ahead on their journey in all types of weather, while I am in favor of waiting for wind and tide. They are for risking all for God in an instant; and I am for taking advantage of all I can to secure my life and property. They hold on to their beliefs, even though all other men oppose them. But I'm for religion that is tolerant of the times and not a threat to my safety. They are for Religion when he dresses in rags and is considered contemptible. But I am for him when he walks in his silver slippers, in the sunshine, and with applause."

Mr. Hold-the-World held up his hand. "Yes, but hold on a moment, my good Mr. By-ends. For my part, I can only consider him a fool who has the freedom to keep what he has but is so unwise as to lose it. Instead, let us be wise as serpents. It is best to make hay while the sun shines. You see how the bee lies dormant over the winter and stirs again only when it is profitable and pleasurable to do so. Sometimes God sends rain and sometimes sunshine. If some people are such fools as to go through the rain, let us be content to take fair weather as our portion.

"For my part, the religion I like best enjoys the security of God's good blessings poured out on us. When you think about it, it stands to reason that since God has given us the good things of this life, then He would want us to continue to enjoy them for His sake.

"Abraham and Solomon grew rich through Religion. And Job says 'that a good man shall store up gold as dust.' If this is so, he couldn't be much like the men before us, if they are anything like you have described them."

"I think that we all agree in this matter," Mr. Save-all said. "Therefore, there is no more need to talk about it."

Mr. Money-love nodded. "You're right. Nothing more needs to be said about this matter. For he who doesn't believe the Scripture or reason, both of which we have on our side, will not appreciate his own liberty or care for his safety."

"My brother," By-ends said. "As you see, we are all going on pilgrimage and so to better distract ourselves from things that are bad, let me ask you this question. Suppose a man who is a minister of religion, or a tradesman, or of some other profession, learns about the prospect of a possible promotion. Let's say this promotion would offer him the good blessings of this life. Yet he can only gain this advantage by appearing extraordinarily zealous in certain points of religion which he had previously neglected. Shouldn't he use this means to attain his end and still remain a righteous and honest man?"

"I understand the point of your question," Mr. Money-love said. "With the permission of these fine gentlemen ...." He made a wide sweeping gesture to include all the men around him. "I will endeavor to give you an answer.

"First, let's look at the example of the minister himself. Suppose a pastor, a reputable man in charge of a small congregation that provides meager financial support, has his eye trained on a bigger, more prestigious, and far more materially wealthy opportunity. Let's say he learns he has a chance of getting this new position if he studies more, preaches more frequently and zealously, and because of the expectations of the people he is required to adjust his stand regarding some of his principles. The way I see it is that there is no reason why a man should not pursue this course of action, provided he receives a call. Yes, and besides this there are many more reasons he should seek this advancement in his career provided he is an honest man. Here are some of the reasons.

1. His desire for a more prosperous congregation is lawful. This is beyond contradiction, for it is providence that set this opportunity before him. So let him pursue it with all his might, without questioning his conscience.

2. Besides, his desire after that larger congregation causes him to be more studious, a more earnest preacher, etc., with the result that he becomes a better man. Yes, he is able to improve himself! And this is certainly according to God's will.

3. Now, as for his complying with the expectation of his people, by deserting some of his principles in order to serve them, I argue this: First, that it reveals he has a self-denying temperament. Secondly, it shows he has a sweet and winning demeanor. And thirdly, it proves he is more qualified for the ministerial office.

4. I conclude, then, that a pastor who exchanges a small congregation for a larger, should not be judged for so doing as being covetous, but rather, since he is determined to improve himself and his trade in this way, should be considered in the same way as anyone who pursues his call and who has an opportunity at hand to do good.

"And now to address the second part of the question, which concerns the tradesman you mentioned. Suppose such a person in his business has poor profitability in the world and has to scrape just to get by. But by becoming religious this same person may find more opportunities to make a better living and fix his financial problems, perhaps by taking for himself a rich wife, or by drawing more and far better customers to his shop. Again, as far as I can see, there is no reason this course should not be pursued. And this is why:

It is virtuous to become religious, by whatever means a man may use.

Plus, it's not against the law to marry a rich wife, and in this way increase the profitability of his business.

Besides, the man who reaps such benefits as these by becoming religious, obtains that which is good by means that are good and as a result becomes good himself. As a result he has a good wife, good customers,

Mr. Money-love's lesson

good profitability, and all these by becoming religious. In other words, to become religious to get all these things is a good and profitable pursuit."

This answer offered by Mr. Money-love to Mr. By-ends' question received loud applause by them all. Therefore, the entire group of four concluded that the entire answer was most sensible and worthwhile. And because they were convinced no man could contradict such an argument, and because Christian and Hopeful were still within calling distance, they wholeheartedly agreed to challenge them with the question as soon as they overtook them, especially because of the opposition Mr. By-ends had faced when he had talked with them earlier. So they called after them.

Christian and Hopeful stopped and waited until the four men caught up to them. However, on their way, the challengers had decided that rather than have Mr. By-ends present the question, it would be more profitable for Mr. Hold-the-World to offer it to the two pilgrims. For they supposed their answer to him would be less likely to rekindle the fiery feelings that had been expressed between Mr. By-ends and them earlier when they had parted ways.

So they approached each other and after a short round of greetings, Mr. Hold-the-World proposed the question to Christian and his companion. Then he asked them to answer it if they could.

Christian didn't hesitate to answer. He said, "Even a babe in religion could answer ten thousand questions such as this one. For if it is unlawful to follow Christ for loaves of bread (*Jesus answered them and said, Verily, verily, I say unto you, Ye seek me, not because ye have seen the signs, but because ye ate of the loaves and were filled.* – John 6:26), how much more detestable is it to make of a man and religion a fake cover and decoy used just to get and enjoy the things of this world! The only ones who hold such an opinion are the heathen, hypocrites, devils, and wizards.

"Heathens: for when Hamor and Shechem had a covetous eye toward the daughter and cattle of Jacob and saw that there was no way for them to get what they wanted unless they were circumcised, they said to their companions, 'If every male among us is circumcised, as they are circumcised, won't their cattle, material possessions, and every beast they own be ours?' What they sought to obtain were the daughters and cattle of Jacob, and they used their religion as a fake cover to try to get them. (*Then Hamor and Shechem, his son, came unto the gate of their city and communed with the men of their city, saying, These men are peaceable with us; therefore let them dwell in the land and trade therein; for the land, behold, it is large enough for them; let us take their daughters to us for wives, and let us give them our daughters. Only with this condition will these men consent to dwell with us that we may be one people: if every male among us be circumcised as they are circumcised. Shall not their livestock and their substance and every beast of theirs be ours? Only let us consent unto them, and they will dwell with us. And unto Hamor and unto Shechem, his son, hearkened all that went out of the gate of his city; and every male was circumcised, all that went out of the gate of his city.* – Gen. 34:20-24)

"The hypocritical Pharisees were also of this religion, but their long showy prayers were nothing but a sham they used for the purpose of getting widows' houses, and their judgment was a greater damnation was from God. (*Beware of the scribes, who desire to walk in long robes and love greetings in the markets and the first seats in the synagogues and the first places at suppers; who devour the houses of the widows and for a pretext make long prayers: the same shall receive greater damnation.* – Luke 20:46, 47)

"Judas the devil was also of this religion, for he desired the money bag and its contents, but he was lost, cast away, and the very son of perdition.

(This he said, not that he cared for the poor, but because he was a thief and had the bag and would take from what was put therein. – John 12:6)

"Simon the wizard was of this religion too; for he wanted to have the power of the Holy Ghost and hoped he might buy it with money. For this reason he received his sentence from Peter's mouth. *(Saying, Give me also this power, that on whomsoever I lay hands, he may receive the Holy Spirit. But Peter said unto him, Thy money perish with thee because thou hast thought that the gift of God may be purchased with money. Thou hast neither part nor lot in this matter, for thy heart is not right in the sight of God. Repent therefore of this thy wickedness and pray God, if perhaps this thought of thine heart may be forgiven thee. – Acts 8:19-22)*

"Neither does it escape my attention that the man who takes up religion for the profit of the world, will throw away that religion to please the world. For Judas became religious for worldly gain, and he sold out that religion and his Master for just that.

"So to answer the question positively, as I perceive, what you have done is heathenish, hypocritical, and devilish, and your reward will be according to your works."

The four men stood staring at one another, without knowing how to answer Christian. Hopeful also approved of the soundness of Christian's answer and so a heavy silence hung between them. Mr. By-ends and his company staggered in the face of such a response and purposely lagged behind, wishing that Christian and Hopeful might easily get ahead of them.

Christian turned to Hopeful and said, "If these men cannot stand before the sentence of men, what will they do when they are confronted with the sentence of God? And if they don't know how to answer when dealt with by vessels of clay, what will they do when they are rebuked by the flames of a devouring fire?"

So Christian and Hopeful walked ahead of them again, and went on until they came to a subtle plain called Ease, which they journeyed across with much satisfaction. However, the plain was so narrow they quickly crossed it and reached the other side.

Now at the farther side of that plain was a little hill called Lucre and within that hill was a silver mine. Some pilgrims who had formerly gone that way had turned aside to see the mine because of its rarity. However, for some who ventured too near the brim of the pit, the deceitful ground beneath their feet broke under them. Some were slain and some had been maimed there. Those who were injured were never free of the influence of the mine's wound until their dying day.

Then I saw in my dream that a little off the road, right next to the silver mine, stood a man by the name of Demas. This gentleman called to passing pilgrims to come and see. In this manner he called to Christian and his companion, Hopeful. "Hello friends! Turn in here and I will show you something remarkable."

Christian called back to him. "What could be so deserving of our attention as to cause us to turn from the way to see it?"

Demas motioned toward the pit. "Here is a silver mine. At this very moment some are digging in it for treasure. If you will come, with a little effort, you may be able to richly provide for yourselves."

Hopeful looked at Christian with wide eyes. "Let's go see."

Christian shook his head. "Not me!" he said. "I have heard of this place and about the many who have been slain here. Besides, that treasure is a snare to those who seek it, for it hinders them in their pilgrimage."

Then Christian called to Demas, and said, "Is this not a dangerous place?

Demas tempts Christian and Hopeful

Has it not hindered many in their pilgrimage?" (*For those that desire to be rich fall into temptation and a snare, and into many foolish and hurtful lusts which drown men in destruction and perdition. – 1 Tim. 6:9*)[9]

"Not very dangerous," Demas said, "except to those who are careless." But his face blushed as he spoke the words.

Then Christian addressed Hopeful confidentially. "Let's not take one step off the way to wander from this path, but instead let us stay true to our way."

Hopeful looked over his shoulder behind them. "I guarantee you when By-ends comes to this place, if he is offered the same invitation he will turn in here to get a closer look."

"I don't doubt it." Christian took in a deep breath and let out a sigh. "There's no doubt of it, for his principles lead him that way, and I wager a hundred to one that he dies there."

Demas persisted and called to the two pilgrims again. "Won't you even come over just to look?"

Christian answered bluntly. "Demas, you are an enemy to those who pursue the right ways of the Lord of this way. I know you already have been rebuked yourself for turning aside here by one of his Majesty's judges. (*For Demas has forsaken me, having loved this present world. – 2 Tim. 4:10*) So why do you seek to bring us into the same condemnation? Besides, if we were to turn aside here, our Lord the King would certainly hear about it and reveal our shame. Our desire is to stand with boldness before him."

Demas cried out to them again claiming he belonged to their brotherhood. Then he said, "If you'll wait for just a short time, I'll join you on the pilgrimage."

In response Christian said, "What is your name? Isn't it the same name by which I have already called you?"

"Yes, my name is Demas. I am the son of Abraham."

"I know you," Christian answered. "Gehazi was your great-grandfather, and Judas your father, and you have continued to walk in their ways. What you are suggesting is nothing more than one of your devilish pranks. Your father was hanged as a traitor, and you deserve no better reward. (*Then Judas, who had betrayed him, when he saw that he was condemned, repented and returned the thirty pieces of silver to the princes of the priests and the elders,*

---

9   Original: *For, behold, they have left because of the destruction; Egypt shall gather them up, Memphis shall bury them: nettles shall possess in inheritance that which is desirable of their silver; thorns shall grow up in their dwellings – Hosea 9:6.*

saying, I have sinned in that I have betrayed the innocent blood. And they said, What is that to us? Thou shalt see to it. And casting down the pieces of silver in the temple, he departed and went and hanged himself. – Matt. 27:3-5) Be assured that when we have an audience with the King, we will tell him of your behavior." So Christian and Hopeful continued on their way, but by this time By-ends and his companions had come within sight again.

Christian and Hopeful watched as the trailing party arrived at the silver mine. As soon as Demas called to them, they left the way and went over to him. Now, whether they fell into the pit by looking over the brink, or they went down to dig, or whether they were smothered at the bottom by the poisonous fumes that often arise in those depths, I do not know. While I am not certain of the specifics, I did notice that they were never seen again in the way.

Then sang Christian this song:

> "By-ends and silver-Demas both agree
> One calls, the other runs, that he may be
> A sharer in his lucre: so these two
> Take up in this world and no farther go."

Now in my dream, I saw that just on the other side of this plain, the pilgrims came to a place where an old monument stood right beside the highway. At the sight of it they were both concerned because of the strangeness of its shape, for it seemed to them as if it had been a woman transformed into the shape of a pillar. The two of them stood intently looking at it, but for a time they didn't know what to think of it.

After some time Hopeful spotted an inscription on the head of the monument, but it was written in an unusual style of writing. So being no scholar, he called to Christian to see if he could understand the meaning. Christian examined it and after a little studying of the letters, he found them to mean "Remember Lot's wife."

So he read it to his traveling companion and together they concluded that it was the pillar of salt into which Lot's wife had been turned because she looked back, with a covetous heart when she was fleeing from Sodom for safety. (*Then the wife of Lot looked back from behind him, and she became a pillar of salt.* – Gen. 19:26) This amazing sight stimulated the following discussion.

"Ah, my brother, this is a timely sight." Christian started. "For it came to us at just the right time as it follows the invitation which Demas offered us to come over to view the hill Lucre. Had we gone over as he desired, and as you were inclined to do, my brother, I suppose we might have been made a similar spectacle for all those who come after us to see."

"I am sorry I was so foolish." He stared at the pillar. "I wonder why I

The pillar of salt

am not now petrified as Lot's wife. For in what way was there a difference between her sin and mine? She only looked back, while I had a desire to go see the mine. Let grace be adored here, and let me be ashamed that such a thought ever entered my heart."

"Let us take notice of what we see here, and how we can profit from it in the future." He pointed toward the pillar which was once Lot's wife. "This woman escaped one judgment, for she did not suffer the destruction of Sodom. Yet she was destroyed by another as we see here. She was turned into a pillar of salt."

Hopeful nodded. "True. And may she be both a warning and an example to us. A warning that we should shun her sin and an example of what judgment will overtake anyone who does not heed the warning. In the same way, Korah, Dathan, and Abiram, with the two hundred and fifty men who perished in their sin, were also an example to others to beware. (*And it came to pass as he had made an end of speaking all these words that the ground broke open under them; the earth opened her mouth and swallowed them up, and their houses and all the men of Korah and all their goods.* – Num. 16:31, 32)

"But above all, I ponder one particular thing. How is it that Demas and his friends can stand so confidently over there looking for treasure, while this woman did nothing but look behind her? For we do not read that she stepped one foot out of the way and yet she was turned into a pillar of salt. The judgment which overtook her remains as an example to all who see it to this day. And truly, all they have to do is lift up their eyes and they can't help but see her."

Christian looked thoughtful. "It is an astonishing thing to contemplate, and it indicates that their hearts have grown desperate in this case. It is fitting to compare them with one who picks pockets in the presence of the judge, or the thief who cuts purse strings under the shadow of the gallows.

"It is said of the men of Sodom that they were 'sinners exceedingly' because they were sinners 'before the Lord,' that is, in his sight. And yet he had shown them kindnesses, for the land of Sodom was like the garden of Eden. Remember that Lot looked around and saw that the whole plain of the Jordan toward Zoar was well watered, like the garden of the Lord, like the land of Egypt. ([This was] *before the LORD destroyed Sodom and Gomorrah . . . . Then Lot chose for himself all the plain of the Jordan, and*

Lot journeyed east; and they separated themselves the one from the other. Abram dwelt in the land of Canaan, and Lot dwelt in the cities of the plain and pitched his tents toward Sodom. But the men of Sodom were wicked and sinners before the LORD exceedingly. – Gen. 13:10-13) Therefore, this provoked him all the more to jealousy and made their plague as hot as the fire of the Lord out of heaven could make it. It is reasonable to conclude that those who sin in the sight of God, and in spite of such examples being set continually before them to warn them, still do the opposite. People such as these must be judged with the greatest severity."

"There's no doubt what you have said is the truth," Hopeful said. "But what a mercy is it, that neither you, but especially I ..." He placed his hand on his chest. "... am not made such an example as this woman! This occasion gives us an opportunity to thank God, to fear before him, and always to remember Lot's wife."

I saw then that the two pilgrims went on their way to a pleasant river, which David the king called "the river of God"; but John, "the river of the water of life." (*And he showed me a pure river of water of life, clear as crystal, proceeding out of the throne of God and of the Lamb.* – Rev. 22:1) Their way followed along the bank of this river. Christian and his companion, Hopeful, walked it with great delight. They also drank of the water of the river, which was pleasant and refreshing to their weary spirits.

On the banks of this river, on both sides, stood green trees with all kinds of fruit, and they ate the leaves to prevent gluttony and which offered other medicinal benefits. On either side of the river there was also a meadow, dotted with lilies and curiously beautiful. It was green all year long. In this meadow they lay down and slept, for in this place they could lie down safely. (*He makes me to lie down in green pastures; he leads me beside the still waters.* – Psalm 23:2) When they awoke they gathered fruit from the trees and drank of the water of the river again and once again lay down to sleep. Thus they did this for several days and nights. Then they sang:

> "Behold, how these Crystal Streams do glide,
>   To comfort pilgrims by the highway-side.
> The meadows green, besides their fragrant smell,
>   Yield dainties for them; And he that can tell
> What pleasant fruit, yes, leaves these trees do yield,
>   Will soon sell all, that he may buy this field."

The pilgrims rest by the River of the Water of Life

So when they were willing to go on, for they weren't as yet at their journey's end, they ate and drank, and departed.

Now I beheld in my dream that they had not journeyed far when the river divided and began to flow in two different directions. They were sorry to see it for they dared not go out of the way. Now the way led away from the river and was rough, and their feet grew tender because of their travels. So the souls of the pilgrims became more and more discouraged because of the ruggedness of the way. (*And they journeyed from Mount Hor by the way of the Red sea, to go around the land of Edom, and the soul of the people was much discouraged because of the way.* – Num. 21:4)

Still they went on and wished for a better way. A little ahead of them, to the left of the road stretched a fenced meadow accessed by a stile. That meadow is called By-path Meadow.

Christian said to Hopeful, "If this meadow lies alongside our way, let's cross over into it."

So he walked over to the stile to investigate, and saw that a pathway on the other side of the fence seemed to run parallel with the way.

"It's exactly what I wished for." Christian pointed to the path on the other side of the fence. "Here the going is much easier. Come on Hopeful, let's cross over."

"But . . ." Hopeful's mouth screwed to one side. "What if this path should lead us out of the way?"

"That's not likely," Christian said. "Look, doesn't it run alongside our way, but just on the other side of the fence?"

So Christian's argument persuaded Hopeful, and he followed him over the stile. Once they had crossed over and were walking on the parallel path, they found it much easier on their feet. Besides that, they spotted a man walking the path ahead of them. His name was Vain-Confidence. They called after him and asked him where that way led.

He said, "To the Celestial Gate."

Christian smiled at Hopeful. "See! Didn't I tell you so? With this advice you can be sure we are going the right direction." So they followed Vain-Confidence who went before them.

But once night fell, it grew very dark. In fact, it was so dark they could no longer see the man walking before them. The man himself, Vain-Confidence by name, could not see the way before him and he fell into a deep pit. This pit was dug in that place purposefully by the prince of those grounds to catch vain-glorious fools so they would be dashed to pieces. And so it happened to Vain-Confidence when he fell. (*He that trusts in his own heart is a fool, but whosoever walks in wisdom, he shall be saved. – Prov. 28:26*)[10]

Now, Christian and Hopeful heard him fall. So they called out to him to figure out what had happened, but there was no answer, only a groaning.

Hopeful said, "Where are we now?"

Christian was silent, for he was wondering if he had led his friend out of the way. And now it began to rain with thunder and lightning in a most dreadful manner. Water rose and began to flood the path.

Hopeful groaned inwardly and said, "Oh, if only I had stayed on the way!"

"Who could have thought that this path would have led us out of the way?" Christian asked.

Hopeful said, "From the beginning I was afraid that this would happen, and so I gave you that gentle warning. I would have spoken a little more directly, but you are older than me in the faith."

"Good brother, please don't be offended. I am sorry I have brought you out of the way and exposed you to such impending danger. I plead with you, my brother, forgive me. I did not act with evil intent."

"Be comforted, my brother, for I forgive you," Hopeful answered. "And I also believe that this shall work out for our good."

10   Original: *For the governors of this people are deceivers, and those who are governed by them are lost* – Isa. 9:16.

Christian said, "I am glad I have a merciful brother traveling with me, but we must not stand here like this. We must try to go back to the right way."

"In that case, brother Christian, let me lead the way."

"No." Christian reached out in the dark and placed his hand on Hopeful's arm. "If you please, let me go first. Then if we happen to run into any danger, I will encounter it first since I am the one responsible for leading us out of the way."

"No," said Hopeful over the sound of rising water. "You shall not go first, because your mind is troubled and for this reason it may lead you further out of the way."

Then for encouragement they heard the voice of one saying, "Let your heart be set toward the highway, even the way that you formerly went. Turn and go back again." (*Establish signs, make thee high markers; consider the highway with great care, even the way which thou didst come. – Jer. 31:21*)

But by this time the flood waters had risen much higher and made the way back very dangerous. Then I understood that it is easier to go out of the way when we are in it, than it is to go in when we are out. Yet the two pilgrims made every effort to go back. It was so dark and the flood so high, that in their attempt to go back they could have easily been drowned nine or ten times.

They could not, with all the skill they had, get back to the stile that night. Therefore they finally found refuge under a little shelter. They sat down there till the break of day but being weary they fell asleep.

Not far from the place where they lay, there was a castle called Doubting Castle. The owner of it was Giant Despair and it was on his grounds they now slept. And so early in the morning when the giant got up and walked up and down in his fields he caught Christian and Hopeful asleep on his property.

With a grim, surly voice the giant ordered them to wake up and he asked, "Where are you from, and what are you doing on my property?"

The two explained they were pilgrims who had lost their way.

Then Giant Despair said, "You have trespassed against me by trampling upon and lying on my grounds. Therefore you must come along with me."

So Christian and Hopeful were forced to go with the giant because he was stronger than them. As they walked along, they had very little to say, for they recognized their current circumstances were their fault.

The pilgrims found asleep by Giant Despair

The giant drove them ahead of himself and eventually secured them in a very dark dungeon in his castle. The spirits of the two prisoners found the dungeon to be nasty and stinking. But here they lay from Wednesday morning until Saturday night, without receiving one bit of bread or drop to drink. They remained in the dark all that time, and no one even came to ask how they were. Therefore, they found themselves in this evil place far from friends and acquaintances. (*Thou hast put lover and friend far from me, and placed my acquaintances into darkness.* – Psalm 88:18) Christian's sorrow multiplied in this place, because it was through his hasty advice that they were brought into this distressing state of affairs.

Now Giant Despair had a wife, and her name was Diffidence. So when the giant went to bed that evening he told his wife what he had done, explaining that he had taken a couple of prisoners and thrown them into his dungeon for trespassing on his grounds. Then he asked for advice. "What do you think I should do with these prisoners tomorrow?"

"Who are they?" she asked. "And where have they come from?"

He told her, and she advised him that when he arose in the morning he should beat them without mercy.

So when he arose in the morning, he grabbed his dreadful crab-tree club and went straightaway down into the dungeon to the prisoners. He began to beat them as if they were misbehaving dogs, although they had shown him no disrespect. The giant continued to beat them so severely, that they were no longer able to try to protect themselves or even to move upon the floor. Once he had finished, the giant walked out and left them there to commiserate over their misery and to mourn under their distress. So for the rest of that day heavy sighs and bitter cries occupied their time.

The next night, Diffidence talked with her husband again about the prisoners. When she learned that they were still alive she advised her husband to recommend to Christian and Hopeful that they commit suicide.

In the morning, he went to the prisoners in the same gruff manner as before. When he saw they were in extreme pain because of the wounds he had inflicted the day before, he told them, "Since you are never likely to get out of this place, your best alternative is to make an end of yourselves. You can use a knife, noose, or poison. For why should you choose to live seeing life is filled with so much bitterness?"

The prisoners asked that he let them go. With that the giant scowled as if he were ready to rush upon them to finish them off right then and there. But he fell into one of his fits, for he sometimes experienced seizures on sunshiny days during which he lost the use of his hands for a time. Therefore he withdrew from the dungeon and left the prisoners to consider what they should do. Christian and Hopeful talked between themselves as to whether it would be best to take the giant's advice or not and it led into an intense conversation. "Brother," said Christian. "What shall we do? The life we now live in this place is miserable. For my part, I don't know whether it is better to live like this or to die by our own hand. My soul chooses strangling rather than life, and the grave seems more desirable for me than this dungeon. (*And my soul thought it better to be strangled and desired death more than my bones.* – Job 7:15) Shall we accept the giant's advice?"

Hopeful let out a thoughtful sigh. "It is true that our present condition is dreadful, and death would be far more welcomed to me than to live in this continual misery. However, let us consider what the Lord of the country to which we are going has said. He declares 'You shall not commit murder,' not just to another man's person, but we are forbidden to take the giant's advice to kill ourselves as well.

"Also, let us consider again, that Giant Despair does not have authority over the law of our Lord. As far as I can understand, others have been captured by him just like we have, and yet they have escaped out of his hands. Who knows if perhaps God who made the world might cause the Giant Despair to die? Or that perhaps at some time or another in the future he may forget to lock us in? Or that he may in the near future have another paralyzing fit while he is here with us in the dungeon and then lose the use of his limbs? If that should ever come to pass again, for my part, I am determined to bolster my courage and to muster all my effort to escape from his hand. I was a fool not to have tried to do it earlier. However, my brother, let us be patient and continue to endure. The opportunity may

Christian and Hopeful in the castle of Giant Despair

come that could provide us with a happy release, but it shall not be by our own murders."

With these words, Hopeful calmed Christian's mind for the present so that they continued to endure the darkness that day, in their sad and doleful condition. Well, towards evening the giant went down into the dungeon again, to see if his prisoners had taken his advice. But when he walked into the dungeon he found them alive, but just barely so, because they were in such need of bread and water. Plus, the brutal wounds they had received when he beat them left them unable to do much other than to breathe a little.

But as I said, he found them alive and it put him in a furious rage and he threatened them because they had disobeyed his advice. "It will be worse for you now than if you had never been born."

At this the two terrified pilgrims trembled, and I think Christian fell into a swoon. But when he revived a little they renewed their discussion about the giant's advice and whether it might be best now to take it or not. Once again Christian seemed in favor of doing it; but Hopeful made a second reply against it.

"My brother," he said. "Think about how valiant you have been on this journey until now. Apollyon could not crush you, nor could all that you heard, saw, or felt, in the Valley of the Shadow of Death. What hardship, terror, and amazement you have already gone through! Are you now nothing but a bundle of fears? You see that I am imprisoned in the dungeon with you, and I am a far weaker man by nature than you are. Also this giant has wounded me as well as you, and has also withheld bread and water from my mouth. Together we mourn without the light, but still let us exercise a little more patience. Remember how you played the man at Vanity Fair and were neither afraid of the shackles nor the cage. You weren't even afraid of bloody death. Therefore let us, at least, avoid the giant's advice and bear up with patience as well as we can."

Night fell again and the giant and his wife, Diffidence, were in bed. She asked him about the prisoners and if they had taken his advice and killed themselves.

"They are sturdy scoundrels," he replied. "They choose to bear all hardships rather than to take their own lives."

"Take them into the castle yard tomorrow and show them the bones and skulls of those whom you have already dispatched, and promise them that before two weeks go by you will tear them in pieces as you have done to other pilgrims before them."

When the morning arrived, the giant went to Christian and Hopeful again and took them into the castle yard. He showed them all the bones and skulls just as his wife had told him to do. "These," he said, "were pilgrims once, just as you are. And they trespassed on my grounds, just as you have done. When I saw fit I tore them into pieces and within ten days I will do the same to you. Now get back down to your cell again." With that he beat them all the way to the dungeon. They lay in the dank darkness all day on Saturday in a most miserable condition, just like before.

That night when Mrs. Diffidence and her husband the giant went to bed, they began to discuss their prisoners again. The old giant was amazed that he could not bring them to an end either by his blows or his advice.

With that his wife replied, "I fear they live in hopes that someone will come to deliver them, or that they have picklocks hidden on their person which they hope to use to escape."

"I hadn't thought of that," the giant said. "But since you have presented this possibility, my dear, I will search them in the morning."

On Saturday, about midnight, Christian and Hopeful began to pray, and they continued in prayer until almost the break of day.

A little before dawn good Christian, as one half-amazed, broke out into this passionate exclamation. "What a fool I have been to lie in a stinking dungeon like this, when I could just as well walk free! I have a key in my pocket next to my heart called Promise that will, I am sure, open any lock in Doubting Castle."

"That is good news, good brother; pluck it from your pocket and try it."

So Christian pulled the key from his chest pocket and fit it into the lock on the dungeon door. As he turned the key the bolt released and the door flew open with ease. Christian and Hopeful both fled the dark cell. Then he went to the outward door that led into the castle yard. He tried his key and it opened that door also. From there he made haste to the outer iron gate, for he knew he must open that gate to escape, but he struggled with that lock for it was desperately hard, but finally the key opened it.

They thrust the gate open to make their escape, but as it opened the gate made such a creaking noise that it woke Giant Despair. He hastily left his bed and pursued his prisoners, but he felt paralysis overcoming his limbs, for one of his fits came over him again and made it impossible for him to go after them. So Christian and Hopeful hurried on until they came to the King's highway. Once again they were safe, because they were out of the Giant's jurisdiction.

Now, when they had crossed over the stile, they began to consider what they could do at that location to prevent pilgrims coming after them from being deceived and falling into the hands of Giant Despair. They agreed between themselves to erect a pillar with a clear message engraved on its side saying: "Over this stile is the way to Doubting Castle, which is kept by Giant Despair, who despises the King of the Celestial country and seeks to destroy his holy pilgrims." As a result, many who have followed after them have read what was written and escaped the danger. Once they finished this project, they sang the following song:

> *"Out of the way we went and then we found*
> *What it meant to tread upon forbidden ground*
> *And let those who come after have a care,*
> *Lest heedlessness makes them, as we, to fare*
> *Lest they, for trespassing, his prisoners are,*
> *Whose castle's Doubting and whose name's Despair."*

Christian and Hopeful escape from Doubting Castle

The Eighth Stage

————∽————

hey went until they came to the Delectable Mountains, which belong to the Lord of that hill which we spoke about earlier. So they went up to the mountains to look at the gardens and orchards, the vineyards and fountains of water. There they also drank, washed themselves, and freely ate of the vineyards.

On the tops of these mountains were shepherds feeding their flocks, and they stood by the side of the highway. So the pilgrims approached them to stand and talk as is the custom for weary travelers. They leaned upon their staffs, and asked, "Whose Delectable Mountains are these? And who owns these sheep that are feeding here?"

"These mountains are Emmanuel's land," the shepherds answered. "They are within sight of his city and the sheep also are his. He laid down his life for them." (*I AM the good shepherd; the good shepherd gives his life for the sheep. As the Father knows me, even so I know the Father, and I lay down my soul for the sheep. – John 10:11, 15*)

"Is this the way to the Celestial City?" Christian asked.

The shepherds said, "You are heading in the right direction."

"How far do we have to go?"

"It is too far for any except those who shall certainly arrive there."

Christian looked at the way ahead and asked, "Is the way safe or dangerous?"

"Safe for those for whom it is to be safe but transgressors undoubtedly fall along the way." (*Who is wise that he might understand this? and prudent that he might know this? for the ways of the LORD are right, and the just shall walk in them; but the rebellious shall fall therein. – Hos. 14:9*)

Christian considered the shepherds' words and asked, "Is there a place where pilgrims who are weary and faint can find temporary rest in the way?"

The shepherds nodded. "The Lord of these mountains has given us orders not to be forgetful to entertain strangers. (*Do not forget to show hospitality; for thereby some, having entertained angels, were kept. – Heb. 13:2)* Therefore this good place is at your disposal."

I saw also in my dream that when the shepherds perceived that Christian and Hopeful were travelers, they asked them some questions, which the pilgrims answered just as they had in other places all the way. The shepherds asked, "Where are you from?" and "How did you enter into the way?" And, "By what means have you persevered so far, for few travelers who begin to come here ever show their face on these mountains."

But when the shepherds heard their answers, they were pleased with them. Their countenance turned favorable, and they looked very lovingly upon the two of them and said, "Welcome to the Delectable Mountains."

The shepherds whose names were Knowledge, Experience, Watchful, and Sincere, took them by the hand and led them to their tents where they partook of a feast. The shepherds said, "We would be content for you to stay here a while and to become acquainted with us, and even more we recommend you enjoy the comfort provided by the bounty of these Delectable Mountains." Christian and Hopeful told them that they would be happy to stay, and then went to bed because it was very late.

Then I saw in my dream that, in the morning, the shepherds invited Christian and Hopeful to walk with them upon the mountains. So they joined them and walked along together for a while, enjoying the pleasant view on every side. Then the shepherds said to each other, "Shall we show these pilgrims some of the wonders that are to be seen here?"

They agreed they should and took them first to the top of a hill called Error, which was very steep on the farthest side. "Look down to the bottom," they said. So Christian and Hopeful peered down and saw several men dashed all to pieces at the bottom, for they had fallen from the top.

Christian looked from the bodies to the shepherds and asked, "What does this mean?"

The shepherds answered, "Have you not heard about those led into error, by listening to Hymenaeus and Philetus concerning the faith of the resurrection of the body?" (*And that word will eat away as gangrene, of whom are Hymenaeus and Philetus, who have erred from the truth, saying that the resurrection is already past and have overthrown the faith of some. – 2 Tim. 2:17, 18*)

"Yes," Christian and Hopeful answered in unison.

The shepherds show the pilgrims the hill Error

The shepherds replied, "They are those you see dashed in pieces at the bottom of this mountain. And they have remained unburied to this day, as you can see, to serve as an example to others to take care that they don't climb too high or come too near the brink of this mountain."

Then I saw the shepherds take them to the top of another mountain named Caution. There the shepherds told them to look into the distance. So when Christian and Hopeful looked afar, they thought they perceived several men walking up and down among a number of tombs located there. As they watched they noticed the men were blind, because they stumbled sometimes over the tombs and were unable to get out from among them.

Once again Christian asked, "What means this?"

The shepherds answered them with another question. "A little below these mountains did you notice a stile that led into a meadow on the left hand of this way?"

The two pilgrims glanced at each other and back at the shepherds. "Yes."

"From that stile," the shepherds said, "there goes a path that leads directly to Doubting Castle, which is kept by Giant Despair; and these men ..." They pointed to the blind wandering among the tombs, "... came once on pilgrimage, just as you do now. That is until they came to that same stile. Because the right way was rough in that place, they chose to leave the way and cross over into that meadow.

"There they were taken by Giant Despair and cast into Doubting Castle, where they were kept in the dungeon. Eventually he put out their eyes and led them among those tombs, where he has left them to wander to this very day so that the saying of the wise man might be fulfilled: 'He who wanders out of the way of understanding shall remain in the congregation of the dead.'" (*The man that wanders out of the way of wisdom shall end up in the congregation of the dead.* – Prov. 21:16)

Christian and Hopeful looked at each another with tears streaming down their cheeks, but they said nothing to the shepherds.

Then I saw in my dream that the shepherds led them to another place at the bottom of the valley, where there was a door on the side of a hill. The shepherds opened the door and told them to look in. They looked in and it was very dark and smoky. From within the darkness, they also thought they heard the rumbling sound of fire accompanied by tormented cries. And the smell of brimstone wafted from the door. Christian turned to the shepherds and asked, "What does this mean?"

The shepherds told them, "This is a by-way to hell, where hypocrites enter in. This includes those who sell their birthright with Esau, those who sell their Master with Judas, those who blaspheme the gospel with Alexander, and those who lie and deceive with Ananias and Sapphira his wife."

Then Hopeful said, "I notice that every one of these put on a show of going on a pilgrimage just like we are doing. Is that so?"

The shepherds nodded. "Yes, and they traveled for quite a long time, too."

"Exactly how far is it possible for them to go on in pilgrimage, since they were miserably cast away?"

"Some farther and some not so far as these mountains."

Then the pilgrims spoke one to the other. "We certainly have need to cry to the Strong for strength."

The shepherds nodded their agreement. "Yes, and you will have need to draw on that strength once you have it, too."

By this time the pilgrims had a desire to press forward on their journey, and the shepherds agreed that they should. So they all walked together towards the end of the mountains. Then the shepherds said one to another,

"Let us show them the gates of the Celestial City, if they have skill to look through our perspective glass."

The pilgrims eagerly accepted the invitation, and so they were led to the top of a high hill called Clear and were handed the glass to look through. They attempted to look through it, but the memory of the last thing the shepherds had shown them made their hands shake so much that they could not look steadily through the glass. However, even with shaky hands they thought they saw something like the gate and also some of the glory of the place. Then they prepared to depart and sang this song:

"Thus by the shepherds secrets are revealed,
  Which from all other men are kept concealed
 Come to the shepherds then, if you would see
   Things deep, things hid, and that mysterious be."

When they were about to depart, one of the shepherds gave them written instructions of the way ahead. Another cautioned them to beware of the Flatterer. The third told them to take care not to sleep upon Enchanted Ground. And the fourth bid them God speed. So I awoke from my dream.

The Ninth Stage

———∽———

slept and dreamed again and saw the same two pilgrims going down the mountains along the highway towards the Celestial City. A little below these mountains, on the left hand, lies the country of Conceit. From it originates a crooked lane along which pilgrims walk because it enters into the way. Here they met with a very lively young man named Ignorance who came out of that country.

So Christian asked him, "Where are you coming from? And where are you going?"

"Sir, I was born in the country that lies there." He pointed left toward the country of Conceit. "And I am going to the Celestial City."

"But how do you think you will be admitted at the gate? Don't you think you may run into some difficulty there?"

Ignorance shrugged. "Not really. I will get in the same way other good people do."

"But what have you to show at that gate? What qualification can you show so the gate should be opened to you?" Christian asked.

Ignorance held his head high and said, "I know my Lord's will and have lived a good life and I have repaid every man to whom I owe a debt. I pray, fast, pay tithes, and give alms, and have left the land of my birth for the place to which I am going."

Christian's brow knit into a slight frown. "But you did not enter in at the wicket gate, which is at the head of this straight way. Instead, you came here by means of that crooked lane. I'm afraid that whatever you may think of yourself, that when the day of reckoning comes, you will be charged as a thief and a robber, instead of being admitted into the Celestial City."

"Gentlemen, you are utter strangers to me!" Ignorance said. "I don't know you, so be content to follow your religion and I will follow mine. I hope all will be well. And as for the gate that you talk about, all the world knows that is a great distance away from our country. I cannot imagine that any man in all our regions knows the way to it. Plus there isn't really any need for them to do so since we have, as you see, a fine, pleasant, green lane that comes down from our country into the way right here."

When Christian saw that the man was wise in his own conceit, he whispered to Hopeful, "There is more hope for a fool than for him." (*Seest thou a man wise in his own conceit? there is more hope of a fool than of him.* – Prov. 26:12) And then he added, "When he who is a fool walks along the way, he

lacks wisdom and demonstrates to everyone that he is a fool. (*Even when the fool walks by the way, he lacks prudence, and he says unto every one that he is a fool.* – Eccles. 10:3) What do you think? Should we talk any more with him? Or should we walk ahead of him for now and give him time to think about what he has already heard? And then shall we wait for him again, after some time to see if talking to him a little at a time can do him any good?"

Hopeful whispered in return, "Let Ignorance think on what we've said for a little while and hopefully he will not refuse to accept our good counsel, lest he

Ignorance

remain still ignorant of what is the greatest gain. God says, 'Those who have no understanding (although he made them), those he will not save.'"

Hopeful further added, "I don't think it is a good idea to tell him everything at once. Rather, if you agree, I suggest we leave him for a while and talk to him later when he may be able to receive it."

So the two pilgrims went on ahead and Ignorance followed after them. When they had put some distance between them, they entered into a very dark lane where they met a man whom seven demons had bound with seven strong cords. The demons were carrying him back to the door they saw on the side of the hill when they were escorted by the shepherds. (*Then it goes and takes with itself seven other spirits worse than itself, and they enter in and dwell there; and the last state of that man is worse than the first. Even so shall it also be unto this wicked generation.* – Matt. 12:45)

Good Christian and his companion, Hopeful, began to tremble. Yet as the devils led the man away, Christian looked to see if he knew him. He thought it might be one Turn-away who lived in the town of Apostasy. But he wasn't able to get a clear view to identify his face, because he hung his head like a thief who has been found out. However, once he had passed by, Hopeful watched as he was taken away and spotted a label on his back with this inscription: "Wanton professor and damnable apostate."

Christian leaned toward Hopeful and said, "Now I remember what he told me about something that happened to a good man in this region. The name of the man was Little-Faith, but he was a good man who lived in the town of Sincere. What happened to him was this:

"There is an entrance to the straightaway here that comes down from the Broadway-gate, a lane called Dead-Man's lane. It's called this because of the murders commonly committed there.

"So this Little-Faith, while on pilgrimage just as we are now, happened to sit down for a time and fell sleep. At that time three sturdy scoundrels came down the lane from Broadway-gate. They were three brothers and their names were Faint-Heart, Mistrust, and Guilt. When they spotted Little-Faith asleep they sprinted toward him. Now the good man had just awakened from his sleep and was just getting up to continue his journey. The three men came up to him and ordered him to stand. At this Little-Faith turned as white as a sheet since he didn't have the strength to fight or flee.

"Faint-Heart said, 'Hand over your purse.'

"But Little-Faith hesitated, for he was very reluctant to lose his money. Mistrust stepped close to him and thrust his hand into Little-Faith's pocket.

"Little-Faith cried out, 'Thieves! Thieves!'

"Guilt struck Little-Faith on the head with a great club that was in his hand and knocked him flat to the ground, where he lay bleeding profusely and in danger of dying. The thieves just stood by watching him bleed to death, but then heard someone coming on the road. They were afraid it might be Great-Grace who lives in the town of Good-Confidence. They quickly departed and left this good man to fend for himself.

Little-Faith is robbed

"After a while Little-Faith began to revive. He scrambled to his feet and staggered on his way."

Hopeful asked, "Did they take all he had?"

Christian shook his head. "No, they never ransacked the pocket where he held his jewels, so those he was able to keep. But, as I was told, the good man was very much troubled over his loss. For the thieves took most of his spending money. Like I said, they did not get his jewels, but other than that he had very little money left. It was scarcely enough to support him to the end of his journey.

"It's sad to say, if I wasn't misinformed, he was forced to beg along the way to keep himself alive, for he wasn't able to sell his jewels. So he continued to beg and scratched to do what he could to exist. He went, as we say, with many a hungry belly for most of the rest of the way." (*And if the righteous are saved with difficulty, where shall the unfaithful and the sinner appear? – 1 Peter 4:18*)

"But isn't it remarkable that they didn't rob him of his certificate, which he must have to receive his admittance at the Celestial Gate?" Hopeful asked.

"Yes," Christian said. "It is remarkable, but they did not get it. Though they didn't miss it through any cunning on the part of Little-Faith, for he had been so dismayed by their assault that he didn't have the strength or skill to hide anything. So it was really more a question of good providence rather than any endeavor on his part that they missed such a good thing." (*The Lord knows how to deliver the godly out of temptations and to reserve the unjust unto the day of judgment to be punished.* – 2 Peter 2:9)

"But it must be a comfort to him that they did not get his jewels from him," Hopeful said.

Christian sighed. "It might have been a great comfort to him if he had appreciated this fact as he should have, but those who told me this story said he was so disheartened because they took away his money that he made little use of the jewels and hardly even mentioned them the rest of the way. And when he did think on his precious jewels and he began to be comforted, they only reminded him of his loss again and filled him with depressing thoughts that consumed him."

Hopeful shook his head. "How sad for that poor man; such a situation could be nothing but a continual source of great grief to him."

"Grief?" Christian asked. "Yes he was deeply distressed! I think any of us would feel that way if we had been robbed and wounded like him, and in a strange place as he was. It is a wonder he did not die with grief, poor man. I was also told that he spread gloomy and bitter complaints concerning his misfortune almost all the rest of the way. He explained all the details to all who encountered him about where he was robbed and how, and who they were that did it. He recounted what he had lost, how he was assaulted, and that he had hardly escaped with life."

"It is a wonder, though, that the demands of traveling did not force him to sell or pawn some of his jewels so the pressures along the way might be relieved somewhat."

Christian looked mildly surprised. "You talk with about as much wisdom as a newly hatched chick with shell stuck to his head to this very day. For what reason would he ever want to pawn his jewels? And to whom would he sell them? In all that country where he was robbed, his jewels were not even counted as valuable nor did he want the type of relief which the citizens living there might offer to him. Besides, if his jewels had been missing when he reached the gate of the Celestial City, he knew he would have been excluded from receiving an inheritance there. That would have been worse for him than meeting up with the villainy of ten thousand thieves."

"Why are you being so sharp with me, my brother?" Hopeful asked. "Esau sold his birthright and for a mere bowl of pottage (*Then Jacob gave Esau of the bread and of the pottage of lentils; and he ate and drank, and rose up, and went away. Thus Esau despised his birthright. – Gen.* 25:34),[11] and that birthright was his greatest jewel. So if he sold such a precious thing, then why couldn't Little-Faith do the same?"

"Esau did sell his birthright," Christian said, "and so have many others besides. By doing so they exclude themselves from the chief blessing, just as that indulgent coward did. However, there is a fundamental difference between Esau and Little-Faith, and also between their spiritual conditions. For Esau's birthright was typical, but Little-Faith's jewels were not so.

"Esau's appetite was his god, but Little-Faith's was not so. Esau's lack lay in his fleshly appetite. Little-Faith's did not. Besides, Esau saw no further than the fulfilling of his lusts saying, 'For I am at the point of death, and what good will this birthright do me?' (Gen. 25:32)

"But Little-Faith, though it was appointed for him to have but a little faith, was by his little faith kept from such extravagances. And by faith, as little as it was, he recognized his jewels were precious and that he should not sell them as Esau did his birthright. However, you do not read anywhere that Esau had faith, not even a little. Therefore it's not surprising in the case of Esau that he was swayed by his flesh. For when the flesh alone controls a man, that man has no faith to help him resist selling his birthright and his soul to the devil of hell. For such a person is similar to the ass, who in her periods of heat cannot be made to change direction; when their minds are set upon their lusts, they will have them, whatever they cost. (*A wild ass used to the wilderness that breathes according to the desire of her soul; from her lust, who shall stop her? All those that seek her will not weary themselves; in her month they shall find her. – Jer.* 2:24)

"But Little-Faith was of a different disposition. His mind was focused on things divine. His livelihood was based upon spiritual things from above. Therefore, for what purpose would a person with this temperament sell his jewels? If there had been anyone who would have even bought them, it would have only served to fill his mind with empty things. Will a man give a penny to fill his belly with hay? Or can you persuade the turtledove

---

11   Original: *Lest there be any fornicator or profane person as Esau, who for one morsel of food sold his birthright* – Heb. 12:16.

to live upon carrion, like the crow? Though faithless ones can pawn, or mortgage, or sell what they have, and even themselves to boot, for carnal lusts, yet those who have faith, saving faith, even if just a little of it, cannot do so. This, therefore, Hopeful, is your mistake."

"I honestly acknowledge it," Hopeful said. "But at the same time, your stern response almost made me angry."

Christian's brows raised in surprise. "I was rather harsh, but all I did was to compare you to birds that are especially lively, which run to and fro in untrodden paths with the shell upon their heads like a newborn chick! But let us leave that matter behind us and consider the matter under debate and all shall be well between you and me."

"But, Christian, these three fellows that attacked Little-Faith; I am persuaded in my heart they were nothing but cowards. Otherwise, do you think they would have been so quick to run at the sound of someone coming along on the road? Why didn't Little-Faith pull together greater courage? He might, in my opinion, have been able to resist them for at least one skirmish and then have yielded when they overwhelmed him."

"Certainly, many have called such assailants cowards, but when they come face to face with them in an assault, few have found that to be the case. As for a courageous heart, Little-Faith had no such thing. And I believe, my brother, that if the same thing happened to you, you would also have surrendered quickly. To be truthful, while you are upset about this matter now when these scoundrels are far from us, I think you might have second thoughts about how bravely you would confront them if they should suddenly appear to you as they did to him.

"But consider again that they are, in fact, hired thieves who serve under the king of the bottomless pit. And he, if needed, will come quickly to their aid himself, and his voice is like the roaring of a lion." (*Be temperate and vigilant because your adversary the devil, as a roaring lion, walks about, seeking whom he may devour. – 1 Peter 5:8*)

"I myself have been engaged in a similar conflict as Little-Faith faced, and I found it to be a terrifying experience. These three villains set upon me, and I began to resist them like a Christian should, but they were quick to call for help and their master came to their aid right away. As the saying goes, I would have given my life for a penny, but God had other plans and I was clothed with armor that had been tested. And even though I was well equipped, I found it hard work to prove myself as a manly pilgrim. No one can understand what it is like in such combat until he experiences being in the thick of the battle himself."

Hopeful responded. "Well, of course these scoundrels ran when they thought that Great-Grace was drawing close in the way."

Christian agreed. "True. In the past, they and their master have often fled when there is the prospect of Great-Grace appearing, and that's no surprise, for he is known as the King's champion. But I trust you are willing to make some distinction between Little-Faith and the King's champion. All the King's subjects are not his champions; nor can they accomplish such valiant feats of war as he when they are tested by assailants. Is it reasonable to think that a little child should handle Goliath as David did? Is it right to expect a wren to have the strength of an ox? Some pilgrims are strong while others are weak; some have great faith, some have little. This man, Little-Faith, was one of the weaker kind, and therefore he suffered exhausting humiliation."

Hopeful let out a deep sigh. "I still wish it had been Great-Grace who appeared, for the sake of those scoundrels."

Christian rested his hand on his cheek and shook his head thoughtfully. "If he had arrived during that skirmish, he might have had his hands full. For I must tell you that even though Great-Grace is highly skilled with his weapons, as long as he keeps his sword sharpened he can do very well against such opponents. But if Faint-Heart, Mistrust, or Guilt can penetrate his armor, he will find the going hard and may even take a fall. And when a man is down, what can he do?

"Whoever looks very closely at Great-Grace's face, will see those scars and cuts there that clearly prove what I'm saying to be true. In fact, during one engagement he had with the enemy, I heard it said that while he was in the battle he cried out, 'We despaired even of life.'

"And isn't it true that these powerful rogues and their accomplices even made David groan, mourn, and roar with anguish? Yes, and also Heman (*O LORD God of my saving health, I cry day and night before Thee; let my prayer come before thee; incline thine ear unto my cry; for my soul is full of troubles, and my life draws near unto Sheol.* – Psalm 88:1-3) and Hezekiah. Even though they were regarded as champions in their days, they were forced to rouse themselves because of the seriousness of the assault. But in spite of taking a fearless stand, they had their coats soiled and torn by them. Peter, upon one occasion, tried to do what he could do in a similar situation. Even though he is considered the prince of the apostles, these same assailants roughed him up to the point that they made him afraid of a pitiful girl.

"Besides, the king of the scoundrels is always at their beck and call. He is never out of earshot, and if at any time they are losing the battle, whenever possible he comes to help them. For this reason it has been said of him, 'The sword of him who attempts to strike him cannot succeed; nor can the spear, the dart, or the javelin. He regards iron as straw, and bronze as rotten wood. The arrow cannot make him flee. Sling-stones are turned by him into stubble. Darts are counted as straw. He laughs at the rattling of the javelin.' (*When one catches up to him, no sword or spear or dart or coat of mail shall endure against him. He esteems iron as straw and bronze as rotten wood. The arrow cannot make him flee; with him, slingstones are turned into stubble. He counts any weapon as stubble; he laughs at the shaking of a spear.* – Job 41:26-29) What can a man do in this case?

"It is true; if a man has full access to Job's horse and has skill and courage to ride him, he might accomplish notable deeds for his king. About his stallion it is said, his neck is clothed with thunder. He will not be afraid like a grasshopper and the snorting of his nostrils is terrible. He paws in the valley while rejoicing in his strength. He goes on from there to engage the armed men. He mocks at fear and is frightened by nothing. Not even the sword turns him back. The quiver rattles against him, as do the flashing spear and the shield. He races over the ground with fierceness and rage, and he doesn't stop at the sound of the trumpet. Instead, at the sound of the trumpet he says, 'Aha,' and is drawn to the scent of distant battle, the thundering of captains and the shouting of the battle cry. (*Hast thou given the horse strength? Hast thou clothed his neck with thunder? Canst thou make him leap as a grasshopper? The glory of his nostrils is formidable. He paws at the earth and rejoices in his strength; he goes forth to meet the armed men. He mocks fear and is not afraid; neither does he turn his face from the sword. The quiver rattles against him, the glittering spear and the shield. He swallows the ground with fierceness and rage; the sound of the shofar does not trouble him; for the blasts of the shofar fill him with courage;*

he smells the battle afar off, the thunder of the princes and the sound of the battle-cry. – Job 39:19-25)

"But for such footmen as you and I, let us never desire to meet with an enemy or promote ourselves as if we could do better when we hear of others who have suffered defeat. Nor should we entertain thoughts of our own spiritual manhood as better than it is, for those who think this way often suffer the worst when tested. Take Peter for example, who I mentioned earlier. He would strut, yes, he would. Because of his proud attitude he fostered thoughts of himself as being more than ready to stand in defense of his Master compared to all other men. But who was more defeated than he was when these villains were on the attack?

"Therefore, when we hear of such robberies taking place along the King's highway, there are two things we should do.

"First, let us go out well equipped and be sure to take a shield with us, for it was for lack of a shield that made it impossible for the hearty assailant of Leviathan to make him yield. For, it is true, that if we lack this weapon he will not fear us at all. Therefore, one of the King's champions has said, 'Above all, take the shield of faith, with which you shall be able to extinguish the fiery darts of the wicked' (Eph. 6:16).

"Second, it is also good for us to request a convoy of the King, and that he will go with us himself. This prospect made David rejoice when in the Valley of the Shadow of Death, and Moses expressed his desire, too, for dying where he stood, rather than to go one step without his God. (*And he said unto him, If thy presence is not to go before us, do not bring us out of here.* – Exod. 33:15)

"Oh, my brother, if our King will go along with us, why should we be afraid of even ten thousands who plot against us? (*I laid me down and slept; I awaked, for the LORD sustained me. I will not be afraid of ten thousands of people that have set themselves against me round about.* – Psalm 3:5-6) And on the other hand, without him the proud only find refuge under the slain. (*They shall bow down among the prisoners, and they shall fall among the slain. For all this his anger is not turned away, but his hand is stretched out still.* – Isa. 10:4)

"I, for my part, have been in the thick of the battle before now and as you can see I am still alive through the goodness of Him who is best. Yet, I cannot boast at all in my own spiritual strength. In fact, I would be glad if I never met with any more such clashes, though I fear we have not yet passed beyond all danger. However, since the lion and the bear have not as yet devoured me, I have hope God will also deliver us from the next uncircumcised Philistine." Then Christian sang:

> "Poor Little-Faith has been among the thieves!
> Was robbed! Remember this – all who believe,
> And get more faith; shall a victor be
> Over ten thousand else scarce over three."

So they walked on and Ignorance followed. Christian and Hopeful continued, until they came to a place where another path joined with the straight way. The new path appeared to be as straight as the way which they had been following, so the two of them stood still pondering the choice and not knowing which of the two to take.

As they were thinking about the way, a dark man wearing a very light robe walked up to them, and asked them why they stood there.

"We're going to the Celestial City," they answered. "But we don't know which of these ways to take."

"Follow me," said the man. "It is the way in which I am going."

So the two pilgrims followed him in the new way which had joined the road. A little at a time it curved until it turned them so far that they veered away from the Celestial City. In a little time, their faces were completely turned away from it. And yet they followed him. But by and by, before they were aware of the man's deception, he led them both into a net that encompassed them. They both became so entangled that they didn't know what to do. Then the white robe fell off the dark man's back and they began to understand where they were. Therefore the two pilgrims lay crying there for some time, because they didn't know how to escape.

Then Christian said to Hopeful, "Now do I see that I have been caught in an error. Didn't the shepherds urge us to beware of the Flatterer? Today we have discovered the truth in what the wise man says: 'A man who flatterers his neighbor, spreads a net for his feet'" (Prov. 29:5).

"Yes," Hopeful said. "And they also gave us written instructions with directions about the way to make sure of our safe arrival. But we have forgotten to study them and so have not kept ourselves from the paths of the destroyer. In this David was wiser than us for he said, 'Concerning the works of men, by the word of your lips I have kept myself from the paths of the Destroyer.'" (*Concerning the works of men, by the word of thy lips I have observed the ways of the violent. – Psalm 17:4*) So the two of them lay entangled in the net grumbling and complaining.

At last they noticed a Shining One coming towards them, a whip of small cords in his hand. When he came close to the place where they were stuck in the net, he asked them where they had come from and what they did

Christian and Hopeful delivered from the net

there. They told him they were poor pilgrims going to Zion, but had been led out of the way by a man clothed in white. "He told us to follow him since he was going to Zion, too."

The man with the whip said, "It is Flatterer, a false apostle, who has transformed himself into an angel of light." (*For these false apostles are deceitful workers, transforming themselves into apostles of Christ. And it is no marvel, for Satan himself transforms himself into an angel of light. – 2 Cor. 11:13, 14*) So he tore the net and freed the pilgrims.

"Follow me," he said to them, "that I may set you in your way again." So he led them back to the true straightaway which they had left in order to follow the Flatterer. Then he asked them, "Where did you stay last night?"

They said, "With the shepherds upon the Delectable Mountains."

He asked if the shepherds had given them written instructions including a map for the way.

"Yes," they answered.

The Shining One pressed further. "When you pondered the way to go, didn't you take out the instructions to learn the way to go?"

The two red-faced pilgrims answered, "No."

"But why not?"

"We forgot."

Then he asked, "Did the shepherds not urge you to beware of the Flatterer?"

"Yes they did," the pilgrims answered. "But we did not imagine that this fine-spoken man dressed in white could possibly be him." (*And I beseech you, brethren, mark those who cause dissensions and offences outside of the doctrine which ye have learned, and avoid them. For they that are such do not serve our Lord Jesus Christ, but their own belly and by smooth words and blessings deceive the hearts of the simple. – Rom. 16:17, 18*)

Then I saw in my dream that the Shining One commanded Christian and Hopeful to lie down. When they did he severely chastised them, to teach them the good way in which they should walk (*And it shall be if the wicked man is worthy to be beaten the judge shall cause him to lie down and to be beaten in his presence, according to his fault, by a certain number. – Deut. 25:2*); and as he chastised them, he said, "Those whom I love, I reprimand and discipline; be zealous, therefore, and repent" (Rev. 3:19).

Having done this, he told them to go on their way, and to specifically pay attention to the other directions of the shepherds. So they thanked him for all his kindness and went along the right way, softly singing.

> "*Come toward this place, you who walk along the way,*
> *See how the pilgrims fare who go astray.*
> *They are caught in an entangling net,*
> *'Cause good counsel they lightly did forget:*
> *'Tis true, they were rescued but yet you see,*
> *They're scourged to boot; let this your caution be.*"

Now, after a while, they noticed someone in the distance coming toward them quietly and alone along the highway to meet them. Then Christian said to his companion, Hopeful, "Ahead of us is a man with his back towards Zion, and he is coming to meet us."

Hopeful said, "I see him. Let us be very careful now, lest he should prove to be another Flatterer also."

So the man drew nearer and nearer until he finally came right up to them. His name was Atheist, and he asked them where they were going.

"We are going to Mount Zion," Christian said.

Atheist burst into a howling laughter.

Christian glanced at Hopeful and back at Atheist with a scowl. "What's the meaning of your laughter?"

Atheist caught his breath and wiped a tear from the corner of his eyes. "I can't help but laugh. It's obvious what ignorant persons both of you are. You've taken upon yourselves this tedious journey that will provide you with nothing but your trouble and pains on a fruitless journey."

"Why do you say that?" Christian asked. "Don't you think we will be received at our destination?"

"Received!" Atheist rolled his eyes as if Christian were a fool. "There is no such a place as the one you dream about in all this world."

"But there is in the world to come," Christian said.

"When I was back home in my own country I heard about this place you are talking about and for that reason I set out to look for this Celestial City, and have been seeking it now for over twenty years. But from that first day on which I departed, until now, I have found no such place." (*The labour of the foolish wearies all of them because they do not know how to go to the city. –* Eccles. 10:15)

Christian gestured toward both Hopeful and himself. "Both of us have heard and believe that there is such a place to be found."

"If I hadn't first believed as you do when I left home, I would not have come this far in my search. You would think I would have found such a place by now if it existed. For I have traveled farther than you have, and now I am going back home where I hope to refresh myself with the things I had cast aside for the empty hope of that which I never found."

Then Christian turned to his companion, Hopeful. "Is what this man said true?"

"Be very careful," Hopeful warned. "This man is one of the Flatterers. Remember what it cost us once already for listening to another sweet-talker like this one." He shook his head in disbelief. "What a thing to say that there is no Mount Zion! Didn't we see the gate of the city ourselves from the Delectable Mountains? Furthermore, are we not now to walk by faith? (*For we walk by faith, not by sight. –* 2 Cor. 5:7) Let us go on, lest the man with the whip should catch up to us again."

A hint of concern showed on Hopeful's face. "But you should have been the one teaching me this lesson, so listen carefully and let me plainly address you. 'My son, stop listening to the instruction that causes you to depart from the words of knowledge.' (*Cease, my son, to hear the teaching that induces one to deviate from the reasons of wisdom.* – Prov. 19:27) I say, my brother, do not listen to him! Rather, let us believe to the saving of the soul."

Christian studied the ground for a moment and looked back at Hopeful. "My brother, let me confess that I did not put the question to you because of my own doubt of the truth. Instead, I intended to test you and to obtain from you a response that would show the real commitment of your heart." He nodded toward Atheist. "As for this man, I know he is blinded by the god of this world. As for you and me, let's go forward holding on to the knowledge that we believe the truth, and no lie can be part of the truth." (*I have not written unto you as if ye ignore the truth, but as unto those that know it, and that no lie is of the truth.* – 1 John 2:21)

Atheist

Hopeful smiled and clapped him on the back. "Now I do rejoice in hope of the glory of God." The two pilgrims turned away from the man, Atheist, and he loudly laughed at them and walked away not just from them, but also from the Celestial City.

Then in my dream I saw the two pilgrims travel on until they came into a certain region where the air naturally tended to make strangers passing through drowsy. And here Hopeful began to feel lethargic and sleepy. He said to Christian, "I have now become so drowsy I can scarcely hold my eyes open." He rubbed his eyes and looked around. "Let us lie down here and take one nap."

Christian shook his head. "In no way should we stop to sleep here," he said. "If we stop to sleep here, we may never awake."

"Why do you say that, my brother?" Hopeful looked at Christian with heavy-lidded eyes. "Sleep is sweet to the working man. If we take a nap, we may feel refreshed."

"Don't you remember what one of the shepherds told us?" Christian said. "He said to beware of the Enchanted Ground. By this he meant that we should be careful not to doze there. 'So let us not sleep, as do others; but let us watch and be sober'" (1 Thess. 5:6).

Hopeful bobbed his head in agreement. "I confess I'm at fault. Had I been traveling alone and fallen asleep, I would have run the danger of death. I see now that what the wise man says is true: 'Two are better than one.' (*Two are better than one because they have a better reward for their labour. – Eccles. 4:9*) At this point in our journey your company has been a continual blessing, and you shall have a good reward for your efforts."

"Now, then." Christian rubbed his palms together enthusiastically. "To prevent drowsiness in this place, let us engage in good conversation."

"With all my heart," the other said.

"Where shall we begin?"

"Why don't we start with where God began with us," Hopeful suggested. "But, if you please, I'd prefer if you begin."

"Very well," Christian said. "I will sing you first this song.

> "*When saints do sleepy grow, let them come hither,*
> *And hear how these two pilgrims talk together;*
> *Yes, let them learn of them in any wise way,*
> *To keep open their drowsy, slumbering eyes.*
> *Saints' fellowship, if it be managed well,*
> *Keeps them awake and that in spite of hell.*"

Then Christian decided to start their discussion with a question. "How did you first come to think of doing what you do now?"

"Do you mean how I first became concerned about the condition of my soul?"

"Yes," Christian said. "That's exactly what I mean."

"For a long time, I continued to delight in those things which were on display and marketed at our fair," Hopeful began. "Things which I believe now would have drowned me in damnation and destruction, if I had continued in them still."

"What types of things were they?"

Hopeful gestured with his palms toward the sky and shrugged. "All the treasures and riches of the world." He let his arms drop as he shook his head. "I also delighted in much rebelling, partying, drinking, swearing, lying, lewdness, and much more. All of which tended to destroy my soul. But at last I discovered by listening to and considering spiritual truth, that this ungodly lifestyle would eventually lead to my death. (*What fruit had ye then in those things of which ye are now ashamed? for the end of those things is death. But now freed from sin and made slaves to God, ye have as your fruit sanctification and as the end, everlasting life. For the wages of sin is death, but the grace of God is eternal life in Christ Jesus our Lord. – Rom. 6:21-23*)

"I further understood that for such things as these the wrath of God comes upon the children of disobedience. (*Let no one deceive you with vain words, for because of these things the wrath of God comes upon the sons of disobedience. – Eph. 5:6*) Such truths I heard from you and also from beloved Faithful, who was put to death for his faith and good living in Vanity Fair."

"And with this new understanding, did you fall under the power of this conviction?"

"No," Hopeful admitted. "At that time, I wasn't willing to know about the evil of sin or the damnation that results from obeying it. Instead, when troubled by the Word of truth I endeavored to shut my eyes to its revealing light."

"But what was the cause of your stubborn resistance to these first workings of God's blessed Spirit upon you?"

"It was more than one cause," Hopeful said. "First of all, I was ignorant that this was the work of God upon me. I never understood that God begins the conversion with a sinner by using awakenings toward sin. Second, sin was still very sweet to my flesh, and I was very reluctant to let go of it. Thirdly, I didn't know how to part with my old friends, because their friendship and lifestyle were still desirable to me. And lastly, the times in which convictions grasped me were so troublesome and fearful to my heart that I could not endure them, or even the mere remembrance of them."

"So are you saying that sometimes you were able to get rid of your troubling thoughts?"

Hopeful nodded. "Yes, but then they would come into my mind again and I would be just as bad … no worse … than I was before."

"Why, what was it that brought your sins to mind again?"

"Many things such as:

If I merely met a good man in the streets; or,

If I heard anyone read from the Bible; or,

If my head began to ache; or,

If I was told that some of my neighbors were sick; or,

If I heard the bell toll for someone who had died; or,

If I thought of myself dying; or,

If I heard that others happened to die suddenly.

"But especially when I considered my own pending appointment with judgment to come."

"And at any time could you easily be relieved of the guilt of sin, when it confronted you by any of these ways?" Christian wanted to know.

"No, not recently anyway. For they grabbed hold of my conscience and if I even thought of going back to sin, though my mind was in opposition to it, it resulted in double torment to me."

"And what did you think of doing then?"

Hopeful said, "I decided I must make every effort to fix and improve my life or else I thought I was sure to be damned."

"And did you actually follow through on this resolve and try to improve your ways?"

"Yes," Hopeful said quite enthusiastically. "And I fled from, not only my sins, but sinful company, too. Plus I devoted myself to religious duties such as praying, reading the Bible, weeping for my sin, speaking the truth to my neighbors, and more. I was involved with so many of these types of activities that they are too numerous to mention."

"And did you think all was well then and that you were better off because of this religious involvement?"

Hopeful shrugged. "Yes, for a while. But eventually greater trouble overwhelmed me again. It reached a whole new level that rose above that of all my reformations."

"How could that possibly come about, since you had reformed your ways and improved your life?"

"Actually, several things brought this upon me," Hopeful said, "especially such sayings as these: 'All our righteous deeds are like filthy rags.' (*But we were all as an unclean thing, and all our righteousnesses as filthy rags; and we all fell as the leaves of a tree; and our iniquities, like the wind, have taken us away. – Isa. 64:6*) 'By the works of the law shall no flesh be justified.' (*Knowing that a man is not justified by the works of the law, but by the faith of Jesus Christ, even we have believed in Jesus Christ, that we might be justified by the faith of Christ, and not by the works of the law; for by the works of the law shall no flesh be justified.* – Gal. 2:16)

"'When you have done all these things, say, We are unprofitable.' (*So likewise ye, when ye shall have done all those things which are commanded you, say, We are unprofitable slaves: we have done that which was our duty to do.* – Luke 17:10) With these sayings and many more like them I began to reason with myself like this: If all my righteous deeds are like filthy rags; if no one can be justified by the deeds of the law; and if when we have done all, we are still unprofitable, then it is but foolishness to think of heaven by means of the law.

"I also thought about things this way: If a man runs up a hundred-pound debt at a local shop and after that pays cash for everything else he buys, his old debt still stands in the book unsettled. The shopkeeper may sue him for it, and throw him into prison till he pays the debt."

"Well, I understand what you're saying, but how did this apply to you?" Christian asked.

"Let me take you through my reasoning on this and you will understand," Hopeful said. "As I pondered this, I realized my sins caused me to be greatly indebted in God's book, and all of my current reforming will not pay off what I owe. Therefore, I wondered what the use is of all my present current efforts to improve. For how shall I escape from the damnation that I brought on myself because of my former transgressions?"

Christian nodded thoughtfully. "That is a very good application. Please go on."

"Well, another thing that troubled me was that even in my latest efforts to change …" Hopeful paused, searching for the right words. "… when I took a closer look at the best of what I do now, I still see sin, new sin which mixes itself with the best of what I do now. So now I am forced to conclude, that in my former fond conceits regarding myself and the debt I owe, I had committed enough sin in one day to send me to hell, even if all the rest of my former life had been faultless."

"And what did you do then?"

"What did I do!" Hopeful's voice raised. "I was at a loss as to what to do. I had no idea which way to turn, until I shared my troubled thoughts with Faithful; for he and I were well acquainted. He told me that unless I could obtain the righteousness of a man that had never sinned, then neither my own righteousness nor that of all the world could save me."

"And were you convinced that what he spoke was true?"

Hopeful ran his fingers through his hair and let his arm drop to his side. "Truthfully, if he had told me this when I was pleased and satisfied with my own efforts to improve, I would have called him a fool for his trouble. But now, having seen my own corruption and the sin which is attached to even my best performances, I have been forced to agree with his opinion."

"But when he first suggested this to you did you think that such a man could be found?" Christian asked. "One who could be rightly described as sinless?"

Hopeful shook his head in short side-to-side movements. "I must confess that at first his words sounded strange; but after a little more talk and time spent with Faithful in fellowship, I became fully convicted that he was right."

Christian asked, "And did you ask him who this man was and to explain how you must be justified by him?"

"Yes, and he told me it was the Lord Jesus, who dwells on the right hand of the Most High. (*But this man, after he had offered one sacrifice for sins for ever, is seated at the right hand of God, waiting for that which follows, that is, until his enemies are made his footstool. For by one offering he has perfected for ever those that are sanctified. Likewise the Holy Spirit gives us the same witness, who afterwards said, This is the testament that I will make with them after those days, saith the Lord, I will give my laws in their hearts, and in their souls will I write them; and their sins and iniquities will I remember no more. Now where remission of these is, there is no more offering for sin. Having therefore, brethren, boldness to enter into the sanctuary by the blood of Jesus, by a new and living way, which he has consecrated for us, through the veil, that is to say, his flesh; and having that great priest over the house of God. – Heb. 10:12-21*)

"And so he explained that you must be justified by Him, by trusting in what He accomplished when He suffered by hanging on the tree. (*But to him that does not work, but believes in him that justifies the ungodly, the faith is counted as righteousness. – Rom. 4:5*) So I asked how that man's righteousness could be effective in justifying another such as myself before God. And he told me He was the mighty God and that He died that death not for Himself but for me; to whom His obedient atoning work and its worthiness would be credited if I believed on Him."

"And what did you do then?"

"I offered my objections as to why I should not believe, because I thought this Christ was not willing to save me."

"And what did Faithful say to you then?"

A smile tugged at the corner of Hopeful's mouth. "He urged me to go

Faithful instructs Hopeful

to Him and find out for myself. But I said it was presumptuous to do so. Faithful said it wasn't because I was invited to come. (*Come unto me, all ye that labour and are heavy laden, and I will give you rest.* – Matt. 11:28)

"Then he gave me a book of Jesus in which were His very words. He gave me this book to encourage me to freely come to Him. He said that every jot and tittle in this book were more firmly established than heaven and earth. (*The heaven and the earth shall pass away, but my words shall not pass away.* – Matt. 24:35) Then I asked him what I must do when I came to Christ, and he told me I must fall to my knees (*O come, let us worship and bow down; let us kneel before the LORD our maker.* – Psalm 95:6), and plead with all my heart and soul (*Then ye shall call upon me, and ye shall walk in my ways and pray unto me, and I will hearken unto you. And ye shall seek me, and find me, for ye shall seek me with all your heart.* – Jer. 29:12, 13), that the Father would reveal Him to me.

"Then I asked him how I must make my petition to this Jesus, and Faithful said, 'Go, and you shall find him sitting on a mercy seat, where he sits all the year long to give pardon and forgiveness to those who come.' (*And there I will meet with thee, and I will speak with thee from above the seat of reconciliation, from between the two cherubim which are upon the ark of the testimony, of all things which I will give thee in commandment unto the sons of Israel.* – Exod. 25:22)

"I told him I didn't know what to say when I did come, and Faithful told me to say something to this effect: 'God be merciful to me a sinner and enable me to know and believe in Jesus Christ. For I understand that if His righteousness was not available, or if I didn't have faith in that righteousness, then I would be utterly cast away. Lord, I have heard that you are a merciful God, and have ordained that your Son Jesus Christ should be the Savior of the world. And additionally, you are willing to grant Him and His salvation upon such a poor sinner as myself – and I am indeed a poor sinner. Therefore, Lord, take this opportunity to magnify your grace in the salvation of my soul, through thy Son Jesus Christ. Amen.'"

"And did you do exactly as you were told?"

Hopeful's head bobbed earnestly. "Oh yes, over, and over, and over."

"And did the Father reveal the Son to you?" Christian asked.

Hopeful's face grew thoughtful. "Not the first, nor second, nor third, nor fourth, nor fifth, no, nor even the sixth occasion either."

"What did you do then?"

"What did I do?" Hopeful's brows knit together. "Well, I didn't know what to do."

Christian asked. "Did you ever have thoughts of giving up on praying?"

"Yes, at least a hundred times and then another hundred."

"And what was the reason you did not give up?" Christian prodded.

Hopeful shrugged. "I believed what he had told me was true, that is, that without the righteousness of this Christ, all the world could not save me. Therefore, I thought to myself, if I stop praying, then I die, and I can only die at the throne of grace. And in addition to this came the thought that 'if it delays, then wait for it; because it will certainly come and will not delay.' (*For the vision is yet for an appointed time, but at the end it shall speak and not lie; though it tarry, wait for it because it will surely come; wait for it.* – Hab. 2:3) So I continued praying until the Father showed me his Son."

"And how was He revealed unto you?"

"I did not see him with my physical eyes, but rather with the eyes of my understanding. (*Illuminating the eyes of your understanding, that ye may know what is the hope of his calling and what are the riches of the glory of his inheritance in the saints and what is the exceeding greatness of his power in us who believe, by the operation of the power of his strength.* – Eph. 1:18, 19)

"Now this is how it happened. One day I was very sad. I think I was sadder than at any other time in my life, and this bout of sadness was the result of a fresh insight of the greatness and vileness of my sins. And as I was anticipating nothing but hell and the everlasting damnation of my soul, suddenly, I thought I saw the Lord Jesus looking down from heaven upon me. And he called to me saying, 'Believe on the Lord Jesus Christ, and you shall be saved.' (*And they said, Believe on the Lord Jesus Christ, and thou shalt be saved, and thy house. – Acts 16:31*)

"But I replied, 'Lord, I am a great, a very great sinner.' And he answered, 'My grace is sufficient for you.' (*And he said unto me, My grace is sufficient for thee; for my strength is made perfect in weakness. Most gladly, therefore, I will rather glory in my weaknesses that the power of Christ may dwell in me. – 2 Cor. 12:9*)

"Then I said, 'But, Lord, what exactly is believing?' Then suddenly I understood that saying, 'He who comes to me shall never hunger, and he who believes on me shall never thirst.' (*And Jesus said unto them, I AM the bread of life; he that comes to me shall never hunger, and he that believes in me shall never thirst. – John 6:35*) I understood that believing and coming were the same thing. Therefore the one who comes to Christ, that is, the one who runs to him in his heart and earnestly longs after salvation by Christ, he is one who truly believes in Christ. Then tears brimmed in my eyes and I asked, 'But, Lord, may such a great sinner as I am truly be accepted by you and be saved by you?'

"And I heard him say, 'And him who comes to me, I will in no way cast out.' (*All that the Father gives me shall come to me, and he that comes to me I will in no wise cast out. – John 6:37*)

"Then I said, 'But Lord, how must I properly think about you in my coming to you, in order that my faith may be placed properly upon you?'

"Then he said, 'Christ Jesus came into the world to save sinners.' (*This is a faithful saying and worthy of acceptation by all, that Christ Jesus came into the world to save sinners, of whom I am first. – 1 Tim. 1:15*) He is the end of the law for righteousness to everyone who believes. (*For Christ is the end of the law, to give righteousness to every one that believes. – Rom. 10:4*) He died for our sins and rose again for our justification. (*Who was delivered for our offenses and was raised again for our justification. – Rom. 4:25*) He loved us and washed us from our sins in his own blood. (*And from Jesus, the Christ, who is the faithful witness and the first begotten of the dead and the prince of the kings of the earth. Unto him that loved us and washed us from our sins with his own blood. –* Rev. 1:5) He is the Mediator between God and us. (*For there is only one God and likewise only one mediator between God and men, the man Christ Jesus. –* 1 Tim. 2:5) He lives forever to make intercession for us. (*Therefore he is able also to save to the uttermost those that come unto God by him, seeing he ever lives to make intercession for them. –* Heb. 7:25)

"From all of this I understood that I must look for righteousness in His person and for satisfaction for my sins by His blood. What He did in obedience to his Father's law by submitting to its resulting penalty was not for Himself but was for those of us who accept it for our salvation with thankfulness. As a result my heart became full of joy. Tears streamed down my face and my affections overflowed with love for the name, people, and ways of Jesus Christ."

"This was truly a revelation of Christ to your soul," Christian said. "But tell me more. Particularly the details of what effect this encounter had upon your spirit."

Hopeful pulled in a deep breath and let it out thoughtfully. "It made me see that all the world, despite all its righteousness, is in a state of condemnation. It made me see that God the Father, while being just, can justify the believing sinner. It made me greatly ashamed of the vileness of my former lifestyle and amazed me with the sense of my own ignorance. For until this time, my heart never contemplated the beauty of Jesus Christ.

"It made me love a holy life and long to do something for the honor and glory of the name of the Lord Jesus. Yes, I now considered that if I had a thousand gallons of blood in my body, I would willingly spill it all for the sake of the Lord Jesus."

I saw then in my dream that Hopeful looked back and saw Ignorance, whom they had left behind, following after them. Hopeful said to Christian, "Look how far in the distance that youngster is lagging behind us."

Christian looked back and spotted the lad. "Yes, yes, I see him, but he doesn't care for our company."

"But I am sure that it would not have hurt him, if he had decided to walk with us to this point."

A slight smile played across Christian's lips. "That is true, but I am sure he thinks very differently."

"Yes," Hopeful returned the smile. "I agree with you. However, let us wait for him to catch up."

So the two pilgrims slowed their pace and stopped to wait for Ignorance. Christian called to him. "Man, come walk with us. Why do you stay so behind?"

Ignorance called back to him. "Because I take pleasure in walking alone, and even more so than in company, unless I find some pleasant travelers."

Christian turned to Hopeful and said under his breath. "Didn't I tell you that he doesn't care for our company? However, come on and join me in a conversation with him to better pass away the time in this solitary place." As Ignorance drew near, Christian said to him, "My friend, how are you doing? How is your relationship between God and your soul?"

Ignorance shrugged as he looked from Hopeful to Christian. "I have hope that it is well for now. My mind is always full of good ideas and beliefs to comfort me as I walk."

"What kind of good ideas and beliefs?" Christian asked. "Please tell us more."

Ignorance stood a little straighter. "Why, I think about God and heaven."

Christian tapped his finger to his lips as if lost in thought for a moment and then said, "So do the devils and souls damned to hell."

Ignorance jutted his chin and held it higher. "But I think of them and desire them."

"So do many who are never likely to reside there," Christian said. "The soul of the sluggard desires and hath nothing." (*The soul of the sluggard desires, and attains nothing: but the soul of the diligent shall be made fat.* – Prov. 13:4)

"But I think about them and leave all that I have for them in order to obtain them," Ignorance countered.

"I doubt that very much." Christian's mouth pulled to one side. "To leave all is much harder to do than many understand. Tell me why or by what evidence you have been so persuaded as to leave all for God and heaven."

"My heart tells me so."

Christian said, "The wise man says, 'He who trusts in his own heart is a fool.'" (*He that trusts in his own heart is a fool, but whosoever walks in wisdom, he shall be saved.* – Prov. 28:26)

Ignorance's lower lip curled in a pout. "That saying speaks of an evil heart but mine is not evil; it is good."

"But how can you prove that your heart is good?"

"It comforts and assures me concerning my hope of reaching heaven." Ignorance punctuated his statement with a nod of his head.

"That may well be, but the heart can be deceitful," Christian said. "For a man's heart may minister comfort with regard to his hope of something, even though he has no grounds to expect the fulfillment of that hope."

"But my heart and life are in agreement with one another; and therefore my hope is well grounded."

Christian asked, "Who told you that your heart and life are in harmony?"

Tiny frown lines gathered between Ignorance's brows. "My heart tells me so."

"My dear fellow, ask yourself whether or not you are a thief. Your heart may tell you one thing, but it is the Word of God that must bear witness in this matter; any other testimony is of no value."

Ignorance sighed deeply. "But is it not a good heart that produces good thoughts? And is it not a good life that is in harmony with God's commandments?"

"Yes," Christian admitted. "It is a good heart that produces good thoughts and a good life that is in harmony with God's commandments. But it is one thing to really have these qualities and another only to think so."

Ignorance crossed his arms in front of his chest. "Then tell me, what counts to you as good thoughts and a life according to God's commandments?"

"There are good thoughts of various kinds," Christian said. "Some with regard to ourselves, some God, some Christ, and some in regard to other things."

"What are good thoughts with regard to ourselves?"

"Those that are in agreement with the Word of God," Christian replied.

"When do thoughts of ourselves agree with the Word of God?"

Christian glanced at Hopeful and back at Ignorance. "When we pass the same judgment upon ourselves that the Word of God passes on us. Let me explain what I mean. The Word of God says of the natural man, 'There is no one who is righteous, there are none who do good.' It also says that 'The imagination of the heart of man is only evil, and continually so.' (*And GOD saw that the wickedness of man was great in the earth and that every*

imagination of the thoughts of his heart was only evil continually. – Gen. 6:5)
And again, 'The imagination of man's heart is evil from his youth' (Gen.
8:21). Now, then, when we think of ourselves in this sense, then our thoughts
are good ones because they are in accordance with the Word of God."

Ignorance stubbornly propped his fists on his hips. "I will never believe
that my heart is that bad."

Christian shook his head sadly. "If that is the case, then you have never
had one good thought concerning yourself in your whole life. But let me
go on. As the Word of God passes judgment upon our hearts, so it also
passes a judgment upon our actions. When the thoughts of our hearts and
actions agree with the judgment which the Word brings on both, then both
are good because they are in agreement with that Word."

Ignorance said, "What do you mean?"

"Why, the Word of God says that man's ways are crooked ways, not
good but perverse," Christian explained. "It also says that their nature is
to veer out of the good way and that they have no inclination to know it.
(*They are all gone out of the way; they are together become unprofitable;
there is no one that does good, no, not one.* – Rom. 3:12) When a man thinks
about his actions in this way, with a heart full of humiliation reflected in
his thoughts, then he has good thoughts about his ways. His thoughts now
agree with the judgment of the Word of God."

"Then exactly what are good thoughts concerning God?" Ignorance
wanted to know.

Christian said, "They are similar to what I have said concerning ourselves.
When our thoughts of God agree with what the Word says about Him, then
they are good thoughts. That means when we think of His character and
attributes as the Word teaches.

"However, to speak of Him concerning ourselves, when we understand
that He knows us better than we know ourselves, and that He can see sin in
us when and where we can see none in ourselves; and when we understand
that He knows our inmost thoughts, and that He at all times sees into the
depths of our heart; and when we think that all our righteousness stinks
in His nostrils, and that for this reason even with our best performance we
still cannot stand before Him with any confidence, then our thoughts are
good, though I cannot talk about this in detail right now."

"Do you think that I am such a fool as to regard God as not being able to see any further than I can? Do you believe that I would hope to come to God for acceptance of only my best performances?"

"Then tell me," Christian said. "Tell me what you think in this matter."

"I'll keep it brief and to the point," Ignorance said. "I think I must believe in Christ for justification."

"But how?" Christian pressed. "How could you think that you must believe in Christ, when you don't see your need of him? You see neither your original sin nor your actual transgressions. Rather, you have such a high opinion of yourself and of what you do that you plainly qualify as one who has never seen the necessity of Christ's personal righteousness to justify you before God. How then can you say, 'I believe in Christ'?"

"In spite of what you say, I believe well enough."

"Exactly what do you believe?" Christian asked.

"I believe that Christ died for sinners; and that I shall be justified before God from the curse of the law, through his gracious acceptance of my obedience to his laws. In other words, Christ makes my religious duties acceptable to his Father by virtue of his merits and so shall I be justified."

"Let me give you an answer to this confession of your faith," Christian said.

"You believe with a false faith; for this faith is nowhere described in the Word of God.

"You believe with a false faith, because it takes away the personal righteousness of Christ and applies it to yourself. Your faith makes Christ a justifier of your actions. In contrast, true faith is a faith in Christ as your justification, knowing that your own works are filthy rags. (*to him that works not, but believes on him that justifies the ungodly, his faith is counted for righteousness.* – Romans 4:5)

"Therefore this faith is deceitful and the type which will leave you under the wrath of God Almighty at his final Day of Judgment. For true justifying faith directs the soul, being sensible to its lost condition by the law, to flee for refuge to Christ's righteousness. Now this righteousness of Christ is not an act of grace by which he makes your obedience a justifying work acceptable to God. Rather it is his personal obedience to the law in doing and suffering for us which this same law justly required at our hands. True faith accepts this righteousness of Christ as if were a skirt by which the soul can be completely covered. In this way the soul is presented as spotless before God. It is accepted by God, and he acquits such a covered person from condemnation."

"What are you saying?" Ignorance asked in a louder voice. "Would you have us trust in what Christ in his own person has done without us? This conceit would encourage the loosening of the reins of our lust, and allow us to live as we are inclined. For what does it matter how we live, when we may be justified by Christ's personal righteousness – when all we have to do is simply believe it?"

"You are fittingly named Ignorance," Christian said. "For you are also ignorant as a person. Even your answer demonstrates this to be true. You are ignorant of what justifying righteousness is, and equally ignorant about how your soul may be safe from the severe wrath of God through the faith in it. Yes, you are also ignorant of the true effects of saving faith in this righteousness of Christ, which include the conquest and winning over of the heart to God in Christ, to love his name, his Word, ways, and people, and not as you ignorantly imagine."

Hopeful nudged Christian and said, "Ask him if ever he had Christ revealed to him from heaven."

But Ignorance heard the question and said, "What now? Are you a man influenced by revelations? I believe that what you ... and you ..." He pointed at Hopeful and also at Christian. "... and all the rest of what you say about this matter is nothing more than the fruit of a muddled mind."

Hopeful said, "Why, Jesus Christ is so hid in God from the natural understanding of the flesh that

Christian instructs Ignorance

he cannot be savingly known by any man, unless God the Father reveals him to the man."

Ignorance jabbed his finger in Hopeful's direction again. "That is your faith, but it is certainly not mine. However, I have no doubt that my faith is as good as yours, though in no way do I have as many fanciful notions in my head so as you do."

"Allow me to add something here," Christian said. "You should not speak so disdainfully of this matter, for I will boldly affirm, even as my good companion has done, that no man can know Jesus Christ except through the revelation of the Father.

"Yes, and I will also say that even the faith that lays hold of Christ, assuming it is true faith, must be forged by the exceeding greatness of his mighty power. (*That the God of our Lord Jesus Christ, the Father of glory, may give unto you the spirit of wisdom and revelation in the knowledge of him; illuminating the eyes of your understanding, that ye may know what is the hope of his calling and what are the riches of the glory of his inheritance in the saints and what is the exceeding greatness of his power in us who believe, by the operation of the power of his strength. – Eph. 1:17-19*)

"Now regarding the working of this faith, I perceive, poor Ignorance, that you are totally ignorant of it. Therefore, wake up and see your own wretchedness, and flee to the Lord Jesus. For only by his righteousness, which is the righteousness of God (for he himself is God), shall you be delivered from condemnation."

Ignorance motioned with the wave of his hand for them to go ahead without him. "You go so fast I cannot keep up with you. So you go on before me and I will follow from behind at a distance."

Christian and Hopeful said:

> "Well, Ignorance, will you yet foolish be
> To slight good counsel, ten times given thee?
> And if you yet refuse it, you shall know,
> Before long the evil of your doing so.
> Remember, man, in time; stoop, do not fear,
> Good counsel taken well, saves, therefore hear;
> But if you yet shall slight it, you will be
> The loser, Ignorance, I'll warrant thee."

The Tenth Stage

hen Christian addressed his companion. "Well, come with me my good friend, Hopeful, for I see that you and I must walk by ourselves again."

So I saw in my dream that they went on ahead at a strong pace while Ignorance limped along behind them. Then Christian said, "I feel great pity for this poor man, because his journey will come to a sorrowful end."

"Unfortunately, in our town there is an abundance of people in his condition – whole families – yes, even whole streets with many being pilgrims, too. So if there are many like him in our parts, how many do you think must there be in the place where he was born?" Hopeful asked.

"Indeed, this is true," Christian said, "for the Word says, 'He has blinded their eyes, lest they should see.' But, now we are by ourselves, tell me what do you think of such men? Do you think that at any time they have convictions of sin and so as a consequence have fears about the danger of their condition?"

"No, I would rather that you answer that question yourself, for you are older and have more experience."

"Very well," Christian said. "I would say, in my opinion, that sometimes they may have such fears. But because they are naturally ignorant of spiritual truth, they do not understand that such convictions contribute to their good. Therefore, they desperately seek to stifle them while they presumptuously continue to flatter themselves concerning the good state of their own hearts."

Hopeful's head bobbed his agreement. "I do believe, as you say, that fear tends to benefit men and to make them right at the beginning of their pilgrimage and to prompt them to go the right way."

Christian grew enthusiastic. "Without a doubt this is what happens, if it is the right fear. For the Word says so. 'The fear of the Lord is the beginning of wisdom.'" (*The fear of the LORD is the beginning of knowledge, but fools despise wisdom and chastening.* – Prov. 1:7)

"How would you describe right fear?" Hopeful asked.

"I'd say you can know that it is true or right fear based on three things: By its arousal. It is caused by conviction of sin.

It drives the soul to believe in Christ for salvation.

It gives birth to and maintains in the soul a great reverence of God, his Word, and ways. So this soul is kept tender, by making it afraid to turn to the right or left from these affections to anything that may dishonor God, break its peace, grieve the Spirit, or cause the enemy to speak of God with reproach."

"Well said, Christian. I believe you have spoken the truth. Have we now almost passed through the Enchanted Ground?"

"Why? Are you weary of this conversation?"

"No, not at all," Hopeful said. "I would just like to know where we are."

"We don't have more than two miles further to go now. Nevertheless, let's return to our topic of discussion.

"Now, the ignorant generally don't know that such convictions of sin tend to cause them to fear and is for their good. Therefore they seek to stifle them."

"In what ways do they seek to stifle them?" Hopeful asked.

"There are four ways:

"They think that those fears are created by the Devil, though in fact they are truly from God. In thinking this way they resist them as things that would cause their defeat.

"They also think that these fears tend to spoil their faith, when, even though as deluded poor men, they do not have any faith at all. Therefore they harden their hearts against them.

"They presume they should not have fears and therefore, in spite of them, they put on a vain show of confidence.

"They see that those fears tend to strip away their pathetic displays of self-righteousness, and therefore they resist them with all their might."

Hopeful said, "I confess to knowing something of this myself, for before I knew the truth about myself my condition was just as pathetic."

"Well, let us leave our neighbor Ignorance by himself at this time and decide upon another question profitable for discussion."

"I agree wholeheartedly," Hopeful said. "But again I ask that you begin."

"Well then," Christian said. "About ten years ago, did you know a man by the name of Temporary in your parts? He was a man enthusiastic about religion then."

"Know him! I certainly did! He lived in Graceless, a town about two miles from Honesty, and he lived next door to a man by the name of Turnback."

"That's right. Turnback actually lived under the same roof with him. Well, at one time that man was very much awakened spiritually. I believe at that time he had some awareness of his sins and of the wages that were due in this regard."

"I hold the same opinion," Hopeful agreed. "For since my house was not more than three miles from him, he would often come to me with many tears. Truly I pitied the man and was not altogether without hope for him; but one may see, it is not every one who cries, 'Lord, Lord!' who proves to be a genuine Christian."

Christian nodded in understanding. "He once told me that he was determined to go on pilgrimage, just as we are now; but all of a sudden he grew acquainted with one Save-self, and then he became a stranger to me."

"Since we are talking about him," Hopeful said, "let us spend a little time to ask the reason for his sudden backsliding and for others like him."

"This may be very profitable, Hopeful, but I ask that you begin this time."

"Very well," Hopeful said. "In my judgment, I see four reasons for it:

Though the consciences of such men are awakened, yet their minds are not changed. Therefore, when the power of guilt diminishes, the very thing that provoked them to be religious ceases to have any effect. For this reason, they naturally turn to their former course again. We see the same reaction with a dog that is sick and vomits up what he has eaten. So long as his sickness prevails, he vomits and throws up everything in his stomach. Not that he does this of a free mind (if we may say a dog has a mind), but rather because of his troubling stomach.

"However, when his sickness passes and his stomach feels better, he turns around and licks up all his vomit and so what is written is true: 'The dog is turned to his own vomit again.' (*But it has happened unto them according to the true proverb, The dog returns unto his own vomit, and the sow that was washed to her wallowing in the mire.* – 2 Peter 2:22) Now, I say a person may be enthusiastic about heaven, but only because they sense and fear the torments of hell. But as their sense and fear of damnation chills and cools, in the same way their desires for heaven and salvation cool also. So then it comes to pass, that when their guilt and fear is gone, their desires for heaven and happiness die, and they return to their former course in life again.

"Another reason is this. They have mindless fears that overwhelm them. I'm talking about fears they have of men, now. 'For the fear of man brings a snare.' (*The fear of man brings a snare, but whosoever puts his trust in the LORD shall be lifted up.* – Prov. 29:25) So then, though they seem to be enthusiastic for heaven so long as the threat of hell's flames are real to them, when that terror has lessened in their way of thinking they have second thoughts. They begin to think it unwise to run after something they know little about and risk losing all. A second idea they begin to entertain is that it is not prudent to bring themselves into unavoidable and unnecessary troubles and as a result they fall in with the world again.

"The shame that attends religion also lies as a roadblock in their way. They are proud and haughty, and religion, as they see it, is low and contemptible. Therefore when they have lost their sense of hell and the wrath to come, they return again to their former ways.

"Guilt and the thought of terror are distressing to them. They prefer not to see their misery before they come into it. Though perhaps when they first catch sight of it, it might make them flee to where the righteous flee and are safe. But because they shun the thoughts of guilt and terror, as I hinted before, once they get rid of their original arousals about the terrors and wrath of God, they harden their hearts gladly and choose ways that will harden them more and more."

Christian patted Hopeful on the back. "You are pretty close to the heart of this matter, for at the bottom of this problem is a lack of a change in their mind and will. Therefore they are like the criminal who stands before the judge shaking and trembling. He seems to heartily repent, but in the end he is truly motivated by his fear of the noose instead of any abhorrence of his crime. This is evident when he is set free and he returns to being a thief and a rogue. However, if his mind was changed he would live differently."

Hopeful agreed and said, "Now that I have shown you the reason of their backsliding I ask that you show me the modus of his falling away." Hopeful gestured to Christian to continue.

"I will do so most willingly," Christian said and started to make his points one at a time, counting them off on his fingers.

"They draw most of their thoughts from the remembrance of God, death, and judgment to come.

"Then they gradually neglect private duties such as personal prayer, curbing their lusts, watchfulness, sorrow for sin, and the like.

"Then they shun the company of lively and whole-hearted Christians.

"After that, they grow cold to public duty, such as conscientious listening, reading of the Word, godly corporate gathering, and the like.

"They then begin to find fault or pick holes, as we say, in the lives of some of the godly, so that they may claim religion is stained based on some weaknesses they have noticed in these believers, and they then justify putting religion behind their backs.

"Then they begin to adhere to and associate with, carnal, immoral, and unrestrained men.

"They give way to carnal and depraved conversations in secret, and they are glad if they can find similar practices in any who are considered reputable, for these hypocrites encourage them to be all the more bold.

"After this they begin to play with little sins openly.

"And then, being hardened, they show themselves as they are. Therefore, being flung again into the gulf of misery, unless a miracle of grace prevents it, they eternally perish in their own deception."

Now I saw in my dream, that by this time the pilgrims had traveled over the Enchanted Ground and were entering into the country of Beulah. (*Thou shalt no longer be termed Forsaken; neither shall thy land any longer be termed Desolate; but thou shalt be called Hephzibah and thy land Beulah; for the will of the LORD shall be in thee, and thy land shall be married. For as a young man marries a virgin, so shall thy sons marry thee; and as the bridegroom rejoices with the bride, so shall thy God rejoice with thee.*

I have set watchmen upon thy walls, O Jerusalem, which shall never hold their peace day nor night; ye that make mention of the LORD, do not keep silent and give him no rest, until he establishes and until he makes Jerusalem a praise in the earth. The LORD has sworn by his right hand, and by the arm of his strength, Surely I will no longer give thy wheat to be food for thine enemies; and the sons of the stranger shall not drink thy wine, for which thou hast laboured: But those that have gathered it shall eat it and praise the LORD; and those that have brought it together shall drink it in the courts of my holiness.

Go through, go through the gates; prepare ye the way of the people; clear up, clear up the highway; gather out the stones; lift up a banner as an example for the people. Behold, the LORD has caused it to be heard unto the end of the earth; Say unto the daughter of Zion, Behold, thy Saviour comes; behold that his reward is with him, and his work before him. And they shall call them, The holy people, The redeemed of the LORD; and thou shalt be called, Sought out, A city not forsaken. – Isa. 62:4-12)

With the way lying directly through it, the air in that place was very sweet and pleasant, and so they rested and refreshed themselves there for a time. Here they heard the continual singing of birds and every day enjoyed various blooming flowers in the land. They also heard the voice of the turtledove in this country where the sun shines night and day.

Therefore it was beyond the Valley of the Shadow of Death and out of the reach of Giant Despair. In fact, from this place they couldn't even see Doubting Castle. Here the pilgrims were within sight of the Celestial City where they were going. Here, too, they met some of the inhabitants of that place. For in this land the Shining Ones frequently walked, because it was upon the borders of heaven. In this land, also, the contract between the Bride and the Bridegroom was renewed. Yes, here, "as the bridegroom rejoices over the bride, so does God rejoice over them."

Here they had no lack of corn and wine, for in this place they began to reap an abundance of what they had sought for throughout their entire pilgrimage. Here they heard voices drifting from out of the city, loud voices proclaiming, "Say to the daughter of Zion, Behold, your salvation comes! Behold, His reward is with Him!" Here all the inhabitants of the country called them "the holy People, the redeemed of the Lord, sought out," etc.

Now, as they walked in this land, they experienced more rejoicing than in other parts that were more remote from the kingdom to which they were headed. But now drawing nearer to the city, they had a more perfect view of it. It was built of pearls and precious stones, and the streets were paved with gold. As a result the natural glory of the city and the reflection of the sunbeams upon it made Christian homesick with longing for it. Hopeful also had a fit or two of the same sickness. Therefore the two of them stood for a while in front of the vista and continued to cry out because of their pangs, "If you see my Beloved, tell him that I am sick of love."

But, being a little strengthened and better able to endure their sickness, they walked along their way and came nearer and nearer to the Celestial City. On either side were orchards, vineyards, and gardens, and their gates opened into the highway.

Now, as they came closer to these places, they noticed the Gardener standing in the way, so they asked him, "Whose goodly vineyards and gardens are these?"

He answered, "They are the King's and are planted here for his own pleasure and also for the comfort of pilgrims." So the Gardener led them into the vineyards and invited them to refresh themselves with the surrounding delicacies. (*Whether therefore ye eat or drink or whatever ye do, do everything for the glory of God. – 1 Cor. 10:31*)[12] He also pointed out to them the King's walks and arbors which he enjoyed. So here Christian and Hopeful lingered and slept.

Now I saw in my dream, that they talked more in their sleep at this time than they had ever done in all their journey. As I pondered the reason for this, the Gardener said to me, "Why do you deeply ponder this matter? It is the nature of the fruit of the grapes of these vineyards, 'to go down so sweetly as to cause the lips of them who are asleep to speak.'" (*And thy palate like the best wine that goes into my beloved sweetly and causes the lips of those that are asleep to speak. – Song of Sol. 7:9*)

So I saw that when they awoke, they prepared themselves to go up to the city. But, as I said before, the reflection of the sun upon the city which was pure gold (*the city was of pure gold, like unto clean glass. – Rev. 21:18*) was so extremely glorious that they could not face it directly to look at it as yet. Instead, they viewed it through an instrument made for that purpose. (*For now we see as through a mirror, in darkness, but then we shall see face to face. – 1 Cor. 13:12*)[13] So I saw that as they went on their way, two Shining Ones met them. They were dressed in clothing that shone like gold and their faces glowed radiantly as light.

These men asked the pilgrims where they came from and they told

---

12   Original: *When thou comest into thy neighbour's vineyard, then thou may eat grapes, thy fill at thine own pleasure; but thou shalt not put any in thy vessel* – Deut. 23:24.

13   Original: *Therefore we all, beholding as in a glass the glory of the Lord with uncovered face, are transformed from glory to glory into the same likeness, even as by the Spirit of the Lord* – 2 Cor. 3:18.

Christian and Hopeful meet two men of the Land of Beulah

them. The Shining Ones also asked them where they had lodged, as well as what difficulties and dangers they had met with along the way and what comforts and pleasures they had experienced. And so Christian and Hopeful told them.

Then the two Shining Ones said to them, "You have only two more difficulties to deal with, and then you will enter the City."

Christian and his companion asked the men to go along with them. The men told them they would, but said, "You must obtain it by your own faith."

So I saw in my dream that they went on together, until they came in sight of the gate. Between them and the gate was a river, but there was no bridge crossing over it, and the river was very deep. The sight of this river greatly stunned the pilgrims, but the men who walked with them said, "You must go through the river or you cannot come at the gate."

The pilgrims began to inquire, "Isn't there another way to the gate?"

The two Shining Ones answered, "Yes, but no one has been permitted to use it except for two. Only Enoch and Elijah have trod that path since the foundation of the world. It shall not be used again until the last trumpet sounds."

A helpless feeling washed over the two pilgrims, especially Christian. They looked this way and that but no alternative way could be found that would allow them to avoid the river. Then the pilgrims asked, "Is the water all the same depth?"

The Shining Ones said, "No." They could offer no further help or guidance except to say, "You shall find it deeper or shallower as you believe in the King of the place."

With this the pilgrims resigned themselves to face the water. Upon entering, Christian began to sink and cried out to his good friend Hopeful. "I sink in the deep water! The billows go over my head; all his waves go over me!"

Then Hopeful said, "Be courageous, my brother. I feel the bottom, and it is firm."

Christian cried out further. "Ah, my friend, the sorrows of death have totally encompassed me! I shall not see the land that flows with milk and honey!"

And with those words a great darkness and horror fell upon Christian, so that he could not see before him. To a large degree he lost his senses, so that he was unable to remember or talk intelligently about any of those sweet refreshments that he had experienced along the way of his pilgrimage.

Rather, all the words he spoke revealed his present terror of mind and

The pilgrims cross the River of Death

the fear that he would die in that river and never gain entrance into the Celestial City. Those who stood by could see he was greatly troubled with thoughts of the sins he had committed, both before and since he became a pilgrim. It was also clear that he was troubled with visions of demons and evil spirits. The words he spoke reflected this over and over.

Therefore Hopeful struggled in his attempts to keep his brother's head above water. Sometimes Christian would seem to have sunk down for good but after a short time, he would rise to the surface again as one half-dead. Hopeful attempted to comfort him, saying, "Brother, I see the gate and men standing nearby to welcome us!"

But Christian answered, "It is you ... it is you they are waiting for, for you have been hopeful ever since I first knew you."

"And so have you," Hopeful said.

"Ah, brother." Christian's face looked deeply troubled. "Surely if I was right with the King he would rise now to rescue me, but on account of my sins he has brought me into this snare and abandoned me."

Then Hopeful said, "My brother, you have quite forgotten the text where it is said of the wicked, 'There is no pain in their death, but their strength is firm; they are not troubled as other men, neither are they plagued like other men' (Psalm 73:4, 5).

"These troubles and distresses you are experiencing in these waters are no indication that God has abandoned you. Rather, they are sent to test you to see whether or not you will recall the evidences of his past goodness and rely upon him in your present distresses."

Then I saw in my dream that Christian was deep in thought awhile and Hopeful continued to speak to him. "Be courageous. Jesus Christ makes you whole."

With that Christian broke out in a loud voice and said, "Oh, I see him again! And he tells me, 'When you pass through the waters I will be with you, and through the rivers and they shall not overflow you.'" (*When thou dost pass through the waters, I will be with thee; and through the rivers, they shall not overflow thee; when thou dost walk through the fire, thou shalt not be burned; neither shall the flame kindle upon thee. – Isa. 43:2*)

Then the two pilgrims both took courage, and the enemy became as still as a stone, until they had crossed over. Christian discovered solid ground for his feet to stand upon, and so it turned out that once he found his footing that the rest of the river was actually shallow and the two of them crossed over.

Now, upon the bank of the river on the other side, Christian and Hopeful saw the two Shining Ones waiting to welcome them. Therefore, when the pilgrims came out of the river, these Shining Ones greeted them saying, "We are ministering spirits sent forth to serve those who shall be the heirs of salvation."

Then they proceeded towards the gate. Now you must note that the city stood upon a mighty hill, but the pilgrims went up that hill with ease because they had the two Shining Ones to lead them upward by holding their arms. Plus they had also left their mortal garments behind them in the river, for even though they went into the river with them, they came out without

The pilgrims approach the gate of the Holy City

them. Therefore they continued to climb with much agility and speed, even though the foundation upon which the city was built was higher than the clouds. So they went up through the region of the air, sweetly talking as they went, being comforted because they had safely crossed over the river and were being escorted by such glorious companions.

The conversation they had with the Shining Ones was about the glory of the place. They told the pilgrims that the beauty and glory of it was inexpressible. They went on to say, "In Mount Zion you shall find the heavenly Jerusalem, the innumerable company of angels, and the spirits of just men made perfect." (*But ye are come unto Mount Sion and unto the city of the living God, the heavenly Jerusalem, and to an innumerable company of angels, to the congregation of the called out ones of the firstborn, who are registered in the heavens and to God the Judge of all and to the spirits of just men made perfect and to Jesus, the mediator of the new testament and to the blood of sprinkling, that speaks better than that of Abel. – Heb. 12:22-24*)

"You are going now," they said, "to the paradise of God, in which you shall see the Tree of Life, and eat of its never-fading fruits. When you arrive there you shall be given white robes, and every day your walk and talk shall be with the King, even for all the days of eternity. (*He that has an ear let him hear what the Spirit saith unto the congregations; To him that overcomes I will give to eat of the tree of life, which is in the midst of the paradise of God. – Rev. 2:7*) There you no longer see former things such as you saw when you were in the lower region upon earth; that is, sorrow, sickness, affliction, and death, for the former things have passed away. (*And God shall wipe away all tears from their eyes; and death shall be no more neither shall there be any more sorrow nor crying nor pain; for the former things are passed away. – Rev. 21:4*) Rather, you are now going to Abraham, to Isaac, and Jacob, and to the prophets, men whom God has taken away from the evil to come, for they are now 'resting upon their beds, each one walking in his righteousness.'"

Then Christian and Hopeful asked, "What will we be doing in the holy place?"

To this they were given the answer, "There you must receive the comfort that results from all your toil and have joy in place of all your sorrow. You must reap what you have sown, even the fruit of all your prayers, tears, and sufferings for the King along the way. (*Do not deceive yourselves; God is not mocked: for whatever a man sows that shall he also reap. For he that sows to his flesh shall of the flesh reap corruption, but he that sows in the Spirit shall of the Spirit reap eternal life.* – Gal. 6:7, 8) In that place you will wear crowns of gold and enjoy the perpetual sight and vision of the Holy One, for there you shall see him as he is. (*Beloved, now we are the sons of God, and it is not yet made manifest what we shall be; but we know that if he shall appear, we shall be like him; for we shall see him as he is.* – 1 John 3:2)

"There you shall also serve him continually with praise, shouting, and thanksgiving; that is he whom you desired to serve in the world, though with much difficulty because of the weakness of your flesh. There your eyes shall be delighted with seeing and your ears with hearing the pleasant voice of the Mighty One. There you shall enjoy your friends again who have arrived here before you, and in the same way, there you shall joyfully welcome everyone who follows after you into the holy place. You will also be clothed with glory and majesty and appropriately equipped to ride out with the King of Glory.

"In the future, when he shall come with the sound of the trumpet in the clouds, as upon the wings of the wind, you shall come with him. When he sits upon the throne of judgment, you shall sit by him; and when he passes sentence upon all the workers of iniquity, whether angels or men, you shall also have a voice in that judgment because they were his and your enemies. Also when he returns to the city again, you shall go with him with the sound of the trumpet, and be with him forever." (*Do ye not know that the saints shall judge the world? and if the world shall be judged by you, are ye unworthy to judge the smallest matters? Know ye not that we shall judge angels? how much more the things that pertain to this life?*– 1 Cor. 6:2, 3)

Now while they were drawing near to the gate a company of the heavenly host came out to meet them. To this multitude the other two Shining Ones said, "These are the men who have loved our Lord when they were in the world and who have left all for his holy name. He has sent us to fetch them, and we have brought them this far on their desired journey so that they may go in with joy and look their Redeemer in the face." Then the heavenly host gave a great shout, saying, "Blessed are they who are called to the marriage supper of the Lamb" (Rev. 19:9).

At this time, there also came out to meet them several of the King's trumpeters clothed in white, shining garments. With loud, melodious noises they raised their trumpets to the heavens where it echoed with their sound. These trumpeters greeted Christian and Hopeful with ten thousand welcomes from the world; and this they did with shouting and the sound of trumpets.

Once this was done they surrounded them on every side. Some went ahead of them, some followed behind, and some were on the right hand and others on the left, as a guard through the upper regions, continually sounding the melodious noise, sending notes on high as they went. So this very sight could be seen as if heaven itself had come down to meet them. Therefore, they walked on together; and as they walked these trumpeters often combined the joyful music with looks and gestures to signify to Christian and Hopeful just how welcome they were and how happy they were to meet them. It was as if these two pilgrims were in heaven, before they even came to it, being surrounded with the sight of angels and the sound of their melodious notes.

Here also they were now able to view the city itself, and they thought they heard all the bells pealing inside to welcome them. But, above all, warm and joyful thoughts consumed them as to how they would live there with such heavenly company for all eternity. Oh, with what language or pen can their glorious joy be sufficiently expressed! And thus they came up to the gate.

Now when they came up to the gate, there was inscribed over it in letters of gold: "Blessed are those who do his commandments, those who have rightful access to the Tree of Life and may enter in through the gates into the city."

Then I saw in my dream that the shining men told the pilgrims to call out at the gate. When they did, some from above looked over the gate, namely, Enoch, Moses, and Elijah. The Shining Ones said, "These pilgrims have come from the City of Destruction for the love they bear to the King of this place." Then each of the pilgrims gave his certificate which he had received at the beginning. These were carried in to the King, who, when he read them said, "Where are these men?"

To whom it was answered, "They are standing outside the gate."

The King commanded the gate to open, and he declared, "The righteous nation that keeps the truth may enter in." (*Open ye the gates, that the righteous nation which keeps the truth may enter in.* – Isa. 26:2)

Now I saw in my dream that Christian and Hopeful went in at the gate and as they entered they were transfigured; and they were dressed in garments that shone like gold. They were also met by those who gave them harps and crowns. The harps were given to offer praise with and the crowns were a token of honor.

Then I heard in my dream all the bells in the city ringing again for joy and that it was said to the pilgrims to "enter into the joy of your Lord."

I also heard the men themselves singing out with a loud voice, saying, "Blessing, honor, glory, and power, be unto Him who sits upon the throne and unto the Lamb, forever and ever."

Now, just as the gates were opened to let the men inside, I looked in after them and witnessed the city shining like the sun! The streets were paved with gold, and many men walked along them, with crowns on their heads, palms in their hands, and carrying golden harps which they used to sing praises.

Among the inhabitants, there were also those who had wings, and they answered one another without pause, saying, "Holy, holy, holy is the Lord." Following that they shut the gates, and after what I had seen, I wished that I had been among them.

Now, while I was gazing upon all these things I turned my head to look back and saw Ignorance come up to the riverbank. He soon crossed over, and without half the difficulty with which Christian and Hopeful had met. For it happened that in that place there was one Vain-Hope, a ferryman, who with his boat helped him over. So I watched as he ascended the hill, to come up to the gate. Only he came alone, for not a single man came out to meet him with the least encouragement. When he came up to the gate, he looked up to the writing inscribed above the gate and began to knock, supposing that he should quickly be permitted entrance. But the men who peered over the top of the gate asked, "Where did you come from? And what is your desire?"

He answered, "I have eaten and drank in the presence of the King, and he has taught in our streets."

Then they asked him for his certificate, so that they might go in and show it to the King. But Ignorance fumbled in his breast pocket for it but found none. The men tending the gate said, "Don't you have one?" Ignorance had no answer, not even a word.

So the men of the gate told the King, but he would not come down to see him. Instead he commanded the two Shining Ones, who had conducted Christian and Hopeful to the city, to go out and take Ignorance and to bind him hand and foot and have him taken away.

At that, the two Shining Ones took him up, and carried him through the air to the door that I saw in the side of the hill and put him in there. I realized that there was a way to hell, even from the gate of heaven, as well as from the City of Destruction. So I awoke, and behold it was a dream.

Ignorance is thrust into hell

Conclusion

Now, reader, I have told my dream to you,
  See if you can interpret it to me,
Or to yourself, or your neighbor: but take heed
  Of misinterpreting; for that, instead
Of doing good, will but yourself abuse,
  By misinterpreting, evil ensues.

Pay attention, that you do not become extreme
  In playing with the outside of my dream;
Nor let my figure or similitude
  Make you laugh or start a feud.
Leave this for boys and fools; but as for thee,
  Do you yourself the substance of my matter see?

Open the curtains, look within my veil,
  Turn up my metaphors, and do not fail.
If you seek them, such things you will find
  As will be helpful to an honest mind.

What of my scum you find there, be bold
  To throw it away, but yet preserve the gold.
What if my gold be wrapped up in ore?
  None throws away the apple for the core
But if you cast it all away as vain,
  I know not but it will make me dream again.

Part II

———∽———

At this point and in this manner I set forth the story of Christian's wife and children and how they set out on their own dangerous journey in pursuit of a safe arrival at the desired country.

I have used similitudes. (*I have also spoken by the prophets, and I have multiplied visions, and used similitudes, by the hand of the prophets. – Hos. 12:10*)

Introduction

———— ⌀ ————

ourteous companions,

Some time has passed since I told you my dream about Christian the pilgrim and about his dangerous journey towards the Celestial country. While it was pleasant to me I also hope it was profitable to you. At that time, I also went on to tell you what I saw concerning his wife and children, and how unwilling they were to go with him on pilgrimage. As a result he was forced to go on his journey without them, for he dared not run the danger of that destruction which he feared would come by staying with them in the City of Destruction. Therefore, as I showed you then, he left them and departed.

Now it so happened that through a growing number of things to accomplish, I have been kept extremely busy, which greatly hindered any chance for me to travel into those parts where he went. Until now, I had no opportunity to make further review about those whom he left behind, so that I might give you an update of what became of them. However, recently I had some concerns and so I went down again toward the city.

Now, I took up lodging in the woods about a mile from that place, and as I slept I dreamed again. In my dream, an aged gentleman came by where I lay, and, because he planned to go part of the way I was traveling, it seemed to me that I got up and went with him. So as travelers usually do, we walked and fell into a conversation. Our talk happened to center on Christian and his travels and this is how I began the discussion with the old man, Mr. Sagacity:

"Sir," I said. "What town is that there below, that lies on the left hand of our way?"

Mr. Sagacity said, "It is the City of Destruction, a populous place, but possessed with a very ill-conditioned and idle sort of people."

"I thought it was," I said. "I went once through that town myself; and therefore what you say is true."

"Too true!" Mr. Sagacity shook his head. "I wish I could continue to speak the truth and have better things to say about those who live there."

"Well, sir," I said. "I can see that you are a well-meaning man, and that you are one who takes pleasure in hearing and telling about that which is good. Please tell me, did you ever hear what happened some time ago to a man from this town, whose name was Christian? For he went on a pilgrimage up towards the higher regions."

Mr. Sagacity's eyes grew wide. "Hear of him! Yes, I certainly did. I also heard of the disturbances, troubles, wars, captivities, cries, groans, frights, and fears, with which he met and experienced on his journey. Besides, I must tell you, all our country rings with tales of him and his adventures. But there ..." He gestured toward the City of Destruction. "There are few houses in the city where people have heard of him and what he did. However, some have sought after and got the records of his pilgrimage; and I think I may accurately say that his hazardous journey has garnered many well-wishers to his ways. For though he was considered a fool by most men when he lived here, now that he is gone he is highly commended by them all. For it is said he lives bravely where he is, and many of them who are determined to never risk his hazards have gained the benefit of water for their own mouths through his rewards."

"They may," I said, "clearly believe that he lives well where he is; for he now lives at and in the fountain of life. He has what he has without labor and sorrow, for there is no grief mixed with this. But, please tell me what the people have to say about him."

"Say!" Mr. Sagacity's eyebrows arched. "The people talk strangely about him. Some say he now walks in white (*Yet thou hast a few persons in Sardis who have not defiled their garments, and they shall walk with me in white, for they are worthy.* - Rev. 3:4); that he has a chain of gold about his neck, and a crown of gold surrounded with pearls, upon his head. Others say, that the Shining Ones, who sometimes showed themselves to him in his journey, have become his companions, and that he is as familiar with them where he is, just like neighbors are with one another here.

"Besides this, it is confidently said concerning him that the King of the place where he is has already bestowed upon him a very rich and pleasant dwelling at court, and he eats and drinks with him every day. Plus he also walks and talks with him and receives smiles and favors from Him who is Judge of all there. (*Thus saith the LORD of the hosts; If thou wilt walk in my ways, and if thou wilt keep my charge, then thou shalt also govern my house and shalt also keep my courts, and I will give thee a place among these that are here. – Zech. 3:7*)

"Besides this, it is expected by some that his Prince, the Lord of that country, will shortly come into these parts and will know the reason, if they can give any, why his neighbors showed him so little support and held him in such ridicule, when they understood he would be a pilgrim. (*And Enoch also, the seventh from Adam, prophesied of these, saying, Behold, the Lord comes with ten thousands of his saints to execute judgment upon all and to convince all that are ungodly among them of all their ungodly deeds which they have unfaithfully committed and of all the hard words which the unfaithful sinners have spoken against him. – Jude 14, 15*)

"For they say, that now his Prince shows him much fondness and that his Sovereign is very concerned with the indignities and humiliations that were cast upon Christian when he became a pilgrim. He will look upon these actions as if they were done to him. (*He that hears you hears me, and he that despises you despises me, and he that despises me despises him that sent me. – Luke 10:16*) And this is no surprise, for it was because of the love that Christian had for his Prince that he attempted all that occurred during his pilgrimage."

"I dare say I am glad that's the end of it for the poor man's sake, for he now has rest from his labor," I said. "And he now reaps the benefit of his tears with joy, has moved beyond the gunshot of his enemies, and is out of the reach of them who hate him. (*Those that sow with tears shall reap with joy. He that goes forth and weeps, bearing the precious seed, shall doubtless come again with rejoicing, bringing his sheaves with him. – Psalm 126:5, 6*) I also am glad that a rumor of these things is heard throughout this country. Who knows; it may have a good effect on some of those who are left behind. But please, sir, while it is fresh in my mind, have you heard anything about his wife and children? Poor hearts! I've wondered often about what has become of them."

"Who?" Mr. Sagacity asked. "You mean Christiana and her sons? It looks like they will do as well as Christian did himself. For though they all played the fool at first and in no way would be persuaded by either Christian's tears or pleas, they had second thoughts and responded wonderfully. They have already packed up and headed out after him."

"Better and better," I said. The news both pleased and surprised me. "You mean to say his wife and children have all left Destruction?"

Mr. Sagacity gave an earnest nod. "It is true: I can tell you the whole story – every detail, for I was right there at the moment it happened and am thoroughly acquainted with all the details of the matter."

"Then since you were there," I said, "you may report it for a truth."

"You need not have any misgivings when affirming it," Mr. Sagacity said. "I mean, the fact is that they have all gone on pilgrimage, both the good woman and her four boys. And since we are, as I understand it, going some considerable distance together, I will give you an account of the whole matter and how it came about.

"His wife was called Christiana from the day she and her children took to a pilgrim's life. After her husband had gone over the river and she heard no more of him she started pondering all that had happened. First, because she had lost her husband and that the loving bond of that relationship was now utterly broken between them. For you know," Mr. Sagacity said to me, "nature can do no less than to entertain the living with many heartfelt and heavy reflections, in the remembrance of the loss of a loved one. In this way, the loss of her husband cost her many a tear. But her thoughts stirred her heart in other ways as well. Christiana began to ask herself whether her unbecoming behavior towards her husband was not one reason that she saw him no more and that for this reason he had been taken away from her in such a manner. With these thoughts came swarms of memories of all her unkind, unnatural, and ungodly demeanor toward her dear friend and husband. These thoughts clogged her conscience and loaded her down with guilt.

"In the same way, she was greatly broken and distressed as she recalled all these things too, with restless groans, salty tears, and the mourning of her husband. She regretted how she had hardened her heart against all his pleas and loving persuasions trying to get her and her sons to go with him. All the things Christian had said and done before her while his burden hung on his back returned to her thoughts now like a flash of lightning rending the hold on her heart to pieces. She especially remembered that bitter outcry of his: 'What shall I do to be saved?' Now his words continued to ring in her ears most dolefully.

"Then said she to her children, 'Sons, we are all ruined. I have sinned away your father, and he is gone. He would have had us go with him, but I refused to go along. In this way, I have also hindered you from receiving true life.' With that tears fell from the boys' eyes and they cried out that they wished to go after their father.

"'Oh,' said Christiana, 'if only it had been our lot to go with him! Then perhaps it would have fared well with us more so than what it is like now. For, formerly, concerning the troubles of your father, I foolishly imagined that they were the product of a foolish notion he had, or that he was overcome with a depressed mood. Yet now I find his frame of mind was not due to foolish imaginations, for they sprang from another cause; that is to say, that the light of life was given him (*Then Jesus spoke again unto them, saying, I AM the light of the world; he that follows me shall not walk in darkness but shall have the light of life.* – John 8:12), and by the help of which,

Christiana's thoughts began to work in her mind

as I understand now, he has escaped the snares of death.' (*The fear of the LORD is a fountain of life, to depart from the snares of death.* – Prov. 14:27)

"Then Christiana and the boys all wept again and cried out, 'Oh, may trouble happen to the day!' The next night Christiana had a dream in which she saw a large parchment opened before her. It held a recorded summary of her ways; and to her way of thinking the crimes looked very black against her. She cried out aloud in her sleep, 'Lord, have mercy upon me a sinner!' (*And the publican, standing afar off, would not lift up so much as his eyes unto heaven, but smote upon his breast, saying, God, reconcile me, a sinner.* – Luke 18:13) And the children heard her.

"After this she thought she saw two very offensive ones standing beside her, speaking between themselves. 'What shall we do with this woman? For she cries out for mercy whether awake or asleep. If she is allowed to go on like this, we shall lose her as we have lost her husband. Therefore we must, by one way or another, seek to distract her from the thoughts of what shall happen in the hereafter, or else all the world cannot prevent her from becoming a pilgrim.'

Christiana's dream

"She awoke in a great sweat with trembling, but after a while she drifted to sleep again. And while asleep, she thought she saw Christian, her husband, in a place of bliss among many immortals, with a harp in his hand, standing and playing upon it before One who sat on a throne. In her dream, her husband bowed his head with his face to the pavement that rested under his Prince's feet, saying, 'I heartily thank my Lord and King for bringing me into this place.' Then a company of those who stood round about them shouted, and strummed their harps, but no man living could tell what they said except for Christian and his companions.

"The next morning, when she was up and had prayed to God, she talked with her children for a while, until someone knocked hard at the door. She called out, 'If you come in God's name, come in.'

"So the man at the door said, 'Amen' and opened the door. He greeted her with, 'Peace be to this house.' When he finished saying this he looked directly at Christiana and said, 'Christiana, do you know why I have come?'

"Christiana blushed and trembled, and her heart began to grow warm with desires to know where he had come from and what his errand to her might be.

"He said to her, 'My name is Secret. I dwell with those on high. Where I dwell it is talked of that you have a desire to go there. There is also another report that says you are aware of the evil you have formerly committed against your husband, in hardening your heart against his way, and in keeping these children in their ignorance. Christiana, the Merciful One has sent me to tell you, that he is a God ready to forgive, and that he takes delight to increase in number the pardon of offenses. He would also have you know that he invites you to come into his presence, to his table, and that he will feed you with the best food of his house and with the heritage of Jacob your father.

"'There is Christian, your husband, who with a great number of companions has beheld that face which ministers life to those who look upon his face; and they will all be glad when they hear the sound of your feet step over your Father's threshold.'

"At this Christiana was greatly embarrassed by this visitor's words and bowed her head to the ground. Secret then proceeded to say, 'Christiana, here is also a letter for you, which I have brought from your husband's King.' So she took it, and opened it. It released a fragrance that smelled of the best perfume. (*Because of the savour of thy good ointments (ointment poured forth is thy name), therefore have the virgins loved thee.* – Song of Sol. 1:3)

"The letter was written in letters of gold and explained that the King wanted her to do as her husband Christian had done, for that was the way to come to his city and to dwell in his presence with joy forever. At reading this Christiana was quite overcome and cried out to her visitor, 'Sir, will you carry me and my children with you, so that we may also go and worship the King?'

"Then the visitor said, 'Christiana, the bitter is before the sweet. You must first go through troubles, just as your husband did, before you can enter this Celestial City. Therefore I suggest you do as your husband Christian did. Go to the wicket gate which you can see in the distance.' He pointed to the spot across the plain. 'For that gate stands at the start of the way up which you must go, and I wish you all good speed in your journey. I also advise you to put this letter in the pocket next to your heart, and that you read the contents of it to yourself and to your children, until you know it by heart. For it is one of the songs that you must sing while you are in this house of your pilgrimage (*Thy statutes have been my songs in the house of my pilgrimage.* – Psalm 119:54), and you must also be prepared to present it at the further gate at your journey's end.'"

Now in my dream as this old gentleman told me the story he seemed to be greatly affected by it, but he pressed on with the story. "So Christiana called her sons together, and began to speak to them. 'My sons, I have, as you may have noticed lately, been under much anguish in my soul about the death of your father. This torment is not due to any doubt that he is happy, for I am satisfied that he is well where he is. I have also been very disturbed with the thoughts of my own state and yours which I truly believe by nature are miserable. My behavior also toward your father in his distress is a great load to my conscience; for I hardened both my own heart and yours against him and refused to go with him on pilgrimage.

"'The thoughts of these things would now kill me outright, except for a dream which I had last night and for the encouragement which this stranger has given me this morning.' She gestured toward Secret.

"'Come, my children,' she said. 'Let us pack up, and go to the gate that leads to the Celestial country, so that we may see your father and be with him and his companions in peace, according to the laws of that land.' Her children burst into tears of joy that their mother's heart was so inclined.

"So their visitor bid them farewell and together the family made preparations to set out for their journey. When they were almost ready to leave, two of the women who were Christiana's neighbors came up to her house and knocked at her door. When Christiana opened the door she said to the two women, 'If you come in God's name, come in.'

"These words stunned the women, for they were not used to this kind of language and certainly didn't expect it to drop from the lips of Christiana.

Yet they came inside, and to their surprise they found the good woman preparing to depart from her house.

"'Neighbor, what is the meaning of this?' they asked."

"Christiana answered and said to the oldest of the two, whose name was Mrs. Timorous, 'I am preparing for a journey.'

"This Timorous was daughter to him who met Christian up on the Hill Difficulty, the very same man who would have had him go back for fear of the lions.

"Mrs. Timorous frowned. 'For what journey? Where are you planning to go?'

"Christiana said, 'To go after my good husband.' But the words barely escaped her lips when she dropped to her chair and wept.

"Mrs. Timorous pressed her hand to her bosom and stood with her chin held high. 'I certainly hope not, good neighbor. Please, for the sake of your poor children, do not do such an unwomanly thing! Your children need you here.'

"Christiana looked up at her neighbor and wiped her tears with the

Mrs. Timorous and Mercy find Christiana packing up

corner of her apron. 'No, you misunderstand. My children shall go with me, for not one of them is willing to stay behind.'

"Mrs. Timorous's lips tightened as if she'd taken a sip of vinegar. 'I wonder deep down who or what has put such a notion into your mind!'

"'Oh, neighbor,' Christiana said. 'If you knew what I do now, I have no doubt that you would go along with me.'

"Mrs. Timorous crossed her arms. 'Please tell me what new knowledge you have that has stirred the idea to leave your friends and tempts you to go nobody knows where.'

"Then Christiana replied, 'Mrs. Timorous, I have been deeply troubled since my husband's departure from me but especially since he went over the river. What troubles me the most is my rude behavior toward him when he was under his distress. Besides, now I am feeling just as he did then. Nothing will help me except going on pilgrimage.

"'Last night I dreamed I saw him. Oh, how I longed for my soul to be with him! He lives in the presence of the King of the country! He sits and eats with him at his table. He has become a companion of immortals and a house has been given to him to live in – a house that when compared to the best palace on earth makes the earthly house seem to be nothing but a dunghill. (*For we know that if the earthly house of this our habitation were dissolved, we have a building of God, a house not made with hands, eternal in the heavens. For in this we groan, earnestly desiring to be clothed upon with our house which is from heaven, if so be that we shall be found clothed and not naked. For we that are in this tabernacle do groan, being burdened, for we do not desire to be unclothed, but to be clothed upon with life swallowing up that which is mortal. – 2 Cor. 5:1-4*)

"'The Prince of the place has also sent for me, with promise of receiving me as a guest, if I come to him. His messenger was here just a short time ago and brought me a letter, which invites me to come.' She plucked the letter from her pocket and read it out loud, and then asked her neighbors, 'What do you say to this?'

"'Oh, the madness!' Mrs. Timorous threw her arms toward the ceiling and wailed. 'The same madness has possessed both you and your husband, to run yourselves purposefully into such difficulties! You have heard, I am sure, the problems your husband met with, from his very first step on his way. Our neighbor Obstinate can certainly testify to how poorly it went as he left on his journey, for he was with him. And Pliable too, but the two of them came to their senses and like wise men returned to Destruction when they were afraid to go any further.'

"'Over and above that,' her neighbor said, 'we also heard how he met with the lions, Apollyon, the Shadow of Death, and many other things. Plus don't forget the danger he met with at Vanity Fair! And think of how hard put he was being a man. How can you being but a poor woman expect to endure such a thing? And think about these four sweet children of yours. They are your flesh and your bones. Therefore, even though you might be so rash as to go on such a journey yourself, for the sake of your children reconsider and stay at home.'

"But Christiana stood and smoothed her apron. 'Don't tempt me, my neighbor. I have now been shown the value of this journey and the gain I shall receive. I would be a fool of the greatest size if I should lose heart now and not strike out on this opportunity. And for all those troubles which you remind me I am likely to meet with in the way, they are so far from being a discouragement to me that they show me I am making the right choice. The bitter must come before the sweet, and that also will make the sweet the sweeter. Therefore, since you didn't come to my house in God's name, as I said, I ask you to leave and not to alarm me further.'

"Then Mrs. Timorous loathed Christiana and said to her fellow neighbor, 'Come, Mercy, let us leave her to her own undoing, since she scorns our advice and company.' She spun on her heels and took a step toward the door.

"But Mercy stood firm, for she could not so readily conform to her neighbor's wishes, for two reasons. First, her sense of pity and kindness ached for Christiana. So she said to herself, *If my neighbor Christiana feels she needs to go, I will go a little way with her and help her.* Second, that same sense of pity and kindness hungered within her own soul, for what Christiana had said had taken hold upon her own mind. Therefore she thought, *I will talk more with this Christiana and if I find truth and life in what she has to say, I shall also go along with her wholeheartedly.* It was after thinking these things through that she answered her neighbor Mrs. Timorous:

"'Neighbor,' Mercy said, 'I did indeed come with you to see Christiana this morning, and since she is, as you see, making her last preparations to depart this country, I think I'll walk a little with her this sunshiny morning to help her on her way.' But Mercy chose not to mention her second reason and just kept it to herself.

"'Well!' Mrs. Timorous faced Mercy with her chin held high and her nostrils flaring. 'I see clearly that you have a mind to go a fooling too.' She shook her finger toward her neighbor. 'But be wise and listen to me. While we are out of danger, we are out, but when we are in, we are in.' With that, Mrs. Timorous turned her back to them, walked out the door, and returned to her house. So Christiana busied herself in preparation for her journey.

"When Mrs. Timorous arrived home she quickly sent for some of her neighbors, including: Mrs. Bat's-Eyes, Mrs. Inconsiderate, Mrs. Light-Mind, and Mrs. Know-Nothing. When they had all gathered at her house, she started to tell them the story of Christiana and her intended journey.

"She said, 'Neighbors, having little to do this morning, I went to visit Christiana. When I came to the door I knocked, as is our custom. She

Mrs. Timorous and her neighbors

answered, 'If you come in God's name, come in.' It seemed a bit odd, but I went in thinking all was well. However, when I walked in I found her preparing to leave town along with her children. So I asked her what she was doing. And she told me, in short, that she had decided to go on pilgrimage, just like her husband had done. She also told me of a dream she had, and how the King of the country where her husband was had sent an inviting letter to come there.'

"Mrs. Know-Nothing asked, 'Do you think she will go?'

"Mrs. Timorous let out a deep sigh and nodded. 'Yes, she will go whatever comes; that's all there is to it. I think I knew it most of all when I tried to persuade her to stay at home by reminding her of all the troubles she was likely to meet with on the way. Instead of discouraging her, my great argument only encouraged her to move forward on her journey. For she told me in so many words that the bitter goes before the sweet; and because it does it makes the sweet the sweeter.'

"Mrs. Bat's-Eyes pursed her lips. 'That blind and foolish woman! You mean to say she takes no warning from her husband's afflictions? For my part, I'd say that if he were here again, he would be content to relax here unharmed and never to endure so many hazards for nothing.'

"Mrs. Inconsiderate also replied with a dismissive wave of her hand. 'Away with such fantastical fools from the town, and good riddance! However, as far as I'm concerned, I think she should stay here where she lives. But who could bear to live by her? For she will either be dull, un-neighborly, or talk about matters nobody can put up with. Therefore, as far as I'm concerned, I will never be sorry to see her leave. Let her go, and let someone better come in her place. Let's face it; it has never been good since these whimsical fools have lived among us.'

"Then Mrs. Light-Mind joined the conversation. 'Come, come; let us put this kind of talk behind us. Yesterday I spent the day at Madam Wanton's, where we were as merry as the maids. And who do you think should be there along with me, but Mrs. Love-the-Flesh and three or four more, with Mrs. Lechery, Mrs. Filth, and some others. So we enjoyed music and dancing, and whatever else we could think of to give us pleasure. And I dare say, my lady herself is an admirable well-bred gentlewoman, and Mr. Lechery is a handsome fellow.'"

The First Stage

———— ∽ ————

y this time Christiana had gotten underway on her journey along with her children and Mercy went along with them also. "And, Mercy," Christiana said, "I take this as an unexpected favor, that you should set forth like this to accompany me a little in the way."

Young Mercy smiled, for she was but a young maid. "If I thought it would lead to anything of good consequence to go along with you, I would never go near the town again."

"Well, Mercy," Christiana said. "Join with me, for I know well what awaits at the end of our pilgrimage. My husband is in a place where he would not be even if he had all the gold in the Spanish mines. And you won't be rejected either for you go upon my invitation. The King who has sent for me and my children delights in mercy. Besides, if you are willing, I will hire you and you shall come with me as my servant. Yet we will have all things in common between you and me. Just come along with me."

Lines of thought marked Mercy's young brow. "But how shall I be certain that I would also be received with hospitality? If I had such a hope as this – but from one with authority, I wouldn't hesitate at all. I would go being helped by Him who can help, even though the way is ever so wearisome."

"Well, my dear, loving Mercy," Christiana said. "I'll tell you what you should do. Go with me to the wicket gate, and there I will further ask for you. If you do not receive encouragement to continue with me on pilgrimage, I will be content for you to return to your home. I will also pay you for the kindness which you have shown to me and my children, by coming with us and supporting us in the way you have."

Mercy clasped her hands beneath her chin and said, "Then I shall go to the wicket gate and will accept what comes next. May the Lord grant that my portion fall there and that the King of heaven shall have his affections upon me."

Christiana's face beamed with gladness, not only because she had a traveling companion, but also because she had succeeded in making this poor maid fall in love with her own salvation. So they went on together, and Mercy began to weep.

Christiana looked at her friend and asked, "Why are you weeping like this my sister?"

"I can't help it," Mercy said. "I am compelled to cry and weep when I consider what a state and condition my poor relatives and friends are in. You know – the ones who remain behind in our sinful town. What makes my sorrow and regret all the more heavy is that they have no instructor or anyone to tell them what is to come."

"Compassion becomes pilgrims," Christiana said. "And you weep for you family and friends, as my good Christian did for me when he left me.

Christiana and her family, with Mercy, set out

He grieved and wept because I would not listen to him or pay attention. I treated him as if what he had to say was of no interest, but his Lord of ours gathered up his tears and put them into his bottle. And now you and I, plus my sweet children, are reaping the fruit and benefit of them. I hope, Mercy, that these tears of yours will not be lost, for the truth has said that 'they who sow in tears shall reap in joy.' And 'he who goes forth and weeps, bearing precious seed, shall without a doubt come again with rejoicing, bringing his sheaves with him'" (Psalm 126:5, 6).

Then Mercy said:

> "Let the Most Blessed be my guide, if it be His will,
>> Unto His gate, into His fold, and up to His holy hill.
> And let Him never allow me to turn aside or veer,
>> From his free grace and holy ways, whatever I suffer.
> And let Him gather those of mine whom I have left behind;
>> Lord, please make them be thine, with all their heart and mind."

Now my old friend continued with the tale of Christiana's pilgrimage and said that when she came to the Slough of Despond, she slowed and came to a stop. For, she said, "This is the place in which my dear husband was almost smothered with mud." Nevertheless, she also recognized the command of the King to make this place good for pilgrims, and yet it was worse than before. So I asked if that was true.

"Yes," said the old gentleman. "Too true. For many pretend to be the King's workers, and say that they are for restoring the King's highways, but they bring dirt and dung instead of stones, and as a result cause more damage rather than repair."

Therefore it was here at the Slough of Despond where Christiana and her boys came to a stop. But Mercy said, "Come, let us risk going forward, but let us be cautious." Then they looked carefully where they stepped, and shifted their path and reeled from one side to the other with doubt. The experience left Christiana feeling like she had been mired in the Slough, more than once or twice, but eventually they did cross over.

They had no sooner reached the other side when they thought they heard someone say, "Blessed is she who believes, for there shall be a completion of those things which were told her from the Lord" (Luke 1:45).

Hearing these words, they continued on their way, and Mercy said to

Christiana, "If I had as good a cause to hope for a loving reception at the wicket gate as you, I don't think any Slough of Despond would be able to discourage me."

"Well," said Christiana. "You know your affliction, and I know mine." She placed her hand on Mercy's shoulder. "We shall all have enough misfortune before we reach our journey's end, my good friend. For can you imagine people like us who plan to reach such excellent glories as we do, and who are subject to envy because of the happiness we have without enemies who hate us? They will assault us with fears and snares and with troubles and afflictions."

And now Mr. Sagacity left me to dream out my dream by myself. Therefore, it seemed to me that I saw Christiana, Mercy, and the boys, all go up to the gate. When they came to it, they entered into a short debate about how they should conduct their affairs when calling at the gate. For instance, they discussed what should be said to the one who opened the gate and who should do the talking. So they concluded, since Christiana was the eldest, that she should be the one to knock for entrance, and that she should also speak for the rest of them to the man who opened the gate.

So Christiana began to knock, and just like her poor husband, she knocked and knocked again. But instead of a person answering the knock, they all thought they heard the sound of a dog barking in their direction. It wasn't just any bark, but the deep sound of an enormous dog. This filled the women and children with dread. They dared not knock any more, for fear the mastiff would stir at the noise and rapidly overtake them.

Due to this turn of events, they were greatly confused and unsure of what they should do next. They dared not knock, for fear of the dog. They dared not go back, for fear the keeper of that gate should see them as they left and then be offended with them. Finally, they thought about knocking again, but this time they knocked more passionately than they did the first time. The Keeper of the gate answered. "Who is there?" And at the sound of the gatekeeper's voice the dog ran off to bark elsewhere and the gatekeeper opened the gate to them.

Christiana bowed low and said, "Lord, please don't be offended with your handmaidens, because we have knocked at his princely gate."

Then the Keeper said, "From what place have you come? And what is it that you want?"

Christiana answered, "We have come from the same place from which Christian came, and for the same business. To be clear, we are asking that if it pleases you, that we be graciously admitted by this gate into the way that leads to the Celestial City. And I answer, my Lord, in regarding the second question, that I am Christiana, once the wife of Christian, who now has arrived above."

With that the Keeper of the gate gaped in wonder, saying, "What? Did the one who abhorred that life just a short time ago now become a pilgrim?"

She bowed her head, and said, "Yes, and so are these my sweet children also."

He reached out and took her by the hand and led her in and also said, "Permit the little children to come unto me." And with that he shut up the gate. Then he called to a trumpeter who was situated above, over the gate, to receive Christiana with shouting and the sound of a joyful trumpet. So he obeyed and sounded the trumpet which filled the air with pleasant music.

Now all this time poor Mercy stood outside the gate trembling and crying, for she feared she had been rejected. But when Christiana had gained admittance for herself and her boys, she began to make intercession for Mercy.

Christiana said, "My Lord, I have a companion who still stands outside the gate, who has come here for the same reason as myself. She is feeling quite discouraged, because she thinks she has come here without an invitation, while I was sent for by my husband's King."

Mercy began to be very impatient and each minute seemed as long as an hour to her. Therefore she prevented Christiana from a fuller interceding for her, by knocking at the gate herself. And she knocked so loud that she made Christiana jump.

Then the Keeper of the gate asked, "Who is there?"

And Christiana said, "It is my friend."

So he opened the gate and looked out, but Mercy had fallen down unconscious outside the gate because she had fainted for fear that the gate would not be opened to her. The Keeper reached down and took her by the hand. He said, "Young woman, I command you to get up."

Mercy opened her eyes and said, "Oh, sir, I am faint. There is hardly a trace of life left in me."

But the Keeper answered her that one once said, "When my soul fainted within me I remembered the Lord, and my prayer came unto you, into your holy temple" (Jonah 2:7). The Keeper told her, "Fear not, but stand upon your feet and tell me why you have come here."

Mercy stood on shaking legs and said, "I have come for that which I was never invited like my friend Christiana was. Hers was from the King, and my invite was but from her. Therefore I fear I have ventured here without permission."

"Did she desire you to come with her to this place?" the Keeper asked.

Mercy gave an earnest nod. "Yes, and as my Lord sees, I have come. And if there is any grace and forgiveness of sins to spare, I request that your poor handmaid may be a partaker of it."

The Keeper of the gate finds Mercy fainting outside

The Keeper took Mercy again by the hand and led her gently inside the wicket gate. He said, "I pray for all who believe on Me." (*I pray for them; I do not pray for the world, but for those whom thou hast given me; for they are thine.* – John 17:9) Then He said to others who stood nearby, "Fetch something and give it to Mercy to smell, to help stop her from fainting." So they fetched a bundle of myrrh and she inhaled deeply of its fragrance and a short while later was revived.

And so Christiana and her boys, and Mercy, were all received by the Lord at the head of the way, and they were spoken kindly to by Him. They also said to Him, "We are sorry for our sins, and beg of our Lord His pardon, and further information regarding what we must do."

He said, "I grant pardon by word and deed. By word in the promise of forgiveness, by deed in the way I obtained it. Take the first from My lips with a kiss, and the other as it shall be revealed." (*And having said this, he showed them his hands and his side. Then the disciples were glad when they saw the Lord.* – John 20:20)

Now I saw in my dream that He spoke many good words to them, by which they were greatly gladdened. He also brought them up to the top of the gate, and showed them at what time they were saved and also told them that this sight would comfort them again as they went along in the way.

So He left them awhile in a summer parlor below, where they refreshed themselves and discussed what had happened. Christiana began and said, "O how glad am I that we have gotten in here."

Mercy agreed, but said, "You may very well be glad, but I have even more cause to leap for joy."

Christiana considered the time she spent knocking at the gate and said, "I thought at one time, as I stood knocking at the gate and no one answered, that all our labor had been for nothing, especially when that ugly mongrel made such a loud, deep barking against us."

Mercy said, "My worst fear came after I saw you were taken into His favor. When you disappeared through the gate I thought I had been left behind. At the time I thought what is written had been fulfilled: *Two women shall be grinding at the mill; the one shall be taken, and the other left* (Matt. 24:41). I made quite a commotion but refrained from crying out, 'Ruined! Destroyed!' I was afraid to knock at the gate again; but when I looked up and saw what was written over the gate, I took courage. I also decided I must either knock again or die. So I knocked, but I can't begin to tell how my spirit struggled between life and death."

Christiana asked, "Couldn't you tell how loudly you knocked? I can tell you that your knocks were so earnest that they startled me. I thought that I had never heard such knocking in all my life. In fact I thought perhaps you would enter the Gate by force or take the kingdom by storm." (*From the days of John the Baptist until now, life is given unto the kingdom of the heavens, and the valiant take hold of it. – Matt. 11:12*)

"Regrettably for someone in my situation, what else could I do?" Mercy asked. "You saw that the door shut after you entered, and I stood on the other side along with that cruel dog. No one could be more faint-hearted than me, but who in my situation would not have knocked with all their might? But please tell me what did my Lord say about my rudeness? Was He angry with me?"

A grin tugged at the corner of Christiana's mouth. "When He heard your unwieldy noise, He smiled a most wonderful smile. I believe what you did pleased Him, for He showed no sign to the contrary. But I wonder in my heart why He keeps such a dog. I have to say that if I had known that before we came to the gate, I'm not sure I would have had courage enough to have attempted any of this. But now we are *in* ..." She grabbed Mercy's shoulders. "We are in! And deep down I've never been happier."

Mercy's head bobbed in agreement. "Please, next time He comes down be sure to ask Him why He keeps such a filthy mongrel in His yard." She paused for a moment and said, "I hope He will not take it wrong."

"Yes, do ask Him," the children said in unison, "and persuade Him to hang the mongrel, for we are afraid he will bite us in the future."

So finally He came down to them again. When Mercy saw Him she fell to the ground on her face before Him and worshiped. She said, "Let my Lord accept the sacrifice of praise which I now offer to Him with my lips."

So He said to her, "Peace be to you; stand up."

But she continued to lay face down and said, "You are always righteous, O Lord, when I bring my case before you; yet I will speak with you about your judgments." (*Righteous art thou, O LORD, even though I dispute with thee: even so, I will speak judgments with thee. – Jer. 12:1*)

She peeked up at Him and asked, "Why do you keep such a cruel a dog in your yard? At the sight of it women and children such as us are ready to flee from your gate in fear."

He said, "That dog has another owner who lives in the castle which you see there in the distance. He just keeps him close to another man's property, and my pilgrims hear his barking but can still come up to the walls of this place. While that is neither bad nor good, he has frightened many an honest pilgrim by the deep booming of his barking.

"The fact is that the owner of the dog doesn't keep him out of any goodwill to Me or mine, but with the sole intent to keep pilgrims from coming to Me. It is his hope that pilgrims may be too afraid to come and knock at this gate when they hear the ferocious bark of his dog. Sometimes the dog has even broken out and harassed some whom I loved, but for now I accept it patiently.

"I also give my pilgrims timely help, so that they are not transferred to his power to do with as his doggish nature would prompt him to do. But if you had been my purchased one before you met the dog, I trust, you would not have been afraid.

"The beggars who go from door to door are willing to run the hazard of the bawling, barking, and biting of a dog rather than lose possible donations. So shall a dog, a dog in another man's yard, a dog whose barking I turn to the profit of pilgrims, keep any from coming to me? I deliver them from the lions, and my precious ones from the power of the dog." (*Save me from the lion's mouth and from the horns of the unicorns. I will declare thy name unto my brethren; in the midst of the congregation I will praise thee.* – Psalm 22:21, 22)

Mercy sat up and said, "I confess my ignorance. I spoke about things which I did not understand. I acknowledge that You do all things well."

Then Christiana began to talk of their journey and to ask for directions. So He fed them and washed their feet, and set them in the way of His steps, in the same way He had done for her husband at the start of his pilgrimage.

The Second Stage

o I saw in my dream, that they walked on their way and enjoyed very comfortable weather.

Then Christiana began to sing, saying:

"Blessed be the day that I began
A pilgrim for to be;
And blessed also be the man
Who to that place moved me.

'Tis true, it was long before I began
To seek to live forever;
But now I run as fast as I can
'Tis better late than never.

Our tears to joy, our fears to faith,
Are turned, as we see;
Thus our beginning (as one says)
Shows what our end will be."

Now there was, on the other side of the wall that fenced in the way which Christiana and her companions traveled, a garden that belonged to the one who owned the barking dog. It happened that some branches of fruit trees that grew in that garden hung over the wall with fruit dangling from the branches. Being ripe the pilgrims found them and gathered them up and ate them to their harm.

Christiana's boys, as boys tend to do, were delighted with the trees and the fruit that hung on them. So they plucked the fruit and began to eat. Their mother scolded them, but the boys went on eating their fill of the fruit.

"Well," she said, "my sons, you sin! That fruit does not belong to us!" But she didn't know that it belonged to the enemy. I'll guarantee you, if she had known, she would have been ready to die for fear. But that passed, and they went on their way.

The children eat of the enemy's fruit

Now, once they had traveled about two bow-shots from the place where they had entered into the way, they spotted two very ugly men walking swiftly toward them. When they spotted them, Christiana and Mercy, her friend, covered themselves with their veils and kept walking on their journey. The children also continued along the way and eventually they met up with the two ugly men who had come down to meet them. They walked up to the women as if they would embrace them, but Christiana said, "Stand back or go peaceably on your way."

But these two acted like men who are deaf, for they ignored Christiana's words and began to lay hands upon them. Christiana became very angry and kicked at them with her feet. Mercy, also, fought back as well as she could and did what she could to divide them.

Christiana warned them again. "Stand back and be gone, for we don't have any money. Being pilgrims, as you see, we live on the charity of our friends."

Then one of the two unattractive men said, "We don't attack you for money! Rather we have come to tell you that if you will just grant one small request which we shall ask of you, we will make women of you forever."

Now Christiana could only imagine what they might possibly mean by that, so she said, "We will neither hear, consider, or yield to what you plan to ask. We are in a hurry and cannot stay. Our business is a business of life and death." Once again, she and her companion made another attempt to go past them again, but they stood menacingly in their way.

One of the men said, "We don't intend to hurt you. It is another thing we want from you."

"You would have us body and soul," Christiana said, "for I know this is the reason you have come after us, but we would rather die right here and right now, than to permit ourselves to be brought into such snares and run a risk to our well-being in the future."

With that they both screamed out and cried, "Murder! Murder!" And so they placed themselves under those laws that are provided for the protection of women. (*But if the man found a betrothed damsel in the field and the man forced her and lay with her; then only the man that lay with her shall die; but unto the damsel thou shalt do nothing; there is in the damsel no sin worthy of death; for as when a man rises against his neighbour and murders him, even so is this matter. For he found her in the field and the betrothed damsel cried out, and there was no one to save her. – Deut. 22:25-27*) But the men still approached them with malice and planned to triumph over them. The two women, therefore, cried out again.

Now like I said, the women and children were not yet far from the gate through which they entered the way, and their screams were heard by those in the house. Therefore a man hurried out of the house for he knew that it was Christiana's voice he heard, and so he hurried to aid her. But by the time the Reliever was within sight of them, the women were caught up in a great scuffle with the two ugly men while the children stood by crying.

The Reliever who came to save them from the attack called out to the ruffians saying, "What are you doing? Would you make my Lord's people sin?"

He attempted to overtake them, but the two men made their escape over the wall into the garden of the man who owned the great dog, and once there the dog became their protector. With the ugly men gone, this Reliever walked up to the women and asked them how they were.

"We thank your Prince!" the women answered. "We do pretty well; we have only been somewhat frightened. Thank you so much for coming to help us. If you hadn't we would surely have been overcome."

So, after a few more words, this Reliever said, "When you were visitors at the gate I marveled that you knew you were weak women and that you didn't petition the Lord for a conductor so that you might avoid troubles and dangers such as these. He would have granted you one, if you had asked."

Christiana brushed dust from her dress. "Unfortunately, we were so preoccupied with our present blessing that we didn't think about the dangers to come. Besides, who could have imagined that such naughty ones could have lurked so near the King's palace? Indeed, it would have been best if we had we asked our Lord for a conductor, but since our Lord knew it would be for our profit, I wonder why he didn't send one along with us."

The Reliever said, "It is not always necessary to grant things not asked for, for by doing so such things are often viewed as of little value or are taken for granted. However, when the need of something is sensed, that thing becomes valued in the eyes of the one who has recognized the need. And when the value which it is properly due is perceived, it will consequently be used after that point because it is recognized as something of worth. Had my Lord granted you a conductor, you would not have regretted your oversight in not asking for one, as now you have occasion to do. So all things work for good and tend to make you more wary."

"Shall we go back again to my Lord, and confess our folly, and ask for one?" Christiana asked.

"I will present Him with your confession of your folly," the Reliever said. "You do not need to go back again, for in all places where you shall go, you will find no lack at all. In every one of my Lord's lodgings, which He has prepared for the reception of His pilgrims, there is enough to furnish them against all such attempts as the one you just experienced. But, as I said, He will be asked of by the pilgrims, to do it for them. (*Thus hath the Lord GOD said; I will yet be enquired of by the house of Israel, to do it for them; I will multiply men like flocks.* – Ezek. 36:37) And it is a poor thing that is not worth asking for." When he had said this, he went back to his place and the pilgrims went on their way.

Then Mercy said, "Suddenly I feel such a void here among us! I made a whole list of reasons for why I thought we had been past all danger. In fact, I actually thought we would never see such trouble again."

"Your innocence, my sister," said Christiana to Mercy, "may excuse you of much, but as for me, my fault is so much greater. You see, I saw this danger before I even stepped out the door, and yet I didn't plan for it when I could have made provision for it. I bear much blame."

Mercy gave Christiana a questioning look. "How could you possibly know such things before you left home? Please tell me the answer to this riddle."

Christiana said, "Of course I will tell you, dear friend. You see, before I ever set foot from the door of my home, I had a dream about this one night as I lay in my bed. In it I saw two men, like these who assaulted us. They stood at the foot of my bed plotting how they might prevent my salvation. This happened at a time when I was very troubled, and here is what I heard them say. 'What shall we do with this woman? For she cries out for forgiveness whether awake or asleep. If she is allowed to go on like this, we shall lose her as we have lost her husband.'

"You would think this might have made me pay attention to what I needed to bring for this pilgrimage, while I had all the provision I might need for the asking."

"Well," Mercy said. "Due to this oversight we have been ministered to and had an opportunity to see our own imperfections. For our Lord has used these circumstances to make clear in our sight the riches of His grace. And as we can see, He has followed us with unasked-for kindness and delivered us for His good pleasure from the hands of these men who were stronger than us."

Now as they talked and walked for a little more time, they drew near to a house which stood in the way. This house had been built to offer relief for pilgrims passing this way. You can find out more about the house of the Interpreter in the first part of these records of the Pilgrim's Progress.

They walked towards the house, and when they came to the door they overheard voices in the house. They listened and thought they heard Christiana mentioned by name, for you must know that talk of her and her children's going on pilgrimage had gone on ahead of her. Those in the house talked about how hearing this news was very pleasing to them, because she was Christian's wife and the same woman who had been unwilling to hear of going on pilgrimage some time ago.

Therefore, Christiana and Mercy stood outside the door listening to the good people inside the house commending her, though they had no idea she was at the door. Finally, Christiana knocked, in the same way she had knocked at the wicket gate.

A young damsel came and opened the door and looked from Christiana to Mercy. Then the damsel said to them, "With whom would you like to speak?"

Christiana answered, "We understand that this is a privileged place for those who have become pilgrims, and as such we now stand at this door. Therefore we ask that we may come in at this time to partake in your hospitality; for as you can see it is getting late and we are reluctant to go any further tonight."

The young woman at the door was named Innocent. She asked, "Please tell me your name, so that I may tell it to my Lord within the house."

Christiana said, "My name is Christiana. I was the wife of that pilgrim who some years ago traveled this way and these are his four children." Christiana motioned toward Mercy and said, "This young woman is also my companion and is going on pilgrimage, too."

Then Innocent ran into the house and said to the others, "You won't believe who is at the door! It is Christiana, her children, and her companion, all waiting for admission here."

All those in the house jumped for joy and went and told their Master that Christiana and the others were there. So he came to the door and upon seeing her and the others, he said, "Are you that Christiana whom Christian, the good man, left behind when he accepted a pilgrim's life for himself?"

Christiana nodded. "I am that woman who was so hard-hearted as to neglect my husband when he was in distress. I left him to go on his journey alone, and these are his four children. However, I now also have come on pilgrimage, for I am convinced that this is the only right way."

The Interpreter said, "Then it is fulfilled which is written of the man who said to his son, 'Go work today in my vineyard; and he said to his father, I will not, but afterwards repented and went'" (Matt. 21:29).

Christiana said, "So be it. Amen. God made it a true saying regarding me and granted that I may be found at last in peace with Him, without spot, and blameless."

"But why do you stand at the door?" the Interpreter asked. "Come in, daughter of Abraham. We were just talking about you, but now you have come to us for advice as to how you are to journey as a pilgrim." He gestured for her to step inside and waved her children and Mercy to enter as well. "Come, children, come in. Come, maiden, come in." And so they all entered into the house.

Once they were inside, they were invited to sit down and rest. When they did, those who ministered to pilgrims in the house came into the room to see them. One smiled, then another smiled, until they all beamed with joy because Christiana had become a pilgrim. They also looked at the boys and gently stroked the children's faces with their hand, in a gesture of kind welcome. They also lovingly greeted Mercy and offered all of them a warm welcome into their Master's house.

After they greeted one another, since supper wasn't ready yet, the Interpreter took them into his Significant Rooms. He showed them what

The man could look no way but downwards, at the muck-rake in his hands

Christian, Christiana's husband, had seen when he had visited the house. They saw the man in the cage, the man and his dream, the man who cut his way through his enemies, and the picture of the biggest of them all, along with the rest of those things that were so profitable to Christian when he had visited.

After they had seen all these things and Christiana and those with her had time to think about all they witnessed, the Interpreter took them aside again. First, he brought them into a room where there was a man who couldn't look any way but down and in his hand he held a muck-rake. One stood above the man's head holding a celestial crown and He offered him that crown for his muck-rake. But the man didn't look up or regard the one holding the crown in any way. Instead, he only raked bits of straw, small sticks, and dust from the floor.

Then Christiana said, "I believe I understand the meaning of this somewhat; that this is a figure of a man of this world ... is it not, good sir?"

"You are right," the Interpreter said. "He and his muck-rake show his carnal mind. You see how he pays more attention to raking up straws, sticks, and the dust of the floor, than to what He who calls to him from above with the celestial crown in His hand has to say? It is to show that heaven is nothing but a fable to some people, and that things here in this world are the only things considered important to them. Now, when you saw that the man with the rake could only look down, it was to let you see that when earthly things hold power over men's minds, they completely carry their hearts away from God."

Then Christiana said, "Oh, deliver me from this muck-rake." (*Remove far from me vanity and lies: give me neither poverty nor riches; feed me with the bread of my judgment.* – Prov. 30:8)

"That prayer," the Interpreter said, "is so little used that it is almost rusty. And 'Give me not riches,' is such a scarce prayer that it is only prayed by one in ten thousand. Instead, straw, sticks, and dust are sought after as great things by most."

With that Christiana and Mercy wept and said, "Alas, it is too true!"

After the Interpreter had shown them this, he brought them into the very best room in the house. It was a magnificent room, and he invited them to look around and see if they could find anything useful there. They looked and looked, but there was nothing to be seen except a very large spider on the wall, which they chose to overlook.

Mercy looked back at the Interpreter and said, "Sir, I see nothing." But Christiana didn't say a word.

The Interpreter said, "Look again."

So Mercy looked again and said, "There is nothing here but an ugly spider, who hangs by her hands upon the wall."

The Interpreter asked, "Is there only one spider in this entire spacious room?"

Then tears brimmed in Christiana's eyes, for she was a woman quick to understand. She said, "Lord, there are more here than one and such spiders whose venom is far more destructive than hers."

The Interpreter looked pleased and said, "You have spoken the truth."

Mercy blushed and the boys covered their faces with their hands for they all began to understand the riddle now.

The Interpreter said, "The spider takes hold with her hands, as you see, and is in kings' palaces." (*The spider takes hold with her hands and is in kings' palaces.* – Prov. 30:28) Therefore, this is recorded only to show you how full you are of the venom of sin. However, by the hand of Faith, you may lay hold of and live in the best room in the King's house above."

"I thought it was something like this," Christiana said. "But I could not figure it all out. I thought we were like spiders and that we looked like ugly creatures, no matter what fine room we were in. But to think that by this spider – that venomous and ugly creature, we were to learn how to act in faith, that I did not understand. Yet the fact that she has taken hold and lives in the best room in the house shows that God has made nothing in vain."

Their hearts filled with gladness as they looked at each other with tear-filled eyes and then bowed before the Interpreter.

He brought them into yet another room. In this room, they found a hen and chicks and told the pilgrims to observe them for a while. One of the chicks went to the trough to drink and every time she drank, she lifted up her head and her eyes toward heaven.

The Interpreter said, "See what this little chick does and learn from her. Your mercies come from above. Acknowledge this by receiving them with eyes turned to heaven."

Again he told the pilgrims to observe and watch, and so they paid attention again to the hen and chicks. They noticed that the hen used a fourfold vocal pattern to communicate with her chicks.

1. She had a common call she used all throughout the day.

2. She had a special call which she only used once in a while.

3. She had a brooding note. (*O Jerusalem, Jerusalem, thou that didst kill the prophets and stone those who are sent unto thee, how often I desired to gather thy children together, even as a hen gathers her chickens under her wings, and ye would not!* – Matt. 23:37)

4. She had an outcry.

"Now," said the Interpreter, "compare this hen to your King and these chicks to his obedient ones. For just as the chicks are answerable to the hen, the King himself has methods which he uses to call his people. By his common call he gives nothing, and by his special call he always has something to give. He also has a brooding voice he uses for those who are under his wing and an outcry which sounds the alarm when he sees the enemy coming. I am going to lead you into the next room where such things are, because you are women, and they are easy for you."

Christiana nodded and said, "Please let us see some more."

So he led them into the slaughter-house, where a butcher was killing a sheep, and the sheep was quiet and patiently accepted her death. The Interpreter said, "You must learn from this sheep to suffer and to put up with wrongs without murmurings and complaints. Look how quietly she accepts her death, without objection. She permits her skin to be pulled over her ears. Your King calls you his sheep."

The Interpreter's garden

After this he led the pilgrims into his garden, amid a great variety of flowers. He said, "Do you see all these?"

Christiana said, "Yes."

He gestured to the colorful display and said, "These flowers are diverse in size, quality, color, smell, and strength. Some are better than others and where the gardener planted them, there they stand, and they do not quarrel with another."

Again, he brought the pilgrims into his field, which he had sown with wheat and corn. But when they looked at the crops the tops were cut off and only the straw remained. He said, "This ground was fertilized, ploughed, and sowed, but what shall we do with the crop?"

Christiana thought for a moment and said, "Burn some and make compost of the rest."

The Interpreter said, "What you need to look for is the fruit. You see, lack of fruit will condemn it to the fire and to be trampled underfoot by men. Be careful that in this matter you don't condemn yourselves."

Then, as they were coming back from the field, they saw a little robin with a great spider in his mouth. So the Interpreter pointed to the bird and said, "Look here."

The pilgrims looked and Mercy wondered what it meant, but Christiana said, "What a disgrace to see such a pretty little bird as the robin red-breast in this way. He is a favorite bird to many because they are easy to love, for they are rather sociable toward people! I had thought they lived on crumbs of bread, or upon other such harmless matter. I admit I like him less than I did, now."

The Interpreter replied, "This robin is a good example, very suitable as an illustration of some who teach publicly. For by their appearance they are, as this robin, notably pretty because of their color and bearing. They also seem to have a very great love for teachers who are sincere. Above all else, they show a desire to associate with such teachers ... to be in their company, as if they could live upon the good man's crumbs. They also pretend that this is the reason they frequent the house of the godly and the decrees of the Lord. But when they are by themselves, as the robin, they catch and gobble up spiders; they change their diet, drink iniquity, and swallow down sin like water."

So, when they arrived back at the house they went inside, but because supper wasn't ready yet, Christiana desired for the Interpreter to show or tell some other worthwhile and valuable things.

This pleased the Interpreter. He said, "The fatter the sow is the more she desires the mire. The fatter the ox the more playfully he goes to the slaughter, and the healthier the lustful man is the more prone he is to evil. There is a desire in women to walk free and to discover something never before seen or known, and it is a properly becoming thing to be adorned with that which, in God's sight, is of great price. It is easier watching a night or two, than it is to sit up a whole year together. In the same way, it is easier for one to begin to profess well than it is to continue faithfully on as he should to the end.

"Every shipmaster, when in a storm, willingly casts items of the smallest value overboard, but who will throw the best out first? None; except for those who do not fear God. One leak will sink a ship, and one sin will destroy a sinner. He who forgets his friend is ungrateful to him, but he who forgets his Savior is unmerciful to himself.

"He who lives in sin and looks for future happiness is like a person who sows weeds and plans to fill his barn with wheat or barley. If a man wants to live well until he reaches his last day of life, he should remember each day may be his last and live accordingly. Backbiting and shifting thoughts prove sin is in the world. But if the world, which God sets light by, is counted as a thing of worth in the eyes of men, then in comparison what is heaven which God commends as worthy of notice? If the life that is fraught with so many troubles is so odious as to be let go by us, what is the life above? Everybody is willing to praise the goodness of men publicly, but who is there who is as impressed with the goodness of God as he should be? We seldom sit down to a meal just to eat and leave; in the same way in Jesus Christ there is more merit and righteousness than the whole world has need of."

When the Interpreter had finished speaking, he took the pilgrims out into his garden again, and led them to a tree. The inside of the tree had rotted away and yet it grew and had leaves. Mercy asked, "What does this mean?"

The Interpreter said, "This tree, which is pleasing to the eye on the outside, but is rotten inside, may be compared to many who are in the garden of God. I speak of those who with their mouths speak highly of God, but in fact do nothing for him. Their outer appearance looks good, but their heart is good for nothing but to be tinder for the Devil's tinder-box."

By this time, supper had been prepared and the table spread with a wide variety of dishes. And after one of them gave thanks, they sat down to eat. According to the Interpreter's usual hospitality, they enjoyed music played by the minstrels. Among them was one who sang with a very fine voice. His song was this:

"The Lord alone sustains me,
  And it is he who does me feed;
How can I then want anything,
  Of which I stand in need?"

When the song and music ended, the Interpreter asked Christiana what it was that first moved her to take up a pilgrim's life.

Christiana answered, "First, I thought about the loss of my husband whom I heartily grieved for, because he had changed. But all that was only natural affection. Then I thought about the troubles and pilgrimage of my husband, and how I had treated him like a rude, ill-bred man. So then guilt took hold of my mind. It would have drawn me into the pond, except for a timely dream I had about the well-being of my husband and a letter sent to me by the King of that country where my husband dwells, to come to him. The dream and the letter worked together and so shaped my thoughts that they compelled me to this way."

"You didn't meet with any opposition before you left your home?" the Interpreter asked.

Christiana said, "Yes I did. A neighbor of mine, one Mrs. Timorous – she was related to the man who tried to persuade my husband to go back, for fear of the lions. In the same way, she also tried to deceive me by calling my intended pilgrimage a desperate adventure, and urged me in every way she could to discourage me from it. She reminded me of the hardships and troubles my husband met with in the way; but I got over all that pretty well. The thing that troubled me most was a dream I had of two ugly ones, who I thought plotted about how to make me fail in my journey. It still runs through my mind, and makes me wary of every person I meet, for fear that they should plan to do me harm and to cause me to turn out of the way.

"I'll tell you this, my Lord, though I wouldn't want everybody to know about it. Mercy and I were so violently assaulted between the wicket gate and arriving here that we cried out murder. And the two who assaulted us looked like the two I saw in my dream."

The Interpreter said, "Your beginning is good; and nearer the end you shall increase greatly." He turned and addressed Mercy and in the same way asked her, "And what moved you to come here, dear one?"

Mercy blushed and trembled, and stood silent for a while for she didn't know what to say because her experience was so different from Christiana's.

The Interpreter encouraged her and said, "Don't be afraid; only believe, and speak your mind."

She took a deep breath, let it out slowly, and said, "Truly, sir, my lack of experience is what makes me want to be silent. This lack also fills me with fears of coming short at the end. I can't tell you about visions and dreams, like my friend Christiana can, nor do I know what it is to weep because I refused the advice of good relatives."

"What was it, then, dear heart?" the Interpreter asked. "What is it that made you do what you have done?"

"Why, it was when our friend here was packing up to leave our town." Mercy motioned toward Christiana. "It just so happens that I and another of our neighbors happened to stop by to see her at that time. We knocked at the door and went in to her house. As soon as we did, we saw her preparing to leave and asked what she was doing. She told us she had been sent for to come join her husband. She explained how she had seen him in a dream, living in an unusual place, among immortals, wearing a crown, playing a harp, eating and drinking at his Prince's table, and singing praises to him for bringing him there. While she was telling us these things, my heart burned within me. I thought, 'If this is true, I will leave my father and my mother, and the land of my birth and, if I may, I will go along with Christiana.' (*Wherever thou goest, I will go; and wherever thou shalt lodge, I will lodge; thy people shall be my people and thy God my God. –* Ruth 1:16b)

"So I asked her more about the truth of these matters and whether or not she would let me go with her, for I recognized there was no longer any way to live in our town without the danger of ruin. But as I walked away from our town, I did so with a heavy heart, not because I was unwilling to leave, but I grieved for the many relatives I was leaving behind. But I came along with all the desire of my heart and will go, if I may, with Christiana to her husband and his King."

The Interpreter said, "You have started out well, for you have given credit to the truth. You are a Ruth, who because she loved Naomi and the Lord her God, left her father and mother, and the land of her birth to come out and go with a people she didn't previously know. The Lord compensate your work and a full reward be given to you from the Lord God of Israel, under whose wings you have come to trust." (*It has fully been showed me all that thou hast done unto thy mother-in-law since the death of thy husband and how thou hast left thy father and thy mother and the land of thy nativity and art come three days ago unto a people whom thou didst not know before. Let the LORD recompense thy work and a full reward be given thee of the LORD God of Israel, under whose wings thou art come to cover thyself.* – Ruth 2:11, 12)

When they finished eating and were getting ready for bed, the women were in their own room and the boys by themselves in another room. When Mercy climbed into bed, she could not sleep because she was so excited and full of joy. For now that all her doubts had finally been removed, she lay in the bed blessing and praising God, who had showed her such favor.

In the morning, they arose with the sun and prepared to leave, but the Interpreter wanted them to linger a while longer. "For, you must go forth in an orderly manner."

Then he said to the young woman, Innocent, who had opened the door to them when they first arrived, "Take them into the garden to the bath, and there wash them and make them clean from the soil which clings to them from traveling."

Innocent did as she was told and led the pilgrims into the garden to the bath. She told them that they must wash there and become clean, for her Master wanted the women to do that and then to come back to his house before going on pilgrimage.

The women went in and washed, and the boys did the same, and all came out of that bath sweet smelling and clean, and much invigorated and strengthened. When they walked back into the house they looked much better than when they went out to wash.

When they returned from the garden bath, the Interpreter took them and looked at each one of them. He smiled his approval and said, "Fair as the moon." Then he called for the seal with which those who were washed in his bath used to be sealed. So the seal was brought, and he set his mark upon them, so they might be known in the places where they were yet to go. Now the seal was the substance and sum of the Passover which the children of Israel ate when they came out of the land of Egypt. (*And it shall be for a sign unto thee upon thy hand and for a memorial before thine eyes, that the LORD's law may be in thy mouth; for with a strong hand the LORD has brought thee out of Egypt.* – Exod. 13:9) At that time the mark was set between their eyes and was a seal that greatly added to their beauty like an ornament for their faces. It also added to their earnestness and made their countenance more like that of angels.

Then the Interpreter spoke again to the young woman who waited upon these women and said, "Go into the vestry and select garments for these people."

She fetched white apparel for each one of them and laid them down before the Interpreter. Then he commanded the pilgrims to put the fine, white, clean linen garments on. When the women were dressed in this way, they seemed to be a terror to each other, for neither could see the glory each one had in herself, but they could see it in each other. Because of this they began to honor each other more than themselves.

"For, you are fairer than I am," said one, while the other said, "You are more becoming than I am." The children also stood amazed, to see what garments they were brought.

Great Heart becomes the pilgrims' guide

The Third Stage

———⌇———

The Interpreter then called for a man-servant of his by the name of Great Heart and told him, "Take a sword, helmet, and shield and take these my daughters, and conduct them to the house called Beautiful, which is the place they will rest next."

Great Heart gathered his weapons and went before them and the Interpreter called, "God speed." The others who also belonged to the family who resided in the house also sent them away with many good wishes. So the pilgrims once again went on their way and sang:

"This place has been our second stage:
   Here we have heard and seen
Good things that from age to age to others hid have been.
   The dunghill-raker, spider, hen, the chicks, also, to me
Have taught a lesson; let me then conformed to it be.
   The butcher, garden, and the field; the robin and his bait,
Also the rotten tree, yields for me an argument of weight,
   To move me to watch and pray, to strive to be sincere,
To take my cross up daily and serve the Lord with fear."

Now I saw in my dream that the small group of pilgrims went on with Great Heart before them. Eventually they reached the place where Christian's burden fell off his back and tumbled into a sepulchre. Here they paused and blessed God.

Christiana said, "Standing here, I remember what was said to us at the gate – specifically that we would obtain pardon by word and deed – that is, by the promise and by deed. I know something of what the promise is, but what is it to have pardon by deed? And in what way was it obtained, Mr. Great Heart? I believe you know, so if you please, I'd love to hear your thoughts on the subject."

Great Heart said, "Pardon by the deed done is pardon which is obtained for another who has need of it, not for the person pardoned. This is how I have obtained it. To speak to the question on a larger scale, the pardon that you, Mercy, and these boys have attained was obtained by another; namely by him who let you in at the gate. And he has obtained it in two ways. He has allowed his righteousness to cover you and spilled his blood to wash you."

Christiana said, "But if he parts with his righteousness in order to give it to us, what will he have for himself?"

Great Heart said, "He has more righteousness than you need or than he needs for himself."

"Please, can you explain this in a way that I can understand?"

Mr. Great Heart

Great Heart said, "I will do so gladly, but first I must explain that the one we are about to speak about is like no other. He has two natures which can be clearly seen as different but which are impossible to divide. Each nature has its own righteousness which is essential because if you took either away, that nature would die. We don't have this righteousness, but it can be put on us so we can be made to live accordingly. For apart from this, there is a righteousness this person has which joins his two natures in one person. This is not the righteousness of God separate from the man; nor is it the righteousness of the man separate from God. It is a righteousness which joins both natures and is essential for Him in preparation to fulfill the role of the mediator which He has been given by God.

"If he loses His first sort of righteousness, He stops being God. If He loses the second type, He loses the purity of His humanity. And if He loses the third sort, which comes through actions and following the revealed will of God in obedience, then we lose the sort He puts upon sinners so their sins are covered. Therefore He said, 'As by one man's disobedience many were made sinners, so by the obedience of one shall many be made righteous'" (Rom. 5:19).

Christiana asked, "Does that mean the other types of righteousness are of no use to us?"

"They are," Great Heart said, "for while they are essential to His nature and task, and cannot be passed on to another, they are what make the righteousness that justifies us work for the forgiveness of sin. The righteousness of His godliness gives power to our obedience, and the righteousness of His humanity allows His obedience to justify, and the righteousness that joins His two natures, provides the authority to perform the work for which it was ordained.

"So then, there is a righteousness of which Christ, as God, has no need. For without it, He is God. There is a righteousness that Christ, as man, has no need of because He is perfect man without it. Again, there is a righteousness of which Christ, as God-man, does not need Himself because He is God without it.

"There is also a righteousness that Christ, as God, and as God-man, has no need of for Himself, and therefore He can spare it for us and gives this justifying righteousness freely. For this reason, it is called the gift of righteousness. Since Christ Jesus the Lord is by the law God, this righteousness must be given away. For the law not only binds those who are under it to act in conformity to the law, but to do so in love. (*For if by one offense, death reigned because of one man; much more those who receive the abundance of grace and of gifts and of righteousness shall reign in life by one, Jesus the Christ.* – Rom. 5:17)

"So the law says that a man who has two coats should give one to him who doesn't have one. Now, our Lord in fact had two coats, one for Himself and one to spare. Therefore, He freely places one on those who have none. And in this way, Christiana and Mercy, and the rest of you who are here, your pardon comes by deed … by the work of another man. Your Lord Christ is He who worked and gives away what He worked for to the next poor beggar He meets.

"But, in order to pardon through deed there must be a price paid to God, and something prepared to cover us as well. Sin has brought a just curse of a righteous law, and now from this curse we must be justified by way of redemption – a price being paid for the evil we have done. This price is the blood of your Lord, who came and stood in your stead and died in your place for your sins.

"In this way He ransomed you from your transgressions by blood, and covered your polluted and deformed souls with righteousness. (*Blessed are those whose iniquities are forgiven and whose sins are covered.* – Rom. 4:7)[14] Because of this, God passes over you and will not hurt you when He comes to judge the world." (*When he sees the blood upon the lintel and on the two side posts, the LORD will pass over that door and will not allow the destroyer to come in unto your houses to smite you.* – Exod. 12:23b)[15]

Christiana looked at Great Heart with wide eyes filled with awe. "This is wonderful! Now I see and understand that we needed to learn about being pardoned by word and deed." She turned her gaze upon Mercy. "Good Mercy, let's make sure to keep this in mind and you too, my children, don't forget what we've learned here." Then she turned her attention back to Great Heart and said, "But, sir, wasn't this what made my good Christian's burden fall from his shoulders and made him leap for joy?"

Great Heart nodded. "Yes, it was the belief in this that cut those strings that could not be cut any other way, and it was to show him the proof of this truth that he was permitted to carry his burden to the cross."

"I thought so," Christiana said. "While in my heart I was calm and joyous before, now it is ten times calmer and happier than ever. And I think what I am feeling, though I have only felt it a little so far, reveals that if the most burdened man in the world was here and saw and believed as I now do, it would make his heart even more merry and carefree."

Great Heart looked about as he considered Christiana's words. "These things not only bring comfort and the easing of our burden, but they create a love within us. For who can think about the pardon that comes through the promise without being affected by the way and means of his redemption, and in return love the man who accomplished it for him?"

Christiana said, "True, I feel as if it makes my heart bleed to think that he bled for me. Oh, you loving One! Oh, you blessed One! You deserve to have me; you have paid the price for me. You deserve all of me, for you

---

14   Original: *Who is he that condemns them? Christ, Jesus, is he who died and, even more, he that also rose again, who furthermore is at the right hand of God, who also makes entreaty for us* – Rom. 8:34.

15   Original: *Christ has redeemed us from the curse of the law, being made a curse for us, (for it is written, Cursed is every one that hangs on a tree)* – Gal. 3:13.

have indeed paid for me ten thousand times more than I am worth. It's no wonder that this brought tears to my husband's eyes and made him hike along lightly on his journey. I believe he wished I were with him, but vile wretch that I was I let him go all alone. Oh, Mercy, I wish your father and mother were here, and Mrs. Timorous, too! In fact, I wish with all my heart that Madam Wanton was here, too. Surely, surely, their hearts would be affected. Neither the fear of the one, nor the powerful lusts of the other could succeed in making them refuse the opportunity to become good pilgrims and to return home again."

Great Heart smiled. "Now you speak in the warmth of your love. Do you think it will always be like this with you? The fact is that this is not communicated to everyone, not even to everyone who saw your Jesus bleed. There were some who stood by and saw the blood run from His heart to the ground, and yet were so unaffected that instead of weeping, they laughed at Him. Instead of becoming His disciples they hardened their hearts against Him. As a result, my daughters, all you have is the result of a unique impression made by divine contemplation upon what I have spoken to you. Remember what you learned about the hen and how her common call gave no food to her chicks. Therefore this is known to you by a special grace."

Now I saw in my dream that the pilgrims went on until they came to the place where Simple, Sloth, and Presumption lay asleep. As Christiana walked by on pilgrimage she spotted them hanging up in irons a little way off on the other side of the way.

Mercy looked at Great Heart and asked him, "Who are these three men and for what reason are they hung there?"

Great Heart said, "These three are men with very bad traits. They have no desire to be pilgrims, and whomever they can hinder, they hinder. They want to be lazy and foolish, and they try to persuade others to be the same, and at the same time they teach all will be all right in the end. They were asleep when Christian went by, and now as you go by they are hanged."

Mercy's brow furrowed as she looked upon the three. "You mean to say they persuade anyone to be of their opinion?"

Great Heart glanced at the ground and back at the three. "Yes, sadly enough they have turned several out of the way. There was Slow-pace whom they persuaded to pick up their practices. They also succeeded with Short-wind, No-heart, Linger-after-Lust, Sleepy-head, and with a young woman named Dull. They all turned out of the way to become like them. Besides this, they said bad things about your Lord, convincing others that He was a slave driver. They also spread bad things about the Good Land, saying, it was not half so good as some pretended, and they began to slander His servants. They even called the best of them meddlesome busybodies. Even more, they called the bread of God husks; and the good things He gives His children imaginary. They finished by saying the travel and hardship pilgrims endure is pointless and serves no purpose."

"No!" Christiana covered her mouth in astonishment. "If this is how they were, I will never grieve for such as them. They have only received what they deserve, and I think it is good that they hang so near the highway so others may see them and be warned. But wouldn't it be better, if their crimes were engraved on a plate of iron or brass and left here as a caution to other bad men?"

Great Heart said, "It already exists, as you will see if you travel a little further to the wall."

Mercy said, "Let them hang and their names rot, and may their crimes live forever against them. I can't help but consider it a great kindness that they were hung before we came here. Who knows what else they might have done to such poor women as Christiana and me?" Then she turned it into a song, saying:

> "Now you three hang there and be a sign
>   To all who shall against the truth combine.
> And let him who comes after, fear this end,
>   If unto pilgrims, he is not a friend.
> And you, my soul, of all such men beware,
>   That unto holiness combatants are."

And so the pilgrims went on from there, until they came to the foot of the Hill Difficulty where the good Mr. Great Heart again took the opportunity to tell them what happened when Christian had traveled this way. First he led them to the spring. "Look," he said. "This is the spring from which Christian drank before he went up this hill. Then the water was clear and good, but now it is dirty and muddied with the feet of some who do not want pilgrims to come here and quench their thirst." (*Does it seem a small thing unto you that ye eat of the good pastures, but ye also tread down with your feet the residue of your pastures? and that in drinking of the deep waters, ye must also foul the residue with your feet? And my sheep eat that which ye have trodden with your feet, and they drink that which ye have fouled with your feet.* – Ezek. 34:18, 19)

At that time Mercy said, "Why do you sound so uneasy?"

Their guide did not answer her directly, but only said, "It will do best if you collect it into a vessel that is sweet and good, for that allows the dirt to sink to the bottom and the water to become clearer." So Christiana and her companions scooped up the water and put it into an earthen pot, and let it stand until the dirt settled to the bottom before they drank from it.

Next Great Heart showed them the two by-ways located at the foot of the hill – the very by-ways where Formality and Hypocrisy lost themselves. He said, "These are dangerous paths. Two men who were here when Christian came by chose to follow those paths, and even though they have since been blocked off with chains, posts, and a ditch, there are still those who will choose to venture here rather than to put forth the effort required to go up this hill."

Christiana said, "The way of transgressors is hard. (*Good understanding brings forth grace: but the way of transgressors is hard.* – Prov. 13:15) It is a wonder anyone can get into these ways without danger of breaking their necks."

"You are right, but yet they will venture onto these ways," Great Heart said. "And if any of the King's servants happen to see them, they call out to them and tell them they are going the wrong way and tell them to beware of the danger. But they answer with reproachful words and say such things as, 'The words you have spoken to us in the name of the King, we will not listen to; but we will certainly do whatever we decide for ourselves.' (*As for the word that thou hast spoken unto us in the name of the LORD, we will not hearken unto thee. But we will certainly do whatsoever thing goes forth out of our own mouth to burn incense unto the queen of heaven and to pour out drink offerings unto her as we have done, we, and our fathers, our kings, and our princes, in the cities of Judah, and in the streets of Jerusalem; for then had we plenty of victuals, and were well, and saw no evil.* – Jer. 44:16, 17)

"Now if you look a little further, you can see these ways have been made secure in an effort to warn travelers, not only by these posts, the ditch, and chain, but also by being barricaded. Yet even with all this, some still choose to go there."

Christiana shook her head sadly. "They are idle and hate putting forth the effort needed to climb the hill. So as a result they get what is written: 'The way of the lazy man is a thorny hedge.' (*The way of the slothful man is as a hedge of thorns, but the path of the righteous is made plain.* – Prov. 15:19) They choose rather to walk into a trap than to go up this hill in order to follow the rest of the path to the Celestial City."

Then the pilgrims set out and began to walk up the hill. Before they reached the top, Christiana began to pant and said, "I dare say this hill is hard work! No wonder those who love an easy life more than their souls choose to follow the flatter path."

Mercy agreed and said, "I must sit down." And the smallest of the children began to cry.

"Come, come," Great Heart said. "Don't sit down here; for just a little further up the hill is the Prince's shelter." Then he took the little boy by the hand and led him up to it.

Great Heart helps the pilgrims climb the hill Difficulty

When they came to the shelter, they were all very happy to sit down, for they were sweltering hot. Mercy said, "How sweet is rest after working so hard (*Come unto me, all ye that labour and are heavy laden, and I will give you rest.* – Matt. 11:28), and how good it is that the Prince of pilgrims provides such resting places! I've heard a lot about this shelter, but I've never seen it before. Be careful not to fall asleep, though, for I heard that it cost poor Christian dearly."

Then Great Heart said to the little ones, "Come on boys, how are you doing? What do you think of going on pilgrimage now?"

The youngest, named James, said, "Sir, I was almost ready to give up; so I thank you for lending me a hand when I needed it. It reminds me of what my mother told me – that the way to heaven is like a ladder and the way to hell is like the downward slope of a hill." He looked up at Great Heart and said, "But I'd rather go up the ladder to life than down the hill to death."

Mercy said, "The proverb says, 'To go down the hill is easy.'"

James added, "The day is coming when, in my opinion, going down the hill will be the hardest of all."

"That's a good boy," Great Heart said. "You have given Mercy a right answer." Mercy smiled, and the little boy blushed.

"Come," Christiana said. "Eat a bit to sweeten your mouths, while you sit here to rest your legs, for I have a piece of pomegranate which the Interpreter gave me as I was leaving his house. He also gave me a piece of honeycomb and a little bottle of spirits."

"I thought he gave you something, when I saw him call you aside," Mercy said.

"Yes, so he did." Christiana nodded. "It's just like I said before we left home. You will share in all the good I have, because you so willingly agreed to become my companion." Then she shared the food with Mercy and the boys and they ate. Christiana said to Great Heart, "Sir, will you join us and have something to eat?"

But he answered, "You go ahead and eat it, for you are going on pilgrimage, but as your conductor, I shall return home. What you have to eat may do you much good, while at home I can eat the same every day."

The Fourth Stage

———— ⌒ ————

ow they ate and drank and chatted a little longer, until their guide said, "It's getting late; it's best if we get ready to go. So they got up to go, and the young boys went before the others. When Christiana set out she forgot to take her bottle of spirits with her, so she sent her little boy back to fetch it.

Mercy said, "I think this is a place where things get lost. It was here that Christian lost his scroll, and here Christiana left her bottle behind." She turned her attention to Great Heart and asked, "Sir, what is the cause of this?"

Their guide said, "The cause is sleep or forgetfulness. Some sleep when they should stay awake; and some forget when they should remember. This is why it often happens at resting places that some pilgrims come away losers. Pilgrims should pay careful attention and remember what they have already received during the good times. When they don't, their happiness ends in tears, and their sunshine is clouded just as you witnessed happened in Christian's story when he visited this place."

When they came to the place where Mistrust and Timorous met Christian to persuade him to go back for fear of the lions, they saw something like a stage, and in front of it, towards the road, stood a large sign with a verse written on it, and beneath the verse was the explanation of why the stage was there. The verse read:

> "Let him who sees this stage, take care
>   Of what he says and thinks;
> If he doesn't, he'll come here,
>   Just like some did long ago."

The words underneath the verse explained, "This stage was built to punish those who, through cowardice or lack of faith, become too afraid to go further on pilgrimage. This is the stage where Mistrust and Timorous were burned through the tongue with a hot iron for trying to hinder Christian on his journey."

Mercy said, "This is much like the saying of the Beloved: 'What shall be given to you, or what shall be done to you, you false tongue? Sharp arrows of the mighty with coals of juniper'" (Psalm 120:3, 4).

So they went on until they came within sight of the lions. Now Great Heart was a strong man, so he was not afraid of the lions, but when the rest of them approached the place where the lions were, the boys were still walking ahead of the others. However, once they spotted the lions they quickly cringed and hurried to follow behind the others, for they were afraid of the lions. So when they hurried to fall in step behind the others, Great Heart smiled. He said, "Tell me boys, how is it that you love to take the lead when there's no danger approaching, and yet love to hurry behind as soon as the lions appeared?"

Now, as they drew nearer to the lions, Great Heart pulled his sword and held it at the ready, with the intent to use it to make a way for the pilgrims in spite of the lions. Suddenly a giant man appeared. He was bloody because he had slain pilgrims and his name was Grim. He asked, "What is the reason you have come here?"

The pilgrims' guide, Great Heart, said, "These women and children are going on pilgrimage, and this is the way they must go. And they will go this way in spite of you and the lions."

The giant Grim said, "This is not their way! They shall not enter in. I am coming forth to stand against them and will back the lions."

Now to tell the truth, because of the fierceness of the lions, and the dour bearing of the giant who backed them, this way had few travelers in recent times, and it was almost overgrown with grass.

Christiana said, "Though the highway has been unoccupied lately, and even though other travelers have chosen to walk the by-paths, it must not be so this time for I am risen a mother in Israel." (*The highways ceased, and those that walked went astray through crooked paths. The inhabitants of the villages ceased; they had ceased in Israel until I Deborah arose, I arose a mother in Israel.* – Judges 5:6b, 7)

Then Grim swore by the lions that the way should remain untraveled, and so he told them to turn aside because he would not allow them to pass that way.

But Great Heart, the pilgrims' guide and conductor, made his first approach toward Grim and came against him and his sword struck so heavily that he was forced to retreat.

The giant stood breathing heavily and said, "Will you slay me here on my own ground?"

Great Heart said, "It is the King's highway we are on, and it is you who have placed lions in this way. But these women and these children, though they are weak, shall not veer from the way in spite of your lions." And with that he struck the giant again with a downright blow. The giant dropped to his knees. With another blow he broke his helmet, and with the next he cut off an arm. The giant roared so hideously that his voice frightened the women, and yet at the same time they were relieved to see him sprawling upon the ground.

Death of giant Grim

Now the lions were chained, and so they could do nothing on their own. Therefore, when old Grim, who intended to back them, fell dead, Great Heart urged the pilgrims forward. "Come and follow me, the lions will not hurt you." So they hurried along, though the women trembled as they passed by them, and the boys looked as if they would die, but they all got by without further hurt.

Now, they were soon within sight of the Porter's lodge, and they hurried to arrive at the gate before dark, for it is dangerous to travel there at night. So when they arrived at the gate, Great Heart immediately knocked. The Porter cried out, "Who is there?"

As soon as Great Heart said, "It is I," the Porter knew his voice and came down, for Great Heart had often traveled this way as a guide and had come here as a conductor of pilgrims. The Porter hurried down and opened the gate, but he saw only the guide standing at the gate, for he didn't see the women or children who were standing behind him.

The Porter greeted him. "Hello, Mr. Great Heart, what brings you here so late at night?"

"I have brought some pilgrims here," he said, "pilgrims who my Lord says must lodge here. I would have been here earlier, if I hadn't been opposed by the giant who used to back the lions. But after a long and tedious fight with him, I have cut him down and have brought the pilgrims here in safety."

The Porter said, "Won't you come in and stay till morning?"

Great Heart shook his head. "No, I will return to my Lord tonight."

Christiana cried out, "Oh, sir, I don't want to see you leave us in our pilgrimage. You have been so faithful and loving to us! You have fought so strongly for us, and your advice has been so good in counselling us. I will never forget all you have done for us."

Mercy agreed. "Oh, I wish we could have your company until we reach our journey's end! How can such poor women like us manage our way when it is so full of troubles, without a friend and defender?"

Then James, the youngest of the boys, said, "Please sir, do come with us and help us, because we are so weak and the way so dangerous."

Great Heart looked kindly at the boy and said, "I must do as my Lord commands. If he had asked me to be your guide the whole way, I would willingly have stayed with you. But you made a mistake at the start, for when he told me to come this far with you, then you should have begged him to let me go the entire way with you, and he would have granted your request. However, as things stand now I must go, and so, good Christiana, Mercy, and my brave children, good-bye."

Then the Porter whose name was Mr. Watchful, asked Christiana where she was from and about who her family was. And she said, "I came from the City of Destruction. My husband is dead and I am a widow. His name was Christian the pilgrim."

"Oh!" said the Porter. "Was he your husband?"

A smile flickered on Christiana's lips. "Yes, and these are his children, and this," she pointed to Mercy, "is one of my townswomen."

So the Porter rang his bell, as he did at such times as these, and a young woman by the name of Humble-mind came to the door. The Porter said, "Go announce that Christiana, the wife of Christian, and her children, have come here on pilgrimage."

Humble-mind turned and went back inside, and she told the others in the house that Christiana had arrived with her family. No sooner did she make the announcement when an uproar arose with a clamor of gladness and celebration within the house.

Those inside the house hurried to the Porter, for Christiana was still standing at the door. Then some of the most earnest residents invited her to come into the house. "Come in, Christiana, come in. You blessed woman and wife of that good man, come in, with all who are with you."

So Christiana went inside and the boys and Mercy followed her. Once inside they were taken into a large room, where they were told to sit down. Each one sat, and the chief of the house came into the room to welcome them as guests. Then everyone else joined them, and when they understood who they were, they greeted each other with a kiss and said, "Welcome, you vessels of the grace of God; welcome us as your friends."

By this time, it was somewhat late and the pilgrims were weary from their journey, and also still a little shaken from seeing the fight and the terrible lions, so they just wanted to get ready for bed. Those in the family said, "No, first you must refresh yourselves with a little food," for they had prepared a lamb for them along with the usual sauce (*Then Moses called for all the elders of Israel and said unto them, Draw out and take lambs according to your families and sacrifice the passover.* – Exod. 12:21); for the Porter had heard they were coming, and had told the others to prepare for

The welcome at the palace Beautiful

their arrival. So when they had eaten and ended their prayer with a psalm, they longed to go to bed.

Christiana said, "If we may be so bold as to choose, please let us be in the bedchamber my husband stayed in when he was here."

The others agreed to it and led the group up there, and they all lay in that same room. When they were settled in, Christiana and Mercy started to talk about things that were on their minds. Christiana, with her head upon the pillow, said, "Little did I think when my husband went on pilgrimage, that I would ever have followed him."

Mercy turned to face her. "And I wager you thought it even less likely that you would be lying in his bed, and in his chamber to sleep, as you do now."

Christiana nodded thoughtfully. "I never thought about seeing his face with contentment, and of worshiping the Lord the King with him, and yet now I believe I shall."

Mercy's eyes grew wide. "Listen, do you hear a noise?"

"Yes," Christiana said. "I believe it is a sound of music … for joy that we are here."

Mercy smiled brightly. "It's wonderful! Music in the house! Music in the heart! And music also in heaven, for joy that we are here!" And so the two women talked a while and eventually the two of them drifted off to sleep.

In the morning when they were awake, Christiana said to Mercy, "I heard you laugh in your sleep last night. I suppose you were dreaming. Do you remember what made you laugh?"

Mercy nodded. "I was dreaming and it was a sweet dream, but are you sure I laughed?"

"Oh yes," Christiana said as she sat at the edge of the bed. "You laughed wholeheartedly. Please, Mercy, tell me your dream."

Mercy scooted to the edge of the bed and settled in beside her. "I was dreaming that I sat all alone in a solitary place, and mourned for the hardness of my heart. Now I had not sat there long when it seemed to me many gathered around to see me, and to hear what I had to say. So they listened, and I went on weeping over the hardness of my heart. The reaction of the crowd was mixed. Some laughed at me, some called me a fool, and some began to shove me.

"With that, it seemed to me that I looked up and saw one with wings coming towards me. He came directly to me and said, 'Mercy, what ails you?' When I had told him of my sorrow and the treatment of the people, he said, 'Peace be to you'; he also wiped my eyes with his handkerchief, and dressed me in silver and gold. (*And I washed thee with water and washed away thy blood from upon thee, and I anointed thee with oil. I clothed thee also with broidered work and shod thee with badgers' skin, and I girded thee about with fine linen, and I clothed thee with silk. I decked thee also with ornaments, and I put bracelets upon thy arms and a chain on thy neck.* – Ezek. 16:9-11)

"He put a chain around my neck, and earrings in my ears, and placed a beautiful crown on my head. Then he took me by the hand, and said, 'Mercy, come with me.' So he went up, and I followed him until we came to a golden gate where he knocked.

"When those inside opened the gate, the man went in and I followed him up to a throne. The one who sat upon the throne said to me, 'Welcome, daughter.' The place looked bright and sparkled like the stars … or rather like the sun, and I thought I saw your husband there. Then I awoke from my dream. But did I laugh in my sleep?"

Christiana's eyes grew wide. "Laugh!" She nodded vigorously. "I certainly did hear you laugh. You should have seen yourself! You must forgive me, Mercy, but I have to say that your dream was a good dream. You see, you have begun to find the first part true and in the same way you shall find the second part true in the end as well. 'God speaks once, and even twice, yet man does not understand whether in a dream, in a vision of the night, or when deep sleep overcomes them.' (*Nevertheless, in one or two manners God speaks to the one who does not see. In a dream, in a vision of the night, when deep sleep falls upon men, in slumberings upon the bed.* – Job 33:14, 15) We don't need to be in bed lying awake to talk with God. He can visit us while we sleep and cause us to hear his voice. Our heart often wakes while we sleep and God can speak to that either by words, by proverbs, by signs and similar things, as well as if one was awake."

Mercy pondered Christiana's words and said, "Well, I am glad I had my dream, and I hope before long to be laughing again as I see it fulfilled."

Christiana said, "For now I think it is high time we get out of bed and figure out what we must do."

Mercy didn't make a move to climb from the bed. Instead, she looked at Christiana and said, "If they invite us to stay a while, let's accept. I want to stay here for a time and to get better acquainted with Prudence, Piety, and Charity, for they all seem to be very decent and clear-headed young women."

"We shall see what they want to do," Christiana said. "Now let's get out of bed."

Once they were up and dressed, they went downstairs where the others asked if they had slept well.

"Very well," Mercy said. "It was one of the best night's sleep I've ever had in my life."

Just as they had hoped, Prudence and Piety invited them to stay. "If you are willing to stay here for a while, you can share in all the house provides."

"Yes, we'd be very happy to have you stay," Charity said.

So Christiana and Mercy agreed and stayed there about a month or more, and the time became very beneficial to them. For when Prudence saw how Christiana was bringing up her children, she asked her permission to teach them. So she gave her unrestricted consent and Prudence began with the youngest, whose name was James.

She said to the boy, "Come, James, can you tell me who made you?"

"God the Father, God the Son, and God the Holy Ghost."

"Good boy," she praised him for his answer. "And can you tell me who saved you?"

James nodded and said, "God the Father, God the Son, and God the Holy Ghost."

"That is still a good answer, but can you tell me how God the Father saved you?"

"By his grace," James said.

"And how does God the Son save you?" she asked.

"By his righteousness, death and blood, and life."

"And how does God the Holy Ghost save you?" she asked.

"By his enlightening of understanding through knowledge, by his renewing, and by his salvation."

After this, Prudence said to Christiana, "You are to be commended for bringing up your children in this manner. After talking with James, I don't see the need to ask the rest of the children these questions, since the youngest can answer them so well. So I will move on and talk with the next to the youngest."

So Prudence went to talk with the second youngest, whose name was Joseph. "Come Joseph, will you let me teach you?"

"With all my heart," he said.

She asked him, "What is man?"

"A rational creature made by God, as my brother said."

"So what do you think is meant by this word 'saved'?"

Joseph said, "It means that man, by sin, put himself into a condition of captivity and suffering."

"And what is meant by man's being saved by the Trinity?"

"That sin is such a great and powerful oppressor that no one can pull us out of its clutches except God," Joseph said. "And that God is so good and loving to man, that he is willing to pull him out of this miserable state."

"And what is God's purpose for saving poor men?" Prudence asked.

"To bring glory to his name, his grace, his justice, etc., along with the everlasting happiness of his creature … man."

"Who are they who will be saved?" she asked.

"Those who accept his salvation."

"Good boy, Joseph!" Prudence said. "Your mother has taught you well, and you have listened to what she has said to you."

Then Prudence went to Samuel, who was the second eldest and said, "Come, Samuel, are you willing that I should teach you?"

Samuel said, "Yes, indeed, please do."

She started with, "What is heaven?"

"A place and condition most blessed, because God dwells there."

"What is hell?" she asked.

"A place and state most miserable, because it is the dwelling place of sin, the Devil, and death."

Prudence asked, "And why would you want to go to heaven?"

"So that I may see God, and serve him without weariness." Samuel's eyes focused on Prudence. "And so I may see Christ, and love him forever, and that I may have the fullness of the Holy Spirit in me which I can't fully enjoy here in this world."

Prudence sat up a little straighter. "A very good boy and one who has learned well."

Then Prudence went to the eldest, whose name was Matthew. "Come, Matthew, shall I also teach you?"

"Yes, I'd like that very much."

"Then let's start here," she said. "Was there ever anything that existed before God?"

"No," Matthew said. "For God is eternal. There was nothing except him that existed until the beginning of the first day. For in six days the Lord made heaven and earth, the sea, and all that in them is."

"What do you think of the Bible?"

"It is the holy Word of God," he said.

"Is there nothing written that you don't understand in the Bible?"

"Oh, there is a great deal I don't understand."

"What do you do when you happen across places in the Scripture that you don't understand?" Prudence asked.

"I think God is wiser than I am, so I pray for him to please let me know all that is in it that will be for my benefit."

"What do you believe regarding the resurrection of the dead?" she asked.

"I believe God shall raise those who were buried, in the same nature but without corruption. And I believe this for two reasons: First, because God has promised it, and secondly, because he is able to perform it."

Then Prudence addressed all the boys. "You boys must still listen to your mother, for she can teach you more. You must also diligently pay attention to beneficial talk you'll hear from others, for it is for your sake that they will speak good things. Also be careful to observe what the heavens and the earth teach you, but particularly spend time meditating on that book, the Bible, which was the cause of your father becoming a pilgrim. I, for my part, will teach you what I can while you are here and shall be glad if you ask me questions which lead to godly edifying."

By this time, the pilgrims had been at this place for a week and a visitor, by the name of Mr. Brisk, came to see Mercy. He was a man of some breeding, and he pretended to show good intentions toward her. He also pretended to care about the things of God, but in fact he was a man who stayed very close to the things of this world. So he visited once or twice, and then more, and told Mercy that he loved her. Mercy was an attractive young woman, and therefore all the more alluring.

Mr. Brisk

It so happened that Mercy was one who always kept herself busy. Even when she had nothing to do for herself, she made garments and stockings for others and would give them to those who had need. Mr. Brisk had no idea where or how she disposed of the items she made, but he found it an attractive trait that she was such a hard worker and never idle.

I guarantee she'll be a good housewife, he said to himself.

Mercy talked to the other young women who lived in the house about all that was happening with Mr. Brisk and she asked about him, for they knew him better than she did. They told her he was a very busy young man, and one who pretended to be religious, but they feared he was a stranger to the power of that which is good.

"No!" Mercy said. "Then I won't consider a relationship like that with him, for I have determined never to have a drag on my soul."

Prudence told her, "There's no need to go out of your way to discourage him. If you continue to do as you've been doing for the poor, his commitment will quickly cool."

So the next time he came to the house, he found her at work as was her usual custom, making things for the poor. He asked, "Are you always working?"

"Yes," she said. "Either for myself or for others."

"And how much can you earn in a day?" he asked.

"I do these things, so I may be rich in good works, storing up for myself a good foundation against the time to come, so I may lay up treasures in heaven." (*Charge those that are rich in this world, that they not be highminded, not placing their hope in uncertain riches, but in the living God, who gives us richly all things to enjoy; but charge them to do good, that they be rich in good works, liberal to distribute, willing to communicate, laying up in store for themselves a good foundation against the future, that they may lay hold on eternal life. – 1 Tim. 6:17-19*)

"Why? Please tell me what you do with them," said he.

"Clothe the naked," Mercy said.

With that his countenance fell, and he decided to no longer see her. And when he was asked the reason why, he said, "Mercy is a pretty lass, but troubled with an illness of mind."

When he had left her, Prudence said, "Didn't I tell you that Mr. Brisk would soon reject you? And don't be surprised if he stirs up bad rumors about you; for besides his facade of religion and his seeming love for you, Mercy, the two of you have temperaments that are so different I believe the two will never come together."

Mercy said, "I could have had husbands before now, although I haven't talked about it to anyone. You see, they also did not like my way of thinking, though none of them found fault with my character. As a result, we could not agree and the relationship could not work."

Prudence rested her hand on Mercy's shoulder and said, "Mercy, in our days few are willing to go beyond the title of being religious and to actually practice what is set forth by the Bible. Very few men will be able to accept your moral convictions."

"Well, if nobody will have me ..." Mercy shrugged. "I will die unmarried and my moral convictions will be to me like a husband. For I cannot change my nature, and for as long as I live I do not intend to marry someone who disagrees with me in this. I had a sister named Bountiful, who was married to one of these misers. The two of them could never agree; but because my sister determined to continue to show kindness to the poor, like she had always done, her husband mocked her for kindness and then threw her out of the house."

"I wager he was a churchgoer?" Prudence asked.

Mercy nodded. "Yes, the type of churchgoer you see everywhere these days, but I can't stand any of them."

Now Matthew, Christina's eldest son, became sick, and his sickness was serious. He had excruciating stomach pangs that left him doubled over. Now there lived nearby a man by the name of Mr. Skill. He was old and a well-respected physician. So Christiana called for him and he came. When he entered the room and examined the boy, he concluded that he was sick with colic. He turned to his mother and asked, "What has Matthew eaten lately?"

"Eaten!" Christiana said. "Nothing but wholesome foods."

The physician said, "Your son has eaten something that lies undigested in his stomach, and it will not be passed without help. It must be purged or he will die."

Then Samuel spoke to his mother and said, "Mother, what was it that my brother gathered and ate right after we came through the gate that is at the head of this way? You remember the orchard on the left side of the way which was on the other side of the wall? Some of the branches hung over the wall, and my brother plucked and ate the fruit."

Christiana covered her mouth and looked to the physician with eyes as large as saucers. "He's right! My child did take and eat. That rascal. I told him not to do it, but he ate it anyway."

"I knew he had eaten something that was not wholesome," Mr. Skill said. "That food, specifically, that fruit is the most damaging of all. It is the fruit of Beelzebub's orchard. It's a wonder no one warned you about it because many have died from it."

Christiana began to cry. Between her sniffles she said, "What a naughty boy! And what a careless mother I have been! What am I going to do? How can I help my son?"

Mr. Skill comforted her and said, "Come, come, Christiana, don't be too depressed. There is a chance your son will be well again, but he must purge and vomit."

Christiana looked to the physician with renewed hope. "Please, sir, do everything you can, whatever the cost."

"Don't worry about that," the doctor said. "I hope to keep it reasonable." So he made Matthew a purge made of the blood of a goat, the ashes of a heifer, and some of the juice of hyssop, but it was too weak. (*For the law having a shadow of good things to come, and not the very image of the things, can never make perfect those who come by the same sacrifices which they offer year by year continually. Otherwise, they would cease to offer them, because those that sacrifice, once purged, would have no more conscience of sin. But in these sacrifices each year the same remembrance of sins is made. For the blood of bulls and of goats cannot take away sins. – Heb. 10:1-4*)

Dr. Skill

When Mr. Skill saw that that purge was too weak, he made one of the flesh and blood of Christ (*How much more shall the blood of the Christ, who through the eternal Spirit offered himself without spot to God, purge your conscience from the works of death to serve the living God? – Heb. 9:14*) (you know how physicians give strange medicines to their patients). It was made into pills, with a promise or two, and a proportional quantity of salt. (*For every one shall be salted with fire, and every sacrifice shall be salted with salt. – Mark 9:49*) The boy was to take them three at a time, in half a quarter pint of the tears of repentance. (*And I will pour upon the house of David and upon the inhabitants of Jerusalem the Spirit of grace and of prayer, and they shall look upon me whom they have pierced, and they shall mourn over him as one mourns for his only son, afflicting themselves over him as one afflicts himself over his firstborn. – Zech. 12:10*)

Once this potion had been prepared and brought to Matthew, he was reluctant to take it, even though he felt like the cramping was tearing his insides to pieces. "Come, come," the physician encouraged. "You must take it."

Matthew looked at him with his brow furrowed in distress. "It upsets my stomach."

"You must take it," his mother said.

"But I will only vomit it up again," he said.

"Please, sir," Christiana said to the doctor. "Can you tell me how it tastes?"

"It doesn't have a bad taste."

With that, Christiana touched one of the pills to the tip of her tongue. "Oh, Matthew," she said. "This potion is sweeter than honey. If you love your mother, if you love your brothers, if you love Mercy, and if you love your life, take it." So, with much fussing, after a short prayer for the blessing of God upon it, he took it and it affected him kindly. It caused him to purge, and then he fell asleep and rested quietly. His temperature returned to normal, and his pain disappeared. In a short time he got up and walked about with the support of a staff. He went from room to room and talked with Prudence, Piety, and Charity, about his disease and how he was healed.

So when Matthew was healed, Christiana asked Mr. Skill, "Sir, what is the cost for all your efforts regarding the care for my child?"

"According to the rules, you must pay the Master of Physicians." (*By him therefore let us offer the sacrifice of praise to God continually, that is, the fruit of our lips confessing his name.* – Heb. 13:15)

"But, sir," Christiana said. "What else is this pill good for?"

"It is a universal pill," Mr. Skill said. "It is good against all the diseases pilgrims are confronted with and when it is well prepared, it will keep for time immemorial."

Christiana said, "Please, sir, make me up twelve boxes of these pills; for if I can get these, I will never take another medicine."

Mr. Skill smiled. "These pills are good to prevent diseases as well as to cure when one is sick. I have to say that if a man would just use this medicine as he should, it will make him live forever. (*I AM the living bread which came down from heaven; if anyone eats of this bread, they shall live for ever; and the bread that I will give is my flesh, which I will give for the life of the world.* – John 6:51) However, Christiana, you must not administer these pills in any way other than the way I have prescribed; for if you do, they will do no good."

He gave Christiana medicine for herself, her boys, and for Mercy, and told Matthew to be careful not to eat any more green plums. Then he kissed each one and went his way.

As I mentioned earlier, Prudence had told the boys that if at any time they had beneficial questions to feel free to ask and she would be happy to answer them. After Matthew was well, he went to her and asked why for the most part medicine was bitter tasting.

"It shows how unwelcome the Word of God and the effects are to a fleshly carnal heart."

"And why does the medicine, if it does good, purge and cause one to vomit?"

Prudence said, "To show that the Word, when it works effectually, cleanses the heart and mind. For you see when it comes to purging and vomiting, what the one does to the body, the other does to the soul."

"What should we learn when we see a flame of fire go upwards, or when we see the sweet effects of sunbeams as they strike downwards?"

Prudence said, "When we see fire reaching upward, we learn to reach toward heaven with a fervent hot desire. And by sending the warmth and sweet influence of His sunbeams, we are reminded that although the Savior of the world is high above, He reaches down with His grace and love to us."

"Where do clouds get their water from?"

"Out of the sea," Prudence answered.

"And what may we learn from that?"

"That ministers should draw their doctrine from God," she said.

"And why do the clouds empty themselves upon the earth?"

"Just like clouds get their water from the sea and let it fall to the earth, ministers should give out what they know of God to the world."

Matthew nodded in understanding and asked, "Why does the sun cause a rainbow?"

"To show that the covenant of God's grace is confirmed to us in Christ."

"Why do the springs come to us through the earth from the sea?"

"To show that the grace of God comes to us through the body of Christ."

"And why do some springs rise from the tops of high hills?"

Prudence said, "To show that the Holy Spirit of grace can spring up in those who are great and mighty, as well as in many who are poor and humble."

"Why does fire fasten itself upon the candle wick?"

"To show that unless we have grace kindled in our hearts, there will be no true light of life in us."

"Why does the wick and wax all burn up to maintain the light of the candle?" Matthew pressed with another question.

"To show that body and soul and all should be used to help maintain the light of God's grace within us."

"Why does the pelican pierce her own breast with her bill?" the boy asked.

"To nourish her young ones with her own blood. In this way, she demonstrates how Christ blessed his young … his people whom he loved … and to save them from death by his blood."

"What can we learn when we hear the cock crow?"

Prudence said, "We can learn to remember Peter's sin and Peter's repentance. The cock's crowing also shows that that day is coming, and with that let it also remind you of the last – the terrible Day of Judgment."

Now about this time their month in the house was up, and they told those in the house, that it was time for them to be going. Joseph said to his mother, "Don't forget to write to the Interpreter, to ask him if Mr. Great Heart can be sent to escort us for the rest of the way."

"Good reminder, Joseph. I had almost forgotten." So she drew up a request and asked Watchful, the porter, to send it by a messenger to her good friend the Interpreter.

When it arrived at the Interpreter's house and he read the request, he said to the messenger, "Go tell them that I will send him."

When the family where Christiana was, saw that they were ready to travel on, they called the whole house together to give thanks to their King for sending them such pleasant guests. When they finished they said to Christiana, "Before you leave, may we show you something as we usually do with pilgrims? Something for you to think about as you travel?"

Christiana, her children, and Mercy agreed, so they took them into a closet and showed them one of the apples of the kind Eve ate from and which she also gave to her husband. It was after eating of this fruit that they were both turned out of paradise. They asked Christiana what she thought it was.

Christiana said, "It is either food or poison, I know not which." So they told her all about it, and she held up her hands in wonder. (*And when the woman saw that the tree was good for food, and that it was desirable to the eyes, and a tree of covetousness to understand, she took of its fruit and ate and gave also unto her husband with her; and he ate. – Gen. 3:6)*

They led her to another place where they showed her Jacob's ladder. (*And he dreamed, and behold a ladder set up on the earth, and the top of it reached to heaven; and behold the angels of God ascending and descending on it. – Gen. 28:12)* At that time there were angels climbing up it. So Christiana and the others watched the angels going up the ladder for some time, and then they were to be taken to another place to be shown something else. But James said to his mother, "Please, tell them we want to stay here a little longer, for this is a curious sight." So they stayed a little longer and feasted on the sight of this pleasant scene.

After a time, they led the pilgrims into a place where a golden anchor

Jacob's ladder

hung. They asked Christiana to take it down. For they said, "You shall have it with you, for it is absolutely necessary you have it so you may bring it within the veil (*Which we have as an anchor of the soul, both sure and steadfast, and which enters even into that which is within the veil* – Heb. 6:19), so you are able to stand steadfast in the event you meet with turbulent weather." (*The LORD also shall roar out of Zion and utter his voice from Jerusalem; and the heavens and the earth shall shake; but the LORD will be the hope of his people and the strength of the sons of Israel.* – Joel 3:16) It made the pilgrims happy.

Then they led the pilgrims to the mountain on which Abraham our father offered up Isaac his son, and showed them the altar, the wood, the fire, and the knife used, for they remain there to be seen to this very day. (*And when they came to the place which God had told him of, Abraham built an altar there and laid the wood in order and bound Isaac his son and laid him on the altar upon the wood.* – Gen. 22:9) When they saw these things, they held up their hands and enjoyed spiritual happiness and favor with God. They said, "Oh, what a man was Abraham, who loved his Master and denied himself in such a way!"

After they had showed them all these things, Prudence took them into a dining room, where a pair of excellent virginals[16] stood. She walked over and played one of them and turned the experience of what she had shown them into this excellent song:

> "Eve's apple we have showed you;
>   Of that be you aware.
> And you saw Jacob's ladder too,
>   Upon which angels dare.
>
> An anchor you received have,
>   But let not these suffice,
> Until with Abraham you have gave
>   Your best, a sacrifice."

Now, about this time, someone knocked at the door. When the Porter opened the door it was Great Heart. When he walked in, those in the room were filled with joy that he was there! Just seeing him again reminded them of how just a short while ago he had slain old Grim the giant, and how he had delivered them from the lions.

---

16   A musical instrument.

Great Heart said to Christiana and to Mercy, "My Lord has sent each of you a bottle of wine, and also some parched corn, along with a couple of pomegranates. He has also sent the boys some figs and raisins. All these things are to refresh you as you travel in the way."

Then they headed outside to continue on their journey. Prudence and Piety went along with them. When they came to the gate, Christiana asked the Porter if any other pilgrims had recently gone by.

He said, "No, only one person some time back, who told me that recently there had been a great robbery committed on the King's highway in the direction where they were headed. But, the thieves have been apprehended and will shortly be tried for their lives."

The news frightened Christiana and Mercy, but Matthew said, "Mother, don't be afraid since we have Mr. Great Heart as our guide."

Christiana nodded and looked at the Porter. "Sir, I am so grateful to you for all the kindness you have showed me, since I arrived here. I'm also thankful for how loving and kind you have been to my children. I don't know how I can ever repay your kindness, but I ask that you accept this small token of my respect for you." So she placed a gold angel[17] in his hand.

He bowed low in homage and said, "Let your garments always be white and let your head lack no ointment (Eccles. 9:8). Let Mercy live and not die and let her works not be few." (*Let Reuben live and not die, and let not his men be few. – Deut. 33:6*) And to the boys he said, "Flee youthful lusts, and follow after godliness with those who are earnest and wise (*Flee also youthful lusts, but follow righteousness, faith, charity, peace, with those that call on the Lord out of a pure heart. – 2 Tim. 2:22*); in this way you shall put gladness into your mother's heart and will find praise from all who are sober-minded."

So they thanked the Porter one last time and departed.

---

17   A gold angel was a coin of the value of ten shillings sterling, and according to the comparative value of money in Bunyan's time, equal at least to a guinea at the present time.

The Fifth Stage

---∽---

ow I saw in my dream, that they traveled onward until they came to the brow of the hill where Piety remembered something and cried out, "I forgot to give Christiana and her companions what I had intended to give them for the journey! I will hurry back and fetch it." So she ran and retrieved it, but while she was gone, Christiana thought she heard a most curious melodious note in a grove a little way off on the right side of the way. It was accompanied by words much like these:

> "Through all my life your favor is
> So freely showed to me,
> That in your house for evermore
> My dwelling-place shall be."

She continued to listen and thought she heard another answer it, saying:

> "For why? The Lord our God is good;
> His mercy is forever sure;
> His truth at all times firmly stood,
> And shall from age to age endure."

So Christiana asked Prudence who it was that made those curious notes.

She said, "They are country birds which sing these notes, but only in the spring when the flowers appear, and the sun shines warm. There are spring days when you may hear them all day long. In fact, I often go out to hear them, and we often even keep them tame in our house. For they make excellent company when we are feeling unhappy, and they also make the woods, groves, and other solitary places pleasant to be in." (*For, behold, the winter is past; the rain is over and gone; the flowers appear on the earth; the time of the song is come, and the voice of the turtle dove has been heard in our land.* – Song of Sol. 2:11, 12)

By this time Piety had returned. She said to Christiana, "Look here, what I have brought you! It is a representation of all the things you saw at our house. This way you can look at this whenever you find yourself forgetful. It will help you call to mind these things for your edification and comfort."

Now they followed the way down the hill and into the Valley of Humiliation. It was a steep slippery descent and they trod it very carefully until finally they reached the valley. Piety said to Christiana, "This is the place where Christian your husband met with the foul fiend Apollyon, and where they had that dreadful fight. I know you must have heard about it but don't worry, because as long as you have Great Heart as your guide, we have hope that you will fare better." So when Prudence and Piety had committed the pilgrims over to the oversight of their guide and conductor, Great Heart, he went ahead and they followed.

Then Great Heart said, "We need not be so afraid of this valley, for there is nothing to hurt us here, unless it is something we bring about ourselves. It is true, Christian met with Apollyon, and the two of them fought severely, but that skirmish was the result of those slips he made going down the hill. For you see, those who slip up there, must expect to enter combat here. In fact, this is how the valley got its hard name.

"For the common people, when they hear that some frightful thing has happened to someone in a place such as this, they think the place is haunted with some foul fiend, or evil spirit, when, sadly, it is the fruit of their own doing that such things happen to them there. This Valley of Humiliation is really as fruitful a place as any other over which the crow flies. I am convinced that if we could figure out a way, we may find something from around here that might give us a reason for why Christian was so severely harassed in this place."

Then James pointed ahead and said to his mother, "Look over there, it's a pillar. And it looks like something is written on it. Let's go and see what it says."

So they walked together to the pillar and read these words written on it: "Let Christian's unintentional errors and faults from before he came here, and the battles he met within this place, be a warning to those who come after."

"Look at that." Their guide, Great Heart gestured toward the pillar. "Didn't I tell you there was something around here that would give us an indication of why Christian was so severely harassed in this place?" Then he turned to Christiana and said, "This is no more criticism to Christian

The pillar in the Valley of Humiliation

than to any others who happen to come this way, for it is easier to go up than down this hill. And that can't be said about many hills in the world. But Christian was a good man. He is now at rest and in the end had a brave victory over his enemy. Let Him who lives above grant that we fare no worse than he did when it is our turn to be tried.

"But we will come again to this Valley of Humiliation. It is the best and most fruitful piece of ground in all these parts. As you see, it is fertile and has many meadows. If a man happened to come here in the summertime, as we have done, and if he didn't know anything of what has happened here in the past, he might look around in delight at all he sees. He'd see how green this valley is and how it is adorned with lilies. (*I am the lily of the field and the rose of the valleys.* – Song of Sol. 2:1)

"I have known many hard-working men who have good estates in this Valley of Humiliation, for God resists the proud, but gives grace to the humble. (*But he gives greater grace. Therefore he says, God resists the proud, but gives grace unto the humble.* – James 4:6) It is indeed a very fruitful soil, and it brings forth a bounty. Some have also wished they wouldn't be troubled by any more hills or mountains on the way, and that the next approach to their Father's house was right here. But the way is the way and eventually there is an end."

Now, as they were going along, and talking, they saw a boy feeding his father's sheep. The boy was dressed in very nasty clothes. In contrast, his countenance was very fresh and good-looking. He sat by himself and sang.

Great Heart said, "Listen to what the shepherd's boy sings." So they listened and this is what they heard:

"He who is down, needs fear no fall;
    He who is low, has no pride.
He who is humble ever shall
    Have God to be his guide.

I am content with what I have,
    Whether it be little or much.
Lord, contentment still I crave,
    Because you willingly save such.

Fullness to like kind, a burden is,
    To those who go on pilgrimage.
Here little, and hereafter bliss,
    Is best from Age to Age."

Then the guide said to the pilgrims, "Do you hear him? I have to say that this boy lives a happier life and wears more of that herb called heart-ease in his heart than one dressed in silk and velvet. For now, let us continue our conversation about life in this valley.

"Our Lord formerly had his country house in this valley. He loved being here and to walk these meadows, for he found the air clean and pleasant. Besides, here a man walks free from the noise and hurrying of this life. All the other lands are full of noise and confusion. Only in the Valley of Humiliation is a man not led about in busyness and hindered in his thinking as he is apt to be in other places. This is a valley nobody walks in except for those who love a pilgrim's life. And though Christian had the hard misfortune to meet with Apollyon here and to enter with him in a brisk confrontation, I must tell you that in the past, men have met with angels here (*Yea, he dominated the angel and prevailed; he wept and made supplication unto him; he found him in Bethel, and there he spoke with us; but the LORD is God of the hosts; the LORD is his memorial. – Hos. 12:4, 5*), have found pearls here (*Who, when he had found one pearl of great price, went and sold all that he had and bought it.* – Matt. 13:46), and have found the words of life in this place. (*Lord, to whom shall we go? thou hast the words of eternal life.* – John 6:68)[18]

"And like I told you, our Lord loved to walk here when he had his country house here, but along with that, he has left a yearly income to be faithfully paid at certain times to those who love and walk these grounds and care for them along the way and for their encouragement to continue on in their pilgrimage."

Now, as they went on, Samuel spoke to Great Heart. "Sir," he said. "I understand that my father and Apollyon had their battle in this valley, but where exactly did the fight take place? For I see this valley is large."

Great Heart said, "Your father battled with Apollyon at a place ahead of us where the passage is narrow, just beyond Forgetful Green. In fact, that place is the most dangerous place in all these parts. It is where others have been faced with difficulty, for if at any time pilgrims meet with any violence, it is when they forget what favors they have received and how unworthy they are of them. But we can talk more about the place when we come to it, for I am sure there remains to this day either some sign of the battle, or some monument to testify that such a battle was fought."

Mercy said, "I think I feel as well in this valley as I have felt anywhere else on our entire journey! I think it suits my spirit." She drew in a deep breath of the fresh air. "I love to be in such places, where there is no rattling of coaches or rumbling wheels. I think here one may, with such solitude and so little to disturb, think about what he is, where he came from, what he has done, and to consider what the King has called him to. Here in the quiet seclusion one may think deeply enough to break the heart and melt the spirit, until one's eyes brim like the fish-pools in Heshbon. (*Thy neck is as a tower of ivory; thine eyes like the fishpools in Heshbon by the gate of Bathrabbim; thy nose is as the tower of Lebanon which looks toward Damascus.* – Song of Sol. 7:4)

"Those who walk through this valley in justice and by divine will make it a well. The rain God sends down from heaven upon those who are here also fills the pools. This valley is also where the King will give vineyards

---

18   Original: *But he that sins against me wrongs his own soul; all those that hate me love death* –
      Prov. 8:36.

to those who are His, and those who go through it shall sing, as Christian did even though he met with Apollyon." (*And I will give her vineyards from there, and the valley of Achor for a door of hope; and she shall sing there as in the days of her youth and as in the day when she came up out of the land of Egypt. – Hos. 2:15*)

Great Heart nodded. "This is true. I have gone through this valley many times and never have I been better than when I am here. I have also been a guide to several pilgrims who all say the same thing. 'To this man will I look,' the King said, 'even to the one who is poor and of a repentant spirit, and who trembles at my word'" (Isa. 66:2).

Now they arrived at the place where the battle between Christian and Apollyon had been fought. Great Heart turned to Christiana, her children, and Mercy and said, "This is the place. It was here on this ground that Christian stood when Apollyon came against him." He pointed to some stones stained with blood. "Look here, and here. This is some of your husband's blood upon these stones to this day. Didn't I tell you there would be a sign or monument of the battle still remaining?

"And look over here, some of the pieces from Apollyon's broken darts. And see here." He gestured toward the ground. "You can still see here how they trampled the ground in this spot as they sought firm footing while they fought against each other. And here too, you can see how they split the stones in pieces with their side blows.

"Truly, Christian made sport of the man and proved himself as brave as Hercules. When Apollyon was beaten he retreated to the next valley, which is called the Valley of the Shadow of Death. We shall arrive there soon." Then he motioned to a nearby monument located next to the way. "And look over there; it is the monument to the battle and Christian's victory, and to his fame, throughout all ages."

So they gathered at the monument which stood just on the wayside before them and read the writing which word for word said this:

"Here was a hard battle fought,
    Most strange and yet most true.
Christian and Apollyon fought
    Each other to subdue.

The man so bravely played the man,
  He made the fiend to fly.
Of which a monument I stand,
  The same to testify."

When they traveled on they came upon the borders of the Shadow of Death. This Valley was longer than the other, and a place strangely haunted with evil things as many can testify. Things went better than expected for this group of women and children, because they had daylight, and because Great Heart was their guide.

When they were entering this valley, they thought they heard groaning like that of dying men. They weren't small whimpering sounds but an excessive moaning. Along with this noise, they thought they heard words of grief spoken by someone who sounded like they were being tormented. These sounds made the boys shake with fear, and the color drained from the women's faces until they looked pale, but their guide told them to take courage.

They walked on a little further, and they thought they felt the ground begin to shake like there was a hollow place beneath their feet. Plus they heard a kind of hissing noise like that of serpents. The combination of the two filled them with dread but nothing happened. The boys said, "When will we get to the end of this miserable place?"

Again, Great Heart encouraged them. He told them to take courage and to pay close attention to where they stepped, so they didn't by chance get caught in some snare.

Now James began to feel sick, but I think it was because he was so frightened. His mother pulled out that bottle of spirits she had been given at the Interpreter's house, and she gave some to James along with three of the pills Mr. Skill had prepared. The boy quickly began to feel better. So they went on till they reached about the middle of the valley. Then Christiana said, "I think I see something in the distance on the road ahead, but I can't make out what it is. I've never seen anything like it."

Joseph looked at his mother and asked, "What is it?"

She placed her arm around him and said, "An ugly thing, child; an ugly thing."

"But, Mother, what is it like?" he asked again.

She shook her head as she stared at the thing. "I cannot tell what it is even though we are getting closer to it."

"Well," Mr. Great Heart said. "Those of you who are most afraid stay close to me." So the ugly fiend came toward them and Great Heart met it, but when it came at him it vanished and none could see it. Then they remembered what had been said some time ago: "Resist the devil, and he will flee from you." (*Submit yourselves, therefore, to God. Resist the devil, and he will flee from you. – James 4:7*)

After that experience, they went on feeling a little refreshed, but they hadn't gone far before Mercy looked behind and thought she saw something like a lion but not a lion. It followed after them quickly with great padded footfalls, and it roared with an eerie hollow voice. Every time it roared, it echoed throughout the valley and made the pilgrims' hearts ache, except for the heart of their guide. As the threat drew closer Great Heart dropped back and walked behind the others and made them to walk before him.

The lion quickly cut the distance between them, and Great Heart turned to fight him. (*Be temperate and vigilant because your adversary the devil, as a roaring lion, walks about, seeking whom he may devour, resist him stead-fast in the faith, knowing that the same afflictions are to be accomplished in the company of your brethren that are in the world. – 1 Peter 5:8, 9*) But when the lion-like fiend saw that they had decided to resist him, he drew back and came no further.

Then they continued on again with Great Heart again before them, until they came to a great pit in the road. It took up the entire way from one side to the other, and before they could figure a way to get over it, a great mist and a darkness settled upon them. None of them could see anything, so they stood still in that place.

Then the pilgrims cried out, "Oh dear! What should we do now?"

But their guide said, "Don't fear, just stand still and see what happens."

They stayed there, because their path was damaged, and they couldn't see because of smoke coming from the pit marring the way. As they stood within the smog, they thought they heard another noise, this time like the rushing of the enemies. Gradually the group saw fire and smoke coming from the pit.

Christiana said to Mercy, "Now I see what my poor husband went through. I have heard much about this place, but I was never here until now. Poor man! He was here all alone at night. In fact, it was night for most of the time he walked the way through this valley. And these fiends were active and moving about him as if they would tear him in pieces. Many have spoken about it; but no one knows what the Valley of the Shadow of Death holds for them until they enter it themselves. (*The heart knows the bitterness of his soul, and a stranger shall not intermeddle with his joy.* – Prov. 14:10) To be here is a fearful thing."

Great Heart said, "This is like doing business in deep waters or like going down into the heart of the sea, and like going down to the bottoms of the mountains. Now it seems as if the barriers of earth are about us forever, but let those who walk in darkness and have no light, trust in the name of the Lord and stay upon their God. (*Who is among you that fears the LORD? Hearken unto the voice of his slave. He who walked in darkness and had no light; let him trust in the name of the LORD and stay upon his God.* – Isa. 50:10)

"For my part, as I have told you already, I have often walked through this valley and have faced much harder times than this. Yet you can see I am alive. When I say this, I am not boasting in myself in any way, for I am not my own savior. However, I have faith that we shall be delivered. Come, let us pray for light from him who can lighten our darkness and who can rebuke not only these fiends we are facing right now but all the Satans in hell."

So they cried out and prayed to God, and he sent light and deliverance. There was, now, no hindrance in their way, for the pit that had stopped them was no longer there. They continued on their way through the valley but met with some very bad odors and a detestable stench which annoyed them all a great deal.

Mercy said to Christiana, "Being here is not as pleasant as it was back at the gate, at the Interpreter's, or at the house where we stayed last."

One of the boys, Samuel, said, "Oh, it isn't as bad to go through here as it would be to live here forever. For all we know, one reason we must endure this stench on our way to the house prepared for us is that the home awaiting us might be all the sweeter to us when we arrive."

"Well said, Samuel," their guide said. "You have spoken like a man."

"Well, if ever I get out of this valley," the boy said, "I think I shall prize light a great deal more than I ever have in all my life."

Great Heart said, "We shall be out of here eventually."

They went on and after some time Joseph asked, "Can't we see to the end of this valley yet?"

Great Heart said, "Pay attention to your feet and where you step, for now we shall be walking among the snares." So the pilgrims watched where they stepped as they went on, but even so they were troubled by many snares. When they arrived among the snares, they saw a man thrown into the ditch on the left side of the way, with his flesh all slashed and torn.

Great Heart pointed toward the man and said, "That traveler was named Heedless. He was going this way but has lain there a great while. He had been traveling with a companion by the name of Take-Heed when he was abducted and slain, but Take-Heed escaped their hands. You cannot imagine how many are killed near this place, and yet men set out flippantly on pilgrimage and come without a guide. Poor Christian! It was a wonder he escaped this place, but he was beloved of his God and he also had a good heart. If that wasn't the case he could never have done it."

Now they drew towards the end of this way and came to the cave from which Maul, the giant, came forth when Christian approached on his pilgrimage. This Maul used to mess up young pilgrims with misleading reasoning, and at this time he called Great Heart by his name and said, "How many times have you been forbidden to do these things?"

Great Heart called back, "What things?"

"What things!" the giant roared. "You know what things! But I will put an end to your trade."

As the giant taunted them, the women and children trembled and clustered together, for they didn't know what else to do. Great Heart said, "Please, before we begin, let us understand the stakes for which we must fight."

The giant said, "You rob the country and rob it with the worst kind of thefts."

Great Heart shook his head. "You're only talking in generalities. Get to the point and speak specifics, man."

Then the giant said, "You are a kidnapper! You gather up women and children and carry them into a strange country. As a result you weaken my master's kingdom."

Great Heart replied, "I am a servant of the God of heaven. My business is to persuade sinners to repent. I am commanded to strive to turn men, women, and children, from darkness to light, and from the power of Satan to God. If this is, in fact, the reason for your quarrel, let us fall to it as soon as you are ready."

The giant stepped forward and Great Heart went to meet him. As he did so, he drew his sword while the giant readied his club. Without exchanging any more words they fell to blows. The giant struck the first blow. Great Heart dropped down onto one knee. When they saw this, the women and children cried out.

Great Heart recovered and stood to his full height. He thrust his weapon toward the giant and wounded his arm. In this way, the fight went back and forth for about an hour. As the fight heightened, the breath from the giant's nostrils grew as hot as the heat that radiates from a boiling cauldron.

Then the two of them took a break and sat down to rest. Great Heart took the time to pray, but the women and children did nothing but carry on with sighs and crying, for as long as the battle lasted.

When the giant and Great Heart had rested and caught their breath, they both fell to fighting again. With a blow Great Heart brought the giant

Great Heart kills giant Maul

down to the ground. The giant raised his hand and said, "No, hold on, let me recover."

So Great Heart fairly let him get up, and they started to fight again and the giant narrowly missed breaking Great Heart's skull with his club. When Great Heart saw that, he ran at him hard and fast with all his spirit, and pierced him under the fifth rib. With that, the giant grew faint. His club tumbled from his grasp. Great Heart landed a second blow and severed the head of the giant from his shoulders. The women and children rejoiced, and Great Heart praised God for the deliverance he had brought about.

With the fight finished and the victory won, the pilgrims erected a pillar and fastened the giant's head on it, and under it wrote the following words so those passing by might read it:

> *"He who once wore this head was one*
> *Who often passing pilgrims abused.*
> *He stopped their way, he spared none,*
> *But them afflicted and misused.*
>
> *Until I Great Heart arose,*
> *The pilgrims' guide to be,*
> *Until that time I did him oppose,*
> *That was their enemy."*

The Sixth Stage

ow I saw the pilgrims continue on to the ascent not far from there, for they determined it to be a possibility for pilgrims. This happened to be the place from which Christian had first caught sight of Faithful his brother. It was here the pilgrims sat down, rested, ate, drank, and celebrated because they had been delivered from this dangerous enemy. As they sat there eating, Christiana asked Great Heart whether or not he had been hurt in the battle.

He said, "No, except a little on my flesh, but that's not so bad. For it is proof of my love for my Master and you, and by grace, it shall be a means to increase my reward at the end."

"But weren't you afraid, good sir, when you saw him come at you with his club?" Christiana asked.

Great Heart said, "It is my duty to not trust in my own ability, so that I may rely only on Him who is stronger than all."

Christiana thought about that for a moment. "But what did you think when he brought you down to the ground with that first blow?"

"Why, I thought that in this way my Master was served, and it was He who conquered in the end." (*Always bearing about in the body the dying of the Lord Jesus, that the life also of Jesus might be made manifest in our body. For we who live are always delivered unto death for Jesus' sake that the life also of Jesus might be made manifest in our mortal flesh. – 2 Cor. 4:10, 11*)

Matthew said, "While you all can think what you please, I think God has been wonderfully good to us. He brought us out of this valley and delivered us from the hand of this enemy. As far as I am concerned, I see no reason why we should ever distrust our God again, since He has given us such a testimony of His love now in such a place." Then the group of them got up and continued forward on their journey.

Now a little ahead of them stood an oak. When they came to it they found an old pilgrim fast asleep under it. They recognized he was a pilgrim by his clothes, his staff, and the belt he wore around his waist.

So the guide, Great Heart, woke the old gentleman. As the old man opened his eyes he cried out, "What's the matter? Who are you and what is your business here?"

Great Heart tried to calm the man. "Calm down," he said. "Come on, we here are all friends."

But the old man rushed to his feet and was on guard because he did not know them or what they were.

Old Honest

Then the guide said, "My name is Great Heart. I am the guide of these pilgrims who are going to the Celestial country."

"My name is Mr. Honest," the old pilgrim said. "I ask your forgiveness for my reaction, for I feared you were part of the group who some time ago robbed Little-Faith of his money. Now that I'm more awake and aware of my surroundings, I can see you are more honest people."

Great Heart asked, "What do you think you could have done to help yourself, if we were in fact those people?"

"What could I have done!" the man said. "Why, I would have fought to my last breath, and if I had, I am sure you could never have bested me, for a Christian can never be overcome, unless he surrenders himself."

"Well said, father Honest," Great Heart said, "for by this I know you are a man of the right kind, for you have spoken the truth."

"And by this I also know that you know what true pilgrimage is," the old pilgrim said. "For everyone else thinks we are the quickest of any to overcome."

"Well," Great Heart said. "Now that we have happily met, please let me ask where you are from."

"I came from the town of Stupidity. It's the town just beyond the City of Destruction."

"Oh, you're that countryman?" Great Heart said. "I've heard you called Old Honesty."

The older gentleman blushed. "Not honesty in the abstract but Honest is my name. I have to admit, I wish my nature agreed with my name. But, sir, how is it you have heard of me?"

"I heard of you from my Master," Great Heart said. "He knows everything. But I have often marveled that anyone from your hometown became a pilgrim, for your town is worse than the City of Destruction."

Mr. Honest nodded. "I agree. Those of us from Stupidity lie more often than the sun shines, and because of it we are cold and senseless in heart. But even if a man were inside a mountain of ice, if the Sun of Righteousness arises upon him, his frozen heart will experience a thaw, and that is exactly what happened with me."

"I believe it, father Honest. I believe it. For I know what you say is true."

Then the old gentleman greeted all the pilgrims with a holy kiss of love, asked their names, and how they had fared since they set out on their pilgrimage.

Christiana stepped forward first. "I'm sure you have heard my name, for good Christian was my husband and these four are his children." She motioned toward her boys. You won't believe how the old gentleman reacted to the news of who she was. He skipped, he smiled, and he blessed them with a thousand good wishes.

He said, "I have heard so much about your husband and his travels, and the wars which he endured in his days. Be assured, the name of your husband resounds all through these parts of the world. He is famous for his faith, his courage, his endurance, and his sincerity."

Then he turned to the boys and asked their names, which they told him one by one. He greeted Matthew and said, "Matthew, you are like Matthew the tax collector, not in wickedness but in virtue." (*And as Jesus passed forth from there, he saw a man, named Matthew, sitting at the receipt of custom; and he said unto him, Follow me. And he arose and followed him.* – Matt. 9:9)[19]

---

19   Original: *Philip and Bartholomew; Thomas and Matthew the publican; James the son of Alphaeus, and Lebbaeus, whose surname was Thaddaeus* – Matt. 10:3.

He turned his attention to Samuel and said, "He is like Samuel the prophet, a man of faith and prayer." (*Moses and Aaron are among his priests and Samuel among those that call upon his name; they called upon the LORD, and he answered them.* – Psalm 99:6)

And to Joseph he said, "You are like Joseph in Potiphar's house, pure and one who flees from temptation." (*And it came to pass as she spoke to Joseph day by day, that he did not hearken unto her, to lie by her or to be with her. And it came to pass about this time, that Joseph went into the house to do his business, and none of those of the house were there within. And she caught him by his garment, saying, Lie with me; and he left his garment in her hand and fled and got outside.* – Gen. 39:10-12)

He turned to James, the last of the boys. "You are like James the just and like James the brother of our Lord." (*Is not this the carpenter's son? is not his mother called Mary? and his brothers, James and Joseph and Simon and Judas?* – Matt. 13:55)[20]

Then the boys told him about Mercy and how she had left her town and her family to come along with their mother and them on pilgrimage. At hearing this, the old honest man turned to Mercy and said, "Mercy is your name. By mercy you shall be sustained and carried through all the difficulties that assault you along your way until you come to that place where you will look directly at the Fountain of Mercy with comfort." (*Blessed are the merciful, for they shall obtain mercy.* – Matt. 5:7)

During all this exchange, Great Heart walked along with his companions very pleased and smiling at them. As they walked, Great Heart asked the old gentleman if he knew Mr. Fearing, for he had come on pilgrimage from those same parts as the old man.

"Yes, very well," he said. "He was a man who understood the root of the matter, but he was one of the most troublesome pilgrims I ever met in all my days."

Great Heart said, "I can see you knew him for you have given a very accurate description of his character."

"I more than knew him! I was one of his closest companions. I was with him most near the end, though I was also with him when he first started to think about what would come after this life."

---

20 Original: *And when they were come in, they went up into an upper room, where Peter and James and John and Andrew, Philip and Thomas, Bartholomew and Matthew, James the son of Alphaeus and Simon Zelotes, and Judas the brother of James were* – Acts 1:13.

Great Heart said, "I was his guide from my Master's house to the gates of the Celestial City."

"Then you knew him to be a troublesome one."

"I did." Great Heart nodded. "But I could bear it well enough. Men of my calling are often entrusted to conduct men such as him."

"Well," Mr. Honest said. "Tell us a little about him and how he behaved under your guidance."

"Well, he was always afraid he would fall short of reaching the place he desired to go. Everything frightened him. I heard that he lay roaring at the Slough of Despond for more than a month. In all that time, he didn't dare to move on, even though he witnessed several others crossing the Slough before him. And many of those people offered to lend him assistance but he was too afraid to accept it. He wouldn't go forward and he wouldn't go back again, either. He said he would die if he didn't get to the Celestial City, and yet he was discouraged by every difficulty and stumbled over problems as insignificant as straw when tossed in his way.

"After he had lain at the Slough of Despond a long time, one sunshiny morning he somehow ventured on and finally crossed over, though I don't know the details. He could hardly believe he had reached the other side. I think he had something like a Slough of Despond in his mind – like an internal mire that he carried with him everywhere he went. Otherwise he wouldn't have been so fearful of everything.

"So Mr. Fearing came up to the gate, you know the one I mean, the gate at the beginning of this way. There he stood for quite a while before he found the courage to knock. When the gate was opened, he stepped back and let others go before him and said he wasn't worthy. For, even though he reached the gate before others, many of them went in before him. There at the gate, the poor man stood shaking and cowering. I dare say anyone who saw him would have pitied him. Finally, he reached for the hammer which hung on the gate. He took it and rapped lightly a time or two. The gate opened to him, but he shrunk back again as he had done before.

"This time though, the one who opened the gate stepped out after Mr. Fearing and said, 'You who tremble, what do you want?'

"With that Mr. Fearing fell to the ground. He who spoke to him marveled to see him so faint-hearted, so he said to him, 'Peace be to you. Get up, for I have opened the door to you. Come in, for you are blessed.' With that he got up and went through the gate still trembling. Once he was in, he was too ashamed to show his face.

"Well, you know how it is there. After he had been shown hospitality for a while, he was told it was time to be on his way and also told the way he should take. So Mr. Fearing went on till he reached our house, but when he arrived and my Master came to the Interpreter's door, Mr. Fearing behaved the same fearful way as at the gate. He lay there in the cold for a good while, before he would say anything. He allowed his fear to paralyze him. The nights were long and cold then. And it is sad but true that in his chest pocket Mr. Fearing had a note that would allow him to receive all my Master had to offer. He was ready to grant him the comfort of His house and also to provide him with a brave and valiant guide, because he himself was so chicken-hearted. Yet even though Mr. Fearing understood all this, he was still afraid to call at the door.

"Instead, he lay here and there near the door until the poor man was almost starved, and his depression was so great that even though he saw several others knocking and entering in, he was just too afraid to even try. Finally, I think I looked out of the window and saw a man lying here and there around the door and I went out to him. I asked him what he was doing there, but the poor man looked at me with tear-filled eyes without saying a word. I figured out what he wanted, so I went inside and told the others in the house about him, and we explained the situation to our Lord. So he sent me out again, to invite Mr. Fearing to come in, but I have to say, it wasn't easy. Finally he did come in and my Lord lovingly carried nourishment to him. There wasn't much food at the table, but the Master took some of it and placed it upon the table in front of Mr. Fearing.

"Then Mr. Fearing presented the note from his pocket, and my Lord read it and said his desires would be granted. So when he had been there a good while, Mr. Fearing seemed to gather a little courage and to be a little more comfortable. For my Master, you must know, is one who is very kind and compassionate, especially toward those who are afraid. Therefore, He introduced everything to him in ways that might encourage him the most.

"Well, when he experienced all the things at the house, he was ready to take his journey to the Celestial City as Christian had done before him. My Lord gave him a bottle of spirits and some rich foods to eat. And so we set out together and I led the way, but Mr. Fearing hardly said a thing. Instead he sighed aloud as we walked together.

"When we came to the place where the three fellows were hanged, he said he doubted that he wouldn't end up the same way. Yet he seemed glad when he saw the cross and the sepulchre. There he wanted to linger a little, and it seemed to cheer him up for a little while. When he came to the Hill Difficulty he didn't hesitate at that, nor did he fear the lions very much. This might seem strange for one so fearful, but his troubles were not related to things like these. His fear was about whether or not he would be accepted at the end of his journey.

"I got him in at the House Beautiful, I think before he was really willing. Once he was inside, I introduced him to the young women who lived there, but he was too ashamed to take advantage of their company. He just wanted to be alone, yet he always loved a good talk and often stood out of

Mr. Fearing in the Valley of Humiliation

sight and listened to others' conversations. He also loved to see ancient things and to think about them. After we left that house, he told me he loved the visit. In fact, he enjoyed the last house as well as the one at the gate and the Interpreter's house, but even though he loved the ancient things found in these places, he couldn't find the courage to ask about them.

"When we left the House Beautiful we walked down the hill into the Valley of Humiliation and he entered the valley like one without a care, for he thought he might be happy at last. And, I think there was a kind of understanding between that Valley and him, for I never saw him in better spirits in all his pilgrimage than he was in that Valley.

"Here he lay down and embraced the ground and kissed the flowers. (*It is good for the man if he bears the yoke from his youth. He shall sit alone and keep silence because he has borne it upon him. He shall put his mouth in the dust; if so be there may be hope.* – Lam. 3:27-29) He woke every morning by break of day and regularly walked to and fro in the valley.

"But when he reached the entrance of the Valley of the Shadow of Death, I thought I might lose him. Not that I thought he would turn around to go back, for I knew he abhorred that idea. His problem was that he was ready to die of fear. He cried out, 'Oh, the hobgoblins will get me! The hobgoblins will get me!' I couldn't snap him out of it. He made so much noise! If they happened to hear him, it was enough to encourage them to come and attack us.

"But one thing I noticed as we entered this valley was how quiet it was. I'd never seen it so quiet, before or since. I suppose the Lord specially restrained those enemies and commanded them not to meddle until Mr. Fearing had passed through the valley.

"It would be too tedious to tell you all the details, so I'll just tell you about two more aspects of the journey with Mr. Fearing. The first is when he came to Vanity Fair. You should have seen him there. I thought he was going to fight with all the men in the fair and that we'd end up getting knocked on the head. His temper was hot against their habitual sinful acts. Upon the Enchanted Ground, he was very alert and wakeful, but when he reached the river and realized there was no bridge he again became dejected. 'Now, now,' he said, 'I will be drowned forever and never see the comfort of the face I have come so many miles to behold.'

"And at this time I noticed something very remarkable. At this particular time, the water of that river was lower than I'd ever seen it in all my life. So he finally crossed over without getting much more than his feet wet. When he was going up to the gate, I said good-bye to him and wished him a good reception above. He said, 'I shall, I shall.' Then we parted ways, and I never saw him again."

"So it seems all went well for him in the end?" Mr. Honest asked.

Great Heart nodded. "Absolutely. I never had doubts about him. He was a man of a worthy spirit, but most of the time he felt very low and that made his life very arduous for himself and very troublesome to others. (*O LORD God of my saving health, I cry day and night before Thee; let my prayer come before thee; incline thine ear unto my cry; for my soul is full of troubles, and my life draws near unto Sheol. I am counted with those that go down into the pit; I am as a man that has no strength: Freed among the dead, like the slain that lie in the grave, whom thou dost remember no more; and they are cut off from thy hand. Thou hast laid me in the lowest pit, in darkness, in the deeps. Thy wrath lies hard upon me, and thou hast afflicted me with all thy waves. Selah.* – Psalm 88:1-7)

"He had positive attributes as well. He was more sensitive to sin than many, and he was so afraid of hurting others that he often didn't do things he thought might offend, even if they were lawful." (*It is good neither to eat flesh nor to drink wine nor do any thing by which thy brother stumbles or is offended or is sick.* – Rom. 14:21)

Mr. Honest's brow furrowed. "But why would such a good man be forced to live so much of his life in such a disheartening way?"

"There are two possible reasons," Great Heart said. "One is that the wise God desires it. Some people must make a lot of noise and others must weep. (*Jesus said unto him, If I will that he tarry until I come, what is that to thee? follow thou me.* – John 21:22)[21] The other is best explained if we look at it like music. Think of Mr. Fearing as one who played a deep tone. While he and those like him sound notes that are more doleful than the notes of other music, some say the bass notes are the foundation of music. And for my part, I don't like that statement because, while it reflects a mindful sorrow, it does not address the weakness of mind some experience. The first string the musician usually touches is the bass, when he intends to put all in tune. God also plays upon this string first, when he sets the soul in tune for himself. Only there was the imperfection of Mr. Fearing in that he couldn't play any other music, until later when he neared the end."

[I've made this bold metaphorical statement to help mature the understanding of young readers, and because, in the book of Revelation, the saved are compared to a company of musicians, who play upon their trumpets and harps, and sing their songs before the throne. (*And when he had taken the book, the four animals and the twenty-four elders fell on their faces before the Lamb, each one of them having harps, and golden vials full of incense, which are the prayers of saints.* – Rev. 5:8)]

---

21   Original: *But unto whom shall I liken this generation? It is like unto children sitting in the markets and shouting unto their fellows* – Matt. 11:16.

Mr. Honest said, "By what you have said, Mr. Fearing was a very zealous man. He didn't fear difficulties, lions, or Vanity Fair; it was only sin, death, and hell that filled him with terror, because he had some doubts about his share in that Celestial country."

"You are right," Great Heart said. "Those were the things that troubled him, and they, as you have correctly observed, arose from the weakness of his mind. His fearfulness was not from weakness of spirit pertaining to the practical aspect of living a pilgrim's life. I believe, like the proverb says, that he could have bit a firebrand and withstood it in his own way and not feared it in the least, but the things with which he was oppressed, no man could ever help him shake off easily."

Then Christiana said, "Hearing about Mr. Fearing and his struggles has done me good, because I thought nobody else was like me. But now I see a similarity between this good man and me. We just differed in two ways. His troubles were so great that they showed to everyone around him, but mine I kept inside. His struggle made his life so difficult that he could not knock at the door to the very houses willing to show him hospitality, while my trouble was such that it made me always knock even louder."

Mercy said, "I'd also like to speak my heart if you'll permit me. For I must say, I too am similar to him in another way. For I have always been more afraid of the lake and the loss of a place in paradise than I have been about the loss of other things. Oh, I thought, if only I had the assurance to know I have a place there! It would be enough! I would give up everything I have in all this world to win it."

Matthew said, "I experienced fear too, but for me it was a fear that perhaps I wasn't saved – that I lacked within me the thing that accompanies salvation. But now that I know how it was for Mr. Fearing and that he arrived at the Celestial City and gained admittance, why wouldn't it go well with me, too?"

His brother James said, "No fears, no grace. Though there isn't always grace where there is the fear of hell, you can be sure there is no grace where there is no fear of God."

"Well said, James," Great Heart said. "You have hit the mark of this matter. For the fear of God is the beginning of wisdom. (*The fear of the LORD is the beginning of wisdom, and the knowledge of the holy is understanding.* – Prov. 9:10) Those who haven't reached the beginning don't have the middle nor the end – in other words, until that point they haven't feared hell. We have talked enough about Mr. Fearing for now, but let's finish off our discussion with this farewell to the good man:

> *"Well, Master Fearing, you did fear*
> *Your God and were afraid.*
> *Of doing anything while here,*
> *That would have you betrayed.*
>
> *And you feared the lake and pit,*
> *Would others do so too!*
> *As for them who lack your wit,*
> *They themselves undo."*

Now I saw that they still went on with their talk. For after Great Heart ended the discussion about Mr. Fearing, Mr. Honest began to tell the others of another traveler by the name of Mr. Self-will. "He pretended to be a pilgrim," Mr. Honest said. "But I am convinced that he never came in at the gate that stands at the head of the way."

"Did you ever talk with him about it?" Great Heart asked.

Mr. Honest nodded. "Yes, more than once or twice but he was always self-willed, doing what was right in his own eyes. He didn't care what

Honest tells about one Self-will

others said or did, and he didn't care to enter into discussion or argument regarding the truth, nor was he willing to learn from others' examples. All he did is what he wanted to do and follow his own way and nothing else."

"Please tell me more about the principles he held, for I'm sure you can tell me since you spent time with the man."

Mr. Honest said, "He held that a man could follow the vices as well as the virtues of pilgrims and that if he lived his life doing both he would still certainly be saved."

Great Heart frowned. "How could he think that? I could understand if he had said it is possible for the best pilgrim to be guilty of the vices, as well as to partake of the virtues. If that's what he said then he would have been correct, for while we are on this side of the river we are not expected to live absolutely vice-free; however, we are to watch and strive to live vice-free. But if I understand you correctly, this is not what he meant. But rather he meant that it was allowable for a pilgrim to continue on doing as he pleased, right or wrong."

Mr. Honest bobbed his head earnestly. "Yes, yes, that is exactly what I mean. That's what he believed and that's how he lived his life."

"But what did he base this belief on?" Great Heart asked.

"Why, he said he had Scripture that backed him up and permitted him to live this way."

Great Heart's brows raised in mild surprise. "Really? Scripture? Can you give us a few examples?"

"I will try to explain it as he did. For instance, he said to have other men's wives was permitted because David, God's beloved, had done so. His reasoning was that since David did it, he could do it. He said that having more than one woman was permitted because it was a thing practiced by Solomon. He also said that Sarah and the godly midwives of Egypt lied, and so did Rahab when she hid the spies, and therefore he could lie. He also said that the disciples went at the bidding of their Master and untied the ass that did not belong to them and took it, and so it is fine for him to take what belongs to others, too. He said that Jacob got the inheritance from his father through guile and dishonesty and therefore he could practice such things as well."

Great Heart shook his head thoughtfully. "He has certainly raised the lowest types of behavior as his examples! And you are sure this was his opinion?"

"Yes," Mr. Honest said. "I heard him plead his case for it and he pointed to Scripture to support such beliefs and to bring arguments for it into discussions with others."

Great Heart said, "His is an erroneous opinion that should not be allowed in the world!"

"Let me clarify one thing," Mr. Honest said. "He did not say that this behavior is permitted for everyone, but only for those who did such things before they were saved. For them it is, according to him, permitted to continue doing the same."

"But this is a false conclusion. For it is the same as saying that because good men, until now, have been weak and sinned, that it is okay for them to continue in this way and to do so on purpose and without any shame. Or it is like saying because a child is blown by a blast of wind or stumbles over a stone and falls in the mire and becomes filthy, that he should willfully lie down and wallow like a pig in the muck. Who would have thought that anyone could have been so blinded by the power of lust to this extent? But what is written must be held as true: they 'stumble at the word, being disobedient; to which they were also appointed.' (*And a stone of stumbling and a rock of offense, even to those who stumble at the word, not obeying in that for which they were ordained.* – 1 Peter 2:8)

"His supposing that people who addict themselves to their vices may also have godly virtues is a strong delusion. To eat up the sin of God's people (*They eat up the sin of my people, and in their iniquity they raise up their soul.* – Hos. 4:8), like a dog licks up filth, does not reveal that such a person even possesses virtues. Nor can I believe that one who holds to this opinion can presently have faith or love in him. I know you have made strong objections against him regarding this view. When you did, what could he say for himself?"

Mr. Honest shrugged. "Why, he says to live life based on one's own opinion seems abundantly more honest than to live in a way that is contrary to it."

Great Heart let out a deep sigh. "That is a very wicked answer. For if we freely let our lusts reign, it is sin. While it seems bad to hold back such feeling based on our opinions, yet not to do so is worse. When a person stumbles accidentally it is bad enough, but allowing your lusts to go unbridled leads into the snare."

Mr. Honest said, "There are actually many who think as this man does, who do not speak out like he does, but they do purposely make going on pilgrimage seem of little importance."

Great Heart nodded his head in resignation. "That is the sad truth, 'but he who fears the King of paradise shall come out from those who believe this way.'"

Christiana said, "There are strange opinions in the world. I knew one person who said that there was time enough to repent when it comes time to die."

"That's not very wise," Great Heart said. "If that unwilling man were to plan a journey, and he had a week to run twenty miles to complete the trip, would he defer his journey to the last hour of that week?"

"You're right," Mr. Honest said. "Yet most of those who count themselves pilgrims do just that. I am, as you see, an old man and have been a traveler on this road for many a day; and I have taken notice of many things.

"I have seen some who have set out with so much enthusiasm that it seemed as if they would drive all the world before them, and yet in a few days they died like those in the wilderness who never got to see the promised land. I have also seen some who promised nothing when they first set out to be pilgrims. If you saw pilgrims such as these, you would think them unable to survive a day, and yet they proved very good pilgrims. I have seen some who have run quickly forward only to have them run back quickly again after a little time. I have seen some who have spoken very well of a pilgrim's life at the beginning but after a while have spoken just as much against it. I have also heard some who speak positively when they first set out for paradise. They say, 'there is such a place,' but when they almost get there, they come back again and say, 'there is no such place.' I have heard some boast about what they would do if they should be opposed, who even at a false alarm have fled faith, the pilgrim's way, and all."

Now, as they were on their way a man came running to meet them and said, "Gentlemen, women and children, if you love life, change directions for robbers are before you!"

Great Heart said, "They are the three who formerly assaulted Little-Faith, but we are ready for them." So they cautiously continued on their way and looked this way and that wherever there was a turn or place where the villains could try to ambush them. But whether the robbers had heard of Great Heart's reputation or it was some other reason, the three robbers never even approached the pilgrims.

Christiana wished for an inn to refresh herself and her children because they were weary. Mr. Honest said, "There is an inn a short distance ahead of us, where a very honorable disciple by the name of Gaius dwells." (*Gaius my host, and of the whole congregation, salutes you.* – Rom. 16:23)

They all decided to turn in there and refresh themselves since the old gentleman had given them such a good report. When they came to the door they went in without knocking, for folks didn't used to knock at the door of an inn. Then they called for the master of the house, and he came to them. So they asked if they might spend the night.

Gaius said, "Yes, gentlemen, if you are true believers, for my house is only for pilgrims." This news made Christiana, Mercy, and the boys happy, because the innkeeper showed love for pilgrims. The pilgrims were appointed rooms. Gaius showed one for Christiana, her children and Mercy, and another for Great Heart and Mr. Honest.

Great Heart said, "Good Gaius, do you have anything for supper?" He gestured toward the others. "These pilgrims have come far today and are weary."

"It is late," Gaius said. "Too late to go out to look for food, but what we have you are welcome to, if that will do."

"We will be perfectly content with whatever you have in the house; for as much as I have ascertained, you are never needy if you are satisfied with what is on hand."

Then Gaius went down and spoke to the cook, whose name was, Taste-that-which-is-good, and instructed him to get supper ready for so many pilgrims. When he finished he returned to the pilgrims and said, "Come, my good friends, you are welcome to join me. I am glad I have this house and that I am able to show you hospitality. While supper is being prepared, let us sit and entertain one another with some good discussion, if you please."

The pilgrims all nodded and said they would be delighted to join him.

Gaius opened the discussion by asking about Christiana and the others. "Whose wife is this older woman, and whose daughter is this young woman?"

Great Heart motioned toward Christiana and said, "This woman is the wife of a former pilgrim by the name of Christian and these are his four children." Then he nodded toward Mercy. "The young lady is a friend of hers, one whom she persuaded to come with her on pilgrimage. The boys all take after their father and desire to walk in his steps. And if they come across any place where their father has lain on pilgrimage, or even happen to see the print of his foot, it ministers to them and fills their hearts with joy, and they crave to lie or walk in the same way."

Gaius said, "Is this Christian's wife? And these Christian's children? I knew your husband's father, and also his father's father. Many good men have come from this stock. Their ancestors first lived at Antioch. (*And the disciples were called Christians first in Antioch.* – Acts 11:26) Christian's ancestors, I suppose you have heard your husband talk of them, were very worthy men. They have, above any others I know of, showed themselves men of great virtue and courage for the Lord of the pilgrims, his ways and those who loved him.

"I have heard of many of your husband's ancestors who have stood all manner of trials for the sake of the truth. Stephen, who was one of the first of the family from which your husband's family line sprang, was stoned to death. (*And they stoned Stephen calling upon God and saying, Lord Jesus, receive my spirit. And he kneeled down and cried with a loud voice, Lord, impute not this sin to their charge. And having said this, he fell asleep in the Lord.* – Acts 7:59, 60)

"James, another from that same generation was slain with the edge of the sword. (*And he killed James the brother of John with the sword.* – Acts 12:2). To say nothing of Paul and Peter, men anciently related to the family from which your husband came, and Ignatius, who was thrown to the lions; Romanus, whose flesh was cut by pieces from his bones; and Polycarp, who played the man in the fire when they tried to burn him at the stake. When the flames didn't hurt him they stabbed him.

"Then there was he who was hung up in a basket in the sun for the wasps to eat, and he whom they stuffed into a sack and cast into the sea to be drowned. It would be impossible to count all from that family who suffered injuries and death for the love of a pilgrim's life. And I can't help but be glad to see that your husband has left behind four fine boys such as these. I hope they will endure and carry on their father's name and walk in his steps, and that they eventually arrive at the same final destination as their father."

"In reality, sir," Great Heart said, "The lads are likely to do just that for they seem to enthusiastically choose their father's ways. For this reason Christian's family is likely to continue to spread abroad and to be numerous upon the face of the earth. Let Christiana look for appropriate young women to which her sons may be betrothed, so that the name of their father, and the house of his ancestors may never be forgotten in the world."

Mr. Honest said, "It would be a pity if his family should become extinct."

"It cannot fail, but it may become diminished. But let Christiana take my advice and it will be sustained. And, Christiana …" He turned to speak directly to her. "I am glad to see you and your friend, Mercy, together here. If I may offer advice, I suggest you take Mercy to one of your closest relations. In fact, if she will consider the idea, I suggest she be given to Matthew, your oldest son as a wife. This is the way to preserve future generations here on the earth."

Gaius proposes marriage for Matthew and Mercy

So these two young people were matched and over time they were married but we can tell more about that later.

Gaius's advice continued. "I will now speak on the behalf of women to take away their disgrace. For as death and the curse came into the world by a woman (*And when the woman saw that the tree was good for food, and that it was desirable to the eyes, and a tree of covetousness to understand, she took of its fruit and ate and gave also unto her husband with her; and he ate. – Gen. 3:6*), so life and health also came into the world in the same way. God sent forth His Son, made of a woman. (*But when the fullness of the time was come, God sent forth his Son, born of a woman, born under the law. – Gal. 4:4*)

"It is clear how much women who were born later detested what the first mother did. You can see it in how much women in the Old Testament desired children, for they looked forward to the fact that this or that woman might become the mother of the Savior of the world. I will say again that when the Savior came, women rejoiced in Him more than in either man or angel. (*And she spoke out with a loud voice and said, Blessed art thou among women, and blessed is the fruit of thy womb. And whence is this to me, that the mother of my Lord should come to me? For, behold, as soon as the voice of thy salutation sounded in my ears, the babe leaped in my womb for joy. And blessed is she that believed, for there shall be a performance of those things which were told her from the Lord. Then Mary said, My soul magnifies the Lord. – Luke 1:42-46*)

"I have never read about any man giving even one coin to Christ, while the women who followed Him ministered to Him of their means. (*And certain women, who had been healed of evil spirits and infirmities: Mary called Magdalene, out of whom went seven devils, and Joanna the wife of Chuza, Herod's steward, and Susanna, and many others who ministered unto him of their substance. – Luke 8:2, 3*)

"It was a woman who washed His feet with tears. (*And, behold, a woman who had been a sinner in the city, when she knew that Jesus sat at food in the Pharisee's house, brought an alabaster box of ointment, and stood at his feet behind him weeping and began to wash his feet with tears and wiped them with the hairs of her head and kissed his feet and anointed them with the ointment. Now when the Pharisee who had invited him saw it, he spoke within himself, saying, This man, if he were a prophet, would have known who and what manner of woman this is that touches him, for she is a sinner. And Jesus answering said unto him, Simon, I have something to say unto thee. And he said, Master, say on. There was a certain creditor who had two debtors: the one owed five hundred denarius, and the other fifty. And when they had nothing to pay, he released them both from their debt. Tell me therefore, which of them will love him most? Simon answered and said, I suppose that he to whom he forgave most. And he said unto him, Thou hast rightly judged. And he turned to the woman and said unto Simon, Seest thou this woman? I entered into thy house, thou didst give me no water for my feet; but she has washed my feet with tears and wiped them with the hairs of her head. Thou gavest me no kiss; but this woman since the time I came in has not ceased to kiss my feet. Thou didst not anoint my head with oil; but this woman has anointed my feet with ointment. Therefore I say unto thee, Her sins, which are many, are forgiven; for she loved much; but to whom little is forgiven, the same loves little. And he said unto her, Thy sins are forgiven.* – Luke 7:37-48) And a woman anointed His body at the burial. (*It was that Mary who anointed the Lord with ointment and wiped his feet with her hair whose brother Lazarus was sick.* – John 11:2) It was women who wept when He was going to the cross (*And there followed him a great company of people, and of women, who also bewailed and lamented him.* – Luke 23:27), and women stayed with Him as He hung from the cross. (*And many women were there beholding afar off, who followed Jesus from Galilee, ministering unto him; among whom was Mary Magdalene and Mary the mother of James and Joses and the mother of the sons of Zebedee.* – Matt. 27:55, 56)

"Women also accompanied His body to the sepulchre when He was buried (*And there was Mary Magdalene and the other Mary, sitting over against the sepulchre.* – Matt. 27:61), and women were the first to be with Him on His resurrection morning (*Now upon the first of the sabbaths, very early in the morning they came unto the sepulchre, bringing the spices which they had prepared, and certain others with them.* – Luke 24:1), and women were the first to bring news of His resurrection to His disciples. (*Although also certain women of our company made us astonished, who before daybreak were at the sepulchre; and when they did not find his body, they came, saying that they had also seen a vision of angels, who said that he was alive.* – Luke 24:22, 23) Based on these examples and more, it is clear women are highly favored and sharers with us in the grace of life."

Now the cook sent a message to let them know supper was almost ready and to set the table with a cloth, plates, salt and bread. Matthew said, "Just seeing the tablecloth and all the preparations for supper makes me even hungrier than before."

Gaius said, "Let all the truths of the gospel minister to you in the same way in this life, stirring a greater desire to sit at the supper of the great King in his kingdom. For all preaching, books, and established rites and ceremonies here on earth are like laying the tablecloth, plates and salt upon the table, when compared with the feast which our Lord will prepare for us when we come to his house."

Supper was served. First a right-shoulder roast, which represented a heave offering, was brought to the table, followed by the breast of the wave offering. Each was set on the table to remind the pilgrims to begin their meal with prayer and praise to God, in the same way David lifted the heave-shoulder and wave-breast along with his heart up to God to show where his heart lay. Following this he used to play his harp. (*And the waved breast and elevated shoulder shall ye likewise eat in a clean place, thou and thy sons and thy daughters with thee; for they are thy due and thy sons' due, which are given out of the sacrifices of the peace of the sons of Israel. With the offerings of the fat which are to be lit on fire, they shall bring the shoulder which is to be elevated and the breast which shall be waved as a wave offering before the LORD; and it shall be thine and thy sons' with thee by a perpetual statute, as the LORD has commanded. – Lev. 10:14, 15*) These two dishes were very fresh and good, and they all ate heartily.

Next a bottle of wine, red as blood, was brought to the table. (*And thou didst drink the blood of the grape, pure wine. – Deut. 32:14*)

Gaius said to them, "Drink freely. This is the true juice of the vine that makes the heart of God and man glad." So they drank and were merry.

Next a dish of fresh, delicious milk was served. Gaius said, "Let the boys have that, to help them grow. (*Having therefore left all malice and all guile and hypocrisies and envies and all murmurings, as newborn babes, desire the rational milk of the word, that ye may grow thereby in health. – 1 Peter 2:1, 2*)

Among the courses they brought up a dish of butter and honey. This time Gaius said, "Eat freely of this, for this is good to cheer up and strengthen your mind in understanding and when making judgments. This was our Lord's dish when he was a child. 'Butter and honey shall he eat, that he may know to refuse the evil and choose the good.'" (*He shall eat butter and honey that he may know to refuse the evil and choose the good.* – Isa. 7:15)

Next they brought a dish of fresh, tasty apples to the table. Matthew asked, "May we eat apples since it was by this fruit the serpent deceived our first mother?"

Gaius nodded. "Apples were the fruit by which we were deceived. Yet sin, not apples, has defiled our souls. It is not the actual eating of the apple that corrupts. To eat this fruit does us good, for it is written, 'Drink of his flagons then, you church, his dove, and eat his apples, those who are sick from love'" (Song of Sol. 2:5).

Then Matthew said, "I had misgivings because a while back I was sick because I ate fruit."

Gaius said, "Forbidden fruit will make you sick, but not what our Lord has allowed."

While they were talking about this, another dish was presented. This one was a dish filled with nuts. (*I went down into the garden of nuts to see the fruits of the valley, and to see whether the vines flourished, and the pomegranates budded.* – Song of Sol. 6:11)

Some at the table said, "Nuts ruin tender teeth, especially the teeth of children."

When Gaius heard this he said:

"*Hard texts are nuts (I will not call them cheaters).*
  Hard shells keep the kernel from the eaters.
Open the shells and you shall have the meat.
  These have been brought to the table for you to crack and eat."

Then the pilgrims were very merry and sat at the table a long time talking about many things. Then, the old gentleman, Mr. Honest said, "My good innkeeper, while we crack your nuts, will you please explain this riddle?

"*A man there was, though some did count him mad,*
  The more he cast away, the more he had."

Then they all paid close attention, waiting to see what good words Gaius would have to say. For a moment he sat still. Then he said, "He who gives his goods to the poor shall have it return to him and ten times more."

Joseph's eyes grew wide. "I have to say, sir, I did not think you could have figured it out."

"Oh," Gaius said. "I have been trained up in this way a great while.

Nothing teaches like experience. Through experience, I have gained an understanding of the kindness of the Lord. There are those who scatter and yet increase; and there those who withhold more than they should but it leads to poverty: There are those who make themselves rich, yet have nothing, and those who make themselves poor, yet hath great riches." (*There are those who scatter, and more is added unto them; and there are those who withhold more than is just, but come to poverty. – Prov. 11:24*)

Then Samuel whispered to Christiana, his mother, and said, "Mother, this is a very good man. Let us stay here in his house for a good while, and let my brother Matthew be married here to Mercy, before we go any further."

Gaius overheard Samuel's suggestion and said, "That's a very good idea, my child."

As a result, they stayed there more than a month and Mercy was given to Matthew as his wife. And while they stayed there, Mercy made coats and garments to give to the poor, which gave the pilgrims a very good reputation.

But let's get back to our story. After supper the boys were ready to go to bed, for they were weary from travelling. Gaius called someone to show them to their bedchamber; but Mercy said, "I will tuck them in."

Mercy clothes the poor

She took them to their bedchamber, tucked them in, and they slept well. But the rest of the group sat up all night, for Gaius and the others enjoyed each other's company so much they didn't want to say good-night. After they talked much about their Lord, themselves, and their journey, old Mr. Honest began to nod off.

Great Heart said, "What? Are you getting drowsy? Come on, here's a riddle for you to think about."

"Let us hear it," Mr. Honest said.

Great Heart said, "He who would kill must first be overcome. He who would live abroad first must die at home."

"Ha," said Mr. Honest. "That is a hard one; hard to explain and harder to practice. I will leave it to you, innkeeper, if you please, to expound it, for I would like to hear what you have to say."

"No." Gaius shook his head. "The riddle was put to you and you are expected to answer it."

So the old gentleman answered thus:

> "He first by grace must conquered be,
>   So that sin will mortify;
>   So he who lives would convince me,
>   Unto himself must die."

"That is right," Gaius said. "This answer contains good doctrine and knowledge to be taught to others. Until grace (Jesus Christ) displays itself and overcomes the soul with its glory, it is altogether impossible to oppose sin. For if sin is the cord by which Satan binds the soul, how would it be possible for it to resist before it is loosed from that bondage?

"Secondly, whether by reason or grace, no one will believe that a man who is a slave to his own corruptions can be a living testament of that grace. And talking about this has brought a story worth telling to mind.

"There were two men who went on pilgrimage. One began when he was young; the other when he was old. The young man had strong depravities to grapple with. The old man's were weaker due to the deterioration of nature. The young man walked each day in the same way as the older man. Their walk looked the same, but which of them had their graces shining clearest, since both looked to be alike?"

"The young man's, without a doubt," Mr. Honest said. "For the one who makes the noblest effort against the greatest opposition, provides the strongest evidence; especially when it keeps up with one who is dealing with half as much opposition due to old age.

"I've noticed that old men often think more of themselves, because they no longer struggle with things as they did when younger, but they mistakenly take the decline of nature for a gracious conquest over sinful corruptions. The result is that they have been quick to deceive themselves. Indeed, old gracious men are best able to give advice to those who are young, because they have seen most of the meaninglessness of things. Yet for an old and a young man to set out together, the young one has the advantage of witnessing the clearest discovery of a work of grace within himself, even though the old man's corrupt ways are naturally the lesser of the two."

In this way they sat talking until the break of day. Now, when the family had awakened and were up and about, Christiana told her son James that he should read a chapter, so he read Isaiah 53. When he finished, Mr. Honest asked why it said that the Savior was to come "out of a dry ground"; and also, that "He had no form nor comeliness in Him."

"Start here," Mr. Great Heart said. "As for the dry ground, it refers to the Jews, from which Christ came, for they had almost lost all the sap and spirit of faith. They were spiritually dried up. As to the bit about no form or comeliness, the words are spoken to unbelievers, who judge based on outward appearance even though they desire to see into our Prince's heart. They judge him by his outside; just like people who don't recognize precious stones when they are covered with a homely crust. When they find one they just throw it away like a common stone because they don't know what they have found."

"Well," Gaius said. "While you are here and since I know Mr. Great Heart is good with his weapons, if you'd like, after we have washed up and eaten, we'll go out into the fields to see if we can do some good. You see, about a mile from here there lives one Slay-good, a giant, who annoys those traveling the King's highway in these parts. I have a pretty good idea where his haunt is. He is the master over a number of thieves and it would be a benefit if we could clear these parts of him."

So they all consented and headed out, Mr. Great Heart with his sword, helmet, and shield, and the rest with spears and staves. When they came to the place where he was, they found him with Feeble-mind in his hands, for his servants had captured the poor man along the way and brought him to their master. Now the giant was searching him, and planned to pick his bones when he was done, for he was a flesh eater.

As soon as he saw Mr. Great Heart and his friends at the mouth of his cave, with their weapons, he demanded to know what they wanted.

Mr. Great Heart shouted, "We want you! For we have come to avenge the fights of the many pilgrims whom you have slain, after you dragged them from the King's highway. Therefore come out of your cave to face us." So he armed himself and came out, and they immediately went to battle and fought for more than an hour and finally stopped to catch their breath.

While they paused the giant asked, "Why are you here on my land?"

"To avenge the blood of pilgrims, as I told you before," Great Heart said again. So with that they went to battle again, and the giant pushed Mr. Great Heart back, causing him to lose ground, but he gained it back again. With great confidence he let fly with such bravery at the giant's head and sides that he made the weapon fall from his hand. So he struck the giant and killed him, and cut off his head and brought it back with him to the inn. He also brought along Feeble-mind the pilgrim. When they arrived back at the inn, they showed his head to the family, and then took it outside and set it up as a warning to any who might attempt to do the same in the future.

The pilgrims bring the head of giant Slay-good to the inn

They asked Mr. Feeble-mind how he fell into the giant's hands.

The poor man said, "I am a sickly man, as you see. Since death usually knocks at my door at least once a day, I thought I would never be well at home; so I took up a pilgrim's life. I have traveled here from the town of Uncertain, where I and my father were born. I am a man of no bodily strength at all, nor of mind, but I thought if all I can do is crawl, I'll spend my life in the pilgrim's way.

"When I arrived at the gate at the head of the way, the Lord of that place freely showed me hospitality. He made no objection against my weakly appearance or my feeble mind. Instead, he gave me everything I needed for my journey and told me to hope to the end. When I came to the house of the Interpreter, I received much kindness and because the Hill Difficulty was judged too hard for me, I was carried up it by one of his servants.

"Indeed, pilgrims gave me much relief, though none were willing to go so mildly as I am forced to do. Yet as we crossed paths, they encouraged me to be of good cheer and said, that it was the will of their Lord that comfort should be given to the feeble-minded (*We also exhort you, brethren, that you warn those that are unruly, comfort the fainthearted, support the weak, be patient with everyone.* – 1 Thess. 5:14), and so after that they went along at their own pace. When I came to Assault-lane, this giant met me and told me to prepare for a fight. But, alas, I am one who is feeble." He shrugged. "So he came and took me and I was so arrogant, I thought because I went along willingly that he would not kill me. And when he got me into his den, I really believed I would come out alive again. For I have heard that if a pilgrim keeps his whole heart trained on his Master when he is taken captive by violence, that by the laws of providence, he will not die by the hand of the enemy. I just figured he would rob me, and sure enough that happened, but as you see I have escaped with my life, for which I thank my King as the originator of the plan and you as the means that brought it to fruition. I expect other violence and contention along the way, but I have resolved to run when I can, to go forward even when I cannot run, and to creep along when I must. The main thing I do is to thank him who loved me, for I am fixed. My way is before me, and my mind is focused beyond the river that has no bridge, even though I am, as you see, feeble-minded."

Old Mr. Honest said, "Along your travels weren't you acquainted with Mr. Fearing, who was also a pilgrim?"

"Acquainted with him! Yes, he came from the town of Stupidity, which is just four degrees north of the City of Destruction. Even though it was far from where I was born, we were still well acquainted for he was my uncle, my father's brother. He and I have much the same temperament, and though he was a little shorter than me, we still had much the same complexion."

Mr. Honest said, "I sensed that you knew him and I can see you are related to one another, because you have the same pale complexion as he and the same look around your eyes, plus you sound very much like him when you speak."

"Most people who have known both of us have said that, and besides, what I have seen in him I have, for the most part, found in myself."

"Come, sir," Gaius said. "Be of good cheer for you are welcome by me and my house. Whatever you might think you might need, ask for it freely, and whatever you need my servants to do for you, they will do it gladly."

Then Mr. Feeble-mind said, "This is an unexpected kindness like the sun shining out of a very dark cloud. Did Giant Slay-good intend for me to receive this favor when he stopped me and decided to let me go no further? And after he rifled through my pockets did he intend that I should come to your house and you would be my host? Yet that is what has happened."

Now, just as Mr. Feeble-mind and Gaius were engaged in this conversation, a man ran up to the house and called at the door. He said, "About a mile and a half away there is a pilgrim struck dead in his tracks by a thunderbolt. His name was Mr. Not-right."

"Alas!" Mr. Feeble-mind cried out. "Is he dead? I met him some days ago when he overtook me. We walked together and he kept me company until today. He was with me when Slay-good the giant took me, but he was quick on his feet and escaped before the giant could grab him. But it seems he escaped to die, and I was taken to live."

> *"What one would think seeks to slay outright,*
>   *Often delivers from the saddest plight.*
> *That very Providence whose face is death,*
>   *Often gives life to the lowly, life bequeath.*
> *I was taken while he did escape and flee;*
>   *Hands crossed and gave death to him and life to me."*

Now, about this time Matthew and Mercy were married and Gaius also gave his daughter Phebe to James, Matthew's brother, as his wife. After the

The marriage of Matthew and Mercy

marriage they stayed about ten days more at Gaius's house, spending their time like as pilgrims used to do.

When they were ready to depart, Gaius prepared a feast and they ate, drank, and were merry. Now the time arrived for them to leave, so Mr. Great Heart called for a settling of their account so he could pay for their lodging. But Gaius told him that at his house it was not the custom for pilgrims to pay for hospitality. He boarded them by the year but looked for his pay from the good Samaritan, who had promised to faithfully repay him for the costs when he returned. (*And went to him and bound up his wounds, pouring in oil and wine, and set him on his own beast and brought him to an inn and took care of him. And on the morrow when he departed, he took out two denarius and gave them to the host and said unto him, Take care of him; and whatever thou spendest more, when I come again, I will repay thee.* – Luke 10:34, 35)

Then Great Heart said to him, "Dear friend, you faithfully do whatever you do for the brethren, especially when they are strangers, and they testify about your kindness to the church. You do well to send them on their journey in a manner worthy of the Lord." (*Beloved, thou doest faithfully whatever thou doest regarding the brethren and with the strangers, who have borne witness of thy charity before the congregation, whom if thou wilt help them as is convenient according to God, thou shalt do well.* – 3 John 5, 6)

Then Gaius and his children said good-bye to all of them, and as he said farewell to Mr. Feeble-mind, he also gave him something to drink as he traveled the way. But when they were going out the door, Mr. Feeble-mind lingered in the house. When Mr. Great Heart saw him dawdling he said, "Please come along with us, Mr. Feeble-mind. I will be your conductor and guide, and you shall advance along the way with the rest of the pilgrims."

Mr. Feeble-mind sighed and said, "Alas! I desire a suitable companion, but you are all robust and strong, while as you see, I am weak. Therefore, instead of coming with you now, I plan to follow at my own pace so my many infirmities won't become a burden to you or me. Like I told you, I am a man of a weak and feeble mind, and things that you all can bear upset me and make me weak. As a traveling companion, I don't like laughing; I don't like cheerful clothing, and I don't like useless questions. No, I am such a weak man that things which others have the freedom to do displease me. And I am a very ignorant Christian man, for I still don't know all the truth. Sometimes, if I hear people rejoice in the Lord, it bothers me because I don't feel the same way. I am a weak man among the strong, or like a sick man among the healthy, or as a lamp shunned. I don't know what to do." (*The torch is held in low esteem in the thought of him that is prosperous, which was prepared to guard against a slip of the feet.* – Job 12:5)

"But, brother," Great Heart said. "I have been commissioned to comfort the feeble-minded and to support the weak. You must come along with us. We will wait for you and help you along the way. We will refrain from talking about preconceived notions and practical things that may upset you, and we will avoid opinionated disputes, for we will become all things to you, rather than leave you behind." (*To the weak I became as weak, that I might gain the weak; I am made all things to everyone, that I might by all means save some.* – 1 Cor. 9:22)

They spoke about all this while they stood at Gaius's door, and while they were in the heat of their discussion, Mr. Ready-to-halt came by with his crutches in his hand and he was also going on pilgrimage.

Mr. Feeble-mind turned to the newcomer and said, "Man, how did you get here? I was just complaining about how I didn't have a suitable traveling companion, but my wish has come true with your arrival! Welcome,

welcome, Mr. Ready-to-halt." Mr. Feeble-mind smiled brightly. "I hope you and I can help one another along the way."

Mr. Ready-to-halt said, "I happily welcome your company rather than to travel alone, my good Mr. Feeble-mind. And even though we have just met, I would like to offer you the use of one of my crutches."

Mr. Feeble-mind held up his hand and shook his head. "No thank you. While I appreciate your good intentions, I don't plan to halt before I am lame. Be that as it may, I think when such an occasion arises it may help me against a dog."

Mr. Ready-to-halt nodded. "Well, if either myself or my crutches can be of a benefit to you, we are at your command, good Mr. Feeble-mind."

In this way the group moved forward along the way with Great Heart and Mr. Honest leading the way, Christiana and her children following next, and bringing up the rear Mr. Feeble-mind walked behind along with Mr. Ready-to-halt on his crutches.

Mr. Honest turned to Great Heart and said, "Please sir, now that we are underway, tell us some of the

Feeble-mind welcomes Ready-to-halt

beneficial things you experienced on pilgrimage before you met us."

Great Heart said, "With pleasure. I suppose you have heard about how Christian of old met with Apollyon in the Valley of Humiliation, and about the hard times he had to endure as he made his way through the Valley of the Shadow of Death. Also I'm sure you have heard how Faithful faced difficulty and death by Madam Wanton, with Adam the First, with one Discontent, and Shame; four deceitful villains as a man could ever meet upon the road."

Mr. Honest nodded. "Yes, I have heard of all this but truly good Faithful endured the ultimate hardship with Shame, but he did not grow weary."

"You're right. For as the pilgrim said it correctly when he said he of all men had the wrong name."

"But where did Christian and Faithful meet Talkative?" Mr. Honest asked. "For that man was also notable but not in a good way."

"He was a confident fool, yet many follow his ways," Great Heart said.

"He almost enthralled Faithful with his talk."

"Yes," Great Heart said. "But Christian quickly opened his eyes to the error in what Talkative had to say."

In this manner, they talked and traveled until they came to the place where Evangelist had met with Christian and Faithful, the place in which he had prophesied to them what would happen to them at Vanity Fair. Great Heart pointed out the place. "It was here Christian and Faithful met with Evangelist, who prophesied to them of what troubles they would meet with at Vanity Fair."

"You don't say." Mr. Honest stared about with wide eyes. "I dare say it was difficult news he had to deliver to them."

Mr. Great Heart nodded. "That it was, but he also encouraged them at the same time. But what do we say about them? We say things like they were courageous as lions and set their faces like a flint in the face of adversity. Do you remember how fearless they were when they stood before the judge?"

Mr. Honest rubbed his chin thoughtfully. "Well, Faithful suffered bravely."

"That he did, and as a result the story relates bold changes that came about from it for Hopeful and some others, for they were converted as a result of his death."

Mr. Honest begged Great Heart to continue because he was well acquainted with many of the details he hadn't heard until now.

Great Heart smiled. "Once Christian passed through Vanity Fair he met with other difficulties and people, including one By-ends who was an arch foe."

Mr. Honest's brow wrinkled. "By-ends! Who was he?"

"A very haughty fellow and a downright hypocrite. He is one who shifts his religious views to line up whichever way the world goes, but he is so cunning that he makes sure he never loses profit or suffers for it. He had his mode of religion for every fresh occasion, and his wife was as good at it as he. He flip-flops from one opinion to another and appeals to others to do the same. But as far as I know he came to a bad end with his selfish motives. I didn't ever hear of any of his children truly coming to fear God, either. As far as I know, none of them amounted to anything even by the world's standards."

Now by this time they came within sight of the town of Vanity. When they saw they were so near the town, they talked over how they should pass through the town. Some suggested one thing and others something different. At last Mr. Great Heart said, "I have often guided pilgrims through this town, as you know. For this reason, I am acquainted with one Mr. Mnason, a man originally from Cyprus who is an old disciple. (*There went with us also certain of the disciples of Caesarea and brought with them one Mnason of Cyprus, an old disciple, with whom we should lodge.* – Acts 21:16) We may lodge at his house. If you think that a good option we will turn in there."

Old Honest smiled. "I'm content to do that."

Christiana agreed.

Mr. Feeble-mind was content to stay there, and in the same way they all agreed.

Now you might have guessed, it was evening by the time they reached the outskirts of the town; but Great Heart knew the way to the old man's house. So they went there and Great Heart called at the door and the old man inside recognized his voice. He quickly opened the door, and they all went inside.

Their host, Mnason, asked, "How far have you traveled today?"

"We have traveled from the house of Gaius our friend."

"I declare!" Mnason said. "You have covered a lot of ground. You must be weary. Come sit down." So they eagerly sat down with thanks.

Their guide Great Heart said, "What a warm welcome, Mnason!" He motioned for the others to come in. "Come, this is my friend. He welcomes you all."

"Yes I do," Mnason said. "Whatever you want, just ask for it and we will do what we can to get it for you."

Mr. Honest said, "Our greatest need is lodging and good company and now I hope we have both."

Mnason smiled. "As for lodging you can see for yourself what it is, but as for good company that will come about with time and a little effort."

"Are you willing to have the pilgrims stay here?"

Mnason nodded. "I am." So he led them to their respective places and showed them a very clean upper room, where they might gather to enjoy each other's company and eat together until it was time for bed.

Now they were seated in their places around the table and were in a good mood after their journey. Mr. Honest asked his landlord, Mnason, if there were any amount of good people in the town.

"We have a few," he shrugged. "But there are far less compared with them who live the other side."

Mr. Honest asked, "Is there any way we can go to visit some of them? For the finding of other good men for those who are on pilgrimage is like the appearance of the moon and stars to those sailing upon the seas."

Mnason stamped with his foot and his daughter Grace came up. He said, "Grace, go tell my friends, Mr. Contrite, Mr. Holy-man, Mr. Love-saints, Mr. Dare-not-lie, and Mr. Penitent, that I have a friend or two at my house who have the desire to see them this evening." So Grace left the house and went to call them. In a short time, they all came and after introductions and greetings were exchanged, they sat down together at the table.

Mnason, their landlord, addressed them all. "My neighbors, as you see I have a group of strangers who have come to my house. They are pilgrims who come from far away, and they are going to Mount Zion. But who do you think this is?" He pointed his finger at Christiana. "It is Christiana, the wife of Christian, the famous pilgrim, who, with Faithful his brother was so shamefully treated in our town." His neighbors stood amazed. They said, "We never expected to see Christiana when Grace came to call us to your home. What a pleasant surprise!"

They asked Christiana about her welfare and if the young men with her were her husband's sons. When she told them they were, they said, "May the King whom you love and serve make you young men like your father and bring you where he is in peace."

Once they had all sat down, Mr. Honest asked Mr. Contrite and the rest, about the current situation in their town. Mr. Contrite said, "You can be sure we are fully immersed in the flurry of fair-time. It makes it difficult to keep our hearts and spirits in good order when we are in such a troubled and grieved condition. Those of us who live in such places as this and who have to regularly deal with all the things that go on here need to be reminded every moment of the day to be careful and pay attention to their spiritual health."

"How are your neighbors now? Are things quiet? Are you free from agitation stirred by high emotions?" Mr. Honest asked.

Mr. Contrite said, "They are much more restrained now than they were before. You know how Christian and Faithful were treated in our town; but lately I'd say they have become far more reserved and less aggressive. I think the blood of Faithful is like a load upon them still to this day, for since they burned him they have been ashamed to burn anyone else. In those days when Christian visited us, we were afraid to walk the street, but now we can show our heads without fear. Back then the title of genuine Christian was odious, but now, especially in some parts of our large town, religion is considered honorable."

Honest and Contrite converse

Then Mr. Contrite asked the pilgrims of their own welfare. He said, "Please tell me how things have fared with you thus far on your pilgrimage. And tell me about the country through which you traveled and how the people reacted towards you."

Mr. Honest said, "The same things happened to us as happens to all wayfaring men. Sometimes our way was free of trouble, sometimes it was dangerous; sometimes uphill, and sometimes downhill. We never knew what to expect with any certainty. The wind is not always at our backs, nor is every person we meet a friend within the way. We have met with some notable difficulties already, and while that is behind us, for the most part we find that old saying true that says, a good man must suffer trouble." (*And all that desire to live godly in Christ Jesus shall also suffer persecution. – 2 Tim. 3:12*)

"You talk of difficulties," Mr. Contrite said. "What difficulties have you met along with the rest of it?"

Mr. Honest shook his head. "I'm not the one to ask. For the best account ask Great Heart, our guide."

Great Heart didn't hesitate to answer. He said, "We have been afflicted with difficulties three or four times already. First, Christiana and her children were tormented by two thugs and they feared they would be murdered. We have been harassed by Giant Bloody-man, Giant Maul, and Giant Slaygood. For the last, we turned the circumstances in our favor and instead of him harming us, we attacked him and escaped.

"After that we spent some time at the home of Gaius, my host, and that of the whole church. While we were there we were persuaded to take our weapons with us and to go see if we might come across any who were enemies to pilgrims. We had heard there was a notable one in the region. Now Gaius knew the area where he lived better than me. So we searched and combed the area until we finally discovered the mouth of his cave. We were pleased and bolstered our spirits.

"We approached his den and when we drew close to the mouth of the cave we found he had dragged this poor man," he pointed to Mr. Feeble-mind, "into his cave by mere force. He was about to kill him. We decided to show ourselves, and when he saw us he supposed us to be another prey, as we had hoped. He left the poor man in his hole and came out after us. So we pummeled him and he vigorously fought back, but in the end we brought him down to the ground and cut off his head. We set it up by the wayside to frighten any others who would practice such ungodliness. And to prove I'm telling you the truth, here is the man himself who can affirm every word. For he is the one who was snatched like a lamb from the mouth of the lion."

Mr. Feeble-mind nodded his head. "He speaks the truth, to my cost and comfort. My cost, when he threatened to pick my bones over and over again, and to my comfort, when I saw Mr. Great Heart and his friends equipped with their weapons as they approached so near for my deliverance."

Mr. Holy-man added, "There are two things people who go on pilgrimage need: courage and a life free from moral stain. If they don't have courage, they can never bolster their way; and if they live loose lives, they will make the very name of a pilgrim stink."

"I hope this warning isn't needed among this group," Mr. Love-saints said. "But really there are many who walk the road who rather say they are strangers to pilgrimage than admit they are strangers and pilgrims on the earth."

"That's true." Mr. Dare-not-lie nodded. "They don't have the pilgrim's clothing, nor the pilgrim's courage. They don't walk with an upright heart but walk in a way that is neither straight nor true. One shoe turns inward, the other outward, and their stockings are on the outside, nothing but a torn rag to the ridicule of their Lord."

"These things ought to be disturbing," Mr. Penitent said. "For the pilgrims are not likely to have that grace put upon them and their Pilgrim's Progress as they desire, until the way is cleared of such spots and blemishes." In this way they passed the time talking until supper was set upon the table. Then they went in and ate. The meal refreshed their weary bodies, and they turned in for the night and went to bed.

Now they stayed in the fair a long time at the house of Mr. Mnason. Over time he gave his daughter Grace to Samuel, Christian's son, to be his wife, and his daughter Martha to Joseph. The reason they were able to stay here so long was that things had changed from the time when Christian had visited the Fair.

Therefore, the pilgrims grew to know many of the good people of the town and did for them whatever service they could. Mercy, as was her custom, worked hard to help the poor and their bellies and backs blessed her for it. She was an example to her profession there. And, to tell the truth, Grace, Phebe, and Martha all had an easy-going and pleasing nature. They did much good, each in their own way, and all were very fruitful so that Christian's name, as was said before, was like it was alive in the world.

While they stayed here, a monster came out of the woods and slew many of the people of the town. It would carry away their children and teach them to suckle its whelps. Now, no man in the town dared to face this monster. All of them fled at the very noise of its coming. The monster was unlike any beast on the earth. Its body was like a dragon, and it had seven heads and ten horns. It brought great devastation and destruction to the lives of the children, and yet it was governed by a woman. (*So he carried me away in the spirit into the wilderness: and I saw a woman seated upon a scarlet-coloured beast, full of names of blasphemy, having seven heads and ten horns.* – Rev. 17:3) This monster proposed certain conditions to men, and those men who loved their lives more than their souls, accepted those conditions. So they came under the beast's authority.

Now Great Heart, along with those who came to visit the pilgrims at Mnason's house, agreed to go and engage this beast, thinking they might deliver the people of this town from the paws and mouth of this devouring serpent.

So Great Heart, along with Mr. Contrite, Mr. Holy-man, Mr. Dare-not-lie, and Mr. Penitent, went forth with their weapons to meet the monster. At first the monster was unchecked. He looked upon the pilgrims as enemies with great disdain, but being hardy men skilled with their weapons, they thrashed him until he retreated. Then they returned to Mnason's house.

It is worth noting that the monster had certain seasons when he came out to make his attempts upon the children of the town. During these seasons, these valiant and important pilgrims watched him and continued to assault him. Over time he wasn't just wounded but became lame. As a result, that devastation of the townsmen's children doesn't happen like it used to. Some truly believe that this beast will die of his wounds.

This made Great Heart and his fellow pilgrims famous in this town. Even though many of the people still had an appetite for worldly things, they highly regarded the pilgrims with reverent esteem and respect. For this reason, these pilgrims were not hurt or put under much pressure. However, some of the more vile sort who were as blind as moles and lacked understanding still showed no reverence for these men and paid no attention to their valor and daring adventures.

The pilgrims at the place where Faithful perished

The Seventh Stage

ell, the time finally came when the pilgrims had to be on their way and so they prepared for their journey. Before they left, they sent for their friends, talked with them, and trusted each one to the protection of their Prince. Those who were able brought items with them, things from their own possessions that were suitable for the weak and the strong, for the women and the men. In this way they equipped the pilgrims with the things necessary for their journey. (*Who also honoured us with many gifts; and when we departed, they laded us with such things as were necessary. –* Acts 28:10) When it came time to leave, they set out and their friends accompanied them for as far as was convenient. Before they said good-bye, they once again committed each other to the protection of their King and then parted ways.

In this manner, the small group of pilgrims went on with Great Heart leading the way. Now, the women and children had little physical strength but pressed on the best they could. Mr. Ready-to-halt and Mr. Feeble-mind could sympathize with their condition. Shortly after they were away from the townspeople and their friends, they came to the place where Faithful had been put to death. They stood there and gave thanks to Him who enabled him to bear his cross so well, and in addition they were thankful for how they had benefitted from his suffering and example.

From there they went on. As they walked along they talked about Christian and Faithful, and how Hopeful joined himself to Christian after that Faithful was dead.

Now they came up to the hill Lucre, where the silver mine stood which lured Demas from his pilgrimage. It was the same mine into which some think By-ends fell and perished. The pilgrims recalled these stories and considered all that had happened. When they came to the old pillar of salt monument that stood against the hill Lucre, they stood and looked out at the view of Sodom and its stinking lake. There they marveled, just like

Christian did when he stood in that same place, thinking about how men of such knowledge and maturity could be so blinded by their own greed as to turn aside here. But as they thought more about it, they understood nature is often not influenced by the harm others experience, especially when the thing they are looking at is alluring to one with a foolish eye.

They went on until they reached the river that rests on this side of the Delectable Mountains. Fine trees lined the banks of this river, and when the leaves of these trees were eaten they helped prevent gluttony. Here the meadows remained green all year long, and the pilgrims could lie down safely. (*He makes me to lie down in green pastures; he leads me beside the still waters.* – Psalm 23:2)

By this riverside, in the meadows, there were sheepfolds for sheep, and a house built for the nourishing and raising of those lambs, the babes of women who go on pilgrimage. Also one was here who was entrusted with them, who had compassion and gathered these lambs with his arms, carried them in his bosom, and gently led those who were with young. (*He shall feed his flock like a shepherd; he shall gather the lambs with his arm and carry them in his bosom and shall gently lead those that are with young.* – Isa. 40:11)

Now, Christiana advised her four daughters to place their little ones in the care of this man, so they might be housed, refreshed, assisted, and nourished by these waters and so none of them would lack in the future. If any of them went astray or were lost, this man would bring them back again. He would also bind up their wounds and strengthen them when sick. (*And I will set up shepherds over them which shall feed them; and they shall fear no more nor be dismayed neither shall they be lacking, said the LORD.* – Jer. 23:4)

Here they would never lack food, drink, or clothing. They were kept safe from thieves and robbers, and this man would die before he allowed one of those in his trust to be lost. Besides, here they were guaranteed good instruction, counseling, and they would be taught to walk in right paths, and that, you know, is a no insignificant kindness. Also here, they enjoyed clear waters, pleasant meadows, dainty flowers, and a variety of trees bearing healthy fruit, not fruit like Matthew ate which fell over the wall from Beelzebub's garden. This fruit brings about health where there is none; heath that continues and increases as long as the fruit is there. So they were happy to commit their little ones into his care. In fact, it was an encouragement to do so, for all of this was under the charge of the King and there would be no place more hospitable to young children and orphans.

Now they went on and came to By-path Meadow. They arrived at the stile which Christian crossed over with his fellow traveler, Hopeful. It was here those two pilgrims were taken by Giant Despair and put into Doubting Castle. Here the group of pilgrims sat down and talked together about what had happened to Christian and Hopeful here and what was best for them to do now. For they wondered if now that they were so strong and had such Great Heart as their guide, if perhaps it would be best to make an attempt on the giant and to demolish his castle. They also thought that if there were any pilgrims being held in the castle this could be an opportunity to set them free before they journeyed further.

As they talked, one said one thing and another said the opposite. One questioned if it was lawful to step upon unconsecrated ground; another said it might be permitted as long as the end result was good. But Great Heart said, "Though that last claim cannot be true in every case, I do have a commandment to resist sin, to overcome evil, and to fight the good fight of faith. I have to ask, with whom should I fight this good fight, if not with Giant Despair? I will therefore attempt to take his life and to demolish Doubting Castle." Then he asked, "Who will go with me?"

Old Honest said, "I will."

"And so will we," Christiana's four sons, Matthew, Samuel, Joseph, and James said, for they were now young men and strong. (*I write unto you, fathers, that ye have known him that is from the beginning. I write unto you, young men, that ye have overcome the wicked one. I write unto you, little children, that ye have known the Father. I have written unto you, fathers, that ye have known him that is from the beginning. I have written unto you, young men, that ye are strong and the word of God abides in you, and ye have overcome the wicked one. – 1 John 2:13, 14*)

So they left the women at the road, along with them Mr. Feeble-mind and Mr. Ready-to-halt with his crutches. The men were meant to guard the women until the others returned since the Giant Despair lived so near. The plan was for them to stay in the road, for then even a little child could lead them. (*The wolf shall dwell with the lamb, and the leopard shall lie down*

with the kid; and the calf and the young lion and the fatling together; and a
child shall shepherd them. – Isa. 11:6)

Mr. Great Heart, old Honest, and the four young men, headed up to
Doubting Castle to look for Giant Despair. When they arrived at the castle
gate, they knocked for entrance with a most uncommon noise. At that the
old giant came to the gate and Diffidence his wife followed. The giant called
out, "Who and what is he who is so brave as to come to my gate and bother
the Giant Despair in this manner?"

Great Heart replied, "It is I, Great Heart, one of the King of the Celestial
country's guides to pilgrims. I conduct them to their place, and I demand
that you open your gates and let me in. Prepare yourself to fight, for I have
come to take off your head and to demolish Doubting Castle."

Now Giant Despair, because he was a giant, thought that no man could
overcome him. So he reasoned that since in times past he had conquered
angels, why should he be afraid of this man Great Heart? So he equipped
himself with armor and went out to meet Great Heart. He wore a cap of
steel on his head, a breastplate of fire, and shoes made of iron. In his hand
he held a great club. The six men drew up to him, and surrounded him in

Great Heart and the sons of Christiana destroy Doubting Castle

front and behind. When Diffidence the giantess came to help her husband, old Mr. Honest cut her down with one blow. Then the fight grew fierce, and they fought for their lives. Giant Despair was brought down to the ground, but was very reluctant to die. He struggled hard and seemed to have, as they say, as many lives as a cat. Finally Great Heart killed him, but didn't leave until he had severed his head from his shoulders and buried his body under a great pile of stones.

Since Giant Despair was dead, they started demolishing Doubting Castle. It took them seven days to bring it down, and in the process they found two pilgrims alive inside: a Mr. Despondency who was almost starved to death and his daughter Much-afraid. But it would have made you wonder to have seen all the dead bodies scattered here and there in the castle yard, and how full the dungeon was of dead men's bones.

When Great Heart and his companions had performed this heroic act, they took Mr. Despondency and his daughter Much-afraid into their protection, for they were honest people who had been imprisoned in Doubting Castle by that tyrant Giant Despair. They took the head of the giant with them to the road and showed it to their companions who waited for them there and told them what they had done.

Much-afraid

Now, when Feeble-mind and Ready-to-halt saw that it was really the head of Giant Despair, they were very lively and merry. Now Christiana, if needed, could play upon the viol, and her daughter Mercy the lute, so since everyone was so happy, they played them a song and Ready-to-halt danced. He took Despondency's daughter, Much-afraid, by the hand and danced with her in the road. True, he could not dance without using one crutch, but I promise you he handled his footwork well, and the girl was to be commended, for she kept time to the music handsomely.

As for Mr. Despondency, he wasn't as interested in the music. He cared more about eating than dancing, because he was almost starved while held captive in the castle. So Christiana gave him some of her bottle of spirits to help him feel better immediately, and then she prepared him something to eat. In a short time the old gentleman became more himself and revived.

Now I saw in my dream, when all these things had taken place that Great Heart took the head of Giant Despair and set it upon a pole by the side of the highway. He placed it right against the pillar which Christian had erected for a warning to other pilgrims who would come after him when entering into the Giant's grounds.

Beneath it he wrote upon a marble stone these verses:

"This is the head of him whose name only
In former times terrified pilgrims.

His castle's torn down and Diffidence his wife
Brave Mr. Great Heart has deprived of life.

Despondency and his daughter Much-afraid,
Great Heart for them also the man has played.

Whoever doubts this, if he'll just cast his eye
Up here, may his doubts and questions satisfy.

This head also, when doubting cripples dance,
Does show from fears they have deliverance."

When these men had bravely proven themselves against Doubting Castle and had slain Giant Despair, they continued on their journey until they came to the Delectable Mountains, where Christian and Hopeful refreshed themselves with the beautified woods, vineyards, fruits of all sorts, as well as flowers of the place. They also became acquainted with the shepherds there, who welcomed them to the Delectable Mountains, in the same way they had welcomed Christian before.

Now the shepherds were well acquainted with Great Heart, and when they saw him leading such a large group of people they said to him, "Good sir, you have a good-size group here. Where did you find all these people?"

Great Heart replied:

"First, there is Christiana and her train,
Her sons, and her sons' wives, who, like the wain,
Keep by the pole, and do by compass steer
From sin to grace, else they had not been here.

Next here's old Honest, come on pilgrimage,
　　Ready-to-halt too, who I dare engage
True-hearted is, and so is Feeble-mind,
　　Who willing was not to be left behind.

Despondency, good man, is coming after,
　　And so also is Much-afraid, his daughter.
May we have entertainment here, or must
　　We further go? Let's knew whereon to trust."

The shepherds said, "We are comfortable with this group. You are welcome to stay with us; for we have accommodations for the feeble as well as for the strong. Our Prince pays attention to what is done to the least of these. Therefore frailty and sickness must not be a hindrance to our hospitality." (*And the King shall answer and say unto them, Verily I say unto you, Inasmuch as ye have done it unto one of the least of these my brothers, ye have done it unto me.* – Matt. 25:40)

So they ushered them to the palace door and said, "Come in, Mr. Feeble-mind; come in, Mr. Ready-to-halt; come in, Mr. Despondency, and Mrs. Much-afraid his daughter. These, Mr. Great Heart," said the shepherds to the guide, "we call in by name, for they are most likely to draw back. But as for you, and the rest of the group who are strong, we leave you to your usual liberty."

Great Heart said, "This day I see that grace shines in your faces, and that you are truly my Lord's shepherds, for you have not pushed the infirm or diseased with your side or shoulder but instead have scattered flowers on the path at their feet as you should." (*The pure and undefiled religion before God and the Father is this, To visit the fatherless and widows in their tribulation and to keep thyself unspotted from this world.* – James 1:27)[22]

So the feeble and weak went into the palace and Great Heart and the rest followed. When they were inside and seated, the shepherds said to those of the weaker sort, "What is it that you would like to have?" For, the shepherds said all things must be managed to support the weak, as well as to warn the unruly. So they made them a feast of easily digested foods that were tasty and nourishing. After they had eaten they went to lie down, with each one going to their respective and proper place.

22　Original: *Because ye have thrust with side and with shoulder and pushed all the weak with your horns until ye have scattered them outside* – Ezek. 34:21.

When morning came the day was clear. There, high in the mountains as was the custom of the shepherds, they planned to show the pilgrims some rare and uncommon things before their departure. After the pilgrims had refreshed themselves and were ready, the shepherds took them out into the fields and first showed them what they had shown to Christian when he was there.

Then they led them to some new places. The first was Mount Marvel. From here they saw a man in the distance who disturbed the quiet of the hills with words. The pilgrims turned to the shepherds and asked, "What does this mean?"

The shepherds told them, "That man is the son of one Mr. Great-Grace. He is the same man whom you read about in the first part of the records of the Pilgrim's Progress. He teaches pilgrims how to believe down to their core and how to turn one way or the other as they meet difficulties by faith." (*For verily I say unto you that whosoever shall say unto this mountain, Remove thyself and cast thyself into the sea, and shall not doubt in his heart but shall believe that what he says shall be done whatsoever he says shall be done unto him. Therefore I say unto you that everything that ye ask for, praying, believe that ye receive it, and it shall come upon you. – Mark 11:23, 24*)

Then Great Heart said, "I know him; he is a man above many."

Then the shepherds brought them to another place called Mount Innocence. Here they saw a man clothed all in white along with two men by the names of Prejudice and Ill-will. These two men continually threw dirt upon the man in white. Now whatever dirt they threw at him, would just fall off again after a short time and his garment would look as clean and white as if no dirt had ever touched it.

The pilgrims asked, "What means this?"

The shepherds answered, "This man is named Godlyman, and this white garment shows the innocence of his life. Now, those who throw dirt at him are men who hate his good conduct, but as you see the dirt will not stick on his clothes. This is how it shall be with those who live innocently in the world. Whoever tries to make such men dirty, labor in vain, for when such men spend a little time with God, their innocence shall shine forth like light and their righteousness as bright as the sun at noon."

Then they took them to Mount Charity where they showed them a man who had a bundle of cloth lying before him. Out of this cloth he cut coats and other garments for the poor who stood around him, yet his bundle and roll of cloth never became any less.

"What does this mean?" the pilgrims asked.

"This is to show you that one who has a heart to give of his labor to the poor shall never lack. He who waters shall himself be watered, and the cake that the widow gave to the prophet did not result in any less in her barrel."

The shepherds then escorted them to the place where they saw one Fool and one Want-wit washing an Ethiopian with dark skin with the intention of making him white, but the more they washed him the blacker he became. Again they asked the shepherds the meaning of what they saw.

The shepherds said, "This is an example of how it is with the vile person who uses all means in their own strength to get a good name. In the end all their effort only results in making them more abominable. This is how it was with the Pharisees and this is also how it shall be with all hypocrites."

Mercy at the by-way to hell

Then, Mercy, the wife of Matthew, said to Christiana, "Mother, if possible, I would like to see the hole in the hill that is commonly called the by-way to hell."

So her mother revealed her thought to the shepherds and so they went to the door on the side of a hill, opened it, and told Mercy to listen for a while. So she listened and heard one saying, "Cursed be my father for holding me back from the way of peace and life." Another said, "Oh, if only I had been torn in pieces before I had lost my soul to save my life!" And another said, "If I were to live again, how I would deny myself rather than to end up living in this place!" Then a noise emanated from the door as if the very earth groaned and quaked under Mercy's feet.

The color drained from her face and she walked away trembling and said, "Blessed are they who are delivered from this place!"

Now, when the shepherds had shown them all these things, they took them back to the palace and showed them hospitality with all the house had to offer. But Mercy, being a young married woman, longed for something she saw there but was ashamed to ask for it. Christiana could tell something was bothering her and asked her what troubled her because she didn't look well.

Mercy said, "There is a looking-glass which hangs in the dining room." She glanced at her mother-in-law and back at the floor. "I can't stop thinking about it. I feel that if I don't have it I shall miscarry."

Christiana said, "I will mention your desire for the mirror to the shepherds and they will not deny you your desire."

Mercy let out a deep sigh. "I am ashamed to admit to these men that I long for it in such a way."

"No, my daughter, don't feel that way. There is no shame in such longing for it is a virtue to long for such a thing as that."

"If that is the case," Mercy said, "then Mother, if you are willing, please ask the shepherds if they are willing to sell it."

Now the looking-glass was one of a thousand. It had the special ability to reflect a man with his own features exactly, but when it was turned another way it showed one the very face and likeness of the Prince of pilgrims himself. I have talked with those who have seen it firsthand, and they have said they have seen the very crown of thorns upon his head when looking in that mirror. They have also seen the holes in his hands, his feet, and his side. And this mirror has an outstanding feature that reveals him to anyone who has a mind to see him, whether living or dead, on earth or in heaven, in a state of humiliation or in exaltation, or whether they come to suffer or to reign. (*Therefore we all, beholding as in a glass the glory of the Lord with uncovered face, are transformed from glory to glory into the same likeness, even as by the Spirit of the Lord. – 2 Cor. 3:18*)

Christiana went to the shepherds alone (now the names of the shepherds were Knowledge, Experience, Watchful, and Sincere,) and she said, "One of my daughters who is pregnant longs for something that she has seen in this house and she thinks that if she is denied by you that she shall miscarry."

Experience said, "Call her, call her now for she shall assuredly have what we can offer her."

So they called her and said, "Mercy, what is the thing you long to have from the house?"

She blushed but said, "The large looking glass that hangs in the dining room."

Without a word, Sincere ran to get it and brought it back and it was given to her with much joy. Mercy bowed her head, gave thanks, and said, "By this I know that I have obtained approval in your sight."

The shepherds adorn the pilgrims

They also gave to the other young women the things they desired and to their husbands great praise, for they had joined Great Heart in the slaying of Giant Despair and the demolishing of Doubting Castle.

The shepherds hung a necklace around Christiana's neck and did the same with her four daughters. They also placed earrings in their ears and jewels on their foreheads.

When they were ready to go from the house the shepherds let them go in peace, without issuing the same warnings which they had given Christian and his companion when they were there. For these pilgrims had Great Heart as their guide, and he was well acquainted with things and could offer them warnings in a timely fashion when the danger was near or approaching. For the warnings Christian and his companion had received from the shepherds had been forgotten by the time they needed to put them into practice. Therefore, this group of pilgrims had an advantage over them in this way.

From there they went on their way singing these words:

"Behold how suitably the stages are set
For pilgrims to find relief when they enter,
And how they receive us without hindrance,
Who make the other life our target and residence!

What new things they have to us they give,
That we, though pilgrims, joyful lives may live;
They do upon us, too, such things bestow,
That show we are pilgrims wherever we go."

The Eighth Stage

———∽———

When they left the shepherds they quickly arrived at the place where Christian met with Turn-away who lived in the town of Apostasy. Therefore Great Heart, acting as their guide, reminded them of Turn-away. He said, "This is the place where Christian met with one Turn-away, who carried with him the character of his rebellion on his back. And concerning this man I have to tell you, he would not listen to counsel from anyone. Once he started to abandon his faith, no persuasion could stop him. When he came to the place where the cross and sepulchre were, he met with one who told him to look at them. Instead, he only gnashed his teeth, stamped his feet, and said he was determined to return to his own town.

"Before he came to the gate, he met with Evangelist, who offered to lay hands on him and to turn him into the way again, but this Turn-away resisted him. In fact, he showed much violent hatred toward him, and then made his way over the wall and so escaped his hand."

The pilgrims went on considering this, and when they reached the place where Little-Faith had been robbed, they came face to face with a man who had his sword drawn, and his face was covered with blood. Great Heart asked, "Who are you?"

The man said, "My name is Valiant-for-Truth. I am a pilgrim on my way to the Celestial City. Now, as I was in my way, there were three men who attacked me and offered me three options. The first was to join with them. The second was for me to go back from where I came, and the third was to decide whether or not I was ready to die right then and there. (*If they say, Come with us, let us lay in wait for blood; let us ambush the innocent without cause. Let us swallow them up alive as Sheol and whole as those that go down into the pit; We shall find all kinds of riches, we shall fill our houses with spoil. Cast in thy lot among us; let us all have one purse. – Prov. 1:11-14*) To the first I answered that I had been true to my faith for a long time, and so they could not expect me to join with thieves. Then they demanded my answer to the second option, and I told them that I had found no disadvantage in the place from where I had come and that I had not abandoned it at all. It was just that I found it no longer suitable to me and in fact very unprofitable for me. So I had forsaken it for this way.

"Then they asked me for my response to the third option. And I told them my life was valuable and dear and that I would not give it away lightly. Besides that I told them they had no authority to offer such choices to me. I warned them that if they planned to interfere, they did so at their own peril. Then these three, namely, Wild-head, Inconsiderate, and Pragmatic, drew weapons and I also drew mine.

Valiant-for-truth beset by thieves

"So we started to fight and it was one against three. The battle raged for more than three hours. As you can see, they left upon me some of the signs of their valor, and I also marked them with some of mine. They just now left. I suppose they might have heard you coming and so took off."

Great Heart said, "Three against one were pretty great odds."

Valiant-for-Truth nodded. "That's the truth, but whether great or small, odds are nothing to him who has the truth on his side. 'Though a host should encamp against me,' said one (Psalm 27:3), 'my heart shall not fear; though war should rise against me, in this will I be confident.' Besides," he said. "I have read in some records, that one man fought an army, and look how many Samson slew with the jawbone of an ass!"

Then Great Heart asked, "Why didn't you cry out, so someone might have heard you and come to your aid sooner?"

"I called out to my King, who I knew could hear me and provide invisible help," Valiant-for-Truth said. "That was sufficient for me."

Great Heart said to Valiant-for-Truth, "You have behaved in a worthy manner; let me see your sword."

So Valiant-for-Truth showed it to him and he took it into his hand. He studied the blade closely for a moment and said, "Ah-ha, it is a straight Jerusalem blade."

Valiant-for-Truth nodded and said, "That's right; it is. Let a man have one of these blades, with a hand to wield it, and skill to use it, and he may venture upon an angel with it. He has no need to fear holding it, as long as he knows how to apply it. Its edge will never blunt. It will cut flesh and bones, and soul, and spirit, and all." (*For the word of God is alive and efficient and sharper than any twoedged sword, piercing even to the dividing asunder of soul and spirit, and of the joints and marrow, and is a discerner of the thoughts and intents of the heart. – Heb. 4:12*)

"You fought a long time," Great Heart said. "I am surprised you didn't grow weary."

"I fought until my sword clung to my hand. The two melded as if a sword grew out of my arm. When the blood ran through my fingers, I fought with the most courage."

Great Heart said, "You have done well. You have resisted to the point of shedding your blood while striving against sin. Come, you shall live along with us, for we are your companions." Then they took him in, washed his wounds, and gave him what they could from what they had, to refresh him, and from that point they traveled together.

Now, as they went on, Great Heart was delighted in Valiant-for-Truth, for he found him to be one who worked well with his hands, who provided help to the pilgrims who were feeble and weak. As they traveled Great Heart enjoyed his company and asked him about many things. He started out asking what country he was from.

"I am from Dark-land," he said. "I was born there and my father and mother are still living there."

"Dark-land!" Great Heart said. "Isn't that located along the same coast as the City of Destruction?"

"Yes, it is, and the thing that caused me to come on pilgrimage was this. We had a man by the name of Mr. Tell-true come into our area and he told us about what Christian had done and how he left the City of Destruction. He told about how he had left his wife and children and had taken up a pilgrim's life. It was also reported how he had killed a serpent that had resisted him in his journey, and how he reached his intended destination. Mr. Tell-true also told about the welcome he received at all his Lord's lodgings, especially when he came to the gates of the Celestial City, about how he was received with the sound of trumpets by a company of Shining Ones. He also told about how all the bells in the city rang for joy at his reception, and about the golden garments with which he was clothed, along with many other things that I shall refrain from relating right now. In a word, the story of Christian and his travels as I heard it filled my heart with an urgency to follow after him. My father or mother wanted me to stay with them, but I just couldn't do it. So I left them and I have come this far on my way."

The parents of Valiant-for-truth try to dissuade him from going on pilgrimage

Great Heart asked, "You came in at the gate, didn't you?"

"Yes, yes; for the same man also told us, that it all would be for nothing if we did not begin by entering this way at the gate."

Great Heart went to Christiana and said, "Look at how the testimony of your husband's pilgrimage has spread abroad far and near."

Valiant-for-Truth looked at Christiana with wide eyes. "You mean to say that this is Christian's wife?"

Great Heart nodded. "Yes, she is." He also gestured to the young men and said, "And these are his four sons."

Valiant-for-Truth couldn't hide his surprise. "What? They are all going on pilgrimage too?"

Great Heart smiled. "Yes, they truly are following after their father."

"It gladdens my heart," Valiant-for-Truth said. "Can you imagine how joyful Christian will be when he sees his entire family that wouldn't go with him when he left, but who will enter in after him at the gates into the Celestial City?"

"Without a doubt it will be a comfort to him," Great Heart said, "for next to the joy of seeing himself there, it will be a joy to meet his wife and children there."

"As long as you brought that up, please, I'd like to hear your opinion about that. Some question whether we shall know one another when we are there."

Great Heart asked, "Do you think when they arrive that they shall know themselves then, or that they will rejoice to see themselves in that blessedness? And if they shall know themselves in this way, why wouldn't they know others and rejoice in their welfare also? And since relatives are our kin, though that relationship will be suspended there, why wouldn't it be rational to conclude that we shall be more glad to see them there than to see that they are lacking?"

"Well, I can see where you stand on this. Did you have any more to ask me about how I first came on pilgrimage?"

"Yes," Great Heart said. "Were your father and mother willing to see you become a pilgrim?"

Valiant-for-Truth shook his head. "Oh no! They did everything imaginable to persuade me to stay at home."

"Why? What could they say against it?"

"They said it was an idle life and that if I weren't inclined to idleness and laziness, I would never tolerate a pilgrim's condition."

Sadness filled Great Heart's eyes. "And what else did they say?"

"Why, they told me that it was a dangerous way. In fact they said that the way which pilgrims go is the most dangerous way in the world."

Great Heart asked, "Did they explain to you why or how this way is so dangerous?"

"Yes, and they gave me many particulars."

"Like what?" Great Heart asked. "Name some of them."

"They told me of the Slough of Despond, where Christian was almost smothered. They told me about archers standing ready in Beelzebub-castle prepared to shoot any who knock at the wicket gate for entrance. They also told me of the woods and dark mountains, the Hill Difficulty, of the lions, and the three giants: Bloody-man, Maul, and Slay-good. And beyond that they said that there was a foul fiend that haunted the Valley of Humiliation, and that Christian was almost killed by him. 'Besides,' they said, 'you must go over the Valley of the Shadow of Death, where the hobgoblins are, where the light is darkness, where the way is full of snares, pits, and traps.' They told me also of Giant Despair, of Doubting Castle, and of the ruin that the pilgrims met with there. Plus they said I must go over the Enchanted Ground, which was dangerous, and that after all that I would come to a river, over which there was no bridge, and they made sure to tell me that river was located between me and the Celestial country."

"Was that all that they said?"

Valiant-for-Truth shook his head. "No. They also told me that this way was full of deceivers, and people who lay in wait to steer good men out of the path."

A slight frown creased Great Heart's brow. "But how did they know all of this?"

Valiant-for-Truth shrugged. "They told me that Mr. Wordly Wiseman waits along the way, ready to deceive any who come along. They also said Formality and Hypocrisy are continually on the road, as well as others like By-ends, Talkative, or Demas. They said if any of these met up with me they would capture me, and if I escaped them they said the Flatterer would catch me in his net. They also told me that if I met up with green-headed Ignorance, I would imagine I was headed to the gate, but instead

I'd be following him back to the hole in the side of the hill and made to go the by-way to hell."

"I'm sure that was enough to discourage you," Great Heart said. "Was that all they had to say?"

Valiant-for-Truth shook his head. "No, there is more. They also told me about many who from long ago had tried to follow the way and had actually gone a great distance to see if they could find any evidence of the glory so many had talked about so much. According to them, those people came back again saying they had been fools for taking one step on the path. Plus they named several more who had done this including Obstinate and Pliable, Mistrust and Timorous, Turn-away and old Atheist. In fact they listed several more, making sure to explain that some of them had gone quite far to see what they could find, but not one of them found a single advantage to following the way."

"Did they say anything more to discourage you?" Great Heart asked.

"Yes." Valiant-for-Truth nodded. "They told me about a man by the name of Mr. Fearing who was a pilgrim and how he found his way so lonely that he never found a time that he felt comfortable. They also talked about Mr. Despondency who had almost been starved along the way. And I almost forgot this, but they talked about Christian, too. They admitted that much talk surrounded him and his adventures on his way to claim a celestial crown, but that even he had almost drowned in the Black River, and that he never actually went another foot further following that incident. However, it was hushed up."

"Didn't any of these things discourage you?"

Valiant-for-Truth shook his head and smiled. "No not really, because they seemed all to be stories of no value, so I counted them as nothing."

"Tell me," Great Heart said. "How did this thinking come about?"

"Why, I still believed what Mr. Tell-true had told me and that truth carried me beyond all the stories those scoundrels had to tell."

Great Heart clapped him on the back. "Then this was your victory, your faith in action."

"I believe you are right. My faith grew as I walked in the way, fought all those who assaulted me, and by believing, my faith has brought me to this place."

"Who desires to true valor see,
Let him come hither;
Such a one will constant be,
Come wind, come weather

There's no discouragement
That makes him even once relent
His first declared intent
To be a pilgrim.

Who hem him all round
With dismal stories,
That themselves confound,
His strength all the more.

No lion can cause him fright,
He'll even with a giant fight,
But he will have a right
To be a pilgrim.

Hobgoblin nor foul fiend
Can daunt his spirit;
He knows that at the end,
He shall life inherit.

Then fancies fly away,
He'll not fear what men say;
He'll labor night and day
To be a pilgrim."

By this time they arrived at the Enchanted Ground, where the air naturally tended to make a person drowsy. It was totally overgrown with briars and thorns, except for here and there in the area where an enchanted arbor stood. If a man sat or fell asleep in this arbor, some say it raises the question of whether or not they shall ever rise or wake up again in this world.

They went through this forest with Mr. Great Heart leading the way, for he was the guide after all. Mr. Valiant-for-Truth followed behind, as a rearguard, in case some fiend, dragon, giant, or thief, should assault them from behind. Each man walked with his sword drawn in his hand, for they all knew it was a dangerous place. Also, they cheered one another up the best they could. Great Heart commanded Feeble-mind to come up behind him and placed Mr. Despondency under Valiant-for-Truth's watchful care.

Now they had not gone far when a vast misty darkness fell over them. For a great while, they could scarcely see one other. For some time they were forced to feel their way and call out to one another because they couldn't see where they were going. One might think it was miserable going for the best of them at that; it was even worse for the women and children whose feet and hearts were tender. But Great Heart encouraged them on from the front and Valiant-for-Truth did the same from behind so that they walked along at a pretty good pace.

The way grew very wearisome and took them through dirt and mire. There was no inn or house in the area to feed them or offer the feebler pilgrims refreshment. For this reason, they walked along with much grunting, puffing, and sighing. One tumbled over a bush and another stuck fast in the dirt. One cried out, "I've fallen down!" and another, "The bushes have caught me and hold me fast. I can't get away from them!" And another would answer, "Where are you?" Some of them even lost their shoes in the mire.

Then they arrived at the arbor which offered warm and promising refreshment to the weary pilgrims. It was formed of fine wrought iron with beautiful greens overhead, and furnished with welcoming benches and other seating, including a soft couch perfect for the weary to rest upon. With all things considered you might think this tempted the pilgrims to stop and rest because their journey had become fraught with difficulties. But not even one of them made a move to stop there. And from what I could tell, they continually paid attention to the advice of their guide, and he faithfully warned them of the various dangers present. Usually, when they were nearest to them, the pilgrims boosted one another's spirits and encouraged each other to deny the flesh. This arbor was called The Slothful's Friend and was made purposely to allure, if possible, some of the pilgrims so they would stop and rest when weary.

I saw them in my dream as they went over this lonely Enchanted Ground, until they came to a place where a man could even more easily lose his way. Now, when it was light, their guide could tell them how to miss those ways that led them astray, but in the dark the difficulties brought him to a standstill. He had a map of all ways leading to or from the Celestial City in his pocket, so he lit a light to view the map or his book, which told him to be careful and to make a right-hand turn. And if he had not been careful to check his map, they would in all probability have been smothered in the mud, for just a little before them at the end of the cleanest way was a pit. No one knew how deep it was, for it was full of nothing but mud and had been put there purposely to destroy the pilgrims who fell into it.

I thought to myself, *Whoever goes on pilgrimage should have one of these maps with him, so that he may look at it when he comes to a standstill so he can see what way he must take.*

Then they went on through this Enchanted Ground until they came to where there was another arbor, but it was built along the side of the road. In that arbor two men lay whose names were Heedless and Too-bold. These two had gone this far on pilgrimage, but after growing weary on their journey sat down to rest and had fallen fast asleep.

When the pilgrims saw them, they stood still and shook their heads, for they could see the sleepers were in a pitiful state. Then they talked over what they should do, whether to go on and let them sleep or to try to awaken them. So they decided to go to them and awaken them, if they could. However, they approached with caution, and took care not to dare to sit down or embrace any benefit offered by that arbor.

So they went to the arbor and spoke to the men. They called each one by his name, for Great Heart seemed to know who they were, but the two men did not stir or answer. Then Great Heart shook them, and did whatever he could to wake them.

Without waking, one of them said, "I will pay you when I receive my money."

Great Heart shook his head.

"I will fight so long as I can hold my sword in my hand," the other said.

At that, one of the children laughed.

Then Christiana asked, "What is the meaning of this?"

Great Heart said, "They talk in their sleep. If you strike them, beat them, or whatever else you do to them, they will answer you in this manner. A long time ago one of them said, 'When the waves of the sea beat upon him, he slept upon the mast of a ship (*Yea, thou shalt be as he that lies down in the midst of the sea or as he that sleeps at the rudder. They have stricken me, thou shalt say, and I was not sick; they have beaten me, and I felt it not; when*

I shall awake, I will seek it yet again. – Prov. 23:34, 35); when I awaken, I will seek it yet again.'

"You know, when men talk in their sleep they may say anything, but their words are not governed by faith or reason. Their words are incoherent now," Great Heart said as he pointed to the sleeping men, "as they were between the time they left on pilgrimage and sitting down here. The harm of it is that when thoughtless, unobserving people go on pilgrimage, the odds are twenty to one that they end up like this.

"For this Enchanted Ground is one of the last refuges the enemy has to use against pilgrims. As you see it is strategically located almost at the end of the way to be most advantageous against us. For the enemy thinks, when will these fools be most ready to sit down? It is when they are weary. And when are they most likely to be weary? It is when they are almost at their journey's end. Therefore I say the Enchanted Ground is placed so near to the Beulah land so that it is near the end of their race. Therefore let pilgrims be attentive and observant, or what has happened to these men here will happen to them and none can awaken them."

The pilgrims desired to go continue on their journey and with trembling asked their guide to light a lantern so they might travel the rest of their way with the help of the light. So he lit the lantern and it helped them to see the rest of this way, even though the darkness was very great. (*We have also the most sure word of the prophets, unto which ye do well that ye take heed, as unto a light that shines in a dark place, until the day dawns and the morning star arises in your hearts.* – 2 Peter 1:19) But the children began to grow very weary, and they cried out to him who loves pilgrims and asked him to make their way more comfortable.

When they walked a little further a wind arose that drove away the foggy mist and the air cleared. They could see that they were at the edge of the Enchanted Ground and that they were within the way walking where they should, plus now they could see one another better.

When they were almost at the end of this ground, the continuous sound of a voice could be heard just ahead of them and it raised much concern. They went on and looked for the source and they found a man upon his knees, with hands and eyes lifted up. They thought he was speaking earnestly to the one who was above, but as they drew closer they realized they could not make out what he said. So they tiptoed softly until he had finished.

When the man finished, he got up and began to run toward the Celestial City. Then Great Heart called after him, saying, "Hello, friend, may we accompany you? That is if you are going to the Celestial City as I suppose."

The man stopped and waited for them to catch up with him. But as soon as Mr. Honest saw him, he said, "I know this man."

Valiant-for-Truth said, "Please tell me, who is he?"

"He is someone who comes from the area where I used to live," Mr. Honest said. "His name is Standfast. He is certainly a proper and good pilgrim."

So they came up to one another and Standfast said to old Honest, "Hello, father Honest, is that you?"

"Yes," he said. "It is me."

"I'm so happy to see you here," Mr. Standfast said, "that I have found you on this road."

"And I am just as glad I saw you on your knees," Honest said.

Standfast blushed and said, "You saw me?"

Honest nodded. "Yes, I did and the sight made my heart glad."

"Why? What did you think?" Standfast asked.

"Think!" said old Honest. "What could I think? I thought we had met up with an honest man on the road and should join his company as we travel."

"It would have been wrong if you had thought anything else," Standfast said. "How happy I am! But I confess that I am not always behaving as I should, and I know that I am the one responsible."

"You speak the truth," Honest said. "But your fear further confirms to me that things are right between the Prince of pilgrims and your soul. For he says, 'Blessed is the man who fears always.'" (*Blessed is the man that fears God always, but he that hardens his heart shall fall into evil. – Prov. 28:14*)

"Please tell us why you were down on your knees just now, brother," Valiant-for-Truth said. "Was it due to some special tenderness of heart or did it have to do with a promise or oath?"

Standfast said, "As you can see we were upon the Enchanted Ground, and as I was going along I thought to myself about how dangerous that part of the road was, and how many had come this far on pilgrimage who had been stopped here and destroyed. I also thought about the manner of the death with which this place destroys men. Those who die here don't die from a violent disease. In fact, the death which they die is not heavy or burdensome to them. For he who dies in their sleep, begins that journey with desire and pleasure and submits to the will of that disease–"

Honest interrupted. "Did you see the two men asleep in the arbor?"

"Yes! Yes, I saw Heedless and Too-bold there and for all I know, they will lie there till they rot. (*The memory of the just is blessed, but the name of the wicked shall stink.* – Prov. 10:7) But let me go on with my tale.

"As I was thinking about all this, I saw one woman dressed in old but very pleasing attire. She presented herself to me and offered me three things, that is to say, her body, her purse, and her bed. Now the truth is I was weary and sleepy, and I had no money. I think perhaps the witch knew that. Well, I rejected her offer time after time, but she ignored my resistance and smiled. Then I began to grow angry; but that didn't matter to her at all. She made the same offers again, and said, if I would be ruled by her, she would make me great and happy. She said, 'For, I am the mistress of the world and men are made happy by me.'

"I asked her name and she told me it was Madam Bubble. This set me even further from her; but she still followed me with the same enticements. Then as you saw, I took to my knees and with hands lifted up and cries, I prayed to him who said he would help. So, just as you came up, the woman went her way. Then I continued to give thanks for my great deliverance, for I believe her intentions were no good and that she sought to make stop my journey."

Honest nodded his agreement. "Without doubt her intentions were bad. But wait a minute, now that you talk about her, I think I have either seen her or read some story about her."

"Perhaps you have done both," Standfast said.

"Madam Bubble!" Honest said. "Is she a tall, good-looking woman with a somewhat dark complexion?"

"Yes, you hit it. That's exactly what she looks like."

"Does she speak very smoothly and give you a smile at the end of a sentence?" Honest asked.

"Exactly," Standfast said. "You've described her perfectly for those are her very actions."

"Does she wear a large purse at her side? And does she dip her hand into it often fingering her money, as if it is her heart's delight?"

"Yes," Standfast said. "That is just what she did. You couldn't have described her more accurately if she had stood right here."

Mr. Honest said, "Then he who drew her picture was a good artist, and he who wrote about her told the truth."

Standfast and Madame Bubble

Great Heart said, "This woman is a witch, and it is due to her sorceries that this ground is enchanted. Whoever lays his head down in her lap, might as well lay it down on a block over which an axe hangs. Those who look upon her beauty are counted as enemies of God. She is the one who maintains the great show of richness and elegance of all those who are the enemies of pilgrims. (*Ye adulterers and adulteresses, know ye not that the friendship of the world is enmity with God? Whosoever therefore that desires to be a friend of the world, makes himself the enemy of God.* – James 4:4) She is responsible for buying off many a man from a pilgrim's life, and she is a great gossiper. Both she and her daughters are always at one pilgrim's heels or another.

"They all commend and even prefer things valued and esteemed in this life. She is a bold and brazen woman who is willing to talk with any man. She always disrespects poor pilgrims and mocks them with laughter, while she highly praises the rich. For instance, if there is money in a place and one cunning enough to get it, she will speak well of that calculating person everywhere she goes.

"She loves banqueting and feasting as well and so you'll find her always at one full table or another. In some places she has told people she is a goddess, and for this reason some actually worship her. At times she even openly cheats and will declare that no one can demonstrate a good comparable to hers. She promises to live with children's children, if they will just love her and make her important in their lives. If they do, she offers plentiful gold from her purse in some places and to some people. She loves to be sought after, spoken well of, and to lie in the hearts of men. She is never weary of speaking well of her wares and the people she loves most are those who think best of her. She promises crowns and kingdoms to some, if they will just take her advice. She leads many around with the halter and ten thousand times more to hell."

"Oh," Standfast said. "What a mercy that I resisted her! To think of where she might have drawn me!"

Great Heart said, "Where? No one but God knows where but generally speaking, we can be sure that she would have drawn you into many foolish and hurtful lusts, the sort which drown men in destruction and punishment in hell. (*For those that desire to be rich fall into temptation and a snare, and into many foolish and hurtful lusts which drown men in destruction and perdition. – 1 Tim. 6:9*)

"It was she who set Absalom against his father and Jeroboam against his master. It was she who persuaded Judas to sell his Lord, and she who prevailed with Demas to forsake the godly pilgrim's life. No one can begin to understand all the trouble she causes. She brings about clashes between rulers and subjects, parents and children, neighbor and neighbor, a man and his wife, a man and himself, and even between the flesh and the spirit. Therefore, good Mr. Standfast, live up to your name when you have done all and stand." (*Therefore, take unto you the whole armour of God, that ye may be able to withstand in the evil day and stand fast, all the work having been finished. – Eph. 6:13*)

At this discussion a mixture of joy and trembling broke out among the pilgrims, but in the end they broke out and sang:

"*What danger is the Pilgrim in!*
  How many are his foes!
How many ways there are to sin
  No living mortal knows.

Some in the ditch are pulled aside,
  And can lie struggling in the mire.
Though some shun the frying-pan
  Do leap into the fire."

After this, I watched until they came into the land of Beulah, where the sun shines night and day. Here the weary pilgrims decided to rest a while. Because pilgrims belonged more to this country than any in this world, and because the orchards and vineyards there belonged to the King of the Celestial country, they were permitted to boldly use any of his things. After a short time they were refreshed, for the bells rang and the trumpets sounded a melody continually. Even though they did not sleep, they were refreshed as if they had a sound night's sleep. Those walking in the streets raised their voices and shouted, "More pilgrims have come to our city!"

One answered, "And many have crossed over the river and were let in at the golden gates today!"

They raised their voices again saying, "A legion of Shining Ones has just come to town. By this we know there are more pilgrims upon the road. Here they come to wait for them, for we are ready to comfort them following all their sorrow."

The pilgrims got up and walked here and there as they listened to the heavenly noises filling the streets while celestial visions delighted their eyes. In this land they heard nothing, saw nothing, felt nothing, smelled nothing, and tasted nothing offensive to their stomach or mind. They only tasted of the water of the river which they were to cross over. They thought it tasted a little bitter to the palate, but it proved to be sweeter as it went down.

In this place there was a record kept of the names of those who had been pilgrims in olden times. Along with this record was an account of the history of all the famous acts they had done. The topic of many conversations dealt with the river and its ebb and flow, and how this had affected pilgrims who previously crossed over the river. Some crossed over when the river was almost dry, while it had overflowed its banks for others.

The children of the town went into the King's gardens and gathered fragrant flowers for the pilgrims and with much affection brought them to the pilgrims. Aromatic camphor also grew here along with nard, saffron, calamus, and cinnamon, with all the trees of frankincense, myrrh, and aloes, along with all the chief spices. The pilgrims' bodies were anointed and their chambers perfumed while they stayed there so as to prepare them to go cross the river, when the appointed time arrived.

Now, while they stayed there and waited for the appointed time, a message arrived from the Celestial City and created quite a buzz throughout the town. It contained an important matter for Christiana, the wife of Christian the pilgrim. The one delivering the message asked where she could be found and he was directed to the house where she was. There the messenger delivered this message: "Hello, good woman; I bring you news that the Master calls for you, and expects that you should stand in his presence clothed in immortality within the next ten days."

When he had read this letter to her, he gave her a sure token that he was a true messenger, and was come to bid her make haste to be gone. The token was an arrow with a point sharpened with love, let easily into her heart, which by degrees wrought so effectually with her, that at the time appointed she must be gone.

When Christiana saw that her time had come and that she was the first of this group to be called to cross over, she called for Great Heart her guide. She told him about the message, and he encouraged her, saying he was happy to hear the news and that he would have been just as glad if the message had come for him. Then she asked for his advice as to how to prepare for her journey. So he told her exactly what to do and that those being left behind would accompany her to the riverside.

So Christiana called for her children and gave each of them her blessing and told them she took comfort that they each bore the mark of their master on their foreheads, and that they had kept their garments so white. She was also glad to have them with her at this time. Lastly, she donated to the poor what little she owned and commanded her sons and daughters to be ready for the time when the messenger would come for them.

When she had spoken these words to her guide and her children, she called for Valiant-for-Truth. To him she said, "Sir, you have showed yourself true-hearted everyplace you go. Be faithful unto death and my King will give you a crown of life. (*Fear none of those things which thou shalt suffer; behold, the devil shall cast some of you into prison, that ye may be tried; and ye shall have tribulation ten days; be thou faithful unto death, and I will give thee the crown of life.* – Rev. 2:10) I would also ask that you keep an eye to my children. If you see them grow fainthearted, speak to them and encourage them, including my daughters, my sons' wives."

Christiana calls her children and gives them her blessing

Then to Mr. Standfast she gave a ring, and she called for old Mr. Honest, and said of him, "Behold an Israelite indeed, in whom is no guile!" (John 1:47)

He said, "I wish you a beautiful, clear day when you set out for Mount Zion. I shall be glad to see you go over the river without getting your feet wet."

But she answered, "Wet or dry makes no difference to me. I just long to be gone, no matter what the weather is like for my journey. I have plenty of time to sit down and rest and dry off once I get there."

Then Mr. Ready-to-halt walked into the room to see her. She said to him, "Your journey to get here has been fraught with difficulty, but that will make your rest all the sweeter. Watch and be prepared, for the messenger may come for you at a time when you least expect him."

Ready-to-halt left the room, and in came Mr. Despondency and his daughter Much-afraid. To them, Christiana she said, "You ought to be thankful and forever remember how you were delivered from the hands of Giant Despair and rescued from Doubting Castle. The result of that mercy is that you have been brought safely here. With that in mind, be watchful and cast off your fear and be serious about how you live your life; never lose hope."

Then she turned to Mr. Feeble-mind and said, "You were delivered from the mouth of Giant Slay-good, so that your light might shine among the living and that you would see your King and be strengthened. Only I advise you to repent of your tendency to fear and doubt his goodness, before he sends for you, so you don't find yourself standing before him embarrassed for that fault when he comes."

Now the day drew for Christiana to depart across the river. The road was full of people gathered to see her off on her journey. All along the banks beyond the river, horses and chariots gathered. They had come from above

Christiana enters the River of Death

to accompany her to the city gate. She stepped forward and entered the river, after saying good-bye to those who had followed her. Then she entered the river and the last words she was heard to say were, "I come, Lord, to be with you and bless you!" Those who waited for Christiana across the river carried her out of their sight, and so her children and friends returned to their place.

Christiana called at the gate and entered with all the ceremonies of joy that her husband, Christian, had experienced before her. At her departure her children wept, but Great Heart and Valiant-for-Truth celebrated with joy on a well-tuned cymbal and harp. In this way they all departed to their respective places.

After some time another message was delivered to the town again, and this time the messenger's business was with Mr. Ready-to-halt. The messenger inquired about him, and said, "I have come from him whom you have loved and followed, though upon crutches. My message is to tell you that he expects you at his table to eat with him in his kingdom the day after Easter. Therefore prepare for this journey." He also gave him a token to show he was a true messenger, saying, "I have broken your golden bowl and loosed your silver cord." (*Before the silver chain is broken, and the golden bowl is broken, and the pitcher is broken at the fountain, and the wheel is broken at the cistern. – Eccles. 12:6*)

After this, Mr. Ready-to-halt called for his fellow pilgrims and said, "I have been sent for and God shall surely visit you also." So he asked Valiant-for-Truth to make his will, and because he had nothing to leave those who survived him except his crutches and his good wishes, he said, "These crutches I leave to my son so that he shall walk in my steps, and along with them I leave a hundred warm wishes that he may prove better than I have been."

Then he thanked Great Heart for his conduct and kindness and so then focused on his journey. When he came to the brink of the river, he said, "Now I shall have no more need of these crutches, since across the river chariots and horses await for me to ride upon." The last words he was heard to say were, "Welcome life!" And with this he went his way.

After this, Mr. Feeble-mind had news delivered when the messenger showed up at his chamber door. He came in and said, "I have come to tell you that your Master has need of you, and that in a very short time you must behold his face in brightness. Take this as a token of the truth of my message: 'Those that look out at the windows shall be darkened.'" (*In the day when the keepers of the house shall tremble and the strong men shall bow themselves and the grinders cease because they are few and those that look out of the windows are darkened.* – Eccles. 12:3) Then Mr. Feeble-mind called for his friends and told them about the message, what he was supposed to do, and about the token he had received regarding the truth of the message. Then he said, "Since I have nothing to leave to anyone, what purpose is there for me to make a will? As for my feeble mind, that I will leave behind me, for that I shall certainly have no need of in the place where I am going, nor is it worth presenting to the poorest pilgrims. Therefore, when I am gone, I desire that you, Valiant-for-Truth, would bury it in a dunghill." The day arrived on which he was to depart, and he entered the river just like those before him. His last words were, "Hold out, faith and patience!" So he went over to the other side.

Eventually, in the days after many of the pilgrims had passed away, Mr. Despondency was sent for, because a message had arrived for him. It said, "Trembling man! You are summoned to be ready with the King by the next Lord's day, to shout for joy for your deliverance from all your doubts." The message also said, "And as proof that my message is true, I give him a grasshopper to be a burden unto him." (*When they shall also be afraid of that which is high, and fears shall be in the way, and the almond tree shall flourish, and the grasshopper shall be a burden, and appetite shall fail: because man goes to the home of his age, and the mourners shall go about the streets.* – Eccles. 12:5)

Now when Mr. Despondency's daughter, whose name was Much-afraid, heard what happened, she said she would go with her father. Mr. Despondency said to his friends, "You know how my daughter and I have acted and how difficult and problematic we have been for all of you. My will and my daughter's is that our depression and mindless fears would not be passed on to any one when we leave, for I know that after my death these evils will offer themselves to others. Let me make it clear, these are remnants of behaviors we entertained when we first began to be pilgrims, and after that we were never able to shake free of them. After we depart, they will walk about like ghosts seeking to entertain the thoughts of pilgrims. For our sakes, don't let them do it. Instead, shut the doors on them."

When the time came for them to depart they went up to the brink of the river. The last words of Mr. Despondency were, "Farewell, night! Welcome, day!" His daughter went through the river singing, but no one could understand her words.

Then after some time another messenger arrived in the town asking for Mr. Honest. He came to the house where Honest lived and delivered this message: "You are commanded to be ready in seven days to present yourself before your Lord at his Father's house. And for proof that my message is true I deliver this token. 'All the daughters of music shall be brought low.'" (*And the doors outside shall be shut because the voice of the grinder is low, and he shall rise up at the voice of the bird and all the daughters of song shall be humbled.* – Eccles. 12:4)

Once he received the news, Mr. Honest called for his friends, and said, "I am about to die but shall make no will. As for my honesty, it shall go with me. Let any who live after I am gone be told of this." When the day of his departure arrived, he prepared to cross over the river. At that time the river overflowed its banks in some places; but Mr. Honest, in his lifetime, had spoken to one Good-conscience to meet him there, and there he was ready to lend him his hand and he helped him over. The last words of Mr. Honest were, "Grace reigns!" And in this way he left the world.

After this it was widely announced that Valiant-for-Truth received a summons by the hand of the same messenger. He also received a token that the summons was true. "That his pitcher was broken at the fountain." (*Before the silver chain is broken, and the golden bowl is broken, and the pitcher is broken at the fountain, and the wheel is broken at the cistern.* – Eccles. 12:6) When Valiant-for-Truth understood the message was true, he called for his friends. He let them know he had received a summons. "I am going to my Father's. Even though I arrived here with great difficulty, I don't regret any of the trouble I had to live through to get here.

"I give my sword to the one who follows me in my pilgrimage, and my courage and skill to the one who can get it. My marks and scars I carry with me as a witness that I have fought His battles and now He will be my rewarder." When the day came for him to cross the river, many accompanied him to the riverbank. He stepped into the water and said, "Death, where is your sting?" And as he went deeper, he said, "Grave, where is your victory?" (*O death, where is thy sting? O Hades, where is thy victory?* – 1

Cor. 15:55) So he passed over the river to the sound of trumpets welcoming him to the other side.

Then a summons arrived for Mr. Standfast. This is the same Mr. Standfast whom the rest of the pilgrims found praying upon his knees in the Enchanted Ground. The messenger stood there as Mr. Standfast opened the message and stood reading the contents. The message told him he must prepare for a change of life, for his Master was no longer willing for him to serve from so far away. This Mr. Standfast was put into a muse and thought quietly about what the message meant.

The messenger said, "You needn't doubt the truth of my message; for here is a token of the truth contained in it. 'Your wheel is broken at the cistern.'" (*Before the silver chain is broken, and the golden bowl is broken, and the pitcher is broken at the fountain, and the wheel is broken at the cistern.* – Eccles. 12:6)

Mr. Standfast called to Great Heart, who was their guide, to come near. To him he said, "Sir, although it was not my fortune to be in your good company during most of the days of my pilgrimage, I have to tell you that since I met you, you have been beneficial to me. When I left my home, I left behind a wife and five small children. Let me request that when you return – for I know you return to your Master's house in hopes that you may conduct more pilgrims as guide – I ask that you send a message to my family and let them know all that has and will happen to me. Especially be sure to tell them of my happy arrival to this place as well as my present and blessed condition.

"Also be sure to tell them about Christian and Christiana his wife, and how she and her children came after her husband. Tell them about her happy end and about where she is now. I have next to nothing to send to my family, unless it be prayers and tears for them. You can let them know about that, if perhaps they succeed."

When Mr. Standfast had set things in order, the time came for him to hurry to the river. When he arrived on the riverbank, the water was very calm, so when Mr. Standfast stepped into the water he stood there for a while and talked with his companions who had accompanied him there.

"This river has frightened many, and I admit thoughts of it have often frightened me. But now as I stand here, I think about how my feet are standing on the very ground upon which the feet of the priests who carried the Ark of the Covenant stood as Israel crossed through the Jordan. (*But the priests that bore the ark of the covenant of the LORD stood firm on dry ground in the midst of the Jordan until all the people finished passing the Jordan; and all Israel passed on dry ground. – Josh. 3:17*)

"The waters certainly taste bitter and feel cold to the stomach, yet the thoughts of what I am going to and the party that awaits me on the other side warm my heart like a glowing coal. I see myself at the end of my journey with my hard days behind me. I am going to see that head which was crowned with thorns, and that face which was spit upon for me. Until now, I have lived by faith based on what I've heard; but now where I go I shall live by sight, and shall be with him in whose company I delight myself. I have loved to hear my Lord spoken of, and wherever I have seen the print of his shoe in the earth, have longed to follow in his steps, too. His name has been as sweet to me as a honey pot and more fragrant than any perfume. His voice has been pleasing and I have longed to see his face more than most people desire sunlight. I gathered his words for my food and for antidotes against my weaknesses. He has held me and kept me from mine iniquities, and he has strengthened my steps in his way."

While he talked about these things his countenance changed and he bowed and said, "Take me, for I come to you." And suddenly he could no longer be seen by those standing along this side of the river.

Along the opposite bank it was glorious to see the area filled with horses and chariots, with trumpeters, pipers, singers, and players strumming stringed instruments to welcome the pilgrims as they went up and followed them in at the beautiful gate of the city.

As for Christiana's children, the four boys that Christiana brought, with their wives and children, I can't tell you about them in detail for I didn't stay there. However, since I left that town, I heard someone say they were still alive and living life for the increase of the church, in that place.

In the future, if I have the opportunity to go that way again, I may give those who desire it an account of what I haven't mentioned here. In the meantime I bid my reader farewell.

The end.

Appendices

The Author's Apology For His Book

———— ∽ ————

When I first picked up my pen to write, I had no idea my thoughts would turn into this little book. I started to write and the story flowed as my pen fought to keep up with my ideas. Thoughts came so quickly it almost felt like I had just begun as I finished the last sentence.

The Pilgrim's Progress tells of the journey of saints and the way of glory in a time when the gospel of salvation was readily available. The story naturally took allegorical form, which makes the meaning clear. Following this form, I set more than twenty important truths down within the tale and had twenty more coursing through my head like sparks that fly from coals. I decided the first twenty to be more than sufficient and to save the rest for another time, so readers wouldn't think that I'd go on for an eternity and decide to read another book instead.

Truthfully, as I started the book I had no idea of the scope and depth it would take on. I never entertained thoughts of the whole world reading my work. When I set out to write this story, I didn't do it to please my neighbor, or to gratify myself. In fact, I can't say what my original goal had been. However, I can say it was more than an absent-minded scribbling of whatever came to mind, and it was more than a diversion from thoughts.

As I put pen to paper and started to write, it filled me with an unexpected delight. The story unfolded with my thoughts following a process which drew on knowledge of the truth. To my surprise the result was a story whose length and breadth surpassed my expectations. Soon I held my thoughts on paper and decided to share my musings with others to see if they thought it a crazy allegory or one that held merit. Some suggested I forget about the idea altogether and others encouraged me saying, "John, print it." With mixed responses, I found myself in a dilemma trying to figure out the best thing to do.

Finally, since the feedback was divided, I decided to go ahead and print it. Since some thought I should and others thought I shouldn't, I figured printing the book would be a test to see which of them were right. That way I wouldn't deny those who thought it should be printed. Plus it gave them a way to share in my delight. For those who didn't think I should publish it, I let them know I in no way intended to offend them. I asked them to be patient and not to judge those who were pleased to have the book published. I reminded those against publication that they were in no way compelled to read it. In this way, I decided to leave it to individual preference and conviction.

You see, when it comes to spiritual food, some love the meat, some love to pick the bone, and some hope for a tale that might seem less rigid and which would not require them to change in any way. With this last group, I have to disagree and tell you up front that I do not write in this style. In fact, I write in such a way that I hope the reader will not miss the truth that none are good and we all must be changed.

Let me be clear that my purpose for moving forward is not to be unkind. As an example, think about dark clouds. They bring rain while bright days do not. The point is that dark days or bright, if the rain falls, the earth yields crops. We give praise to God for both the clouds and sunshine and treasure the fruit brought about by both. No one can distinguish the benefit of each, for they work together, and we should not complain about either. This fruit is welcomed by one who is hungry, while one without an appetite spits it out and makes the blessing null.

Consider the ways of a fisherman. To catch the fish he takes steps that engage all his wits. He uses snares, lines, angles, hooks, and nets. Yet, even with all these tools, there will be fish that are not caught by any device one can make. Instead, they must be groped for and even tickled, or they will not be caught no matter what you do.

Think about the one who hunts birds. How does he seek to catch his game? It takes an assortment of tactics and devices like guns, nets, lime-twigs, light, and bell. The fowler creeps along, stands still, and takes on varied postures to remain unnoticed. Yet none of these tactics will make him master of whatever bird he pleases. For instance, while his skills include whistling to lure and catch one bird, the very same tune will cause him to miss another bird.

Here's another thing to think about. If, as myths suggest, a pearl may be found in a toad's head, just as such a precious stone may be found in an oyster shell, that means two things that promise nothing contain something better than gold! Who are we to look with disdain upon an idea rather than to look there for something precious?

So it is with my little book. It may not include pretty pictures to make it attractive, but it does hold a treasure worth looking for.

Some have said, "Well, I am not fully satisfied that your book will stand when soundly tried."

When I asked for more specifics regarding their concern, their objection amounted to things such as "It is dark." Or they pointed to the fact it is only fiction. Their objections lead me to ask, what is wrong with fiction? Some men, by fictional words as dark as mine, make truth, light, and reality radiate and shine by means of parables and allegorical style such as I use.

"But they want solidness," another objected. His concern is based on an idea that such a writing style is weak and that metaphors, allegory, and similitudes are unclear. He went on to say, "They drown the weak" and "Metaphors make us blind."

However, I don't agree. You can write using metaphors and stand firm on what is meant. Weren't God's laws, His gospel laws, in olden times presented using types, shadows, and metaphors? Yet any clear-thinking man would be unwilling to find fault with them, unless he wants to come against the highest wisdom! No, instead he stoops to pick up such valuable things and seeks to understand them. He looks for the value and meaning in things like the pins and loops of the tabernacle construction and how they are a type of the uniting ministry of God's word, or the symbolism of heavenly things represented by calves and sheep, heifers, rams, birds and herbs, and the blood of lambs. God speaks to us in this way, and the one who understands is blessed to find light and grace in it.

Don't think that I want anything less than the truth by choosing this writing style. The message I convey is not superficial. Consider how the Bible speaks truth in parables, while other works that appear truthful are not always true. The story should not be despised because it is allegorical. My dark and cloudy words do hold the truth, and we must be careful how we judge lest we receive things hurtful to us as if they are nothing, while depriving our souls of things that are good.

If you look at the Bible, you'll plainly see that the prophets used metaphors to set forth truth, and the teachings of Christ and his apostles are clothed in the same way. The Holy Scripture has metaphorical aspects and is not often amusing or entertaining. It is full of dark figures and allegories and yet it also illuminates with a luster and radiance that dispels human gloom.

Let the critic of my book look to his own life. Even as a child of God, we all have darker aspects than those in my book and more shining qualities too. So I say, don't be more critical of *The Pilgrim's Progress* than of yourself. Let the work stand to be judged by impartial men. Though dressed in allegorical attire, the truth still helps the troubled and immature far more than Satan's lies. It encourages understanding and brings the will into submission. When it comes to words, the apostle Paul told Timothy to take hold of sound words and to reject old wives' tales. However, he never forbade the use of parables which offer hidden treasures worth digging for with the greatest of care.

Before I conclude, let me ask my godly critics this: Are you offended? Do you wish I had told my story in another style? Or that I had said things in a more direct manner? Let me offer these three things to which I shall submit with respectful deference.

I find nothing in Scripture that denies the use of my allegorical method. In application, I seek the advance of truth this way. I am not denied but have permission and example, too, from those who have pleased God by their words or ways more than people alive today. So in my own way, I expressed my thoughts to declare things most excellent to you.

I find men of high esteem write in their style; yet no one puts down their writing. I agree that the abuse of truth should not be tolerated, and anyone who writes with such intent should not be tolerated. However, writing style is a matter of suitability and taste, so if you object to the style, I ask that you still support the cause of truth.

For this reason let truth be free to venture upon us in whichever way pleases God, for God knows better than any of us how He works. He has taught us first to plough, to guide our minds and pens for His purpose and designs. He uses dishonorable things to usher in the divine.

I find many places in the holy Scripture that use aspects of this writing method in cases where one thing sets the stage for another. I use allegory in the same way. Not to smother Truth's golden beams but to cast its rays like the light of day.

And now, before I close, I want to show the benefit of my book for everyone, and then I'll commit my book and its readers and critics into God's hands which are able to bring down the strong and make the weak stand. This book traces out the way from start to finish for people seeking the everlasting prize. It shows you where we come from, where we go, what we do, and what we leave undone. It demonstrates how we run the race until we are called to the gate of glory.

It shows, too, those who set out for life with all their might as if they can obtain the lasting crown by what they do. In the illustration put forth in my book, readers will also see the reason why those who strive in such a way will die like fools.

This book makes a traveler out of you, and if you are ruled by its counsel and understand its directions, you will be directed to the Holy Land. It will prod the spiritually lazy to be active and the spiritually blind to see. It will remind the forgetful of the things we should never forget. If you're ready for a rare and profitable experience and to find the precious truth within a fictional story, then read my allegorical fancies. They will stick like burs and yet may be comforting to the helpless.

This book is written in such a way that the one who picks it up may think it nothing more than a novelty, but the gospel threads that run through it go deeper to affect the minds of apathetic men. It is able to bolster the depressed, and while it is entertaining to read, it is far from foolish. It's a book for everyone; for those who enjoy riddles and their explanations, and for the deep thinkers who contemplate the meaning behind them. If you love to pick the meat of a matter, live in a dream while awake, or want to laugh one moment and weep the next, this book offers that and more. This story is told in such a way that you'll question whether you are blessed or not by reading the same lines as you comprehend the truth of God with your mind and heart.

The Author's Way

Sending Forth of His Second Part of the Pilgrim

Go now my little book to every place,
Where my first Pilgrim has shown his face
Call at their door: if any say, "Who's there?"
Then answer Christiana is here.
If they call for you, "Come in," then enter thou,
With all your boys, and then as you know how,
Tell who they are, and from where they came.
Perhaps they'll know them by their looks, or name,
But if they should not, ask them yet again.
If formerly they did not entertain,
One Christian, a Pilgrim? If they say
They did, and were delighted in his way;
Then let them know that these related were,
To him, for they his wife and children are.
Tell them, that they have left their house and home;
Are turned Pilgrims who seek a world to come;
And have met with hardships in the way.
They've met with troubles night and day;
They have trod on serpents, fought with devils,
And have also overcome many evils.
Yes, tell them also of the next who have,
Of love to pilgrimage, been courageous and brave
Defenders of that way; and how they still

Refuse this world, to do their Father's will.
Go tell them also of those dainty things
That pilgrimage unto the Pilgrim brings.
Let them be acquainted, too, of how they are
Beloved of their King, under his care;
What goodly mansions he for them provides,
Though they meet with rough winds and swelling tides,
How brave a calm they will enjoy at last,
Who to their Lord and by his ways hold fast.
Perhaps with heart and hand they will embrace
You, as they did my first offspring and will grace
You, and your fellows with much cheer and fare,
As they show well, they of Pilgrims lovers are.

Objection I

But how, if they will not believe of me
That I am truly yours, 'cause some there be
Who counterfeit the Pilgrim and his name,
Seek, by disguise, to seem the very same;
And by that means have wrought themselves into
The hands and houses of I know not who.

Answer

'Tis true, some have, of late, tried to counterfeit
My Pilgrim and to their own work my title set;
Yes, others recycled half my name and title, too,
Stitching them to their books to make them do.
But yet they, by their features do declare
Themselves not mine to be, whose ere they are.
If you meet with such, then your only way
Before them all is to say what you must say
In your own native language, which no man
Now uses, nor with ease can mislead man.
If, after all, they still of you shall doubt,
Thinking that you, like gypsies, go about
In naughty ways the country to defile;

Or that you seek good people to beguile
With things unpardonable, send for me,
And I will testify you pilgrims be;
Yes, I will testify that only you
My Pilgrims are and that alone will do.

Objection II

But yet, perhaps, I may inquire for him
Of those who wish him damned life and limb.
What shall I do, when I at such a door
Ask for Pilgrims and they shall rage the more?

Answer

Fret not, over my Book, for such bugbears
They are nothing but groundless fears.
My Pilgrim's book has traveled sea and land,
Yet could I never come to understand
Why it was slighted or turned out of door
By any Kingdom, were they rich or poor.
In France and Flanders, where men kill each other,
My Pilgrim is esteemed a friend, a brother.
In Holland, too, 'tis said, I am told,
My Pilgrim for some is worth more than gold.
Highlanders and wild Irish can agree
My Pilgrim should familiar with them be.
'Tis in New England under such advance,
It receives so much loving countenance,
As to be trimmed, newly clothed, and decked with gems,
That it might show its features and its limbs.
Yet more, so comely does my Pilgrim walk,
That of him thousands daily sing and talk.
If you draw nearer home, it will appear,
My Pilgrim knows no ground of shame or fear.
City and country will him entertain,
With "Welcome Pilgrim," yes, they can't refrain
From smiling, if my Pilgrim is but nearby,

Or shows his face in any company.
Brave heroics does my Pilgrim hug and love,
Esteem it much, yes, values it above
Things of greater bulk; yes, with delight
Say, my lark's leg is better than a kite.
Young ladies, and young gentlewomen, too,
Do not small kindness to my Pilgrim show;
Their cabinets, their bosoms, and their hearts,
My Pilgrim has; 'cause he to them imparts
His pretty riddles in such wholesome strains,
As yield them profit double to their pains
Of reading, yes, I think I may be bold
To say some prize him far above their gold.
The very children that walk the street,
If they do but my holy Pilgrim meet,
Salute him they will; wish him well, and say,
He is the only young man of the day.
They who have never seen him, yet admire
What they have heard of him and much desire
To have his company, and hear him tell
Those Pilgrim stories which he knows so well.
Yes, some who did not love him at first,
But called him a silly fool, say they must
Now that they have seen and heard him, him commend;
And to those whom they love, they do him send.
Therefore, my second part, you need not be
Afraid to show your head: none can hurt thee,
Who wish but well to him who went before;
'Cause you came after with a second store
Of things as good, as rich, as profitable,
For young, for old, for staggering and stable.

Objection III

But some there are who say,
He laughs too loud
And some do say,

His head is in a cloud.
Others say, his words and stories are so dark,
They know not how, by them, to find his mark.

Answer
One may, I think, say,
Both his laughs and cries
May well be guessed at by his watery eyes.
Some things are of that nature, as to make
One's fancy chuckle, while his heart does ache.
When Jacob saw his Rachel with the sheep,
He did at the same time both kiss and weep.
Whereas some say,
A cloud is in his head,
That shows his wisdom's covered
With its own mantles – and to stir the mind
To search thoroughly after what it gladly would find,
Things that seem to be hidden in words obscure
Do but more the godly mind allure
To study what those sayings should contain,
That speak to us in such a cloudy strain.
I also know an opaque similitude
Will on the curious notion more intrude,
And will penetrate faster in the heart and head,
Than things from images not borrowed.
Therefore, my book, let no discouragement
Hinder your travels. Behold, you art sent
To friends, not foes; to friends who will give place
To you, your pilgrims, and your words embrace.
Besides, what my first Pilgrim left concealed,
For you, my brave second Pilgrim, has revealed;
What Christian left locked up and went his way,
Sweet Christiana opens with her key.

Objection IV

> But some don't love the method of your first:
> They count it romance; throw it away as dust.
> If I should meet with such, what should I say?
> Must I slight them as they slight me or nay?

Answer

> My Christiana, if with such people you do meet,
> By all means, in loving ways, be sure to greet;
> Decide not to return revile for revile,
> But if they frown, please on them smile.
> Perhaps 'tis nature, or some harsh report,
> Has made them thus despise or retort.
> Some don't love fish, some don't love cheese, and some
> Don't love their friends, nor their own house or home;
> Some start at pig, slight chicken, don't love fowl
> More than they love a cuckoo or an owl.
> Leave such, my Christiana, to their choice,
> And seek those who when they find you will rejoice;
> By no means strive, but in most humble ways,
> Present yourself to them in your Pilgrim's guise.
> Go then, my little Book and show to all
> Who entertain and bid you welcome shall,
> What you shall keep shut up from the rest;
> And wish that what you show them may be blessed
> To them for good and make them choose to be
> Pilgrims far better than you or me.
> Go, then I say, tell all men who you art.
> Say, "I am Christiana; and my part
> "Is now, with my four sons, to tell you what
> "It is for men to take a Pilgrim's lot."
> Go, also, tell them who and what they be
> Who now go on pilgrimage with thee.
> Say, "Here's my neighbor Mercy." She is one
> Who for a long time with me a pilgrim gone:
> Come, see her virgin face, and learn

Between idle ones and pilgrims to discern.
Yes, let young damsels learn of her to prize
The world which is to come, in all its ways.
When little tripping maidens follow God,
And leave old doting sinners to his rod,
'Tis like those days in which the young ones cried
"Hosanna!" when the old ones did deride.
Next tell them of old Honest, whom you found
With his white hairs treading the Pilgrim's ground.
Yes, tell them how sincere this man was;
How following his good Lord he bore the cross.
Perhaps with some gray headed, this may succeed
To have them fall in love with Christ and sin to grieve.
Tell them also, how Master Fearing went
On pilgrimage and about the time he spent
In isolation, with fears and cries;
And how, at last, he won the joyful prize.
He was a good man, though much down in spirit;
He is a good man and does life inherit.
Tell them of Master Feeble-mind also,
Who would not travel before but behind would go.
Show them also how he was almost slain,
And how one Great Heart did his life regain.
This man was true of heart; though weak in grace,
One might read true godliness in his face.
Then tell them of Master Ready-to-halt,
A man with crutches but much without fault.
Tell them how Master Feeble-mind and he
Did love and in opinion much agree.
And let all know, though weakness was their chance,
Yet sometimes one could sing and the other dance.
Don't forget Master Valiant-for-Truth,
That man of courage, though very much a youth.
Tell everyone about his spirit – that was so stout,
No man could ever make him face about.
And how Great Heart and he could not forbear,

But pulled down Doubting Castle, slayed Despair!
And don't overlook Master Despondency,
Nor Much-afraid, his daughter, though they lie
Under such guises as may make them look
(To some) as if their God had them forsook.
They went ahead softly but sure; and at the end,
Found that the Lord of Pilgrims was their friend.
When you have told the world all these things,
Then turn about, my book, and touch these strings;
Which, if but touched, will such music make,
They'll make a cripple dance, and a giant quake.
Those questions which lie unspoken within your breast,
Freely propound, expound, and for the rest
Of your mysterious riddles, let them remain
For those whose nimble fancies shall understand gain.
Now may this little book a blessing be
To those who love this little book and me.
And may its buyer have no cause to say,
His money is but lost or thrown away.
Yes, may this second Pilgrim yield that consequence
As may with each good Pilgrim's imagination enhance;
And may it some persuade, who go astray,
To turn their feet and heart to the right way,
Is the hearty prayer of the author,

– John Bunyan.

John Bunyan

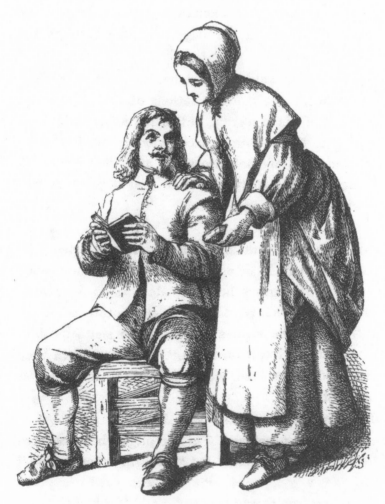

The wife of Bunyan persuades him to read her books

Bunyan reads his Bible

Bunyan listens to the women